# Colombian
# Roulette a novel

Toby
Green

MKUKI NA NYOTA
DAR — ES — SALAAM

PUBLISHED BY

Mkuki na Nyota Publishers Ltd
P. O. Box 4246
Dar es Salaam, Tanzania
www.mkukinanyota.com

© Toby Green 2016

ISBN 978-9987-082-39-1

Visit www.mkukinanyota.com to read more about and to purchase any of Mkuki na Nyota books. You will also find featured authors, interviews and news about other publisher/author events. Sign up for our e-newsletters for updates on new releases and other announcements.

Distributed worldwide outside Africa by African Books Collective.
www.africanbookscollective.com

# Contents

Chapter 1 . . . . . . . . . . . . . . . . . . . . . . . . . . . . . . . . . . . . . . . . . . . . . . . . . . . . . . . .1

Chapter 2 . . . . . . . . . . . . . . . . . . . . . . . . . . . . . . . . . . . . . . . . . . . . . . . . . . . . . . .14

Chapter 3 . . . . . . . . . . . . . . . . . . . . . . . . . . . . . . . . . . . . . . . . . . . . . . . . . . . . . . .25

Chapter 4 . . . . . . . . . . . . . . . . . . . . . . . . . . . . . . . . . . . . . . . . . . . . . . . . . . . . . . .40

Chapter 5 . . . . . . . . . . . . . . . . . . . . . . . . . . . . . . . . . . . . . . . . . . . . . . . . . . . . . . .53

Chapter 6 . . . . . . . . . . . . . . . . . . . . . . . . . . . . . . . . . . . . . . . . . . . . . . . . . . . . . . .68

Chapter 7 . . . . . . . . . . . . . . . . . . . . . . . . . . . . . . . . . . . . . . . . . . . . . . . . . . . . . . .82

Chapter 8 . . . . . . . . . . . . . . . . . . . . . . . . . . . . . . . . . . . . . . . . . . . . . . . . . . . . . . .98

Chapter 9 . . . . . . . . . . . . . . . . . . . . . . . . . . . . . . . . . . . . . . . . . . . . . . . . . . . . . 116

Chapter 10 . . . . . . . . . . . . . . . . . . . . . . . . . . . . . . . . . . . . . . . . . . . . . . . . . . . . 130

Chapter 11 . . . . . . . . . . . . . . . . . . . . . . . . . . . . . . . . . . . . . . . . . . . . . . . . . . . . 147

Chapter 12 . . . . . . . . . . . . . . . . . . . . . . . . . . . . . . . . . . . . . . . . . . . . . . . . . . . . 165

Chapter 13 . . . . . . . . . . . . . . . . . . . . . . . . . . . . . . . . . . . . . . . . . . . . . . . . 181

Chapter 14 . . . . . . . . . . . . . . . . . . . . . . . . . . . . . . . . . . . . . . . . . . . . . . . . 196

Chapter 15 . . . . . . . . . . . . . . . . . . . . . . . . . . . . . . . . . . . . . . . . . . . . . . . . 211

Chapter 16 . . . . . . . . . . . . . . . . . . . . . . . . . . . . . . . . . . . . . . . . . . . . . . . . 227

Chapter 17 . . . . . . . . . . . . . . . . . . . . . . . . . . . . . . . . . . . . . . . . . . . . . . . . 241

Chapter 18 . . . . . . . . . . . . . . . . . . . . . . . . . . . . . . . . . . . . . . . . . . . . . . . . 255

Chapter 19 . . . . . . . . . . . . . . . . . . . . . . . . . . . . . . . . . . . . . . . . . . . . . . . . 267

Chapter 20 . . . . . . . . . . . . . . . . . . . . . . . . . . . . . . . . . . . . . . . . . . . . . . . . 283

Chapter 21 . . . . . . . . . . . . . . . . . . . . . . . . . . . . . . . . . . . . . . . . . . . . . . . . 295

Chapter 22 . . . . . . . . . . . . . . . . . . . . . . . . . . . . . . . . . . . . . . . . . . . . . . . . 309

Chapter 23 . . . . . . . . . . . . . . . . . . . . . . . . . . . . . . . . . . . . . . . . . . . . . . . . 322

Chapter 24 . . . . . . . . . . . . . . . . . . . . . . . . . . . . . . . . . . . . . . . . . . . . . . . . 335

*For Tim*

# CHAPTER 1

Cars back to front and their lights orange to gold to red like an urban sunset. The municipality were doing roadworks again. Here was the traffic paying its road charge before any improvement had been achieved. The cars going to the airport coughed and their effluent hung like a ceiling over western Santa Fé. Chevvies, Toyotas, brand new Mercedes, even some ancient VW Beetles and 2CVs imported God knows how from São Paulo: Julián Restrepo counted them all. It gave him some satisfaction. As a kid he'd been fascinated by cars, long before his dad had stopped repairing them and started owning them. He'd pointed out the makes to his parents in the street, known them all.

His two-way radio crackled. Pancho was asking if anyone was near 46th street in the south. Another driver broke in, no he wasn't, and he wouldn't be going either: he valued his car. It was a respected client, Pancho insisted: someone had to pick her up. He began calling out drivers by name, like a teacher with a register, but Julián wasn't going to be pulled in to drive to the south of the city from where he was. He always made for the airport if he was scratching for a fare. Sooner or later the firm got orders for transfers from the arrivals' hall and if he was nearby he could be the first there. He told Pancho where he was: *Oh yes Julián*, Pancho said, *and I'm sure your first-class tickets are ready now at the American Airlines desk.*

The traffic had come to a complete stop. The yellow taxis looked like stale stains of pollen on the roads. Their horns rang in a syncopated beat, like the merengue music rolling from the roadside stalls. Some of the drivers rolled down their windows and shouted to each other. It was the mayor, his cousin owned the company doing the roadworks. Didn't they know, that was how the contract was made and how things would carry on? It was raining, the heavy cold rain of the high plateau. The rain was dirty, you could feel it on your tongue if you leant out just to look up at the sky and feel its pelting brown tears on your cheek. The rain drummed on the bonnets of the cars and bounced from the tarmac. It muffled the sounds of their horns and magnified the tail-lights of the cars in front. Slowly they were moving again. They'd passed the spot where the road had been reduced to one lane. Julián turned up the volume on his stereo. Soon he heard Pancho's voice again, wheedling and kind, actually there was someone to pick up at the airport, Julián, an English lady off the Continental flight from Miami. Could he make it there in twenty minutes? "For you, fatso, I'll turn up in traditional

Indian clothes as well," Julián answered, even though he hated folklore. And then he was quiet as Pancho gave him more details, thinking of the firm's other drivers all laughing at his joke.

Julián felt safe just then, with the rain hammering his car and so many cars surrounding him. Pancho knew that no one else would be able to pick up this English woman. It was Julián's trick, and it worked well. He'd met quite a few foreigners like that and they usually gave him plenty of work. It was an easy job: charm them on the way from the airport, and give them his card: it worked every time for someone like him, an adept of the easy life, a loafer who'd learnt too many lazy habits from his father and couldn't forget them.

The radio went quiet after a minute and he drove and wondered why there were always so many people going to the airport. Probably somewhere among these taxis there was a runner with a condom in their belly, or a suitcase on their lap, grabbing it tightly between their knees and staring out of the window in fear and silence. He'd had passengers like that once or twice. He remembered one guy, thinking like he spoke, with the high quick accent of the coast, explaining how he ran a small store up there in the north, how he'd saved a little money and was going to visit his cousin in Rotterdam. Julián hadn't replied, chewing gum: the guy had been as likely to have a cousin in Rotterdam as he was to become lead guitarist of an American rock group.

Near the airport, the rain eased. Julián pulled into the car park and wiped his car with one of the cloths he kept in the boot. He sat back in the drivers' seat and wrote the passenger's name on a piece of card in big letters: PAMELA OSWALD, PROCEDENTE DE LONDRES, VIA MIAMI. The plane had already landed so he went to wait next to the arrivals' hall along with others like him. For a long time the passengers streamed out of the baggage claim. Most were returning from shopping trips and visits to family in the States. They were fat and rich. They looked docile, like pets that had been neutered, but of course they weren't. Relatives met them and they soon disappeared. It was the foreigners who spent longer in the arrivals' hall. They went to the row of bureaux de change and then they eyed the taxi drivers. They looked as if their eyes had been caught in the headlights, yet it wasn't quite dark. Although the police now guarded the area, many of them had been told that you had to be careful at the airport. It hadn't been so long ago that there had been some who used to take new arrivals on a millionaires' tour from cashpoint to cashpoint around the city until their credit card limit was used up. People told silly stories, crazy stories, but a story's facts didn't all have to be right for it to be related to the truth. If it wasn't life that you were afraid of there was nothing to scare you.

It took thirty minutes for the arrivals to abate. Julián called Pancho on his cellphone and Pancho told him to wait. "Just charge her extra for the waiting time and we'll split it 50-50," Pancho told him. "That's good business sense." Julián looked at the baggage carousels but he couldn't see anyone. There were some distant voices, though. They were disembodied. He couldn't tell who was making the noise or see the bodies which they belonged to and for all he knew they could have been recordings of people and arguments long gone. It was the sort of thing his father Arturo might have put together, just to spook him. Nothing here was impossible.

At length two more people emerged through customs, both of them foreigners. One was a very tall, very thin man with greying stubble and livid brown eyes. He was talking to a woman with the blonde hair and blue eyes of movies and cigarette adverts, the world that was sold so hard that even Julián saw that it had become a pastiche of itself; her hair was cut into a bob and her eyes seemed to him luminous with an excitement that Julián returned instinctively, and then crushed. He'd lost his bags in Madrid, the tall man was telling the lady in English, his flight from Tenerife had been so late that he'd known they wouldn't make the connection in time. She'd come from London, and the inbound Continental flight to Miami had also been late. She turned and caught sight of Julián's name board: "And that's me," she said to the tall man, "so I'll have to go or this guy will wonder if he'll ever get his fare." She walked up to Julián: "Pamela Oswald, that's me," she said in English, "but I haven't got any bags, they're lost in America," "Lady," Julián answered in his best English, "here, we are in America."

He beckoned her to follow and they crossed the road beside the terminal building and went to the car park. As they crossed the darkened forecourt Julián smiled, for he caught a glimpse of some musicians carrying guitars and panpipes towards the departures hall, in their Indian dress, just as he had threatened to do for Pancho. One of them played a quickening riff on his guitar, a sound heavy with the mountains, as if in welcome. The Englishwoman smiled when she heard this, but Julián told her to ignore them: we can do without them, he said, without explaining why. Then he held open the rear passenger door, in silent coercion, and she climbed into the seat. He manoeuvred the car round, wound down his window and gave the guard 1000 pesos. It was dark by then and the man had raised up the collar of his coat to protect himself from the cold. He stood cowled and beaten with his back to the night like a blackened image of those monks whose prayers so long ago helped the world to keep turning. Julián called out a farewell behind him and then they drove out through the gate and onto the road back towards the city.

The passenger talked a lot. He'd heard enough American music that he understood some of it but listened only with half an ear and her babble saved him from thinking. It was like listening to the radio or watching TV. It was like listening to Pancho. He was still haranguing the firm's drivers because no one wanted to go down to fetch the customer at 46th street in the south. Hell it wasn't that bad, Pancho said, it wasn't like he was sending them to Ciudad Bolívar. Julián broke in then: "Boss," he said, "I've picked up the English lady now, so you can kiss my ass, I'll not be picking up that ride for you." "Watch out Restrepo," came the voice, disembodied and breaking up like those he had heard or thought he had heard at the airport, "don't make your bid for freedom just yet, you can tell what we think of freedom in this snake of a country of ours, we've named the biggest stinking cesspit of a shantytown in the whole of fucking America after the Liberator Bolívar." Julián muted the radio for a moment after that. You had to love Pancho: he was too realistic to have a hope of surviving in this country, the fact that he was there every morning seemed like a daily miracle and was enough to keep all the drivers going.

Once the radio was off he realised that the foreigner had stopped talking. They'd still only reached 45th Avenue so they were a long way from her destination in the Pachinero neighbourhood towards the north of the city. She was looking out at the night sky and its twisting yellow blackness reflecting the streetlights. They were snarled up on a flyover beside some buses, and on one of them he could hear a couple of country people talking, so proud and distinct in their accent even though their region was in an even worse state than Santa Fé. A kid climbed on to the bus to sell some chewing gum but no one paid him any attention. He swung himself off and tried his luck on the next bus. The drivers were kind, they always let the kids on to try to scrape some pesos together, even though they'd like as not be dead before five years were out. Anyway, things weren't as bad as they had been, that was another story doing the rounds.

The Englishwoman leaned forward as they sat stationary in the traffic.

"Perdón," she said, "is there some kind of pharmacy near here?"

"What stuff you want?"

"I got nothing. My bag, everything, it's all lost in America."

"Lady," Julián said, "the whole fucking America is lost."

"I'm sorry?"

"Like I said," Julián answered slowly, "this is America."

They were moving again. What did she want? She asked herself the question aloud and then answered herself: she wanted *something*, a toothbrush, some toothpaste, that would be a start.

"Problem is, is Sunday," Julián told her, "stores are closing early."

"Still, there must be somewhere."

Julián remembered that there was a superstore near 10th Avenue which was open on Sunday evenings. He told her that he had an idea and she sat back in her seat, satisfied. He put the sound back on the two-way radio and called Pancho. He'd call again once he'd collected the fare. It might take an hour. "Make sure she pays for it," Pancho said, "remember where she comes from." Julián switched off without replying and turned down a side street that ran a shortcut through to the supermarket. These weren't the badlands but it was a Sunday night and the streets here were dark and there was no one out and the whole city seemed void of decent humanity as they drove through it. He locked the doors from the driver control. Was this a bad area? she wanted to know. It was safer like this, Julián answered. They passed one teenager walking alone with his head bowed into the wind and covered by a thin baseball cap and he seemed for a moment as lonely as it was possible for any person to be. The pavements were broken and where some houses had been were empty lots of uneven piles of rubble risen like middens of a people long dead and the shops were shuttered and the doors of the small evangelical churches were closed and there were very few cars but for theirs.

He parked the car near a side-door to the supermarket and whistled to two boys who were sitting nearby. There'd be 500 pesos each if they looked after the car. Si señor, they said. One of them removed his baseball cap and scratched his ruffled black hair. Neither of them was older than seven and it was late on a Sunday night and no one cared. As they walked round the store, Julián nudged the Englishwoman's conscience, since it was sure to be rawer than his own: she didn't have to answer to his father, after all. Why didn't they pick up a couple of packs of biscuits? Those boys hadn't eaten.

"That right?" she asked.

"Si señora. They not eating."

"Where are those kids living? Who are their parents?"

5

Julián laughed. "They living here." He looked at her. "You got children, señora?"

She laughed at that. "Not yet," she said. "That's a long way off."

"Is a pity," he said.

"A pity?"

Julián nodded at the kids. "Is a pity here people don't think like you."

She bristled. They picked up some biscuits, some bread, cheese and ham, a bunch of bananas and some oranges and took them to the checkout along with the toiletries that she had chosen for herself. Julián thanked the boy who filled their bags and took the receipt from the girl at the till. He handed it to the security guards to be stamped as they left the building. They walked with the cheap plastic bags swinging and rustling and the city around them cowed in a deceptive stillness, and when they reached the taxi he talked quietly with the boys who had guarded it and handed them a bag with their food and they stood with their heads bowed as if receiving a punishment and not a gift. Their shame forbade them from meeting his eyes or the Englishwoman's and they just nodded and whispered gracias and collected the bag and took it with them into the darkness where they would eat.

"Come on," Julián said, "is not far to where you going."

The Englishwoman opened the passenger door and sat inside and closed it heavy in silence. He drove them east towards the mountains that loomed darkly above the city's pallid glow.

"You live round here?" she asked him.

"Is not too far."

"You born in Santa Fé?"

"No señora. I born in the south. In Rosario. Living here five years now."

"Why d'you move?"

"My father bought this taxi. I came too."

"How's Santa Fé?"

He looked at her, slowing as he drove. He had misjudged her, perhaps. She was not a typical gringa.

"Is better now. Before you standing in the centre. On 7th Avenue. On Caracas. People just come with knife. Asking for money. You collecting a fare and they have gun. They rob you. Taxi drivers killed everywhere. Is very dangerous. Now is better."

For some time she said nothing. Perhaps what he had said had frightened her, but it was impossible to know what she had learnt before she came, if she had known what she was beginning. He asked if anything was wrong but she did not answer him and looked out at the streams of light diverted here and there into buildings and the headlights of cars speeding on into their own pools of darkness.

"Why you come here?" he asked her eventually.

"I always wanted to help. So I came here to do something better, to work."

"You have a job?"

"Yes, in a charity."

"A charity?" he asked. "But is that a job?"

"Of course."

She smiled, and Julián smiled. They both smiled. Then they laughed, at themselves and the distance between them, and their laughter echoed around the taxi as if to make them feel less alone. These gringas were so difficult to understand, they came here to work, they were paid – and it was all for a charity.

They had reached 10th Avenue and its streams of light and traffic and life. They were near some of the private universities and the students here never seemed to sleep. He understood them because they were like him and after they'd got really high they'd waste the darkest hours of the night in their bedrooms, like he did, glowing in the bilious light of their computers where they spent their time in chat rooms making contacts with distant ciphers who they would never see, who would never be more than an electronic presence to them.

Julián switched off the taxi's central locking system and wound down his window and smelt the marijuana on the air. Ten blocks further west it was crack. Everyone was on some kind of high, legal or not. Groups of middle-aged women walked slowly by, smartly dressed, arm in arm, returning from prayer meetings. They stopped at some traffic lights at the junction with 58th street and he turned and looked at Pamela Oswald.

"You here a long time señora?"

"It's a three month work placement," she said. "I'm helping get a new project off the ground in one of the barrios. One for kids who've hurt themselves. Cut themselves up with knives."

"Is it in the south?"

She nodded.

"That sounds good," he said. "There could be a lot of money in that. There's always money in new projects. Money for everyone."

"Not always," she said.

The lights changed and Julián drove forwards, but he still looked at Pamela, this time keeping his eyes on her through the overhead mirror. "My father," he said, "you know, he won money. A lot of money."

"How?"

"The lottery."

"Lucky him. Lucky you."

"Maybe. And since then, he always saying, there can be money in everything. Even a piece of paper can make you rich. There can be money in everything. Even in the south you make money. Somebody like you, you can invest. When you leave, you gonna be rich."

"Well," she said, "that's not why I'm here."

"But it's your job," he said, "and every one want to earn well in their job."

"Not everyone," she said.

"You want a driver to take you tomorrow. To the south?" She didn't answer him. "I can help you," he said. He picked up one of the firm's cards and wrote his cellphone number on the back. "You ever want to go somewhere just call me. You want to see Santa Fé at night, call me. I play guitar. Good band. Rock music."

She thanked him. They were nearly at her destination and he felt sad. Probably she wouldn't call. People just disappeared and that was the way of life. You couldn't blame them and you couldn't blame whatever it was they succumbed to and it wasn't as if there was a shortage of people in his city or in the world: bodies reproduced themselves and their spirits too, in a constant sea of multiplication of the sadness and beauty of the world, without end. He raised the volume up high on the stereo and put on a compilation of his band's music, tapping his finger to the base beat constant like a pulse within him that kept him alive. In spite of everything the music they played was thrilling and hopeful. It wasn't dead like the lives of the parasites who fed from the dead and killed them without seeing them, no, his band were better vampires, they drew their vigour from the force which was life instead of from death: that was why they had called themselves Los Vampiros.

He pulled up the car outside an apartment building on a quiet street. She paid him and then laughed, she didn't have any bags so he couldn't help her with those. Who was she staying with? The family of one of the volunteers at the centre where she was helping. She was paying them a decent rent and they'd promised to give her a different window onto life in the city, one which few foreigners could get.

"Enjoy your stay," he said.

She smiled. "That was your music wasn't it?" He nodded. "Maybe I'll surprise you and ring you up one weekend," she said.

She turned and went to the entrance of the apartment building and pressed the bell. She was buzzed in and then she waved and went inside and the city suddenly seemed quiet, dangerously quiet, but there was a buzzing in his ears and it was not the sound of the music which he helped to make and his love for it which kept him happy but the hum of cars like his and people like him swarming like bees over the ruins of the hive which they had made.

# CHAPTER 2

The stairwell was dark and silent like the windy back streets between the airport and the Pachinero. There was a timer switch for the communal lights but it didn't work and you had to climb the steps as they were; it was impossible to see more than their outlines picked out by some faint luminescence which seemed to come from the steps themselves. Two floors up a glow cast more light. A door had opened onto the darkness and there was a figure there. As she walked up a voice called down: *Come on, it's up here.*

Pamela climbed and the light became brighter, the drab stairwell clearer. She reached the door to the flat. Leila Halabi was waiting, her dark hair falling in loose strands on either side of her face, resting against her angular cheekbones as if to hide them.

"So you decided not to bother bringing any clothes with you, then?" Leila laughed. "You thought, they're all dirty over there, I won't need to change."

"Continental Airlines lost my bag in Miami," Pamela told her.

"Ah, these yanquis," said Leila. "They tell us that they're the best, but we all know better."

"You're right," Pamela answered, smiling, "we all do."

She went into the flat and put the bag which she had used as hand luggage on the chipped wooden floor. She was standing in a large living room. At one end was a dining table embellished with a lace throw and a green-and-white vase. Facing the table was a sofa with deep brown leather cushions which sat beside the window onto the street. A few books were strewn on the coffee table beside the sofa: a history of the independence wars, a picture book on Santa Fé, and a novel called *María* which told anyone who knew Leila how proud she was to be a mother.

The room was still.

"You must be tired," Leila said.

Pamela stretched: "It's not so bad. I'm used to travelling." She walked over to the sofa and sat down. She picked up the novel and looked at it. The dust jacket was blue-and-white and illustrated with a line drawing of a man from a previous era with a flourishing moustache and the air of the patrician. "Where is María?" she asked Leila.

"She's watching TV in her room."

"Did she go to the Centre today?"

"Not today. She prefers to go on Saturdays. That way, she can stay out as late as she likes on Saturday nights."

Pamela put the book down. Suddenly she did feel tired, very tired. It was four in the morning in Britain and she hadn't slept for almost two days. She had been given a send-off and had barely slept all night before leaving at five in the morning for Heathrow, since they'd begun talking politics at midnight around some sofas and bean bags at a friend's flat in Clapham and ended slumped like the dead. But how could she just retire now? She was obliged to be sociable. She looked up at Leila: for a moment she felt angry at her long, sad face, the dark eyes, the sense of vitality and even optimism which spread from her and was the opposite of what she felt: then she repressed the feeling. "I'd like to meet María," she said then.

"I'll go and see if I can get her away from her programme."

Leila turned and went up the corridor that led away from the living room into more darkness. There didn't seem to be many lights on in the flat, in the whole building. Pamela stood and looked between the rungs of the Venetian blind but when she looked outside she could not see many lights there either. The whole new world she had arrived in seemed to have lost itself in this darkness. Of course, it was night. Her mind was void with tiredness. She wasn't even thinking any more.

Pamela was still standing looking out between the rungs of the blind when she heard Leila walking behind her, her feet echoing gently from the floor. "This is María," Leila said.

"Buenas noches, tía."

Pamela looked around. María had long dark curls and a face still rounded with puppy fat. She had wide, deep eyes, the eyes of someone who understood more than she should have done at her age. She did not seem innocent, not exactly, but there was a happiness in the way she embraced Pamela, as if she was genuinely pleased to see her.

"Buenas noches," Pamela replied. Then she laughed: "I'm sorry my Spanish is still not great," she said to Leila. "I've taken some courses. Now I'm hoping it'll get lots better while I'm here with you."

"So are we," said Leila.

María turned to go back to her room and as she went Pamela thought for a moment of the taxi driver who had brought her from the airport. Slowly, she remembered the journey, the bag which was lost. She had arrived with nothing, and it suited her. Perhaps it was what she had really wanted: she had needed to leave a lot behind her, if not everything.

Leila came and sat in an armchair beside the sofa – matching brown leather, part of the suite. Pamela asked her where she had learnt to speak English so well. The office in London and the centre in Santa Fé hadn't said, they'd both just assured her that her landlady would speak her language. Leila told her about her job at one of Santa Fé's universities. She was a materials scientist and most of the journals she had to read were in English. Often she was involved in research projects with North American universities whose professors and researchers would pass through and oversee the work. It was cheaper for them that way, she told Pamela, to devolve the bulk of their actual research to a country like this, where salaries were lower and no one asked too many questions, and people like her were happy to work.

Pamela sat still as a stone, listening. The words seeped in, but she didn't feel receptive. She needed to go to sleep but she felt that she couldn't, not yet. Leila stopped talking, and just looked at her for a moment.

"You're staying for three months, aren't you?" Pamela nodded. "That's fine," Leila said, "I think we're going to get along well." Pamela yawned. "You're tired," Leila told her. "Do you want something to eat before you go to bed? Look, I'll be honest with you. I'm not going to cook for you while you're here. I'm too busy and María never eats anything of mine anyway. The previous lodger, she never ate anything I cooked anyway, so I'm not going to bother for you."

"Who was the previous lodger?"

Leila ignored her, brushing the question away with a gesture of her hand. "There's an old lady downstairs on the first floor, Señora Fonseca," Leila said. "She can cook for you in the evenings if you just give her 5000 pesos a night. But I don't mind getting something together for you tonight."

"Thank you," said Pamela. She followed Leila into the kitchen. 5000 pesos: that was about two dollars, she'd checked the exchange rates as she'd come out of the arrivals' hall at the airport.

"What do you want to eat?" Leila asked, standing next to the fridge and opening the door. "A sandwich?"

"Aren't you going to eat anything?"

"I'm not hungry. I ate a big lunch. Here," Leila said, picking up a short stool with a frayed red leather seat, "sit down. It won't take long."

Pamela sat. The kitchen was cramped and drab. It was divided into two: in the half nearest to the living room were the fridge, the cooker, and the sink: behind the sink was a tiled wall which came up to shoulder height, and behind this was a washing line strung from one side of the room to the other and a large bucket filled with clothes soaking in frothy bubbles and water. A packet of Omo washing powder stood on top of the tiles and behind the bucket were two high windows which gave onto the interior courtyard of the apartment building, onto the night.

Leila filled the kettle with water and put it onto the stove. While it was boiling, she made a sandwich with slices of ham and some avocado. Neither of them spoke and the silence was filled gradually by the gathering murmur of the water from the kettle raising itself to heat and Pamela felt that there was something peaceful and humane between them there in that silence, the sort of thing that she had come to Santa Fé to find.

Leila opened a chipped plywood cupboard and got down some teabags and opened two sachets and put the teabags in two china cups. She took the water off the stove and filled the cups and put them and the sandwich onto a tray.

"We'll eat in the dining room," she told Pamela, "it's easier in there."

"Thank you," Pamela said.

"Stop thanking me," Leila said. "Why are you thanking me? You're paying me, aren't you?"

"Still," Pamela said, "I'd feel bad if I said nothing."

They sat at the dining table and drank their tea. Pamela ate her sandwich. Actually, she was ravenous. She demolished it in two minutes even though Leila had filled it full.

"Of course," Leila said, almost to herself, "travelling is stressful. It gives hunger. You'll want another one."

Pamela tried to demur but Leila had none of it. It wouldn't take a minute, Pamela should just sit and rest. This was her home now, as well, a home for all three of them, Leila, María and Pamela. She'd need to feel at home here, Leila told her, because she'd find her job at the Centre difficult soon enough, there was no doubt of that. Pamela called through to the kitchen: actually, she loved her job, it made her feel alive and as if she was doing something useful.

Leila came back into the living room with the sandwich. "Don't tell me," she said, "you always wanted to save the world." Pamela laughed; she wasn't quite sure how to take it, and the best thing to do was eat. As she ate, she asked Leila, did they often take in lodgers, then? Leila looked distracted, and after a moment rose and went to the door of María's room and asked her something. Then she returned and sat opposite Pamela, in silence.

After she had eaten, Leila carried the tray back into the kitchen and then showed Pamela her room. It was a tidy, square space with a single bed and a bookcase filled with volumes in English and Spanish. Beneath the bookcase was an old PC on a prefabricated desk that had seen better days. There was a built-in wardrobe. Leila smiled at her: she could put her clothes in there, she told Pamela, when they arrived. The bathroom was along the corridor. Could she please remember to put her toilet paper in the plastic bin next to the loo? The pipes would block if she flushed them down. Then the flat would flood with sewage.

"Thank you for everything," Pamela said to her.

"Well," Leila answered, acknowledging her good intentions at last, "we couldn't just let you go out into the city on your own, having no one. You've come here to help us, haven't you? We need to look after you."

She left and went into María's room. Pamela saw the door open and that beyond it was a darkness filled with the pixillated violence of a television screen and the subterranean noise of its commentary. María was lying on her bed, leaning back against the wall. She raised herself slightly as her mother came in. At that point, Pamela looked away. She did not want to intrude on their lives any more than she had done already. She closed the door to her room and sat down on her bed. She looked at the small cloth bag that she had with her, limp and forlorn on the floor. She did not even have any clothes to put away, there was nothing to occupy herself with so that she did not have to be alone with her thoughts.

Pamela realised then that she'd put so much energy into preparing her departure that not once had she thought about arriving. She had been busy liaising with the host institution in Santa Fé and getting materials ready to take out with her, saying goodbye to her friends, moving things out of her flat in Stockwell and into storage. When the centre in Santa Fé had told her that they had found somewhere for her to live she had simply accepted it. It would be a financial arrangement. On the plane, she'd wondered fleetingly what the flat would be like and how she would relate to the owner, but she'd given up the effort. She found it difficult to imagine worlds before she had seen them. But now she had arrived and time seemed to have passed with excruciating slowness ever since she had landed just as you imagined it would at a moment of great importance in life, just as you approached your death, and her whole experience seemed vivid and crystalline like a world seen through a child's eyes before they have conceived the prison of boredom.

She lay down. She needed to go to sleep but first she wanted to wash. She had bought some basic toiletries at the supermarket with the taxi driver, Julián. He was clearly money-orientated, but so many people were. It had been nice of him to give her his card. She might take him up on his offer to learn something about the city with him. It would suit both of them: he'd get some regular fares and she'd learn to see the city in a different way, like a local might.

She opened the door and went to the bathroom where there was a single bare bulb and a chipped sink and a toilet with a flimsy plastic seat and an electric shower. She washed her face and brushed her teeth and then pulled her pants down and sat on the toilet. She realised that she hadn't been to the toilet since about two hours after leaving Miami. She was probably dehydrated. She'd talked quite a lot on the flight with an old Italian woman who was desperate for a cigarette and came to Santa Fé every year to gamble in the casinos. To Pamela it had seemed exciting, but now that she thought about that sort of way of doing things, urinating in the bathroom of people who had little that was excess and seemed to have no need of it, it irritated her.

When she had finished she knocked gently on María's door. Leila called for her to come in and she opened the door and hovered there on the threshold. She did not want to go in any further. Leila and María were lying next to one another on María's bed, their arms linked together, watching a soap opera imported from Argentina. Their limbs seemed loose and rested and their eyes half-closed, or half-open, bidden by sleep. But they did not want to go to sleep. Probably those evenings were the only times they really got to spend together.

"Come in," Leila said again. "I'm sorry," Pamela said. "I didn't want to interrupt. It's just that I'm thirsty. I think I need to drink something before I go to bed." Leila rose somewhat. "It's like I told you, you're in your own home now. Just help yourself to whatever you need." Pamela still hesitated so Leila stood up and led her into the kitchen. "Look," she said, "here are the jugs of water." She pointed to two plastic jugs on the cracked tiles above the sink. "It's boiled water. There are lots of impurities in the tap water of the city although many people drink it." She poured a glass out and handed it to Pamela. "Here you go. Have as much as you like. If you finish the jug, boil up some more water. This is your home now. That means you don't have to wait for me to wait on you, just so that you can thank me."

She watched Pamela drinking. She had not turned the light on and so they stood in darkness with just a glow entering from the inner courtyard and from the television in María's room.

"I've understood now," Pamela told her when she'd drained the glass. "Don't worry about me. I won't get in your way."

She put the empty glass in the sink and followed Leila out of the kitchen.

"What time are you going to the Centre tomorrow?" Leila asked her.

"Not too early," Pamela said. "They know I've arrived late tonight so they're not expecting me much before lunchtime."

"Oh, quite late. If it was earlier, I could help you catch your bus. I don't have to leave too early."

"But people in Santa Fé start early, I've been told," Pamela said.

"Mostly they do," Leila agreed, "but I'm lucky. I run my department. I can manage my own timetable." She looked at Pamela and they stood in silence for a moment in the space beside the dining table in the emptiness of the salón. "But you know how to get to the Centre?" she asked her.

"I've got the number of a taxi driver," Pamela said, "I'll just call him when I'm ready to go."

"Can you trust him?"

"He brought me here from the airport, didn't he?"

"Just be careful," Leila said. She turned to go back into María's room and then stopped: "It made me laugh when you arrived this evening with no bags. A few years back, people's bags often used to go missing the other way, when they were leaving Santa Fé."

"Why?"

"The traffickers had contacts in airports across the world. They had stooges among the baggage handlers who'd slip the drugs into the bags and mark them up for their associates to pick out at the other end. The bag would be lost for 24 hours while the switch was made and then redelivered to the passenger. Everyone knew about it." Leila looked at Pamela then, her smile fading. "But I'm sure that hasn't happened to your stuff. Probably it'll turn up tomorrow."

They said goodnight. Pamela went into her room and closed her door and lay on her bed fully clothed. She had nothing else to sleep in and she snuggled under her blankets and pulled them up to her chin and turned the light off and lay there brooding in the darkness. She began to drift towards sleep, aware that finally she had begun to relax. This was where she had needed to be. She didn't have much that attached her to London. It had been almost a year since she'd had a serious relationship and though her friends were sorry to see her go she sensed that they'd soon get used to her absence. She'd read so much about how terrible the world was becoming but you couldn't really grasp that without working to try and make it better, without coming here. She knew too that the country was said to be so beautiful by those who had seen it. Colleagues in the London office had told her about the forest-covered mountains above Santa Fé, the mountain villages where you might catch a fiesta if you were lucky, and the chasms so bottomless that they seemed to lead beyond the confines of the known world. She fell asleep dreaming of those mountains and of remote farms where Native Americans still rode out horses to check on their livestock and tended vegetable gardens and where you could ride out over the wild pastures and peaks into worlds untainted by reality.

# CHAPTER 3

Bear was a violent bastard but they were all violent bastards in the comuna and a slug in the guts had never stopped a friendship on the hill. Who hadn't seen blood the day they were born, the colour of red Chibcha clay? Everyone heard their mothers' cries at least once even if they never listened again.

Like Bear. Bear stole from his mother's business. A small store selling sweets and salt and tea and beer and cigarettes. A small store without a licence for alcohol and Bear stole without licence and threatened his mother with the authorities if she complained. Hadn't she seen what they did to women caught on the wrong side of the law? Was it imagination she was missing, or brains? There was nothing you could do to stop someone like him walking off with the beer and the cigarettes.

But Bear was the sort of person you wanted on your team. His name had come to him for a reason, his forearms brown with hair before their time, his face rounded and hard. He'd nick the ball and kick his opponent and slip the ball to Elvis and Elvis would score, skipping round defenders as if they were as thin as air, like he was. And everyone was happy when that happened. Everyone. How did you show that you were happy? You slipped off your T-shirt and wheeled around with it and ran faster than everyone like you were some animal on the TV being chased all the time, by the predators who were everywhere, and you picked up a stone from the pitch and threw it at the supporters of the opposition. You ignored the referee. You were able to reach a state where you could ignore everything. Forget everything. That was happiness. Bear was happier than most. Once he picked up a rock instead of a stone and after he had thrown it he laughed and flipped somersaults like he was a pancake tossed by his mother above a flame waxing and waning like a pulse or the lifeforce of the earth entire.

Bear's philosophy was his own. "What's misery?" he asked the team one Saturday before a match. "Misery is not being happy. Look at me. We're not scoring enough goals. I'm unhappy." Crouching down. In hiding although he was an animal that could not be hidden. Although he was the team captain. "I'm miserable," he told them.

Elvis's mother Juaní told him that he should not be in Bear's team. "The boy is lazy," she told Elvis, "he is fourteen. Fifteen. At his age he should be working. Not stealing from his mother." There was no work, his mother knew that, but it did not stop her from criticising. "His mother Teresa was never a friend to us, but I did respect her. She worked like a bitch when he was a child," she told Elvis. "At the Gloria bakery, where his sister works now. From six in the morning until seven at night, seven days a week, with two days off a year. She worked so hard to feed him that she never saw him." She gestured angrily. "That boy doesn't know the meaning of gratitude. Duty. He just likes the sound of his own voice. It makes him feel like he's in the army already. What does he do? Sit around the mechanic's workshop and pretend he's helping."

When she spoke to him like that Elvis listened with his head lowered. He didn't answer back. Not yet. He wasn't old enough. Yet. He knew that his mother was trying to educate him. She was always doing things when she spoke. Emptying water from the bases of soft drinks bottles which she had cut in half and used to catch leaks. Feeding his sister Elvira. Washing Elvira's nappies. Hanging the world out to dry as if it were always wet, or it never stopped raining. Sometimes she got Elvis to do that and he'd carry the kitchen chair outside and use it to climb onto the corrugated iron roof and string out the dirty clothes: it's easier for you than me, his mother used to call out to him, you're so light on your feet, but mind that you peg them out properly. When she harangued him like that, as if he was still seven or eight and not old enough to go his own way, he pretended he had not heard: dreaming that somehow already he had escaped from this, which was his life, and that his mother was not too old for this, that this would not be his lot until death or chance intervened.

One of the questions he brooded on most deeply was why they had called him Elvis. All the other kids on the team had nicknames. Bear. Monkey. Lion. Snake. Animal totems, as if they were straight from the African jungle and did not have a 400-year vintage. The only one who didn't have one was Elvis, and so he hated his name.

"Why?" he asked her one night, after all the chores had been done.

"Because we both loved his music then, just before you were born."

"But I've never heard you play it."

"Things changed after you were born," Juaní told him.

Once his father had brought home a pirated CD of music by Elvis from the coast and had played it in the cheap stereo, just so that his son would know his namesake. But the music had made him cry: didn't they realise that he didn't want to be different, that in the comuna survival wasn't a question of being different, being an individual, but of trying to be the same? But it was too late. Bear said that his name already was like a nickname, that it couldn't be real. It was foreign. And that was why Elvis felt like he'd been at a baptism and others had decided and others had chosen and others had called him something that would always make him different and always make him feel that he was never at home or that somehow his home had been sullied even though this was the only home he could ever have. An alloy in a world of pure metal. Cold. Hard. Frozen rigid from a world that had burned molten, fired him in a kiln.

When he felt that anger he always played better the next day. Really his opponents could have been ghosts. There were so many of them, and he drifted past them as if they could not touch him. So slight that he could not be severed by a violent tackle, so short that he could duck under the arms that grappled with him in the clumsiness of their violence, of their desire to stop him. Perhaps he was so immaterial that he was the one who was the ghost, who had disappeared before them.

For some weeks now Bear had been gearing the team up for their match of the season. The barrio of the Cross lay on the opposite side of a ravine which was the burial place for much of the city's rubbish. It was where cats went after their screaming fights to die, their ears torn and red with dust and blood, their fur lacerated with cuts. The women of the barrios slung their waste there and so did some of the dump trucks that collected from Miraflores where neighbours paid a decent rate to decent businesses whose executives lived in Miraflores too and assured their clientele that their waste was safely disposed of. The wires of the cable car route scratched as the capsules passed over the refuse, heading to and from the city. The ravine must have been beautiful once. Now it echoed with the staccato slaps of plastic in the wind and shards of glass that glittered when the sun shone. It smelt of death and abandonment. No one from Comuna 13 dared cross it and neither did the people of the Cross. Slander ruled between the neighbourhoods that never saw each other. The others were guerrillas, or paramilitaries, or both. It was dangerous to cross the ravine. People could tell a stranger from a distance and they didn't last.

The two neighbourhoods were due to play the coming Sunday. For weeks Bear had been drilling the team. They usually practised behind the terminal for the buses which climbed up the hill from the city centre. Sometimes the bus drivers would come to watch the training as they waited to travel down the hill again and call out encouragement and abuse. Lion, use your head on the ball not your opponent! Run, Monkey, run! Condor, you couldn't save my grandmother's penalty kick! Condor was the goalkeeper, named after the Chilean who had knifed himself with a razor blade and faked an injury in the hope that his team could escape from a defeat in Brazil and so qualify for the World Cup. It had been some time ago, no one was quite sure when, but people in Comuna 13 still remembered and admired the Condor. They dreamed of that sort of salvation through self-mutilation.

Four days before the match, on the Wednesday, Bear arrived at the training session with a crate of beer that he'd stolen from his mother's shop. The team drank and joked with each other. Monkey asked Elvis, was he going to sing a song when they won?

"How can he?" Bear said. "He's got the name, but not the looks. He needs the curls, the sunglasses."

They all looked at Elvis, at his chocolate skin and his eyes the colour of coal and luminous in their darkness.

"Of course I'll play," Elvis said then, cutting in on Bear, "but only if they pay me like the real King."

"Ay Elvis," Bear said, "and where are we going to find that sort of money from? Do you want to turn us into thieves?"

"I thought that had happened already," Elvis answered. He looked at his friends for laughter and then found himself on his back, staring upwards at the darkening sky.

"What are you calling me, a thief?" Bear's hands were on him, closing on his neck, clawing at his ribs. Others were on him. On Bear. Elvis picked himself up as the others held onto Bear and restrained him like a wild animal that had broken loose from its moorings and yearned to destroy all others around it until nothing was left not even a wasteland or a squalid comuna like this where people could live and love and fight in the blind sight of a carefree world. He looked at Bear, at his hands thick and callused by odd jobs at a mechanic's, his light brown eyes squirrely and evasive, intense, afraid.

"There's plenty of money in the city, Bear," Elvis said in the end. "We both know that. It's just that none of it's here. I'm sure you could pay me properly for my song if you tried."

After that he turned and walked away past the parked-up buses and across the street and down the alley past Señora López's store towards home. He was hungry and wanted to eat something and he would have liked to play a game of chess with her son Juanchito but he had no money so he did not stop. Juaní always mocked him for his pretension. Where would chess get him? she used to ask her son. Would people hire him for his skill at sequences of prearranged moves? But that was precisely why he enjoyed the game, and had done ever since a student had come from the local university to run a workshop at the evangelical church two years before: it was only when he played chess that he could pretend that his life was not as it was.

As he walked home from the López store the streets were all dark but there was a glow from somewhere far down in the valley where the centre of the city lay and the lights were always illuminated. He saw the shadows of others like him, hungry young men, standing in the doorways of their mothers' houses and waiting for something to happen to them. For an opportunity. People weren't picky about what an opportunity was. Violence could be an opportunity, if it came on the right terms. Often, it was the only one.

When he got home his father was sitting at the table in the square room which trebled as kitchen, dining room and salon.

"Hello Elvis," the old man said. He looked grey. Beaten. Like a carpet flogged in the street: the bright threads of the highland weavers smothered and still ashen with dust from a volcano that exploded decades before.

"Where have you been?" Elvis asked him.

"Veracruz," the old man said. "They put me on the Veracruz route. I've been going, there and back. There and back. Three times a week. I've been here sometimes. You're never here."

"Neither are you," Elvis answered.

"Are you still at school?"

"Have you brought any money?" Elvis answered.

"Nothing for you. Everything I've got, I've given to your mother. You can ask her."

Elvis went outside into the yard where his mother was cooking on the gas stove in the lean-to.

"I'm hungry, mama."

"There's some food," Juaní answered. "I'll bring you something."

Elvis stood there, silent, listening to the dogs outside, cats fighting down the street and over the roofs. The wind was blowing. His mouth tasted of dust. He was really very hungry. He went into the lean-to and put his arm around his mother's shoulder. She rested against him for a moment.

"It will be ready soon," she told him then. "Go and sit with your father."

"Why?"

"Because he's your father." Elvis said nothing. "Go on," she said. "It will be ready soon."

He did as she asked but he didn't know what to say to the old man who drove inter-city buses for a living. He'd seen the whole of the country where Elvis had yet to leave the city, and rarely went downtown from Comuna 13. He brought money with him whenever he came but that wasn't often and the imperative of earning money to keep his children alive meant that he had hardly been able to help with their education. You had to move to keep alive, but moving took you away from the things you loved most, and perhaps helped to erode them. Elvis felt sad when he looked at him that evening. He saw that the man was getting old. He kept his eyes lowered and did not speak, waiting for his father to say something. But he was mute and by and by Elvis realised that his father was as hungry as he was.

"What brought you back this time?" he asked. His father did not move. Then he took his baseball cap from his head and placed it upturned on the table. His hair was dark and ruffled. Hollows swelled beneath his eyes cast into shadow. It looked as if the old man had been in a fight. "Have you been in trouble?" Elvis asked.

"I haven't slept."

"You never sleep."

"The road was empty. Darkness. Just the mountains black in the night. Bare in the headlights. The bus – the bus was empty."

"That's no surprise, papi. No one has any money. People can't travel."

"That's not it," his father said.

"The family will never close the business," Elvis said. "They want to clean up their money."

But his father didn't answer. He looked away. His eyes were empty and did not receive that which the world offered them.

Elvis rose and went back to the lean-to where his mother was putting corncakes onto a plate. He asked what was wrong. It was something bad, Juani told him. A hippie revolutionary on the bus, some puffed-up kid who claimed he was a Chilean writer: the paramilitaries had been after him. They had wanted to take him off the bus and Elvis's father had called the young man who ran the business, and there had been an argument on the far end of the line and then he had told him to refuse the paramilitaries. There was plenty of money to clean up, and they could not afford the bad publicity.

Elvis felt very sad then. Sad and angry. He went outside and kicked a stone in the yard. When the corncakes were ready he carried them through on a floral plate and put them on the table. They sat wordlessly on the low stools looking at each other and at the holes in the plaster that held together the adobe walls, holes which could as easily have been made by guns as by decay. Juaní brought in a broth and ladled it into two bowls and the two men ate, dipping the corn bread into the broth and feeling some blood inside them.

"So what's new in the comuna?" the old man asked when he had finished, sitting back.

"We're playing the barrio of the Cross on Sunday," Elvis said.

"Will you win?"

"Bear thinks so."

"That fool! Don't listen to him. He's worthless."

"Papi, he's the team captain."

"That won't do you any good," his father said. "No good at all. That boy – he's worth less than my turd."

"He's a good footballer," Elvis said. "He brings beer for the team."

"Why are you defending him? Hasn't he hit you yet?" Elvis looked down. "Of course he has. Do you really think he's your friend? Son, you're a coward." His father stood and picked his cap from the table. "Juaní," he shouted, "all that pain when you had this boy, and for what? You gave birth to a coward, someone who's grateful to be beaten up and thanks the person who hit them. Someone who'll never get out of this place."

Juaní came rushing in when she heard the argument, her face streaked with tears. "Husband," she said, "don't be so angry. Stay."

"I can't. It's an insult to be this boy's father."

He left and slammed the door. They heard his steps outside and they were gone. So much anger. Elvis asked himself why but he had no answer. Both his parents hated Bear and had warned against him. That was how it was in the comuna. Vendettas cut so far that their scars lay deeper than a knife could reach and no one could remember their source or say how they could heal over. No one could imagine them ever disappearing, not even if you tried to amputate the limbs where the scars lay. The time before they had emerged was so remote and beyond meaning that it hung like a legend over them, and that spectre of peace did not console them but was a reminder of all that they had lost. His parents hated Bear and that was enough for them to despise Elvis for the power he had over him.

After his father had gone Juaní turned to him and told him that she had warned him: warned him to keep away from Bear. He thought he was special, she said to him, that because he'd never had a father and still needed one that made him different to every other wretch up in the comuna. But hadn't he realised, that all his friends were the same, that they had to accept it and forget it? Men didn't hang around long up here, she said, looking sadly at her son.

His father did not come back that night. Elvira slept badly. Crying. Elvis turned onto his side and held his blanket to him but it was cold. He shivered. When the night reached its darkest point with the air cutting like a knife he sat up. He needed some money. He needed some help to get out of this place before it consumed him. But there was nothing. His father worked but he had nothing. None of them had anything. There was nothing but the emptiness of the city and the emptiness of the sky above them and the void of space with pinpricks of starlight glowing like the lamps of a lost city or civilisation always beyond reach.

Eventually he slept for a couple of hours but woke when the dogs started to bark. Even before it was day. Purple and then grey and colourless white rode the sky above Comuna 13. Already those who lived there had woken. Some women were crying somewhere in the distance. People had died by night. The burials were already being planned. There could be no peace without the burials. Beyond the cries growled engines. The city, humming already, its noise rising up the hillside with the smoke and the heat. Elvis left the house and walked up the alley and over broken stones and bottle ends rammed like missiles into the ground. He climbed straight on up the hill. If he carried on the city would end and the houses would disappear.

A voice called to him as he went.

"Elvis!" It was Condor. He came running up with his big hands and clapped him on the back. "Where are you going? To school?"

"It's training."

"Training?"

"You didn't see me running?"

Elvis started to jog up the hill and Condor went with him. They ran for a minute and then stopped. The hills curved in an amphitheatre and were green and gold in the dawn sunlight. At points the city flashed silver below them, where the sunlight caught a mirror or a window, singing with a quiet joy so early in the morning.

"Was that your training?" Condor asked.

"Yes."

"You need to look after yourself for the match."

"That's it."

"Don't go to school today or tomorrow," Condor told him. "It's not the time to go to school."

They turned and went back down the hill and parted. Elvis knew that Condor was right. He mooched about at home, practising moves on the chess board, hunger in his stomach like an old friend, nagging, like his mother. He couldn't even go and sit outside one of the supermarkets in Miraflores as he often did, hoping to be given a few pesos for carrying some bags and looking grateful. Juaní telling him to get out of bed. Why wasn't he at school? Which gang was it this time? Juaní looked at him. Angry. Sad. He didn't work and so he'd never change, he'd never improve his lot or hers or Elvira's.

The team met for training on the Thursday and Friday. They practised well. They didn't kick each other, not as hard as they sometimes did. Snake danced on his feet with the ball, slippery, impossible to pin down. Then Elvis took over and slipped like a snake himself between the defenders. He was their secret weapon, Bear said. They all felt confident. On the Saturday, though, Condor didn't show up. Bear sent Elvis to his house but when he got there no one answered the door and he couldn't hear anything. It was unusual. Someone was at home in most houses of the comuna, most of the time. The place was full. If you pulled all the occupants out of a house, as the paramilitaries did sometimes, they tumbled out like beads on a string, always more, more than you were expecting. Why weren't Condor's family at home?

Elvis jogged back to the wasteland where they practised and reported to Bear. He'd be here tomorrow, Bear replied: his life depended on it. None of the others doubted him and they played well on their last practice, the ball zipping across the earth from foot to foot, passed and shared. Near the end of the session, Elvis kicked Bear on his calf but the captain laughed it off: it was like he'd been touched by a piece of paper, he joked. Everyone laughed. Snake stood with his foot on the ball, his long dark hair shaking. Bear's chest wobbling. It was funny. They weren't miserable. It had been a good training session, Bear announced to Elvis in the end: he'd do well to remember that move for tomorrow.

Elvis finished up and walked across the bus park and down the alley. His mother had given him 5000 pesos that morning from the stash his father had brought back from the Veracruz run. Her anger with him hadn't lasted. Usually it only reflected how his father had treated her. He held the crisp note in his hand and went into López's store and sat at a stool beside the counter and ordered a Pilsen and a sandwich. The television was on. The boy López was watching football, Los del Sur against América. The picture was fuzzy. Elvis walked up to the machine and played with the tuning knobs. He turned and went back to his stool and looked at the boy and the boy smiled.

"We're losing 2-0," he told Elvis.

"Shit," said Elvis. He reached out and offered the boy some of his sandwich and they both munched. They could hear the voice of his mother call through then:

"Juanchito," she called, "come and speak to your father on the phone."

Juanchito did as he had been told and Elvis drank his beer. Then Olímpia scored a third goal and their striker took off his shirt and wheeled around the pitch, and Elvis turned to watch him, brooding. He was thinking about his own match. About what he would have to do.

That night he slept badly on his mattress, alternating between excitement and dread. He had no breakfast. The team met at the pitch at lunchtime. They all arrived early except Condor. Condor didn't come. At two o'clock, thirty minutes before kick-off, Elvis ran to Condor's house but it was still empty. At kick-off, Condor still hadn't come. They put Lion in goal as he was the next biggest in the team but he was no goalkeeper. The team from the Cross pulverized them, 6-0, and Bear ran like a beast kicking and hitting and swearing at the referee.

For the last goal, Elvis passed the ball to an opponent who played it through to the Cross's striker. After he'd scored Bear marched up to Elvis and floored him with an uppercut. He stood over Elvis in satisfaction and Elvis remembered his father's hatred and his mother's distrust: too much anger because there was so little of everything else. Bear's eyes were narrow with a hatred and humiliation that would never go away. They burned, like the city, like their hearts dyed red in a fire not of their making. They were sharp as light and yet Bear himself was nothing, less than nothing.

"You fucking asshole," Bear said. "This is all your fault."

He marched off. He'd said nothing about Condor. It was as if Condor didn't exist any more. He'd gone missing but no one cared. People vanished all the time. It was a fact of life. As far as Bear was concerned, you had to blame the living and leave the disappeared out of it.

# CHAPTER 4

Later that night and after others were long asleep Julián returned home from his shift. He parked in the secure car park opposite his father's apartment and said goodnight to Olmos, the security guard. He crossed the street alone. The city hibernated, silent.

He rose to the sixth floor in the lift and stepped out into the corridor. The timer switch was broken and he had to paw his way in darkness like some wretched animal not yet hunted to extinction. Julián opened the door of the apartment. His father Arturo was asleep. He went through the small dining area to his room and switched on his computer to see who was online. Claudio in Buenos Aires, John in Manitoba: no one he wanted to chat to. He surfed the net looking at websites blaming various wars on a conspiracy of American security forces. This was something his English friend Robert Stone had put him on to, but he couldn't believe it.

He surfed for half an hour, amused and agitated. His back curved as he read. Like his mind. He breathed sharply. It was always the same when he returned from work. He could never sleep at once. There was an anxiety that came from touring the streets at night and it could not be purged simply by entering the safety of an apartment protected from the darkness. It was an anxiety that never entirely disappeared.

At the stillest part of the night, he switched off the computer. He went in one movement from the swivel chair onto his narrow bed and texted the Englishman Stone: yes he'd be able to come to meet tomorrow morning at 11 for a band practice. He stripped and climbed into bed naked and shivered for a moment as his body adjusted itself to the new temperature. Then he fell asleep, just as the night was greying.

He must have been cold as he slept. He dreamed that he lived in a cold country where it was never fully light and masked gangs roamed the cities and the fields massacring people beneath skies of clouds tinted purple and red by the dawn or the sunset or the dyes of the mountain weavers and that he Julián Restrepo had been invited with his band to entertain the murderers and had set up a stage or amphitheatre in a field surrounded by trees stripped bare and tall and lifeless and they had played their music for hours and days as the gangs had passed never listening once to a sound which might have made them stop and that finally one gang had stopped and their commander had shouted some orders and they had turned with their guns raised pointing at the stage as if the band had been the hidden target of the murdering, the reason and the justification for its existence. Julián had looked in fear at the eyes of these soldiers who would kill him, interrogating their faces, wanting to shout insults and question their humanity. But he had seen just his own eyes, and his own face.

Arturo woke him as usual with his morning shower. Or rather, the song which accompanied him as he washed, knowing that he was waking his son and delighting in it. Julián stirred and sat up, covered by his duvet. He rose and dressed in a gown and wandered into the kitchen to make himself a tinto. He sat opposite his father but neither of them spoke until Arturo put aside his mug of hot milk.

"How are the classes going?" he asked Julián.

"OK," Julián said, drinking his coffee.

"Have you had any tests this month?"

"Not yet."

"It's a good career, accountancy," Arturo said then, looking without enthusiasm at his son, as if trying to convince himself of what he was saying. "It teaches you about money. Discipline. How to be trusted by others. Who is going to work with an accountant if they don't trust him?" Julián wasn't sure if his father expected an answer or not, but when he didn't carry on he rose. "Where are you going?" Arturo asked him.

"I need more sleep. I have a lecture at 11."

His father nodded. "OK, that's fine. I'm going to fly to Veracruz later. I'll be back tomorrow."

That was typical of his father. What the fuck was he going to do in Veracruz? He had all this money from his lottery win and claimed to invest it in small enterprises around the country. He could have said anything: that his hair was purple, that he was interested in his son, that he had loved his mother: Julián still wouldn't have believed any of it. Why hadn't he invested any of the money in his home city, after all? It was probably because he preferred the black whores of Veracruz to what he got in Rosario.

"Enjoy yourself dad," Julián said, "but don't forget to take precautions."

He went back into his room where he lay for twenty minutes, stirring gently. He almost fell asleep but then he got a strong erection and the image of the Englishwoman he had driven in from the airport came before him. There was no way he'd get to sleep after that.

He climbed out of bed and showered. He dressed and walked down to 11th Avenue where he watched the lines of buses farting black smoke straight up into the clouds above them. He lit a cigarette and after five minutes caught a bus towards the colonial district, walking towards the middle and sitting on the unpadded brown leather seats with his knees squeezed up against the seat-back in front. These buses were made for short people because his compatriots were short, but Julián was taller than most; he habitually lamented his discomfort, but at least he could blame his father for it, and his German grandfather. After half a dozen blocks a middle-aged woman climbed on, her cheeks smudged with mascara. She was well-dressed. Her brown jacket and smart blouse were rumpled. She was crying that she'd been assaulted in the street and the hooligans had taken everything. Could people just lend her 1000 pesos to get home? She came on with the same trick every day, Julián had seen her at least four times before. She was lucky to look rich: it meant she could afford to become old. But she'd aged markedly in the last few months. Julián had noticed new lines around her eyes, when her face arched, pretending.

Once she'd gone, Julián looked out of the window. He texted Stone: he was an hour early, he'd be round for some coffee. The bus stopped in a line of traffic in the streets grey and shuttered. Thugs stood in uniform outside chain-stores, proud of their guns, and watching the people walking past them with purpose on the sidewalks, going about their business. Some of his fellow passengers were sleeping off the work of the night shift which had just finished. Others were texting. Julián looked at the bus and beyond it his city with his eyes empty and drawn, beyond interest. There was nothing for him here. He had to leave.

He got off the bus in the colonial district and walked along 10th street, up the hill towards Montegordo. The shops had opened and some of the cafes were busy. There was a group of three people dressed up in Indian regalia and busking outside one of them, a fancy dress irruption from the past into a world that consumed it. Beyond the buskers, there were some building works at one of the government offices and a cluster of labourers stood outside in orange hats. He walked round them and texted Stone to say that he'd arrived and then his phone rang. It was the Englishwoman, Pamela Oswald. She needed to take a cab to the place where she was working and wondered if he was free? Where was the centre, Julián asked her? It was in the south: 35th Street, by 20th Avenue. Julián told her he'd be there right away: ahorrita.

He went into the cultural centre where he usually met Stone, and sat at a table on the inner courtyard. There weren't many people at the centre, which was housed in what had been the viceroy's residence during colonial times. There were a few researchers in the library, which was in a bare room panelled with hardwoods which had once been the hall for audiences, but there was no one else there.

When Stone arrived the coffees were already there on the glass table.

"Two tintos, Lizard, as promised," Julián told him. "I'm paying."

Stone smiled at him. "You don't change, Julián. Except when you play a guitar, you don't change."

Julián shrugged. He liked the gringo. He was a good bassist. Sometimes he made some joke, about when they made it big in California. Then his eyes opened wide, drugged up, and his wiry frame pulsed, laughing. It was almost the only time that the English guy laughed, and when he did his tongue used to hang out of his mouth, like a lizard's. That was how they'd come by his nickname.

"Shouldn't you be studying?" Stone asked him.

"My dad's gone to Veracruz."

"What for?"

"He says it's to look after his houses there."

"Did you make any money last night?"

"There was one big fare. Someone from England."

"Is that so?"

"She's just rung me. She wants me to take her to her work."

"What does she do?"

Julián shrugged. "I don't know. She said something about a charity. About helping people who'd mutilated themselves. Cut themselves with a knife."

Neither of them said anything for a minute. The sky was still grey and mottled with cloud and the insipid light which rose every day above Santa Fé. They could see out of the main entrance into the cultural centre, towards the rest of the city. 10th Street was quiet. Three students were sitting on a wall with some folders: they were checking over something that they had written, something that seemed important to them. Two soldiers walked past in fatigues and looked at the students with stares thick with hatred and lust. They were walking heavy and purposeful down the hill into the city with bullets clipped around their waists and they did not speak to each other and they looked out for potential dangers and then they carried on. Hoping that the dangers would appear. That they would have to take action.

"What about you?" Stone asked him.

"What about me?"

"Aren't you going to collect her?"

"I've told her I'll be there soon."

"But you won't." Julián said nothing. "It doesn't matter," the Englishman carried on. "She'll probably just think it's an exotic quirk."

"What's that?" Julián asked, and Stone pointed to his watch.

Lizard was right. If he wanted to get to know the English girl better he had to go, and he did want to, he yearned to. He spent most of his life dreaming about leaving his country, going somewhere like England. As he sat there and drained his coffee, Julián felt like a teenager about to lose his virginity. When he felt afraid like that his first thought was to buy something. A new CD. If he brought along something new when he went to collect Pamela it might be impressive.

"Come on, Julián," Stone said. "You can't afford to stay here."

They always joked that Julián was richer than Stone. The lottery layabout, Stone called him, and it was true, ever since his dad had won and moved the family from Rosario to Santa Fé Julián had started spending money on things of no value. Stone always joked that Julián couldn't afford to do this or that when it was Stone who had little money to speak of.

"Why should I go?" Julián asked.

"Because you don't want to be here any more."

"What about the practice?"

"Fuck the rehearsal," Stone said. "Stop thinking about the band all the time."

Julián tried to joke: "You keep saying that when we make it big in California…"

"Fuck that. Even you don't believe that."

Julián stood up. He rang Pamela Oswald and told her that he was stuck in traffic. He'd be with her as soon as he could. Then he looked at Stone. Without a word they walked out of the café and down the hill towards the city which yawned grey and monstrous in the plain below them. They stopped outside Stone's apartment building, beside a shop selling stationery to university students.

"You haven't even met her," Julián said to Stone, resentfully, preparing to say goodbye.

"What did you say she did?"

"An NGO. Helping people who've cut themselves."

"Jasmine went to help at a place like that," Stone said.

Julián winced and looked at Stone's face but he saw no pain at all, only a hardness to match his name. Julián laughed nervously, but Stone was impassive and he turned even before Julián had left and went up to his apartment. He was hard to understand, so happy to help Julián leave when he seemed happy to stay here himself.

Julián walked down to 7th Avenue and caught a bus to the Pachinero. It didn't take long at that time in the morning and within twenty minutes he was ringing the buzzer at the Englishwoman's apartment building. He told her who it was and she came right down. She was dressed in a smart blouse and blue jeans.

"Where's your cab?" she asked Julián when she saw him standing there in his jeans and denim shirt.

"I had problem," he said. "Is gone for its service this morning."

"But how will I get to the rehabilitation centre?"

"Don't worry," Julián said. "Is ready now. We can go."

"Why didn't you tell me?" she asked. "You said you were stuck in traffic."

He looked straight into her blue, deep eyes. They reminded him of a sea he'd seen once, on holiday in the north.

"I didn't want you to go with a stranger," he said.

Softly, she retreated. She came with him and they walked along her street. The apartment building was in a quiet spot but up on 11th Avenue there were restaurants and pharmacies and small supermarkets and the back entrance to the supermarket where teenagers sat drinking and tramps lay sprawled asleep with their faces fringed with stubble curled upon their lips open and breathing in starts the cold air of the city and the plumes of thick black smoke thrown up from the backs of the buses like acid streams of condensation from an unseen ocean of the world, its nether region, puffing past the Avenue in stuttering gasps.

They crossed 11th Avenue and passed the student district and caught a bus north on 9th Avenue. Luckily, Julián's flat wasn't far away. He told her that the mechanic had agreed to drive his car to his building, and when they reached 73rd Street they got out and he took her to the parking lot and unlocked the taxi with his keyfob. He opened the passenger door of the yellow Toyota and Pamela climbed in.

"Where are we going?" he asked her again and she reminded him of the address.

"Is in the south," Julián said.

"What's it like in the south?" Julián looked at her. He couldn't imagine what she knew, really, or what she had guessed. "What's it like?" she asked him again and he could see a slight frown between her eyebrows, like a third eye, as the Buddhists called it, an eye of wisdom and sorrow. He turned the key in the ignition and reversed the car out of its space.

As he put the car into first gear and prepared to drive out he looked at her and answered: "Is not like here."

As they drove along Caracas he watched her drink in the city. This was the first time she had seen it in daylight, of course. It was what they wanted her to see, the city erect with tower blocks rising in clusters of light and glass, the city crammed with cars and yellow taxis like Julián's, crammed with prosperity, and the red buses coursing like blood from station to station, the blood of the city and the country spilt there as if the leaders of the country had taken a knife to a vein and bled it, like some doctor or quackery in times long gone.

Then they passed the city and the policemen on traffic duty and the signs of business and past 5th Street the buildings became lower and they drove along 6th Avenue past the large empty lot in front of the municipal offices where rubbish rustled in the mountain winds and the bare sand along the pavements refused to support grass and then the city tailed off into its greatest extent where the buildings were low and some had been destroyed and the lots remained vacant, as if pulverized by a bomb, and no one had thought them worth rebuilding, no one thought there could be roots or foundations worth extending in the south, and the shadows of what had been lay next to small stores and dignified women waiting for buses and the streets were quieter for though there were cars few people in the south owned them.

At the junction with 35th Street he headed west. They waited at some traffic lights. Julián locked the doors of the car but three men came and rattled the windows and the doors and Julián didn't wait for the lights to change but streaked off to the echo of their anger. He checked his mirror after a few seconds and he could just see them waiting beside the traffic lights, their bodies limp and hungry. They didn't in fact seem as angry as he had expected. They just seemed desperate.

"What work do people do around here?" Pamela asked him then.

"What work?" Julián looked at her.

"Yes."

"What work you think those men do?"

"Not them, "she said. "What about the others?"

"Many is like them. Others drive buses. Working in shops. Security guards. Others like me – driving taxis."

She looked out of the window. They had nearly reached the centre, he told her. Her face seemed to settle, adjust. Soon all of this would be normal to her. She would accept it. No longer would it be a myth or a dream that disappeared if you did not think about it. This would be her reality, day by day.

Julián pulled up outside the centre. There was a low wall where the plaster had broken and much of it was covered with graffiti and murals. He couldn't avoid the representation of the indigenous past today: it kept on assaulting him. At one end there was a painting of snowcapped mountains behind a large lake where the water was deep blue and there was an image of a Native American rising with a golden figure in their hands. At the other end of the wall different artists had competed and there was a riot of colours overlapping and figures where some were crossed out or blurred and others were stronger, had their arms crossed, in defiance, anger or sorrow. There was a rust-coloured metal gate built into the wall and behind it they could hear activity: some shouts, a ball being kicked, a gale of laughter, warmer than the winds of the city.

"This is it," Julián told Pamela. "Are they expecting you?"

"I rang them from my apartment," she said, "just after I'd rung you to book the car." They looked at each other. "How much do I owe you?"

Julián looked at the meter. "Is 30,000 pesos," he said.

She looked in her purse and gave him the money.

"Why don't you come in and see?"

"Me? Why should I?"

"I don't know. I thought it might be interesting for you."

Julián shook his head. "I'll see you some other time," he said. "You'll need a cab again."

He watched as she got out of the car, holding her bag. She did look good. There was something light and hopeful about her as she moved, a graceful optimism that he didn't see often. It was so different to Stone: Stone with his fraught energy always tending to anger, an unpredictable distrust of the world as it presented itself to him. Stone had become cynical but he was able to joke about his cynicism. He was almost like the rest of them.

"Well goodbye," she said.

"You should meet my friend," Julián told Pamela as she was about to walk off. "English friend."

"Who is he?"

"Robert Stone. Is a journalist."

Pamela stopped: her eyes had opened as if he had said something suggestive. "Of course," she said. "I've read his articles. How do you know him?"

"Is in my band. Guitar, like me."

"Your band. You told me about that last night, didn't you?"

"We call him Lizard. He always promise: Lizard say, one day, when we make it big in California…"

"I'd like to meet him," she said.

"We'll go to a party some time," Julián said. "Call me."

He wound down his window and started up the car. He was going to drive straight through all the red lights until he reached the city centre. He sped off, flicking the switch on the radio to the taxi control centre. Where was he?, Pancho wanted to know. When Julián told him he laughed, he'd refused to go to the south just the day before, and that for a respected client. "Don't tell me," he said, "it must be to do with sex and I don't want to know about it." Julián switched off the radio and slowed the car for a moment, feeling the judders of the potholes and the frightening speed of his world which so rarely stopped and allowed him to think about its meaning. Why had he taken Pamela to the south? It was because of the power which she and the other Englishman Stone had over him. Pancho was right. It was about money, sex and money. But his chances of hitting it off were tiny. Was it worth that shadow of hope? What would his father have said? Julián accelerated again, trying to forget about the Englishwoman and his father together. The old man wouldn't care: right then he was probably fucking some black whore in Veracruz and reappearing in his son's life as someone who might look after him was probably the last thing on his mind.

# CHAPTER 5

A streak of light as the metal gate opened and offered a new world. Behind the gate was a patio of sand, long and wide enough for 5-a-side football. On the far side of the patio was a breezeblock wall which rose above head height and was topped by broken glass. On the side nearest the road there was a concrete area for chairs and tables above which was a roof of corrugated iron held up by a lattice of thin wooden beams and some stakes that had been cemented into the concrete. At each end of the patio were long, low buildings where the residents slept and the offices of the centre were housed.

"We've been waiting for you Pamela," a woman said, so short that she barely seemed to come up to Pamela's shoulders. "I'm Ramona."

"Ramona!"

Pamela stepped forward and embraced her. They'd spoken often on the phone, and it was Ramona who had arranged for her to stay at Leila's apartment. Her bearing was as Pamela had imagined, someone professional and in charge.

"We were worried," Ramona said, stepping back. "We thought something might have happened to you on the way here. You took your time."

"I was messed around by the taxi driver."

"There's nothing new there," Ramona said. "Messing people around is the true vocation of taxi drivers in this city."

A group had gathered beside Ramona and were examining Pamela. Inquisitively. Eyeing her hair and the fairness of her skin as if somehow they were her amulets, protection from a world where you needed protection. They were mostly adolescents or young adults. To look at them, they seemed to come from the same world as Ramona – though of course Pamela knew that they did not. None of them were tall, and as she looked at them Pamela realised that many of them were probably older than they seemed.

"Come on," Ramona said then, "I'll show you around."

They crossed the patio and entered the buildings at one end. Ramona pointed out a dormitory where there were twelve beds, six on each side of the room, and blankets piled up like bundles of cloth for sale in a market. A refectory was next to one of the dormitories, and beside the refectory was a kitchen where vast aluminium saucepans stood on the gas cookers. They walked through the kitchen and Ramona opened a door at the far side which led into her office. On Ramona's desk there was a photo of two children sitting on a veranda, somewhere in the countryside. There was a large, cheap wall-clock opposite Ramona's chair. The walls were streaked with dirt, and the paint was fading.

"Sit down, woman," Ramona said, taking her own advice. There were two comfortable chairs in the room, each with a red leather back and solid wooden arms. "They're the only luxuries I have in this place," Ramona said, as she saw Pamela looking at them. "I can deal with most things this country throws at me but I can't stand a bad back."

Pamela sat. She felt exhausted. She wanted to say something but she wasn't sure what she could say. The idea that there was anything she might be able to offer this person who was so clearly in command of her environment seemed ridiculous.

"It's nice to be able to talk to you," she said in the end. "My Spanish isn't as good as I'd hoped it would be."

"Well, learning a language takes time," Ramona said.

"Where did you learn English?"

"In Canada. I completed my studies at York University in Toronto."

"Why did you come back here?"

"I wanted to help my country," Ramona said. "But why did you come here? What are you going to do at my centre?"

That wasn't a question that Pamela had been expecting. She'd been under the impression that her managers in London had arranged everything, and when she had spoken to Ramona on the phone it had all seemed so easy.

"Well," said Pamela, "I'm here to help."

She looked at Ramona, taking her in properly for the first time. Her face seemed almost like a cast from the deep past. She had dark eyes and high cheekbones; she was much shorter than Pamela had imagined, but had a vivid, birdlike presence, an energy that always seemed ready to fly beyond her own confines. She didn't look like someone who would suffer fools.

"I am sure you will help," Ramona told her then. "Certainly, your money is already helping."

She opened a drawer in her desk and took out a red hard-backed folder which she passed to Pamela.

"What's this?"

"Our accounts for this year, so far."

Pamela opened the folder. It was thick with invoices and receipts, and IOUs scrawled in a hurry, probably by Ramona, on the desk that separated them.

"Where does your funding come from?"

"We don't have any funding," Ramona said.

Pamela looked around her. "Then how does this place keep going?"

"Oh that's very simple. When I came back from Canada I worked at the National Archive doing research commissioned by North American professors who were too busy to come here and do the work themselves. There were several of us working there. One had an uncle who owned this place and when he died she inherited it. We were so angry at the state of the country that we decided to get the project started. Whenever foreign researchers come to the archive we invite them to come and see the place and they usually get together some donations when they go back to their own countries. That's how we keep going."

"That's an amazing thing you've done for all these people," Pamela said.

Ramona stood up. "It's just the way this country is," she said. "If we don't help ourselves, no one else is going to do anything. We fire the bullets into our own hearts but we also have to staff the hospitals. We're all open-heart surgeons even if we don't realise it."

She opened the door of the office and they walked back into the kitchen where two women dressed in white overalls and with their hair wrapped in protective plastic had begun to peel vegetables. Two of the saucepans were lit and there was a smell of slowly boiling flesh.

"It's chicken today," Ramona told Pamela. She said a few words to the cooks which Pamela didn't understand and then they embraced Pamela with broad smiles. But Pamela felt that their eyes were distant. "Look," Ramona said, "I'm sure it'll be good to have you around. What do your managers in London want you to do?"

"This is a new project for us," Pamela said. "A new funding stream opened up and our funders want to see real evidence of what we're doing and how we're helping to make things better. I need to scope the impact so that I can write a briefing report when I go back. But I wanted to do more than that, too. I didn't feel I could really do the place justice if I didn't live with you a little time."

"So they're paying you for the whole three months?"

"No," Pamela said. "They wouldn't do that. I've taken my annual holiday and some unpaid leave. They just wanted me to come for two weeks."

"I'm glad you've told me that," Ramona said. "That makes you like us. A real volunteer." She turned and said something to the cooks who stopped working for a minute. "I've just told them: you're not someone with lots of money, you're working hard. Come on." Ramona led her out of the kitchen, past the refectory and the dormitories. "Look, I'm sure there are lots of things you'll be able to do for us," she said. "Your money's going to help us build two new dormitories which we'll need to decorate. We'd really appreciate your help with that."

They stood at the edge of the patio. A football match had started. There were shouts, and the scraping sound of feet turning in the hard sand. Ramona pulled up a chair for Pamela and the two women sat drinking coffee. Ramona turned to the teenage girl who had brought it and said something sharp. She threw the coffee out into the patio and advised Pamela to do the same.

"It's absolutely disgusting. Asqueroso, we say here. I wouldn't drink it if I were you." Pamela said nothing for a moment, watching Ramona. She realised now that she had been deceived and that she was not as she had imagined, not at all as she had imagined. She'd had this idea that women here were oppressed, that men walked all over them, but that wasn't the impression that Ramona had given her, or Leila the night before. "Aren't you going to throw it away?" Ramona repeated.

"The truth is, I need the caffeine."

Ramona lit a cigarette. "You're tired, of course," she said. "It's a long journey."

"I'll get used to it."

"You don't have to come in tomorrow if you don't want to," Ramona said.

"But that's why I'm here."

"Yes," Ramona agreed, slipping back into her chair, "so you say."

Ramona looked away. One of the chefs had appeared in the doorway that led to the refectory and had called to her. Ramona rose and went over, leaving Pamela alone. When she came back she said that she had to get on with some work. Later in the week they could talk about developing a plan for the project which would satisfy requirements back in London. For now, there were other things to do. A boy had arrived the day before; one of her contacts had just called her. Arrangements needed to be made for his transfer from a shanty town to the centre. He had deep wounds in his wrists, girdling them, enveloping his limbs like a sheath.

"We'll talk some more when I've got more time," she informed Pamela.

"What shall I do now?"

"You could probably do with more rest. I'd go back to your apartment if I were you."

Pamela felt that Ramona was trying to get rid of her. It wasn't the reaction she'd been expecting. But what had she been expecting? How much should good intentions really count for? There were some things, whole worlds, that had not been spoken of yet between Ramona and her.

"I'm not tired," Pamela said. "I'd like to see how the centre works."

"Fine," said Ramona, "why don't you go and help in the kitchen? There's plenty of work to do there, as you've seen..." She looked at her watch. "Now I must get on. That boy needs me more than you do."

Pamela tried not to feel irritated. After all, she didn't know the centre. Perhaps she couldn't help with the administration straightaway. She went into the kitchen and smiled at the cooks. She tried some of her Spanish. "Permiso, "she said. "Adelante," said the taller of the two cooks, beckoning her towards them. There was a large mound of potatoes and Pamela took one of them and began to peel it with a knife. The other two women were silent at first, but soon they started to work together. They began to talk again, and Pamela managed to rid herself of the idea that she was interrupting. There was so much to do and this was as good a place to start as any. Slowly she'd accustom herself to the work, she'd feel like she was at home. She'd meet some of the residents and get to understand them.

When the stew was ready Pamela ladled it into bowls and placed a hard circular roll beside the bowl on a tray, ready to be taken into the refectory. When the last tray had been carried through she went in herself. Ramona beckoned her over and she went to sit beside her on the long wooden bench and ate from her tray on the scarred old table, opposite people who ate as she did, mostly in silence. Pamela felt so conspicuous; her skin, her eyes, her hair, her entire being marked by a difference which seemed hard to erase. But though Ramona did not talk to Pamela she managed to include her in what conversation there was, opening her body towards her and resting her hand on her shoulder when she was talking about her to some of the residents. Pamela felt self-conscious, but she tried to raise her head and smile at the others. Ramona seemed to understand her, for when they were leaving she linked her hand with Pamela's to signal her acceptance in a world which itself had needed to struggle so hard to be accepted.

"Come back tomorrow," Ramona told her, and Pamela took the invitation, realising that it was time to leave. Ramona called her a taxi and she rode to Leila's apartment. Leila hadn't cut a spare set of keys yet but she'd told her that María would be at home: she got back from school at around 3 on most afternoons. Pamela rang the bell several times but there was no reply. She walked out into the street and called up to the second-floor window but no one answered. An old lady with permed grey hair and a face drizzled with freckles, like specks of pepper, came and said something.

"I'm looking for María," Pamela said slowly, clearly.

But the old lady spoke no English. She had a key to the apartment block and let them both in and they walked up to the first floor where the old lady opened a door and signalled that Pamela should follow. The apartment had the same layout as Leila's on the floor above, and Pamela stood emptily in the large salon for a moment, looking at the old lady and wondering what she should do. From Caracas, she could hear the rumble of the city buses and their noise made the wooden floor of the apartment judder gently in the afternoon light.

"Siéntese, siéntese," the old lady said, gesturing at a sagging grey armchair beside the window. "Puede esperar tranquilamente. La muchacha volverá más tarde."

Pamela sat and the old lady went into the dark kitchen and lit a match and put a small aluminium kettle on the gas stove and hummed to herself some snatches of what sounded like country music. Pamela could hear all the activity, and she peered in and saw the old lady opening a cupboard and putting a roll of bread on a plate with some jam. The water began to heat in the kettle, ringing distantly like bells in a time and place distant from this one. The light in the apartment was grey and came from a high window that gave onto an interior courtyard that was silent in the gloaming.

She came with a tray towards Pamela. "Siéntese, tranquila," she said. "Aquí puede tomar café. Ya luego vuelve la muchacha."

Pamela smiled in thanks and sipped her coffee. She felt immensely tired. She ate the bread and jam and the sound of her jaws on the food magnified inside her. The old woman neither drank nor ate anything but seemed happy just to serve her and watch her as if she had been some museum exhibit. Of course, English people didn't come to stay often in the apartment block. Was that novelty enough to explain her generosity? Perhaps she was just a good person.

The day outside darkened to night but the old lady made no move to turn on the light. As in Leila's flat they sat in obscurity and the feeling of a cave's light and the stillness of that flat and the strangeness of the old woman's generosity and the immensity of all the stories that lay behind Ramona's work at the centre suddenly made Pamela feel sad.

The old lady rose when the night was pitch and drew the curtains and then turned on one of the lights.

"Gracias," Pamela said.

"Así está mejor," the old lady replied. She laughed: yes, it was much better. "No nos podíamos ni siquiera ver."

After a moment she rose and went back to the kitchen and reheated the water in the kettle. She hadn't turned on the light in the kitchen and moved around in a tenuous illumination that crept in from the salon. Why did all these people never turn the lights on after dark? It was as if they wanted no one to see into their world. Out there in the night and in the city that was their habitat, that was becoming the universal habitat of humanity, there was something that was not right. There was something frightening, that didn't fit with the stories that people liked to tell themselves.

Pamela looked inside her handbag for her phone and made an apologetic gesture. "Claro, claro," said the old lady. "Adelante. Está en su casa." Pamela called Leila and Leila answered. She explained the situation and Leila laughed, her voice breaking up, she was with old Señora Fonseca, of course she was: she's the person I said would cook for you, she reminded Pamela: the old lady knew you were coming, she's a good sort, pass the phone to her and I'll explain. They spoke for some moments and then Señora Fonseca returned the phone to Pamela. Leila said she'd be back in twenty minutes: they'd discuss the arrangement for Pamela's meals when she arrived.

"Claro," the old woman said, "no entendía que no sabías que ibas a comer conmigo. Con la otra muchacha, no hicimos este arreglo." Pamela tried to respond, but her Spanish was so weak that she struggled. The old lady had said something about another person: which other person? "Aquella que estuvo con la Leila antes." Before? Perhaps she was talking about the lodger who had been there before her.

Ten minutes later they heard the door slam at the front of the apartment building and someone ran up the stairs. They hammered on the door and Señora Fonseca opened. It was María. She explained in broken English, her mother had called. She had forgotten that Pamela did not have the key. Her mother had bawled at her down the phone as she so often did, anything could have happened to the foreigner, standing outside in the evening with nowhere to go to and no one to see. After a moment she sighed, and told Pamela that she'd been with her friend Ximena in the top-floor flat next door. She turned to Señora Fonseca and talked to her. Then they all sat down and waited for Leila.

When Leila arrived a few minutes later she swept in and began talking with Señora Fonseca. Pamela felt like a child, knowing that she was being talked about but not really understanding how. Señora Fonseca was looking at her, beneficently, as if she had some maternal interest in her welfare. "Pues, claro," she kept repeating.

Finally, Leila went over to María and gave her a bear hug. "Ay, I love you," she told her in English, apparently for Pamela's benefit, "but you give me so many problems." Pamela rose but Leila motioned to her with her hands. "You sit down," she said, "you're staying for supper."

"Supper?"

"I explained it to you last night," Leila said. "You're going to come and eat here with Señora Fonseca. She's very happy with the arrangement."

"Thank you," Pamela said.

"It starts tonight. You must be hungry."

She was starving, Pamela told her. Leila said something to Señora Fonseca, and the old lady rose and came to give Pamela a hug. "No se preocupe mi niña. Yo le voy a cuidar como si fuera mi propria hija. Voy ahorrita a preparar la cena. Espérese aquí, tranquila." She turned and went into the kitchen, leaving Pamela alone with Leila and María.

"How did you get on today at the centre?" Leila asked her. Pamela told her about her arrival with the taxi driver who had brought her from the airport and about her meeting with Ramona. Probably María could tell her a lot about Ramona, she suggested, and María smiled a shy and distant smile. Her mother put a protective arm around María and smiled, yes of course it was true, María could talk about the centre, but her daughter worked hard at school, every day, and she had other things on her mind. What things? Leila didn't answer but instead she ruffled her daughter's hair and they both rose and María went out of the apartment door and into the stairwell and up towards their flat. She got shy sometimes, Leila told Pamela when her daughter had gone, she shouldn't expect her to talk like an adult, not yet.

They waited for some time while Señora Fonseca prepared the dinner. After a few scattershots at conversation they lapsed into silence and listened to the noise from the street, rising and clear as if those shouts and the laughter and the noise of car and moped engines had travelled across water and Santa Fé had been built like the ancient capital of Mexico in the heart of a lake whose waters were deep and pure, as Tenochtitlán's had been, pure and red with the blood of enemies. Pamela had read about this a few months ago in a history of Latin America, when she'd been trying to get used to the idea of the journey she was to make: now she couldn't get the image of Tenochtitlan out of her mind, it felt like it was about to burst upon her at any time with its difference, its violence, its immeasurable mystery. The city too hummed with a suppressed anger that surprised Pamela when she thought about it then, listening. Perhaps it was just her imagination, thinking of all that blood red and gone. She was reading too much into the city, too much into history, when she'd only been there for a day, when she'd only read a few books.

"Don't feel you have to wait with me," she told Leila after a time.

"I don't," Leila said. "I'm going to eat with you tonight. I'm hungry."

"I did some cooking myself today," Pamela told her.

"Where? At the centre?"

"I helped get the lunch ready."

"That's good," Leila said. "You're joining in already. That's good."

"I took the food in to the refectory and sat next to Ramona at lunchtime," Pamela said, reminding herself of her day, as if otherwise it had been so fluid and intangible that the memory of it might have disappeared altogether.

"Did you talk to any of the residents?"

"I didn't get the chance."

"You didn't ask them why they were there? Why they'd butchered themselves?"

Pamela shook her head. "No," she said, "I didn't."

Señora Fonseca came in then with a tray. She busied herself setting the table, moving between the kitchen and the salon with plates and cutlery. She set their plates on floral mats and then brought through a large bowl of spaghetti bolognese, which she served with some fresh chopped tomatoes and lettuce. "Buen provecho," she said when she had finished, and Leila thanked her. Señora Fonseca sat near them at the table. Wasn't the old lady going to eat? Pamela asked Leila, but Leila shook her head.

They ate in silence. When they had finished, Leila put down her fork and looked at Pamela. Pamela saw anger there. For the first time since she had arrived in Santa Fé she felt afraid, and bewildered. There were many things that she did not understand here: things that she did not understand at all.

"You're upset," she said to Leila.

"Yes."

"It's something I said."

Leila said nothing for a while. "Those kids," she said in the end, "I thought you'd come here to help them?"

"Yes," Pamela said. "That's why I'm here."

Leila stood up; she called out her thanks to Señora Fonseca: "Hasta mañana," the old lady called through from the kitchen. She looked at Pamela. "There are too many people in this country who don't want to ask any questions," she said. "And that's how it's been since my parents arrived in this country in 1948."

"That was a bad year to arrive here," Pamela said, trying to show that she understood Leila's anger.

"1948 was a bad year."

"Where did your family come from?"

Leila looked at Pamela with undisguised disdain. "They came from Palestine. From Ashkelon."

Pamela couldn't bring herself to say anything and afterwards they walked in silence up to Leila's flat and then said goodnight quickly, as if something sordid had passed between them. The truth felt like that sometimes: sordid. Pamela went into her room and lay on her bed and thought of what Leila had said, and of everything that she had not said, of the silence that surrounded her previous lodger, the woman that she thought the old lady Fonseca had tried to tell her about.

By and by she slept but she ground her teeth together and knew she had, for in the morning she woke with her jaw stiff and aching and it reminded her of what her last boyfriend used to say when they woke in the dark London mornings of winter: what was it she found so agonising about her life, about him? It was like sleeping next to a clockwork toy, the teeth of the wheels biting into each other soullessly all night. That was when he'd screamed most, one morning, when she'd ground her teeth into her lips and the sheet was smeared with blood that was not consciously of her making, that had come from some place deep inside her and could not be put back.

# CHAPTER 6

How much did it cost, to live like a dog, in Comuna 13? What was it worth? Life had a meaning there. Sometimes it was the most precious thing on earth. And other times, most times, it was worth nothing. Nothing at all.

When you lived among the rubble and the shards of glass and the middens of plastic echoing like hollow drums in the city's breezes you realised that people were really like dogs. For the dogs lived there too. They loped with broken legs or lay curled among the debris of shacks that had fallen down or collected together to trot with purpose along the dirt roads where fragments of glass glittered in the sunshine. Sometimes you saw them sleeping like old men with their faces long and tired and their eyebrows wrinkled and pulsing.

Elvis had a dog, a mongrel called Chico. He really was little. Small, with a brain to match his size. He lived out in the yard at the back of the house, scratching around against the rusting corrugated iron partition which separated them from their neighbours. But Juaní was soft and often let him in to the house. God knew how she managed to feed him, but she did. She loved his wet black nose and mottled black and white fur and the loyalty which she found in him and nothing else. Chico did not desert them. There weren't many better options than the Jaramillo house anyway. In some houses he would have been kicked, in others starved. So he stayed where he was. The dogs of the hill were a cowardly, reticent bunch. They only really barked if there was a tremor. They could hear things that people could not, the earth grinding, its heart struggling to go on. There were some who thought that dogs could see things that people could not, too. That there were invisible forces who wrapped people up and consigned them to this destiny, and their ancestors to the destiny before theirs.

During the week following the defeat to the barrio of the Cross Elvis hardly left the house. He stayed at home and jested with Chico and sat on the frayed white blanket which covered his bed studying his chess board and playing games against an opponent who was always imaginary. Bear had broken the bridge of his nose when he had hit him. It wasn't a bad break but it made Elvis feel withdrawn and he did not want to leave the house. Not to go to school, and not even to run errands for Juaní. Chico was his friend, that was for certain. He'd never even barked at him. He was always so eager, padding over to him when he came into the yard, nuzzling his wet nose against Elvis's leg and looking at him with doleful dark eyes which suggested that he understood more than he should have done. Elvis didn't want to face anyone in the streets, people who might have shouted abuse at him for having been on the losing team. For having been humiliated by Bear. He was much happier that week being around Chico and when the sky darkened and the dangerous noises of the night began, rising above the tired hum of the city, Elvis felt somehow protected by the world and by his place in it.

But his mother became tired of having him around. Ten days after the match she started encouraging him to clear out.

"You need to go to school," she said. "Get an education."

"What for, mami? So that I can understand why life is shitting on me?"

"Without an education you're nothing. Who knows what it could be useful for? You may need maths to do accounts when you're older. You may need money to help Elvira and me."

"Who will I do accounts for?" Elvis asked. "You're dreaming."

"One thing is clear, that chess isn't going to get you anywhere."

"You don't know, mami."

"What's it teaching you? What skill can you learn?"

"Strategy," Elvis said. And at that he turned his back on his mother and climbed into bed to lie on his lumpy mattress. He pulled the covers up to his chin. It was dark but it was still early and there was the smell of smoke from people's fires in the air. He could hear people out on the street, the rustle of their feet as they walked, soft conversations murmuring so gently that their meaning was lost. The longer that he had stayed at home the more distant the world had become, even though he was so intimate with it and could hear it breathing through the wall beside his bed. He had become scared of it. And the only way to deal with fear was to become angry, to challenge it. Chico was at the bottom of his bed, and he almost kicked the dog off. But then that impulse made him feel very sad and he lay in his bed and sobbed with his chest convulsing and his cheeks wet with tears and he tried to be silent and to stifle his sadness so that it would not infect others, so that he could be alone with it, but he could not and by and by his mother came away from rocking Elvira to sleep and sat by him and laid her hand on his chest until he slept.

The morning was grey and silent when he woke. He rose and dressed and boiled some water on the gas stove to make some warm milk. He opened the packet of milk that stood solitary on the draining board and spooned some into his cup with some sugar. There was some stale bread in a plastic bag next to the stove. He poured the water onto the milk powder and then dipped the bread into the milk to soften it and as he ate it he felt better. As he ate he remembered that he hadn't eaten the previous day either. It was the sort of thing that was easy to forget. You lived with hunger like mice or dogs or some other harmless domestic animal and if you didn't think about it it couldn't eat you. Hunger was a kinder friend than many of the people that Elvis had known.

By the time he had breakfasted and left the house other people were risen in the streets. Faces drawn and sleepshorn upon the dusty streets. Their eyes red with sleeplessness and drink as if they had been snapped still by a camera. Buildings and streets and shopfronts all dark in reflection of a daylight still awaited. Only where someone had wound up the metal shutters and opened their shop was the world any brighter, illuminated by a bare bulb hanging above a desk where the owner waited for custom and did their accounts. But once you passed these orifices of light the darkness returned and people passed as shadows before they disappeared.

Elvis walked five blocks down the hill towards the city and then turned left, towards the barrio of the Cross. The way began to rise gently. This was one of the busier streets of the comuna and there were shops open and people waiting and talking to each other. Here, where there were others, people felt safe at least. Half a block before the street reached the ravine which separated the two neighbourhoods he turned down an alley which led between a Mormon church and a half-finished house whose owner had gone to Santa Fé to try to earn enough money to complete it. The alley opened out into a large square yard where derelict cars had been dumped by some shyster from Miraflores. This was where the mechanic that Bear assisted was based, salvaging parts deemed unsalvageable by richer mechanics and taking them back into the city from which they had come to sell them again. Elvis could see Bear's mousy brown hair as he walked up to the huddle of men surrounding one of the cars, a rust-red Chevrolet dismembered on the wasteland. Bear hadn't seen him yet and for a moment Elvis almost turned and left but then he went on, knowing that for Bear the fight had probably already been forgotten. No doubt, he was already thinking about the next victory. That was what military types did, and Bear had always been a military type, one of those who admired the taste of blood on his hands provided that it belonged to someone else.

When Bear saw him he rose, straightening his back. He looked like a sloth uncurling from his tree, one of those that Elvis had seen in a wildlife documentary which he had watched at López's store. Bear looked at Elvis for some moments. His round, porcine face curved further with a smile. The conversation slipped and Bear rose straighter. Everyone was watching him, not Elvis. They would respond to Elvis as Bear responded to him. This was the meaning of power. They had all stopped except for the Angolan, the mechanic in charge who named himself after his ancestors, who he said had been Angolan slaves who had worked in the silver mines in the colonial era. The Angolan was tall and had thick, strong limbs which were the colour of milky coffee, and he insisted that though he had been born here in his heart he was Angolan. Others laughed at him for it, for what did a place so distant in space and memory have to do with their struggles on the hill? No one on the hill knew or cared much about that. But the Angolan revelled in his difference and kept his nickname: that was the funny thing about time and the ancestors, he said, for it moved in a circle and here he was, like his ancestors, mining metals of which others would reap the benefits.

"Well," Bear said, "the king has come to visit us."

"That's enough of that, Bear," the Angolan snapped into the laughter. "Help me with this gasket."

"Ask the king," Bear said.

"I'm asking you. You're here to earn some pesos, so you need to do some work." He walked round the side of the Chevrolet and opened his toolbox, which was deep with tools that blackened with rust the further down in the box they lay. He picked up a spanner and passed it to Elvis. "Here," he said. "Get to work on one of the other cars. Take it apart and see what you can find." Elvis looked at the spanner. He felt useless. The Angolan looked at him. "You're here to earn some money, aren't you? So get to work."

And so it was the Angolan who was in charge. Of course, he was older than Bear. Bear was a prick. A pubic hair. The Angolan was older, almost a veteran. He had some white hairs among his curls. People who lived that long around here tended to cause fear. You could only live a long time in the hills if you killed people for a living or had other types of protection. The Angolan had always worked hard, and honestly. No one accused him of violence. He probably made enough money to go and live somewhere safer but he never did. He said that he liked it where he was. That was another reason that people were afraid of him.

People listened to the Angolan, and with his protection of Elvis came a measure of security. Bear did not stay for long. Not after the Angolan had put him in his place. There was no money to be made here, he shouted loudly, five minutes after Elvis had started to work on a grey Ford which had split into two. Bear looked across at Elvis, whose head was deep in the bonnet of the front half of the car that was tipping forward gently towards the city's maw: this was a game for losers and jackasses, he shouted. The Angolan rose and watched him go. He lit a cigarette and waved his hand through the smoke so that it scattered through the air and above the city like a cloud. He'd be back, the Angolan muttered, inhaling: most of them came back. Elvis watched him go, too, hoping that the Angolan was wrong, because it took a peculiar form of desperation to get him to confront his enemy, and Elvis was desperate. His formal education was at an end, he knew that. No one was going to help him an inch further if he did not help himself. Now he had to plan his own way through the comuna.

And after Bear had disappeared the gloom finally broke and the greyness of the morning light dispersed as the scavengers worked in teams around the metal carcasses and the sun gradually rose above them like their sentinel and made the stench of the rubbish rise from the ravine so near to them and singed their skins to burn and raised the skyscrapers of the city below them to gleam with a siren brilliance. By mid-morning a pile of serviceable parts had gathered on the hard earth below their feet and the Angolan scooped them up and put them into a heavy twine sack the colour of ash. He told them that he'd be back in the evening after selling what he could through his contacts. He'd distribute the shares that evening and people believed him because he had never failed them. He needed a helper. Someone to carry his sack so that those city boys did not sneer at him any more than they usually did. They paid people better if they didn't think them destitute. That was how this country worked.

The Angolan asked Elvis to go with him and Elvis picked up the sack and he carried it with a sense of pride and belonging. He felt almost as if the tools belonged to him. He had helped to excavate them. They were worldly goods, objects worth more than their appearance suggested. They walked together through the barrio and Elvis felt as if the Angolan was protecting him. No one looked at them. No one threatened to humiliate him. As they went, Elvis felt dimly aware that these were his first independent steps, that he was like a toddler learning to walk, like Elvira. Even though his independence depended on the Angolan.

They waited for the bus in the turning area behind the practice pitch and when it came they boarded and the Angolan paid their fares. They sat together and the Angolan nudged him: Elvis's father was a bus driver wasn't he? Inter-city, Elvis told him. He'd gone again on the Veracruz route. Then he looked away and thought of his father sliding through the mountains and the farmsteads sprinkled like ochre baubles across the hills and the roadside restaurants where the passengers ate and his father too. He hadn't seen him since their argument. Why had he been so angry? Bear was an asshole, everyone knew that, but there was no point in getting angry about him. His father was usually quieter and more modest than that. Then Elvis remembered the fear in his eyes and in his silence when he had sat with him at the table, thinking of that row with his employers. The paramilitaries had wanted to kill that passenger, the hippie writer. Soon, his father feared, they'd want to kill him. Elvis remembered that fear as they slid down the hills into the city and he looked at the cars in their lines like ants climbing closer and closer to their queen, bringing their sacrificial offerings to the group. He held on tight to the back of the seat in front as the bus rattled on the road. His knuckles were almost white, reaped by fear.

They got off at the block beside the car mechanics' workshops, which were all congregated together downtown. A round sack on his back and round bodies and bodies thin as planks boarding up empty houses in front of him as he carried the old parts. Houses that were empty like the bodies in front of him. There were many empty houses in the barrio. Like the one where Condor and his family had lived. Empty houses and the bodies somewhere to match them staring up like residues of memory and the earth, rising with the centuries, layer upon layer of soiled histories that recurred, that time's imported linearity never stamped out.

The Angolan guided him into several stores and he tipped the parts out and the men picked about them, their faces and arms streaked with grease and smeared with sweat. The bag became lighter. By the end of the afternoon they had 100,000 pesos. The Angolan would keep half of it and give the rest to the helpers. It had been a good day's work for everyone. The Angolan invited Elvis to eat dinner at his house when they had finished.

They caught the bus back up the hill. The city was darkening and lights rose from the shacks on the hills like stars in a world inaccessible. Elvis looked away from the window and saw that the Angolan's wrists had deep scars, scars that looked fresh.

"How did you do that?" Elvis asked him.

The Angolan shrugged: "I tripped when I was looking at a car and cut them on the bonnet."

"They're deep scars," Elvis said.

"I didn't do it to myself and that's the truth. I'm not like the others. Like Bear."

"Bear hasn't cut himself."

"That's true. He hasn't. Not yet."

They fell silent as the bus climbed higher and the night became nearer and Elvis began to wonder why so many people were harming themselves, waiting for destruction, any destruction, be it theirs or that of others. The Angolan wasn't the first to mention it. Many people were cutting themselves, like the Chilean goalkeeper Rojas. Sometimes they disappeared afterwards. Some people said that there was a centre somewhere which received them all, some earthly heaven for the tending of the mutilations of this world. But no one knew, for those who went in were never seen again in Comuna 13.

When they reached the turning area they climbed out of the bus and walked across the empty practice pitch drunk in the silver moonlight. Three dogs lay sleeping on some broken bricks at the entrance to an alley which climbed steeply between shacks propped up by palings and covered by corrugated iron roofs held down by lumps of rock. There was light in some of the shacks and people were eating. Broth with corncakes, or some corn on the cob. It made Elvis feel hungry. He turned to the Angolan and asked what they would eat but the Angolan did not know.

They turned into an opening between two houses and followed a path strewn with dog turds until they reached a fence with a gate in it. The gate was secured by an old padlock, which the Angolan opened. They crossed a yard where chickens pecked at corn in the dust and drank water from an upturned plastic compartment recycled from an abandoned fridge. The Angolan knocked at the door and they went inside to find a bare room where there was a small table covered with a plastic tablecloth decorated with red and yellow roses. A middle-aged woman was sitting there in front of a large, steaming saucepan: the Angolan's wife, Rosaura. There were some bowls on the table. It seemed as though the woman had been expecting them for some time.

Rosaura rose to greet them and embraced her husband. The Angolan introduced Elvis and he kissed her on the cheek. Rosaura was tidily presented. Her hair was swept into a bun behind her head and she wore a well-ironed red blouse and a pretty cardigan tied together by a bow beneath her neck. Some strands of her dark hair fell in front of her forehead and she brushed them away after she had greeted Elvis. She seemed younger than the Angolan, although it might just have been that she was less wearied by life.

"Come on," she said to Elvis. "I've been waiting for you for hours."

Elvis sat on the hard bench beside the table and she ladled some broth with a piece of chicken into his bowl. She went over to the cooker and took some corncakes off the stove and put them in a basket, covering them with a cloth to keep them warm. She brought the basket of corncakes over and the men served themselves and dipped them into their soup.

"How did you know I was coming?" Elvis asked as he ate.

"I always bring one of my helpers after I've been into the city," the Angolan answered for his wife.

"Humberto is very set in his pattern of life," Rosaura said, resting against the wall of the shack and watching them eat. "He is regular. Not like the others." The Angolan smiled at this, and gave his wife a look of love that recalled desire. "He's never been any different," she went on, "and I've known him for over thirty years."

The Angolan began to chuckle. "I'm just remembering," he said to Elvis.

"What are you remembering?"

"I'm remembering the night I met Rosaura. She danced like a horse."

Rosaura threw a tea-towel at him and they both laughed. "Don't you believe him," she said to Elvis. "If I danced like a horse, he was the blacksmith."

Then they began to tell Elvis about their lives. They had both been born late in the 1950s. They had lived in small farmsteads and ridden bareback on roan horses between fields of coffee and maize on dirt paths that linked the farmsteads to the road and the violence beyond it. The mountains drifting into haze. Serrated with pinnacles like knives. Knives that cut the crops and dug into the earth. Helped to dig the graves. The first deaths had happened for no reason in the years before they had been born, and people had buried the victims and others had been angry and hidden out higher amid the pinnacles where no one would come to find them and they could store up a revenge that had been building for centuries. God knew how. And when other graves had been dug and whole families had inexplicably disappeared as if already they had been spirits treading lightly amid their neighbours and never destined long for this earth some people had decided to come to the city believing that things would be better there, and their parents had come when each of them had still been young children.

"There was work in the cities," Rosaura said. "Yes, that was how it was."

"And how it is," the Angolan said.

"Though now there are problems in the cities too," Rosaura added. "People in the cities make things and buy things and people in the countryside grow things and die." Elvis was silent, and Rosaura told him not to feel sad for them. "We've had a happy life," she said. "Much happier than our lives were before we moved here."

"Is work good?" Elvis asked the Angolan.

"You've seen for yourself," he said. "I can shift things in the city. People know me. You can work for me and earn something if you want. But you'll never leave this place, of course."

"The only way to leave this place is by dying."

"Oh that's not true," the Angolan answered. "But still, you can stay here like me, and be happy with the world you have."

Rosaura brought in a plate of bananas and Elvis ate two of them. "Are you still hungry?" she asked him.

"I haven't eaten for two days."

Rosaura went to the front door of the house and whistled for a boy, Paco. When Paco appeared she gave him 1000 pesos and told him to go to the store and to buy some biscuits.

"Why haven't you eaten?" she asked Elvis, while Paco was gone.

"My mother hasn't cooked. I expect the money my father gave her has run out."

"Where is he?"

"He's gone again."

"He's a bus driver," the Angolan explained to Rosaura. "On the Veracruz route."

When Paco came back with the biscuits he shared them with Elvis and they ate the lot in ten minutes. Then Elvis rose and said that he needed to get back to his mother. The Angolan gave him 10,000 pesos and he left and walked hunched over in the dark as quickly as he could. No one came for him. He could hear his heart in his head and the blood circling his body with each pulse. Shit, it was great to be alive. Who cared what Bear had said to him, or that the team had lost? It was he who was the one walking home with a full stomach and some money in his pocket. He'd outmanoeuvred Bear that day, his wit had trumped the violence of the other, and he was the one who'd achieve his desire and could survive now in the comuna and look after his family.

He jogged across the practice pitch and up past López's store and went into his house. Elvira was crying and his mother was burping her on her shoulder. He put the money on the table and his mother smiled in some form of happiness that could sustain them all for the next day and longer still. Such a delicate, beautiful thing was happiness. So wonderful to give. Elvis smiled then, thinking of Bear, who had said that happiness was throwing stones at the opposition. What did that asshole know? Bear hadn't taught him as much as he had thought, he realised. He thought of his father somewhere, driving alone through the world by night, and of his own walk through the barrio and of the darkness outside and thought that perhaps he had learnt more from his father than he had ever realised.

"Are you hungry, son?" Juaní asked him, looking at his happiness.

"No, I've eaten. That is for you."

"You've always been a loyal son," she said. "Sometimes I wished I had had a daughter first. Daughters never leave. But you have always been a loyal son."

Elvis walked outside and Chico padded up to him and rested his head against his leg and Elvis looked up at the stars speckling the world with their fleeting light and he thought of the Angolan and of Rosaura and of his father driving the night through and of all those souls and all those paths flickering like stars in the night and turning like the earth on its axis and vanished and gone like Condor and his family, like those who had mutilated themselves, gone to some place which would welcome them but which no one had seen, which no one could say where it was.

# CHAPTER 7

There are some dreams which wake people by night and others through which they sleep soundly. Sometimes life seemed like one of those, where it was impossible to tell the waking and the dreaming states apart. Why was everyone so tired? Why did so few people sleep well? It was peace which helped people to sleep properly, to fall asleep: a Spanish doctor had told Julián that once, as he took him from his apartment beyond the Zona Rosa to the airport. Was there so little peace in the world?

He wasn't any better than most, Julián knew that. The one thing he envied his father was his ability to sleep. He'd have been peaceful enough to do that if he'd won all that money on the lottery like Arturo had. But when Julián got home from his night shifts he'd find it impossible to sleep, even if it was four or five in the morning. He'd drink something, beer or rum, and sit on a padded chair beside his narrow single bed staring at the bilious light from the computer screen. As he surfed, he'd listen to rock music. Finally, when even the computer had managed to send him curling under his blankets, into bed, he dreamt, unsure if he was alive or dead, if dreams were the proper medicine for the living. But he never slept for long and when he woke in the morning to the sound of his father showering and peeled back the blankets to rise and stand beside the computer terminal and look through the rungs of the blind at the city and its people working and the green arms of the mountains to the east wrapping themselves around the sprawl, he always felt shattered.

He spent his days in escape. His father was still paying for his accountancy classes but Julián had fled the private university months before and so long as the fees were paid no one cared. It was the way the world worked. There were several friends like him, people who did not want to do what they were supposed to be doing but did not know how to escape their destinies. That was how he'd met the Chilean Raúl Bontera and Jhonny Cruz. Cruz's parents had a large coffee plantation in the country, and Bontera was coy about where his money had come from. Some said it was over a crooked book deal which he'd made a few years before when he had been living in Buenos Aires. Certainly, Bontera had that sort of flouncing arrogance which the Porteños excelled in, even if he was a Chilean. What tied them together was that all of them had money which didn't belong to them, as they studied for a future in which they didn't believe. So they took lines of coke and snorted like horses and Bontera said that it reminded him of ranches he's seen in Buenos Aires province, when he'd spent some time in Argentina, all those horses unused and snorting in the pastures where they'd been put out to feed, to live, to run and to die in.

The three of them recognised each other as fellows. No wonder they were so angry, and turned to rock music, congregating together in the Colonial district and dreaming they would be picked up by the first promoter of the Rolling Stones, who had moved to Santa Fé and was said to keep his hand in. They'd sit there for hours, trying out verses on each other. Bontera wrote most of the lyrics, fancying himself a poet and reading classical literature when he was in his accountancy lectures to steal as much of it as he could. Then they'd play guitar riffs and drink tinto by day and beer or aguardiente by night.

That was how they had met the Lizard, at the café in the cultural centre in the Colonial district. They'd all noticed him there, someone who had as little apparent purpose in life as they did, wasting their mornings getting high on legal drugs. One morning he asked them to lend him the guitar and he played a few chords, like something out of Eric Clapton, or the old progressives: Emerson, Lake and Palmer: Yes. They had all started laughing, and that was how they'd started their band, Los Vampiros. Somehow, just because it had an Englishman in it, it seemed more authentic. We can touch Pink Floyd now, Jhonny Cruz had laughed to Julián in the back of the bus on the way back from their first rehearsal.

It hadn't taken long for them to gravitate towards the cultural centre, pushed by their own pretensions. It was the sort of building which the city's uninspired photographers used for their postcards, a home for bullies and murderers in the past and for dreamers and layabouts today.

"What do you live from?" Julián had asked Stone one day, since Cruz and Bontera thought the Englishman had to be rich like they were. How else could he sit around all day, living off caffeine?

"I'm like most other people in your city," Stone had replied. "I rise early at five, when the city is already alive. Just like parents and teachers getting ready for school, like everyone else who hasn't died in the night and is packing their kids into minibuses. And while they're doing that, controlling their anger, I'm preparing dispatches in my flat."

"Why so early?" Bontera had wanted to know.

"I came here to live like everyone else."

Cruz had laughed: "There's nothing so great about the way we live."

"My day works better if I begin like everyone else. I can make a few phonecalls, fact-check, and file my stories by ten in the morning, when it's mid-afternoon in London."

"And that's enough to live off?" Julián had asked.

"If I can place two stories a week, that's enough for me. Most of it's bullshit, of course, for PR companies and investors. But since we all feed off bullshit, I don't care. It's a good life.."

Then they had looked outside, almost instinctively, at the light reflecting yellow and red from the brightly painted houses across the street and the day slowly drawing colour and life like Stone did from the sun and the buildings and the people who lived there. They couldn't blame him, he had said then. In the day he could roam down to see the jewellers on 6th Avenue by Tucapel, passing the long red lozenges of the buses queued up on the sidewalks. He'd take a coffee and read the paper. At night the streets became silent, dangerously silent, as if hiding from their sadness and the parties which filled the houses so near to them, deadened by the conflict and the noise of each day's existence and cowed into a stillness so dreamlike that it could only be roughly broken. It was a good place to live.

Julián's friends had thought less of Stone after that. Like most idlers they admired easy money and the freedom it could bring even though like all right-thinking people they hated capitalism. They were disappointed that he wasn't going to be able to buy Los Vampiros stardom. But Julián admired Stone the more, because he worked for the time to be able to create and had devised a world for himself where that was possible. This seemed to him to be the aim of a productive life. He said that to Stone once and the Lizard dismissed him with a wave of his hand: it wasn't so great to be creative, he said, in fact frankly it was a luxury, one that these days was usually bought with someone else's violence, paid for by someone else's misery.

All the same, Stone seemed to like Julián and they built a rapport which may only have been based around the fact that they were both guitarists. That was how Stone knew Julián's dreams, the reasons that he could take nothing seriously in this country and scorned his father's hope to see him qualified as an accountant. Sometimes, late into the night, Julián would finish up his shift at Stone's flat and he'd sit sprawled on his mattress staring up at Stone's map of the world lacerated with the drawing pins that marked his own passage and at the dim bulb roseate with a lampshade with red tassels, unable to repress the sense of soft entropy of his friend's life. And as he sat there, Stone would ply him with aguardiente and give him ideas, while mocking him at the same time.

"So you want to leave this country? You have to spend time. You have to work at it, plot it, like a good story. You need to get to know her."

"Who?"

"The Englishwoman. What's her name? The fascist."

"Oswald."

"That's it, Pamela Oswald."

"Why is she a fascist?"

Stone dismissed the question with a drunken wave of the hand. "You have to get to know her. Show her that you're rich in your own right, that you don't value her for her passport."

"But I do, Lizard. I do."

"Doesn't matter. That's the sort of hypocrisy that would make someone like her feel at home."

But when Julián came one night and mentioned that he'd refused her suggestion that he look around the rehabilitation centre with her, the Lizard laughed: had all that talk of migration, of exile, just been a joke then? When was he going to make her realise that he was interested, pretend that he cared? She gave him a chance and he slammed it back in her face. Perhaps his father was right, he said, and he was just a loser. Julián had felt upset then: he'd looked into Stone's face and seen there the hollowness of triumph, of happiness over another's sadness or failure. It reminded him that he didn't know anything of Stone's life.

That was when his taxi was a release. Jumping in in the evenings. You didn't know what would happen. If life was good the danger was frightening and you turned away from the customers if you didn't like the look of them. Men with a shadow of evasiveness, eyes that looked away when the heart spoke. Thieves dressed as businessmen whose briefcases might have been empty. You didn't know who was buying or who was selling, or why everyone was buying and selling when everyone had so many things already. You just wanted them to go away and to be able to crawl back into that hidden recess of the world where your life was good and you could be at peace. But you needed their fares, you needed people to keep on buying you up, all that consumption mattered if you were going to survive and the world was going to survive when the world was an organism in the process of consuming itself. That was why you hated your customers, why it was so difficult to listen to them. Somehow, their money sustained you. But it also made your thoughts more and more violent.

After Stone had mocked him over the Englishwoman Julián trawled the streets in his taxi. Life was not good, and that was when the job was exciting. Because it was difficult to retain interest in the world when the world had lost interest in you. In his country, the world increasingly seemed to have lost interest in everyone. But that didn't have to be a bad thing, not if it meant that people here learnt at last to take care of themselves. What had the world been to this country over the past five centuries but an abusive tyrant, a drunk rapist, a joker, a lecher, a clown? You could drive the streets of the city for ten hours and these were probably half of the people who'd pay your fares and keep you fed and alive: the two facts were connected. Colombian Roulette, that was what Bontera called it, after a game he'd picked up when he had been living there.

Julián's third client that evening was a smart woman with permed grey hair and layers of foundation and thick-rimmed black spectacles who sobbed in gentle and absorbing trills all the way from the Plaza San Martín to a rundown neighbourhood near the airport where her daughter lived with a layabout husband who beat her and their children and was fired from a succession of jobs in haulage firms and made no secret of the fact that he couldn't wait for his mother-in-law to die so that he could spend the estate. His fifth client was a young rich kid who drank two beers in the taxi and offered one to Julián. He drank it, after the customer had gone. The city blared. A policeman came and knocked on the window and Julián offered him a swig. Then Pancho radioed in and he collected some students going to a party in the Pachinero and then a quiet old man who asked to go to 63rd Street where the drug dealers and transsexuals could be found. And all the time he was remembering what Stone's face had looked like that morning when he had laughed at him about Pamela Oswald, a look of sadness twisted with something unrecognisable, power perhaps, or misery. Something he didn't really understand. Was Stone laughing at him because he'd never leave this country when he always could? Or was he just mad?

He cruised the city until late that night when all the people seemed to have gone and with them their money and the noise of the city had ebbed until all that was there was a shadow of life. Even though after four in the morning there was no one who wanted a lift he trawled the streets for some time and circled the northern reaches of Caracas and cut through from 53rd Street west past the shopping strips where everything was shuttered up and cold. He didn't stop at any of the traffic lights and beside one was a group of homeless people cowled in overcoats and blankets and seeming hollow beneath them as if their spirits had no flesh. One of them looked in through the car window from beneath his hood and his eyes were dark and emptied by the drugs which people took to fend off their loneliness and the hood which protected him from the cold was dark and the world was dark and frightening as Julián bore witness.

After he had passed them he decided to end his shift but he could not bear to be mocked by Stone and so instead went back to his home. When he arrived, it was after five and already there were more cars in the streets. It was almost light. He managed to scorn the computer at first, and instead he sat on his bed and wrote some lyrics for a song, but then he went online and exchanged inanities with someone in Quito and after he logged off at six-thirty he rang Stone and tried the lyrics he'd written out on him.

"Where did they come from?" Stone asked when he had done.

"The city," Julián said. "From what I saw last night."

"And who were the vampires?"

"That was all of us. You and me, Cruz and Bontera, the whole fucking city."

"Terrific," Stone said. "It's the best thing you've ever written. Better than Bontera's stuff, that poetry as he calls it. Much better."

Then Julián went to sleep at seven, after dawn. He slept for two and a half hours and woke with an erection. He tried to remember his dreams but he couldn't. His penis was twitching as he sat up and he tried to ignore it but he couldn't. He calmed down slowly and then he caught a bus to the Colonial district and rang the doorbell of Stone's apartment building. On the street a woman was sweeping the pavement outside her house. Three boys no older than ten sat on the pavement next to her and watched. They were smoking and did not move even when she was right over them with her broom. Her back was bent and taut and it reminded him of the men who carried sacks of food and grain at San Andresito, bending further each moment like a sculptor admiring his work and hammering in extra nails day by day into the tomb which is their lasting creation.

Stone leant out from the upper window and told Julián to come on upstairs. He hadn't finished work yet. Julián climbed up the steep wooden stairs and opened the door into Stone's flat. Stone was sitting at his desk beneath the map of the world, beside the old wooden-framed double window that surveyed the city.

"Just wait a few minutes," he told Julián. "I'm finishing my piece."

Julián went into the kitchen and made himself a cup of coffee. The sink was filled with cups and a saucepan sitting in stale water. There were a few plates standing in the red plastic drying-up rack. A cheap plywood cupboard had been screwed into the wall above the sink and Julián stacked the dry plates and began on the washing up. A few minutes later Stone came in and watched him.

"I'm not hiring a domestic home help, you know," he said, walking back into his living room and standing by the window. He turned to Julián: "I'll bet you've never done the washing up unasked in your own home," he said.

"No I haven't," Julián agreed, "but I'm desperate to leave. I don't care if I help my dad or not."

"So you think that if you make yourself useful here I'll have you instead."

They looked at each other for a moment; it was Julián who looked away, wanting to distract himself with the mess of Stone's life, the clothes piled up on the bedclothes, the books strewn across the floor.

"You really ought to get a home help," he said to Stone, turning back to face him.

"Well," said Stone, "you need to find a woman too. For as long as you don't make that Oswald woman interested you'll be coming round here, annoying me when I'm trying to work."

Julián ignored him. He walked up and stood beside Stone to share his view of the city. Below them Don Octavio was sitting beside his stall selling ice creams, chocolate bars and cigarettes. He sold a packet of Kent to a businessman and put the money into a drawer. A policeman was watching him from across the street and walked over. He exchanged a few words with Don Octavio and Octavio gave him three cigarettes from the open packet of Life which was on the kiosk in front of him.

"Come on," Stone said. "I've had enough of this. Let's go and have a coffee." As they walked down to the street, Julián asked him how his work was going. "It's hard work," Stone said. "No one wants to talk."

"Are you still investigating Jasmine?"

Stone opened the door out into the street. He did not answer. He called out a greeting to Don Octavio and they walked across the street to the cultural centre and sat in the courtyard at a small round table waiting to be served. Stone tapped the table with a pencil, as if he wanted secretly to be a drummer.

"No one's interested," he said by and by. "All I get these days are requests from investors to report on portfolio opportunities. I haven't been able to make any money by writing about Jasmine for over two months."

"You need to do some research," Julián said.

"I've done my research. No one wants to talk."

"But you know who took her?"

"I've got an idea."

"There must be a connection to her work."

"Or to me."

Then Stone laughed: he sat back in his chair and with his laugh he bared his teeth.

"What's so funny?" Julián asked. "You liked her, Lizard."

"Forget it. Let's talk about the band. The next gig."

"There's a private party in a club in the Zona Rosa. In two weeks' time. Saturday week."

"Are we going to play there?"

"Maybe we should. Lots of people will be there. People with connections."

Stone laughed again, more muted: "The sort of people who might know where she has got to," he said.

"Maybe," Julián said. "You'd know more about that than me."

Stone nodded because of course Julián was right: he knew that the whole country was rotten and he didn't care to dig too much in rotten earth because that usually ended badly. But Stone didn't seem to mind and had spent his whole life digging in dirt, like a pig. That was the problem with journalists: they were pigs who dug in filth and lived in filth and slowly came to resemble that filth and fattened themselves from it until they were taken before the executioner's knife, pleading ignorance, like a squealing pig. Julián wondered if Stone could really be any different. It was like asking if mermaids were real: stupid, really stupid. But then he remembered how impressed Pamela Oswald had been when he'd mentioned Stone's name. As if she had read lots of his articles, and admired him. Perhaps he wasn't a pig, at least not yet.

After they'd drunk their coffees they walked down the hill. On the corner of 7th Avenue and the Plaza de Bolívar a tall foreign tourist was talking to a very beautiful black whore. Julián stopped across the road from them, pretending to look at the headlines of the newspapers at a kiosk. He wanted to look at the hooker, thinking all the time of his father, those business trips to Veracruz, where he probably behaved just like this tourist. It reminded him that Stone was right: he really needed to find someone, someone who wasn't just a hooker, who hadn't already been bought like everyone and everything else in this city.

"You're a fucking idealist, Restrepo," Stone said to him as a parting shot, as if reading his thoughts. "A fucking idealist."

"You sound just like my father."

"Shit, that's probably why you like me," Stone said. "I'll see you for band practice. We need to get ready for that party, if we're going to play there."

Julián spent much of the next ten days with Stone, Jhonny Cruz and Bontera. They practised by day while Julián was supposed to be at his accountancy classes. He drove nights as usual and drank coffee laced with cocaine to keep himself awake. It was good money. You could charge a lot to drive at night because the city was afraid and assumed that the taxi drivers were as well. Arturo didn't really complain so long as the money was on the table for the housekeeping at the end of the week. He wasn't going to support his son to be a layabout, he'd made that clear. And he wasn't going to waste money on a maid. As soon as Julián's mother had died, he'd made that clear as well.

A few days before the party in the Zona Rosa, Pamela Oswald rang. She needed a taxi to take her out that evening. Where was she going? Julián asked. Pamela didn't answer at once, and Julián played the question over in his mind, aware that it sounded jealous. It was a dinner with the manager of the rehabilitation centre, she said then: she lived in the Colonial district. How was she getting on there? Julián asked her, and she said that it was fine, that she'd tell him that evening.

It was absurd for him to be jealous, he realised that. He had no claim on her and there had been a note of surprise in her voice when he had asked about her life. But it was right for people like him to take an interest. Otherwise people like Pamela came here and they could just be swallowed up by a great teetering void which hung like a chalice over the mountains of the country, a black hole, a memory. People had to know about their lives. They had to care about them. Otherwise they could just disappear. Like so many others. His father challenged him sometimes about his friends: why were there two foreigners in Los Vampiros, the Chilean and the Englishman? Weren't musicians from his own country good enough?

"They care enough about the country to come and spend some of their lives here," Julián had replied once. "So we owe it to them to take care of them."

"There are many who wouldn't agree with that," Arturo had scoffed, laughing.

"You're right. And that's why people like me have to step up and look after them. Look at Stone. Did you know that his girlfriend had vanished? That right now, he's investigating her disappearance."

"Who was she?"

"An American research scientist who just vanished one day from the office of her research partner at the Universidad de Los Andes. That sort of thing could happen to Bontera and Stone."

"Another foreigner."

"A human being."

"Yes," Arturo had replied, "but people from here, too, are disappearing."

His father despised him, and the Lizard was right, he had to get out. Perhaps he'd been a fool to reject the invitation to look round the rehabilitation centre. But at least now this jealousy of Pamela Oswald was a sign that he cared. About something. That seemed important. Sometimes it seemed as if all the feeling had been stripped from the world. But like most things, Julián knew this to be a mirage. When something appeared to have gone it returned and lay sunk unseen beneath the earth in piles of bones or stored up in the bellies of people as a remembrance of all that had been felt, all that had been lost. It was like all these pseudo-revolutionaries recreating the indigenous past: they wouldn't let anyone forget that there was a different way of being.

He was tired that afternoon. He made his way back from the Colonial district to the flat and slept until just before dark. He had something to eat and collected his taxi from the car park. Olmos asked him if he'd be watching the football that evening from the Copa de Libertadores, América de Rosario were playing a team from Paraguay, Olímpia. He'd be working, Julián replied. He turned out of the parking lot and toured the northern streets of Santa Fé depositing clients here and there until eight o' clock when he drove to the Pachinero and rang the doorbell of the flat where the Englishwoman was living. She came down shortly afterwards, dressed in black jeans and with a dark duffel coat to keep her warm. Julián welcomed her and they drove up to 11th Avenue and then joined the broken chains of light arrowing into the city.

Julián asked Pamela how she was doing and she said that she was fine. How did she find the job, and the country? Pamela attacked him with her enthusiasm. For him, she was everything that was desirable. She leant forward and as she spoke he imagined her breasts, hanging as she spoke, pendulous, desirable: her breasts and those of a thousand J-PEGs. He sat more upright as he drove. She did not seem to notice. She was talking about her job, about how it all seemed so real, now, everything that she had been working for in London. She was humbled by the importance of the work that was done at the centre, by the enormity of the task. People didn't understand, she said, they really didn't. The workers had welcomed her and now they joked with her and treated her like a family member, as one of them, especially as her Spanish was improving day on day.

At length she sat back and Julián drove the car in silence into the city. At a traffic light he lit a cigarette and offered one to Pamela and they both smoked as he pulled away and they were sucked towards the centre.

"Why did you ring me up?" he asked. "I thought I never see you again."

"I wanted to see you," she said.

"Why me?"

She didn't say for a moment. "Perhaps I wanted to show you how I'm getting on. That I'm not alone here any more."

"That's good," Julián said.

"I don't think many people are alone here," Pamela said.

"But the people you working with – how they end up there?"

She didn't answer that; instead she leant forward to give him some directions. They were entering the Colonial district. They had crossed Tucapel and there were shadows of people moving in the dark streets. There was energy. There was laughter.

"She lives up towards the Montegordo," Pamela said.

"She treating you well?"

"Wonderful."

"That's good."

He pulled the car up as she directed him. Still he didn't feel that she had explained why she had rung him up again. Perhaps she'd had a bad experience with a different taxi driver, although it didn't seem like that. Or perhaps this was an opportunity. As she opened the door to get out he told her about his gig that weekend in the Zona Rosa. It wasn't far from her flat. She thanked him and said she'd love to come and that she'd call him on the Saturday to find out the details. Then she paid and walked up to ring the doorbell of an old wooden house like many others in the Colonial district which hid a history like many others of violence and emotions and injustices past and buried behind that old door and in the hearts of the people who lived there, people who Pamela was working with, people who she thought she was helping. The door opened and Pamela went inside, and disappeared.

# CHAPTER 8

On her third Saturday in Santa Fé Pamela woke early. The subdued shudder of the water on the plastic shower curtain echoed through the thin wall as María washed. Pamela could hear her singing a snatch of a song, something that sounded sad, and beautiful. She stretched in her bed, reluctant to emerge from her dreams, pulling the thick blankets around her. She was thinking of food. She was hungry. Perhaps she wasn't eating enough. She rarely ate at the rehabilitation centre because the experience of being there was too exhausting. She only ate by night, at Señora Fonseca's: the old lady gave her plenty to eat, much more than Ramona had done when she had gone to eat with her in the Colonial district, but it still left her feeling hungry.

The night before the old lady Fonseca had given her chicken and rice. She had eaten in the dark pulsing with energy from the city, an energy that had never been requited: eating silently, as she always did when she was there. At first she had thought that this living space was much like Leila's on the floor above, but day by day she realised that it was not. The armchairs were patched and sagging, and there were few books. The walls had not been repainted in many years and the whites were all smudged, like the walls in Ramona's office at the centre. Sadness stuck to the room. During her first few days she had tried asking a few questions about Fonseca's life but the old woman had looked alarmed, as if she had heard something which should not have been there. Her eyes widened, her low forehead bunching with lines like rings on a tree. Pamela had realised that the old lady would never understand her. She was inured to serving, in silence.

The water stopped and Pamela heard the gentle thud as María pulled the shower door open. She sat up and put her feet on the floor. It was cold, not yet light. Had it been a weekday the city would have been alive already. Rubbish trucks collecting the bags which people just slung out on the pavement at Caracas. Waiting for their excess to be silently disposed of. Teams of minibuses racing each other from traffic light to traffic light up the main roads with their excited cargoes of schoolchildren. These were the people who drove María to school. All of them were asleep though, now. All of them except for María and for her.

There was a knock on her door and Pamela opened it, her blue nightshirt hanging crumpled by her knees.

"Vamos, tía," María said. "We need to leave. It's six o'clock."

"I'm coming," Pamela answered.

She tied her hair in a bun and pushed a few strands away from her cheek. She put on her blue jeans and clipped her bra together behind her back. Her lost bags had arrived eventually, two days late: a thickset man had waited silently by the door of the apartment building for her, one of those people you tried to avoid at other times. She put on a red blouse and then went to the bathroom where she washed her face and brushed her teeth. Leila was still sleeping and there was a part of Pamela that wished that she was too. It was going to be a long day, if she went to the party with Julián that night. She hadn't even told Leila about that yet, since she knew that she'd be met with sarcasm: a toyboy already, what was this, her countrymen and English women living down to their bad reputations already? That was the funny thing about Leila, she seemed to have little or no identification with the country, and was as happy talking to Pamela in English as to María in Spanish. She was a chameleon, at home with everything and nothing.

María had made coffee for them both and put it on the table in the salon with some bread and butter. They breakfasted swiftly with just one dim light to guide them. The rungs of the blinds were still closed when they went out of the apartment and down the stairwell. They walked up to 11th Avenue past the string of shops selling rosary beads and biblical charms and sayings of the saints that could tide you through yet another year of life. They waited for a bus and when it came they paid and sat at the back like rebels against a city that had many ways of provoking rebellion. María looked so tired that Pamela left her to sleep. Soon the girl's face was pushed against the window, pressing for release, her cheek distorted by the pressure.

Every time Pamela went through Santa Fé she felt a surge of excitement, like a child again discovering the world. The journey reminded her that she had come here for a purpose, that she needed to gulp up the opportunities that came to her before they were gone. She did not tire of looking out of the window at the city reborn each day with its hustlers and smart students and dignified old ladies emerging from tea shops as if from their natural habitat. The pavements broken up by the passage of so many feet and so much time and so many memories forgotten, pavements which made her think of Brixton and Portobello. And little surprises which she would never have seen in London, like the female foreman of the building site not far from the city centre, giving orders to the workmen. Small vestiges of beauty, someone smiling to themselves as they walked along the pavement and felt far from the world suffering and dirty as they walked through it. It was those small vestiges which reminded her why she was there: that was what she wrote about in her emails.

When they reached Tucapel she woke María. They got off the bus and walked arm in arm to a stop where they caught a bus south. People looked hard at Pamela, distracted by her hair. Leila's daughter seemed more awake, and they amused themselves with talking. Pamela told her about the party that night in the Zona Rosa.

"Who's arranged it?"

"My friend," said Pamela. "He's a guitarist in the band. Why don't you come too?"

But María looked shy, her eyes green and distant. "I'm busy," she said. "I'm going to see Ximena."

"Boys?"

"No!" María laughed. "We just want to watch some films."

"That's OK. It can wait. There will be other times."

"That's good," María said.

"Good?"

"It's good you are here. Otherwise, it is just mami and me."

"Your mother is not easy?"

"As you see, she is an old mother. She was over forty when I was born. And then, she gets sad. That for her is easy."

Pamela did not feel surprised. She could see, it was years since Leila had had a relationship and it wasn't good for her. Just the two of them. The dark flat by night where there was an acid silence or television.

"People need company," she said.

"Otherwise, she comes sad," María said. "She remembers her childhood.   Here in the violencia from other violence."

"I'm sorry," Pamela said.

"Don't misunderstand. The country was good for them. It gave them a home. There was space, too much space. Space which others had left. Here they give you a good welcome, then bury you."

They got off the bus some blocks from the rehabilitation centre. They walked quietly. Already, Pamela had learnt not to be afraid of the south of the city. Ramona laughed at her, she was already more of a local than many of the people who lived here: sometimes taxi drivers didn't want to come, worried that people would attack their car and that things were worse than they really were. It was true, things did go wrong. There'd been an incident a few weeks before when a journalist dressed in a purple dinosaur costume as part of a promotion had been attacked at a local supermarket and forced to flee on a motorcycle. But he'd had an expensive camera with him, something worth a lot of money. If you came with little, and walked slowly, it was like as not that no one would bother you.

They reached the centre in time to help with breakfast.

"Vamos," Ramona said when she saw them. "I may be little but I can eat like an elephant. We're hungry too. We have as much right to eat as the next person."

Pamela and María ran into the kitchen and put on their white tunics and gloves and started loading plates with bread rolls and butter. Pamela mixed together some powdered milk in one of the large saucepans and lit the stove. It was all mayhem: María was running in and out carrying the plates as Pamela filled them. It was as always: never enough helpers and never enough food to go round. She'd seen that already in the first weeks as she'd helped with the accounts and with the cooking and with painting the new dormitories. Ramona had pretended that she'd be in the way but perhaps this had been somehow to protect her from the enormity of what had to be done there.

When finally everything was served she went through to the refectory and sat beside María, opposite one of the residents who everyone called the Tumbera. The Tumbera fixed Pamela with a stare as soon as she had sat down, and Pamela smiled. She hadn't tried to talk to the Tumbera much, but she always tried to be civil. Now the Tumbera surprised her: she could speak English, did Pamela realise that? Pamela did not: where had she learnt? In San Bonifacio, working with the American archaeologists there. Then Pamela remembered, she'd once asked Ramona what the name meant, and Ramona had shaken her head: the keeper of tombs, she had said, she was a funny one, she'd spent years in the south, in San Bonifacio, working with archaeologists in the pre-Hispanic sites there. Pamela thought it sounded fascinating: fascinating, yes, but it wasn't something you'd do if you valued your life, Ramona had told her, the place was crawling with the guerrilla and so the paramilitaries were nearby too: you were lucky to leave it alive if leave you ever did.

"In San Bonifacio," Pamela said now to the Tumbera, draining her milk. "Did you spend long there?"

"Five years."

"Did you like it?"

"The mountains is everywhere. The forest. People is very kind."

She had looks which were all to the contrary of Pamela's, with a pretty, spherical face and dark hair which fell over her forehead in loose strands. Her face was one of those which was like a cast of other faces and beings lost to the earth, sculpted to bring to mind those peoples of desolate antiquity. It contained many faces, many facets of experience. All those years digging up the past and living with the past in the mulchy earth of the south and all the time the thought getting to you, the question of what those people had actually been like. These North American archaeologists came with plenty of money and they said they were thinking, and the people working on the dig too said they were thinking as they layered up the earth in piles, as if from graves freshly dug and awaiting new coffins, but all the time it was apparent that none of them yet really could say how these people so long dead had looked at the world, how they had understood the moment when they had stopped looking. That perspective was too alien, too different: it asked you to accept the limitations of your view of the world, and that was too much for most people.

"It must be beautiful in the south," Pamela said.

"Is OK. Ask María. She knows it too."

Pamela looked at María in surprise. "How's that?"

"It's where Leila was born," María said. "My grandparents ran a shop in Rosario. They both arrived as teenagers and married in the mid-50s, after they'd been here a few years. The Palestinian community was small, and their families had known each other in Ashkelon. They'd been in Rosario ten years or more by the time mami was born, long enough to be part of the community."

"Are they still alive?"

"No. They had hard lives. Vidas muy triste. My grandmother never forgot Ashkelon. She kept a photograph of her family house all her life on her dressing table. Hasta el día de su muerte aguardó esa foto."

María said nothing more, and Pamela boiled with rage, as she always did at evil. Some people were able to turn themselves off from it, ignore it, but she could not: she had to confront it, and her last boyfriend had told her, that was why she was always getting into trouble, why she ground her teeth at night. "You must have visited there, been outside the city sometimes?" she asked María by and by.

"Oh yes. They knew people who had farms. Sugar cane. Not coffee. Sometimes we've been out there and stayed. Ridden horses."

"It must be beautiful," Pamela said again. But neither María nor the Tumbera spoke. After a while María rose and said she was going to prepare lunch. The Tumbera looked at Pamela: "Come on," she said. "I want to show you something."

The refectory was almost empty by then. They rose from the wooden benches and walked along the bare concrete floor, out into the corridor and into the dormitory where the Tumbera slept. She went over to her bed and leant over a bag, rummaging. From the back she looked delicate, like a piece of ancient pottery that you could dig up and shatter at the slightest touch.

"What are you looking for?" Pamela asked.

The Tumbera rose with a small photo album. "Do you remember these?" she asked Pamela.

"Remember them?"

"Photographs. Pieces of paper," the Tumbera said. "Before we all lived...by screens." Pamela did not hide her surprise well, for the Tumbera continued: "Yes, even I know that." She sat down on her blankets and patted the bed beside her: "Come on, sit here."

She began to leaf through the photographs, showing her relics that had been dug up and bones and skeletons of beings and people whose rest had at last been shattered by the children of their assassins. The pictures showed a smiling crowd, a mixture of tall foreigners, Native Americans, mixed race people working on the dig. Everyone looked happy.

"Why did you leave?" Pamela asked.

"Life worked out like that. The money stopped. The professors left."

"Why?"

"It was the guerrilla. They got too involved in the region. They kidnap. One of the North Americans went missing. They rob. Suddenly, no one interested. San Bonifacio...Pah!"

"That's a shame."

"That's what fear does to people."

She looked away. Pamela listened to the sounds outside. Some of the residents were playing football, shouting to each other. The Tumbera was looking out towards the empty space where they were playing but she was not looking. She was living in the past.

"History," Pamela said. "People think too much about it. We need to sort out the injustices in the here and now, not those of the past."

The Tumbera looked at Pamela. She was smiling. There was a tear forming in her eye. Pamela could not bear it and got up, about to make some excuses: she didn't want to have to deal with that emotion. She used to agree with her, the Tumbera told her, but now she wasn't so sure for it had come to seem to her as if every pain and justice was connected in past and present, that the past intruded onto the present at every moment, and that what they were suffering right then, and what she had suffered before she came to the centre, could only happen because they hadn't grieved for everything that had been lost from the past, because the burial hadn't properly been done. So would she go back and work there if she had the chance? The Tumbera put down the photo album in answer to Pamela's question, wiping the tear which had fallen with her hand: was she crazy, did she think she preferred it here? Pamela felt bad, then. She hadn't meant to be rude. She was trying to make conversation, really.

"I'm sorry," she said. "Ramona told me not to ask you how you got here."

"When the dig packed up, my life went wrong. Was in the late 90s. You no idea what it was like here then."

"I've heard it was bad."

"Me – I was excavating the past. Digging into it. Cutting out that earth. And then suddenly – I couldn't do it no more."

The Tumbera rose and went to the window. The football match had finished and the crystalline sounds of people talking and walking had replaced the noise of the match. The Tumbera whistled: "Gorda. La Inglesa te quiere hablar." She turned to Pamela. "Go and see the boss. Go on."

Pamela went. She walked across the yard. Ramona was standing next to some pots of paint, giving instructions to two of the volunteers. She was utterly in command of her environment: a flourishing human being.

"What's up?" Ramona asked her.

"The Tumbera sent me over."

Ramona shrugged. "She's like that," she said. She made as if to go to her office but Pamela stopped her.

"Who gave her that name?" she asked Ramona.

"I did. She was always talking about tombs she'd excavated and the bones she'd seen. She was like a walking tomb, pretending that the dead were like her, sleepwalking among us."

"Has she been here long?"

Ramona shrugged: "Almost a year. She was picked up in Ciudad Bolívar. Too many drugs and not enough food. If she hadn't started cutting into herself, she'd probably be dead by now." Ramona turned and handed the paint pots to the volunteers, giving them some instructions. There was something faintly comical, she was so much shorter than the painters were, but it didn't stop her telling them what to do "Don't worry about her," she said to Pamela then. "She's just one of many, as you've seen. There are others much worse who you haven't spoken to yet. It's not worth spoiling your weekend about."

"No."

"It's that party tonight, isn't it? The one you told me about the other night."

"Yes, I'll ring my friend later."

"Is María going with you?"

"No."

"That's good," Ramona said. "You don't want her to get too close to you, like the last one."

"The last person to stay with Leila?"

Ramona turned to her then. Pamela watched her eyes shine and dim, like shooting stars, assessing how much to illuminate.

"So they told you about her?"

Pamela shrugged. "Not really."

"No," Ramona said. "They wouldn't."

"Who was she?"

Ramona turned to go to her office: "If they won't tell you, I'm not going to," she said.

As Pamela worked she thought about the centre's manager, so admirable in so many ways and yet impossible to be close to. Even when she had gone round for dinner that week she had felt as if she was eating with someone who would give so far but no further. She hadn't even asked Pamela once about her life in England, before coming to Santa Fé. That suited Pamela, of course, but still it was strange. No, Ramona was like an oracle, speaking in riddles and mysteries. Why had she implied that María was untrustworthy if she had sent Pamela to live there in the first place? What or who was the last one? Pamela knew that there had been no other NGO like hers who had tried to help the rehabilitation centre before: no one else had cared enough: no one else was committed.

She texted Julián on the bus as they went home that afternoon and he gave her the directions for that evening. Hasta luego, she texted back with a smile. María asked her about the party that evening and Pamela said she didn't know much about it, really: she wanted to see the taxi driver again, and to meet his friend, who was a famous journalist.

"What's his name?" María asked, as the bus ground to a standstill in the traffic.

"Robert Stone. Though you won't have heard of him. He writes for the international press. Stories about this place."

"What stories?"

"There was a whole series just before I arrived. About some American materials scientist who disappeared."

María started. "But that's my mother's friend. Jasmine Purdue."

"I didn't pay attention to the details. According to Stone, it was all related to the business connections that she had."

"Tiene que ser la Jasmine."

Pamela said nothing. She saw that María was disconcerted that people in the wider world might know something that related to her. It was getting cold, and she zipped up her coat and wrapped her scarf more tightly around her neck: a bright woollen alpaca scarf that she had bought at Brixton Market. The truth was that Stone's stories had tantalised her when she'd first read them and she'd claimed relief when she'd seen that the American's fate was connected to the work she had been doing. Nothing like that was going to happen to her, she'd told her friends back in London. She was trying to help people, she wasn't going there to rape the country: these days people understood the difference.

"What did he say about Jasmine?" María asked then.

It was getting dark and the clouds were massing above the city and over the Montegordo hill, boding night. The city seemed frenetic even though it was a Saturday. People were trying to get home, trying to retire before the dark pressed in. Pamela tried to remember the details of the articles. She looked at María as she thought, but her mind turned too slowly. It was something about a research company based in the States, linked to one of the American universities, and the discovery of a new fibre in the Amazon basin that had a commercial application. But she couldn't remember much, the details of the case had vanished from her mind soon enough.

"I can't remember it all," she said to María. "Did you meet her?"

"She was a good friend of ours. She even came to the centre with me a few times." María paused: they were nearing their stop in the Pachinero and she was getting ready to ring the bell. "She was staying with us. Como tú."

And then it was night and the city luminous and threatening, changing shape like one of those old shamans that Pamela had read about deep in the jungles of Colombia and Peru. It had been sleeping by day. Now, what was it? She had laughed at Ramona, the veiled sense of threat, that something was not right with María, that there could be something dangerous. But she hadn't said anything about this American, Purdue. No one had mentioned it, though her presence had been there from almost the first moment. She was gone from their minds and consciousness if ever she had been there as anything more than a token and now she existed as a cipher, a name. If that was what a memory was. Probably it was a coincidence. But why the silence? Probably because already she was being forgotten, like everything that is past or has disappeared. What is a memory of the dead once the bearers of memory themselves are gone? Inscriptions, anguished markings in nameless cemeteries and readerless books in libraries soon to be scanned into oblivion. A thought that then is gone. The best you could hope for was an urn burial, like the ones that the Tumbera had dug up in San Bonifacio. Those that had disappeared but were never quite forgotten, whose imprint never quite left the earth and its meaning.

She texted Julián from the apartment and he called to collect her at eleven o'clock that night. Pamela said goodbye to Leila, who was sitting alone in the room she shared with María, the blanket pulled around her and her knees tucked up to her chin. She seemed unconcerned: María was next door with Ximena and everything was quiet. Leila told her to be careful and then Pamela was gone, down the steps. Julián drove her north through the rivers of light and darkness and the shadows gathered in a crush like matchsticks in the gloom, pressed together, of people gathered together for safety but tempted by the dark. She asked Julián who would be playing that night and he said that they were, with another band. It'd be rich kids, a private club. Pamela's name was on the guest list.

When they arrived in the Zona Rosa Julián parked at a guarded parking lot and they walked to the club's entrance. Julián gave their names to the bouncers and they were let in to a club like any other, like the ones that Pamela had seen in London. The lights and smoke and people dancing in oblivion on tiered levels, the crush of people by the bar, shaded by the dim brilliance of the spotlights. Pamela smiled: she'd wanted to come along to have a local experience but it seemed like she might have been better staying at Leila's and watching the Argentine soap opera.

Julián led her to the bar and she ordered a rum and coke. As she was drinking some people came by, and Julián introduced her to two of the other band members. Stone wasn't here yet, he said, he was on his way. So Pamela smiled at his friends, and one of them leant over and told her that he was Bontera, that he wrote the lyrics for their band. Pamela tried to seem interested, but she tired as Bontera persisted, coming on to her. His eyes were luminous. He wanted to write songs that were meaningful, he shouted, leaning next to her ear, that offered at least a glimpse of someone living here and now, in Santa Fé, in the early 21st century. Not many people care about that, Pamela suggested and Bontera nodded, getting excited. History had tried to present one outlook as some universal truth: but the only universal truth I'm interested in, he told her, the only universal human right is the one for men and women to hold each other.

Pamela backed away, and tried to turn to Cruz. "He talks too much," she said. Cruz nodded, "He calls himself a poet. That gives him licence." "It's a mistake to give him the opportunity," she said, trying to make a joke, but Cruz shrugged, unwilling to get involved. There was some unspoken hierarchy in their band, perhaps, one that gave Bontera first pickings: was that what Cruz was trying to intimate to her? Or at least was that what Bontera kept on intimating, leaning over towards her? Could he buy her a drink? Not yet, she said. And she wasn't interested in history, anyway, but in what was happening now. Neither was he, Bontera said, not that universal history. His stories picked different perspectives, different outlooks, and welded them into one: that was what he wanted to do with his songs, that was in fact a real history. This, all this, he said, waving at the club and then pointing at himself, is what I call Colombian Roulette, a game I enjoyed when I lived there: you don't know what you're going to get when you come here, it might be beautiful, but it might sure as hell kill you all the same. How is it different to Russian Roulette? Pamela wanted to know. There's one big difference, Bontera told her: in Russian Roulette, you have the safety of the empty chambers.

Pamela turned away, tried not to respond. She looked for Julián and saw him coming towards her with his arm round a friend. It was Stone, he said, introducing them, and that was when she became excited, and left Bontera and Cruz behind her. She moved closer to Stone, flirting. She couldn't help herself. It was exciting to meet someone she'd read about, in the paper.

"I've been reading your pieces," she said to him. "But you didn't say anything about being a musician."

Stone looked at her dismissively, and moved away: "What are you doing in this country, then?"

"I've come to help."

"No, but what are you doing here?" She wondered if he was deaf, but then saw the hardness of his face in the lights.

Pamela felt shocked. He wasn't the person she'd imagined from the articles, not at all. He was so bitter. She felt her body moving away.

"You should try smiling," she said. He did smile then. "The people I work with smile, and they've suffered more than you ever will."

"Of course. I don't doubt you."

They fell into silence and looked at the dance floor. In a corner she could see Bontera and Cruz doing some lines of coke. Her nose twitched, but she repressed the thought quickly: she wasn't here for that.

Stone leant towards her. There was almost a leer in his expression, something she didn't like. He was going to share something with her, something to make her understand this place, understand him. The last private party like this he'd been to had been one of the most scandalous in the history of Santa Fé. It had been given by a plastic surgeon, a member of the elite: the sort of guy who was always expanding the breasts of the oligarchy's women. But this surgeon had not been a happy man. His daughter had been raped six months before by a gang of super rich lowlifes who went around the city's streets raping girls for fun, coming from such powerful families that they knew they could get away with it. The surgeon was very clever, Stone said. Masterful. He said nothing. Bided his time. Then six months later he threw this party. He invited the cream of society. He invited the rapists, slipped a drug into their drinks, and then took them into a back room where he surgically removed their testicles.

Pamela recoiled. Stone was laughing: of course they hadn't known about it at the time, they'd just been having a good time, like everyone else except the rapists: that was justice for you. Pamela smiled weakly. She finished her drink and ordered another rum and coke. Now it was Stone who was moving closer to her. She couldn't tell if he was trying to flirt with her by shocking her or if he was past caring. Perhaps that was what happened to foreign correspondents like Stone. Those who have once cared for everything in the world end by despising everything.

Julián was laughing. He looked at her, leant over, and shouted into her ear.

"You need to be careful with Stone," he said. "The Lizard knows what he wants, and usually gets it."

Pamela appreciated Julián – appreciated that he was not like his friend Bontera, that he had not come on to her, and that he had given her a chance to evade Stone.

"When is the band playing?" she asked him.

"Not until later," he said: "three or four in the morning. I hope you'll still enjoy it, if you and Stone haven't left by then."

"Don't worry," she shouted in his ear, "I'm not going to sleep with him. There's no chance of that."

Perhaps there was a hint of flirtation in that. Julián seemed to move towards her. He wanted her, she sensed that, and she remembered the feeling she had had that morning on the bus, the sense that she had to grab her experience of Santa Fé before it was gone. That was good, Julián said then, she'd made the right choice. They looked at each other. Julián laughed then, his long, aquiline nose and even features softening with the action: she needed to watch out, the last gringa Stone had dated, he'd ended up writing articles about her after she had disappeared from her office in the university.

# CHAPTER 9

A month passed and Elvis became a regular at the Angolan's, bent taut over the bonnets of cars dismembered. Some were drilled with bullet-holes but others had little wrong with them at all. The scavengers of Comuna 13 struggled to understand how they had ended with them in this open-air burial on the hill. But they did not complain. They rifled the parts of the motor and the suspension and the brake parts clean until just the chassis was open to the air.

When times were good and the rich had thrown out more than usual Elvis would see the benefit. Turned into a dog with the sanction of those who could afford morality, a dog which was grateful for bones which had not been chewed through. He'd go and eat with the Angolan and Rosaura, sharing his spoils with Paco afterwards as they picked their way through the alleys and over tin cans and plastic bottles abandoned by chance for the Gods to dispose of. He never arrived at the house drunk, and when he put money on the table his mother said nothing, although it was always gone the next morning. He ate better, filled out. They were able to buy more food for Elvira, too, and Chico got better pickings. Elvira cried less at night, he noticed. He'd always hated his sister for the bawling by night, like an animal. Probably like he had been at her age. He had never realised that it was because she was hungry.

Juaní said nothing to him about his work and she asked him nothing about school since it was better not to ask questions if you were not prepared for the answers. If she had known that he was earning the money honestly, she would have been surprised. She had made her point about the importance of an education but the truth was that when your stomach contracted into a fist that assaulted you at every hour, food mattered more than an education. School was dangerous. If you had any sense, you abandoned school. Although it wasn't as bad as it had been. Juaní told him that one evening, when he'd missed a month already, softly making her point: some years ago, there were schools in the city where pupils died every day, victims of the gangs. That was just how the city had been. No one was especially outraged. Perhaps that was the problem, Juaní said, no one really cared enough, and life had gone on, hadn't it?

And it was during that month, when Elvis finally felt established at work with the Angolan, that the paramilitaries first came through the comuna. They knocked on doors, asking for contributions in the fight against terrorism. There had once been many terrorists in this comuna, they told people. A big war! Bodies. A big cleaning job! Let's hope it doesn't have to be done again. They were all in this together, fighting for the future. They were all in this together.

"What sort of contributions do they want?" Elvis asked his mother when he first heard rumours of the visits.

"They need two things," she told him, "money and recruits. And we have to give them one or the other."

"How can we do that?" he asked her.

"It's a good thing you are working," she told him. "If you'd carried on going to school, we wouldn't have any money to give them."

So that was it: it had become impossible to go to school and stay in the comuna anyway.

"Who are they fighting?" he asked her.

"The poor."

"But we're the poor."

"They always fight the poor," Juaní said. "So many of us are poor. They have the luxury of choice. They've fought us already."

"When was that, mamí?"

Juaní looked at him, her eyes old and the lines around them bunched like whiskers. "It was a long time ago. You probably don't remember."

And down by the turning point for the buses from the city you could watch the dark cars numberless and new wheeling like carrion hawks. Hunting. People tried to keep out of their way. Football practices stopped. Even the dogs seemed scared and retreated into the shadows of houses that had been abandoned to them through fear or violence or bad luck or poverty. Houses like Condor's, which had been dismantled and reused already. Very ecological, the dogs' inheritances, with their mud bricks broken down and crumbling and windows and doors stripped, the roof stripped, the building a skeleton of a home in which they could live. Chico whimpered and spent most of his time hiding under Elvis's feet, as if he could smell the fear. At first Elvis was surprised that the dogs cowered but one afternoon, sneaking down to Señora López's store for a bag of rice, he saw the carcasses of ten mongrels piled up beside the alley. Yes, they'd come here to clean up and that could mean many things. The dogs understood this: they knew when to keep away. Elvis wondered if they weren't the best judges of people he'd met.

Many people left the comuna in those weeks when the paramilitaries were there. No one saw them go except for their families and that was what you could hear in the hills, if you listened carefully enough, the sobs of mothers dispossessed of their sons by men not much older than they. Men who would become mentors and instructors in violence. Men who like their sons would soon be dead and buried by soil dug over their putrefying bodies by other young men whose blood still was hot. Officers and foot soldiers dreaming of the war and of the day when their superiors might hand out some money to them so that they could go and buy electronic goods and women who at least did not have to be taken with violence, even if they had to be paid for. Sometimes you heard rapes on the hill in those weeks, screams muffled by the whirring of the cable car overhead. But it was not as bad as the last time, people said. Not nearly as bad. It was not worth complaining.

What were these new inheritors of the violence? It was plague, some people said. Attendance at church went up. And the priests prayed. As always, they prayed. The women prayed and the men fought. That was life. That was the history of the world. Perhaps a time would come when the men would pray, too, but not in this generation. Not among the paramilitaries. Though sometimes as you saw them in the streets you saw crosses around their necks, totems of beliefs that they had learnt by rote and which were easily sacrificed or co-opted for a new cause.

Through all that time Elvis worked every day. There was no point in hiding for then there would be no money to buy his freedom from the army. The Angolan looked out for him, giving him as much as he could. Rosaura fed him and Paco to save on his other expenses. They did not talk about this, or discuss why. Like all the most important things in life it was never spoken of for words might have robbed the generosity of dignity. Of charity. And all the time Elvis kept accumulating pesos and hiding them where he could in the house, waiting to make his pay off, walking home late at night past posters newly stuck on telegraph poles of young men who had disappeared without warning, whose families were desperate to know what had become of them.

Elvis worked harder than ever before at the cars and twice went with the Angolan into the city to the mechanics' yards where it was amazing how normal life seemed and how people were still listening to the same radio stations and arguing about football matches and talking on their cellphones and withdrawing money at cashpoints and buying food at supermarkets and hailing taxis which edged slowly beside one another in the crawling traffic of the city where plenty of people had money, and plenty of people thought that the world worked well. And Elvis knew that they thought this because they were protected by the paramilitaries, they knew that those envoys of violence were their saviours but that they thought little of them, nothing at all if they could help it, discarding thoughts of their protectors for traditions that were more appeasing of their consciences, that forgave them.

By and by the paramilitaries came. Three of them, pale as moonlight in a scarlet dusk. They stood by the door, guns hanging at their sides like third limbs. Saplings of men, yearning to mature. Juaní listened and kept the door ajar and Elvis skulked on the bench behind the table where the family ate, and he looked at the cracked walls of his home and the calendar poster tacked on there of the city below them, offering the security of modernity and beauty, and he wondered if he would ever see this place again. The men said that the price was 200,000 pesos, twenty days' work, that was how much was needed to cooperate in the fight against terrorism. Elvis had it with him with a little to spare. He rose and gestured to his mother to go and stood looking at the men and handed them the money. But did he have anything else that he should not, a stray dog? Chico was in the corner, whimpering, and they asked Elvis if he was a stray and Elvis said he was not, and they asked him if he was sure, and he shrugged. The youngest of the paramilitaries raised his gun casually and shot the mongrel as it lay there. There was no point in taking chances, he said, dirt had to be cleaned up. Then they thanked him for joining in the fight, such solidarity would not be forgotten, a good deed was not something that vanished, it remained in the world's maw, it could be rekindled, goodness would never die out, but, lamentably, neither would evil. And then when they were gone, Elvis hugged Juaní and they both cried. Elvira had slept gently through the visit but had woken with the gunshot, and now they took it in turns to burp her on their shoulders. She stretched against them, warm and soft.

"Go and sleep," Juaní told him gently. "You must be tired. I will care for her."

"I'm not tired," he said. And so before he slept he picked up Chico's corpse and took it out to the yard. Elvis scrabbled out a shallow grave; Chico's corpse was dirty, heavying now, empty and red. The mongrel was silent as Elvis buried him and felt as if he was leaving his childhood behind him as he did so.

After he had done, he went onto his bed and worked through some moves on his chessboard. Thinking of strategy, always strategy. This was how you could survive in the comuna, only by learning strategy. And survival was not a mean ambition, it held him together and had driven him to supplant Bear and work with the Angolan and to pay money to his enemies.

Eventually he slept until he was woken by the dogs of the hill greeting the dawn. That made him miss Chico with a raw emptiness. He rose and went out into the grey light and listened to people hammering metal distantly and the sounds echoing round the hills like voices of manufactures long past and then he did feel tired, much more so than the night before. A large cross had been painted on the pavement in front of their house, something he had seen across the comuna. The payment of money and young men was like a vote, a decision. Comuna 13 was deciding to side with the forces of law and order, which meant that they accepted the status quo. But people on the hill were not natural conservatives. They came from families which had been in the city for more than thirty years and they were the children of people who had made the move from the farms of their parents to the city. People who had not accepted the status quo and could not accept it here. That was why the co-operatives had formed, the pathways of resistance. That was why the paramilitaries had come.

Elvis continued to work hard with the Angolan, getting stronger and fitter. Now that he had paid, all the money he earned went into food for the household. They were all happier. It had been weeks since his father had appeared, but they had enough money to eat. At times in the morning as the light broke white and clean over the city and the people rose from their sleep and the air of the hill cluttered with coughs and radio programmes and the clucking of chickens pecking at the dust of the back streets another sound joined them, Juaní singing, boleros usually, her voice husky with her age and the build-up of tobacco, husky but beautiful. There was something light about her features, a great weight lifted, the world of her family's survival, which no longer depended on her husband. Her son could care for them too, now. He was beginning to fill out, still slight, but growing. He was becoming a man. Even Bear would not have frightened him if he had seen him by night in the streets on the way back from eating with the Angolan and Rosaura. But the Angolan had been wrong: Bear never had gone back to scrounge for work, and Elvis hadn't seen him for weeks. In fact, no one in the comuna seemed to know where he was, though his mother insisted that he hadn't left with the paramilitaries, and she had refused to join the others and slap a poster of him on a lamp post or telegraph pole asking for news of the disappeared.

Perhaps it was because he felt that he was adopting the role of the provider that Elvis became more curious about his father. He realised that he hardly knew him. A stranger to him all these years, arriving with his eyes and voice heavy, tired by things they would rather not have witnessed or spoken of. Yet once he must have been young, like him. Once he and Juaní must have been in love. One evening when it was late, and Elvira was sleeping in her cot beside Juaní's mattress, rustling against her blankets and tugging them up to her chest, he sat at the table sipping a cup of sweet black tea and asked where they had met and she told him about an Independence Day party one evening twenty years before. He had been a handsome man. Worldly. He had seen things, travelled around the country. His mouth soft and open as he spoke. Compelling because of his enthusiasm, because of the energy with which he lived in the world. She hadn't been wise, hadn't thought about what a life with him would mean. The absence, a sense of desertion slowly drifting between them, as he was away earning money.

Juaní had said all this to Elvis with her back turned, stooped over the sink. Working. She turned, holding a ragged tea towel in her hands. Her face seemed ashen. Drained like the world of life and blood. So much needlessly cast away and nowhere from which to replenish it. She had never spoken like this to him before: never spoken to him like an adult.

"I used to resent it," she told Elvis. She put the tea towel down and went and sat in the broken orange plastic chair that sat beside the door. "I was not clever," she said. "Those weeks away on the buses. His women on the coast. Oh yes, you probably have two or three half-brothers and –sisters there. He brought back the money, but so what?"

She was speaking of him as if he was dead. They both were, he realised. "You needed the money, mami."

"Yes I did. It was only after the attack, though, that I forgave him. He was away in Veracruz and when he heard the news he kept away. Yes, that was when I forgave him. Even though we weren't here then. But everywhere things were bad. Everywhere." She looked at Elvis quickly and then her eyes darted away. He thought he understood her, then, understood her anger. "Things have been better since then," she said. "But you're too young to remember."

That was the second time she'd mentioned this attack. He asked the Angolan about it the next day but the Angolan looked through him as if he hadn't heard. That evening he left the graveyard for cars where he worked and passed beneath the cable cars whirring overhead, down the dust roads which led to the turning area for buses where concrete funnelled the vehicles and their charges down into the city. Then he crossed over to the dust roads which climbed again beyond, and on his way home he called in at López's store and ordered a coke. The boy

Juanchito came and sat beside him on the stools behind the counter. "Qué más?" he said and Elvis shrugged. He passed him the coke and the boy took a swig. His mother called to him from the kitchen: he should stop annoying the customers, they hadn't come to listen to him, by God, they had enough worries. She came and stood beside her son and Elvis, and her son dropped his head and his body fell limp, in its place. Outside a dog barked and Señora López walked through the beads that hung like a rosary of protection across the doorway and shouted into the street, clapping her hands. The dog slipped away and she stood there with her arms akimbo, staring into the darkness.

Elvis put his bottle down on the counter and Señora López turned at the noise. She was a tall, strong woman, almost as dark as that night outside, and she seemed to Elvis to have a limitless capacity to ward off the world as she turned to him then.

"Clear off," she said to her son again and this time the boy obeyed.

"Qué más?" Elvis asked her.

"That boy. He's no good. If he'd been a few years older, like you, they would have taken him."

"People say they've gone away."

"For now. They've never trusted us. How can you trust people who by rights should hate you?"

Elvis looked down at the floor: a spider was dancing across the concrete with surprising grace and he watched it until it had left the shop, slipping under the beads. "I don't remember it when they came before," he said.

"It was some time ago."

"Did anyone come to investigate?"

She laughed then, at his innocence and at the injustice of the world. "Not a chance." Then her face evened. "No, wait. There was some foreigner who came asking questions. About a year later. He came with people from the hill so no one touched him, but no one wanted to talk to him either. What was he going to do? If he'd asked the right questions he'd have ended up in an unmarked grave like the rest of us."

"Who was he?"

"Some English journalist, I think. Some people were excited. They started talking about the royal family in England. You know what people are like here." She shrugged. "Aping those who keep them down."

"So he found nothing out?"

López shrugged. "I don't know. Whether he found it or not, no one did anything. So does it matter?" Then a flicker of memory passed her eyes and she walked over and sat beside Elvis beside the shop counter. "It wasn't his fault, you understand. He said to me, once, that no one would be interested. That no one would care. And he was right."

At that she stopped talking and put her hand on his shoulder, as if she had wished him for a son in Juanchito's stead.

Elvis stood up. "What would you do if you were me?" he asked her.

"I would leave. Go in your father's bus to Veracruz. Forget this place. They may have problems in Veracruz but at least their problems are different."

"But I've never left this city."

"No condition is permanent, Elvis. There can always be something better."

"You're an optimist, then, Señora López."

"By the grace of God, I am."

And outside he walked up the hill towards his house and called his greetings to neighbours and friends resting in their doorways, and he saw their washing rustling on their corrugated iron roofs and heard the scratchy sound of radios and music, cumbia and vallenato, and he could hear the city grinding below as if it had been an animal sighing as it neared its resting place, and further up the hill the lights tailed off into the night and the dust became thicker and the soft pinpricks of the stars glowed, waxing and waning in their luminescence like moons long forgotten or stories long untold of those who have died or been forgotten, buried without memory in a time beyond keening. He looked at it all and thought how beautiful and sad the world was.

When he got home Juaní was waiting for him with her face long and empty. Elvira was crying out. Elvis could see that his mother had tried to comfort her and eventually had tired. The square large room in which they cooked, ate and sat was dark. There was just one candle on the table, the wax molten and splayed. The light of the candle wavered against his mother's face, the flame waxing and waning, almost going out. He had forgotten the tiredness of the house, a small space which communicated its own exhaustion.

He sat down on the orange plastic chair by the door, looking at his mother, the moment of wonder already lost.

"Qué más?" he asked his mother and she said nothing. The radio was on and the announcer was talking of a special day of prayer, the next day, for the children of the city. But the battery was flat and the sounds were slow and difficult to distinguish.

"Did you bring any money?" she asked him. He gave her what he had left. "Usually, you bring more," she commented. Elvis looked at the floor: he wasn't going to explain himself, or justify his luxury, a drink at the store. "Hopefully, there will be some more tomorrow," Juaní said, understanding him.

"Maybe. When papí comes back, there will be more."

"I don't think he will be coming back."

Elvis looked at his mother: "How do you know?"

She rose and turned the radio off, casting them into silence. "I rang the family today. It has been so long since he's come."

"How long has it been?"

"Six weeks. Longer than he's ever been away before."

"Six weeks?"

It did not seem that long: not at all. Elvis realised that he had not missed his father. He was used already to his absence. How had he marked his life, really, except with the act of cruelty that had provoked his naming? He looked up at his mother: Elvira was still crying, but Juaní had not moved to comfort her.

"What did they say?" Elvis asked.

"Just that he doesn't work for them any more."

"What happened to him?"

"That was all they said. 'He doesn't work here any more.'"

Elvis stood up and went to give his mother a hug. Her body seemed older, somehow. Probably it was just his feeling, something not based in reality. But when he stepped back to look at her he felt that she sensed this, too, that this was the moment when her old age had begun, when her past had disappeared together with her husband, even though it could not be buried, since no one could say if he was dead or not, where he might be, in Veracruz, at some farm in between where he had found a new lover, somewhere else in the city, or in an unmarked grave where he would decompose into the earth but never quite be forgotten. You did not forget a time when you had loved, even when it was past. Juaní would not forget. Even though her future looked loveless and increasingly barren, a space where her soul would vanish and find no space for breathing, she would not forget the time when she had loved for it was what might keep her alive.

Still, Elvira was crying. It was Elvis who rose at last, went in the tenuous candlelight to her sponge mattress, picked her up and swung her in his arms, singing to her, trying to feel that love which could be so hard to preserve. He sung her the songs Juaní had sung to him when he had been a baby. He nuzzled his nose in her cheeks and wiped the tears from her gently and felt their cool freshness on his skin as if for the first time, as much in love and devotion as if he had been her father.

# CHAPTER 10

Arturo was not going to support him forever, that much had become clear to Julián. Like most people he knew, he didn't set much importance by reality. So, his father wanted him to train to be an accountant. He wanted him to learn the arts of book-keeping, double-entry, to free up his hand. Like most people with money, he did not want to be bothered with looking after it himself. He wanted his son to wipe his arse until he died, and save on the toilet paper. That was why Julián was more and more interested in becoming a vampire.

There were plenty of videos on vampires on the Internet. Lots of them. You could watch footage of earnest North American zoologists and their forest-dwelling bats and portentous documentaries set in Romania where the mountains and forest and the poverty of the country people reminded Julián of home. Sometimes he replayed the footage late at night at his computer station after he had returned from his shift through the streets dark and void and cold as his dreams of vampires. There was one film in particular, a trashy home video shot in some high-rise, in Belo Horizonte or São Paulo, a Brazilian twist to the Metamorphosis where a bloodsucking debt collector swelled bigger and bigger, devouring the apartment, exploding in cochineal destruction. That was the sort of vampire Julián had had in mind when he'd joined the band, and sometimes he dreamt of it after logging off and climbing into the bed beside the computer, settling down in the confines of his room for what rest he could.

It was actually very easy to escape reality. It was easier day by day. His father wanted him to train as an accountant so that he could escape it in the whorehouses of Veracruz and Julián had no intention of following his prescription. What did Arturo think he was, some kind of doctor? An upstanding member of society, a wealth creator? He was a chancer, an ex-mechanic who'd struck it lucky on the lottery. So Julián kept his head down and lied about his marks and escaped reality in the pre-dawn hours in the Internet, or when he dreamed of emigration. If he could just leave the country and abandon his father he would be able to escape his responsibilities for a while yet, all the petty routines which his father had in mind for him.

The only plans that Julián had just then related to Los Vampiros and Pamela, both of them offering a combination route out of his future if only he had the imagination for it. He played the band's CD round in a random loop in the taxi as he drove, asking his clients what they thought of it. He tried to ignore Pancho if he radioed in with a job that would distract him and then he texted Stone and Jhonny Cruz late at night, after returning from the streets, and called Bontera most mornings. He saw one of the three every day, going to Stone's flat or eating steak with Bontera at the grill house run by Cruz's uncle. Always they were discussing their next gig, and how to promote their CD. How to sell more copies, to sell the idea of the band. Bontera said that what they really should do was establish some kind of festival in the city, the equivalent of a literary *tertulia*: that would bring attention, and impose the authority of their voice. But Cruz laughed him off as a fantasist: start it if you like, he said, but I'll stay here eating steak until you do.

Two weeks after the gig in the Zona Rosa Los Vampiros played another set at a bar in the Colonial district. Pamela had given him her cellphone number and he called and asked her to go. He needed her there, he said, and when she asked why he didn't know what to say. He couldn't say, I'm dreaming of you, dreaming of you because I want to leave my life and start another one, take the band with me but leave the rest to rot. Like some fucking Indian mystic who manages to become reincarnated in the same life. Instead he told her the sort of thing she wanted to hear: that she'd like the place, that it would introduce her to a more authentic local reality, the sort of thing she was looking for.

The venue was set up some steps from the street, which gave on to an open floor where there was a bar at the far wall and some brilliant lighting. On the wall beside the bar was a mural of the Colonial district, drawn in luminous paint that glittered in the moving lights. The place was always crowded: it was a venue for students and artists, the sort of place where no one has money that they have earned themselves.

This time Julián talked to Pamela properly as soon as she arrived. Her rich gringa looks gave status. It was all to the contrary of what had happened in the Zona Rosa. And she responded to him. She did not seem as flirtatious with Stone as on that night, in fact she seemed cold whenever he tried to talk to her and eventually he gave up and sat drinking rum at the bar. She seemed to want to talk to Julián, and although he tried to introduce her properly to Bontera and Jhonny Cruz she didn't seem interested in them. Bontera had told him after the last time, he'd tried his luck, but she'd seemed reserved and distant, as if she hadn't liked what she was hearing. But what had he talked about, Julián had asked him? And then Bontera told him his usual story about narratives, and the fragmentation of the world – the only narrative, he said, that had meaning any more. Asshole, Julián had told him: no wonder you turned her off.

The band weren't due to play their set until two in the morning and before then the management put on some salsa which made it hard to talk. Julián tried to shout into her ear and although she didn't turn away, it was difficult to hear each other. The students danced and flirted. No one seemed to be taking it seriously. No one except for Pamela, since when Julián asked her to dance she stuck rigidly to some steps she must have learnt in a class. Probably a class in London, he shouted to her. But that was the step, the step she had been taught.

Just before they were due to play he took Pamela to have a drink at the bar. She asked him how the band was going and he told her that it was perfect. They were going places. By the end of the year they'd have a recording contract, he was sure of it. She looked impressed by his lies but he couldn't really tell why she found him attractive. Probably it had nothing to do with him and reflected some idea that she had about herself, some idea about her life and its meaning. Would she come with him up the Montegordo hill the next day, on Sunday? Of course she would, she said. She'd take the day off from the centre, ring Ramona and let her know. She couldn't go in every day. Well that was fine, Julián said, just fine: he'd look after her then just as he had when he'd picked her up at the airport and when he'd driven her to the south of the city and to Ramona's by night. He'd look after her. He'd drive her back to the Pachinero that night after the gig, too. You couldn't just go with any taxi driver, he said, just with anyone. Look what happened to the American that Stone was investigating. You needed protection.

He saw that Pamela stiffened when he mentioned the American.

"You're not worried about her, are you?" Julián asked.

"No," she said.

"Have you found out anything more?"

"I read some of Stone's articles, on the Internet."

"Didn't you like them?"

She looked at him, her blue eyes wide, sad and luminescent like a moon in its waning.

"Qué atroz! I looked at them and then at his other articles. Things I had forgotten about since I arrived here."

"Yes," Julián said, "this is a very good country for forgetting. The best."

When eventually they played their set there was some energy that charged between Julián and Stone, something stronger than usual that sprang from one guitar to the other and buzzed in their minds as their fingers grasped for the chords which could touch them and harmonise with the rhythms of Bontera, the voice of Jhonny Cruz lost and low and singing in counterpoint to their music, singing of all the sorrow they felt, all the hope, the endless hope which being alive inspired in them. Because otherwise you could live here and think about everything since 1948, since 1492, all the bodies piled up like matchsticks, eviscerated by history, like the world itself, slowly, a torture, like the trajectory of the human race, sanctifying torture. You could build walls so that this history did not intrude, although inevitably it did when you saw some copper-skinned beggar sitting humbly on the pavement. You could live like that but then you could not really be a human being since every last shred of humanity would at last have disappeared, sublimated into the machines which today made life so possible, and so impossible. So you played and span with the energy, played because this was a good country for forgetting. Because the world was the best world for it, too.

And then late at night when people had begun to leave the bar and walk the shadows of the Colonial district, into the darkness that hung low and touched the streets and the broken pavements, when they were looking for a taxi even though it was so late, and the night had almost kissed the morningtime to waken it, Julián asked Pamela if she was ready to leave. They went to say goodbye to Cruz and Bontera.

"You should come to see me some time," Bontera said; but he winked at Julián as he said it, knowing this was an invitation that would never be taken up.

"We'll come along," Julián said, as if somehow he was already with Pamela.

"Where's Stone?" Pamela asked him as they walked down the steps to the street.

"He left already."

"I don't understand him. I was so excited to meet him. But he's so distant. Cold."

"You have to get to know him."

"He doesn't want to know me."

Julián took her hand as they went into the street. "He has seen much. In this country. Many things. And even before, I think. Though he never speak about that. Things to make you cold."

"Does he have friends?" Pamela asked. "Girlfriends?"

"I don't think he left alone," Julián said. "He not usually leave a gig alone."

Pamela linked her arm through his and they walked along the cold streets which were dark and empty and brooded with threats withheld, and they went down towards the private car park on 4th Avenue where Julián had left his taxi and they felt a cold wind blow down from the Páramo to the north, where the Indians were said to have thrown all their gold to hide it from the Spanish. Lost, like they had been. Like Stone, the voyeur of his country. Like he was, Julián, in the night.

A child came then even more lost than he was, dressed in a shapeless grey shift and emerging from the shadows where he was probably destined to remain forever, his face dark, grimy, streaked, his eyes hungry, speaking for a belly that seemed to have vanished. He asked for some money and Julián put his hand in his pocket and gave him 1000 pesos, a token of his humanity, for that was what it was worth. Pamela pulled him more tightly towards her then, and they went into the car park and Julián greeted the guard and opened the doors to his car and they sat there, still and quiet in the city before the cold sun broke, and Pamela leant across and kissed him.

After they had done they straightened up in the car. Julián climbed into the front seat and opened the passenger door. He stood and leant against the taxi, watching the stars disappear one by one. He tucked his hands into the pockets of his jeans to keep them warm. He did not feel tired but rising with the energy of the day and the hope that perhaps his escape might be nearer. He should make the most of this. She had been receptive, he had felt it from the first moment. They both wanted what the other offered, that which they did not have themselves.

Pamela came out of the taxi then and stood beside him. She linked her arm through his again.

"There's no point in going back to the Pachinero now," he said.

"I have to. My landlady will get worried. And I have to call Ramona."

"Call them."

"I'm tired. I have to work tomorrow."

"But what about the Montegordo? Is just here."

"We can go up another day."

"Sunday is the only day to walk up there. Any other day, they rob you."

"It can't be that bad."

"Why not?"

"I don't believe it." She yawned. Her blonde hair was bunched and ruffled and her face was pale. "Is it beautiful up there? It must be, I suppose."

"Is a good picture of the city," Julián said. "Climbing up there. You see everything. Murderers, rapists, thieves. Politicians. Anyone who needs to ask for forgiveness. If you want to understand this place, you have to go there."

"But what about the view?"

"Is nice too."

"I'd like to go," she said.

"I'll call Stone. He no sleep yet. You can sleep there and then we go."

Stone was awake and they went round to his apartment. Outside the front door Don Octavio had just arrived to set up his kiosk and Julián greeted him and bought a packet of Lucky Strike and then rang the bell. Stone opened the door in his dressing gown with a mug of coffee in his hand.

"I'm working," he told them. "I've got a nine o'clock deadline."

"What about the girl you left with?" Julián asked but Stone ignored him, turning as if to shut the door in their faces. "We need to sleep, Lizard."

Stone stopped: "Well, you can sleep here if you want," he said, "but I'm working. You can go on the bed."

"Is clean?"

Stone looked at him, withering.

"You still on the lookout for work as my domestic?" he asked.

Julián did not answer. He and Pamela followed Stone up the old and uneven wooden stairs and into the apartment and they walked over to the bed and climbed under the large alpaca poncho which Stone used as a bedspread, and they nuzzled into one another in tenderness, animals still as they had been in the taxi, but looking now for security, something calm, that place beyond activity. It was light now and the city had woken and they could hear people selling coffee and peanuts sweet and salted and newspapers and cigarettes, although the sellers of bodies were at last falling asleep, as they were, falling into dreams as Stone worked across the room from them on his story and half a world away in the short-staffed newsdesks of London on a Sunday afternoon someone waited to see what he might have discovered.

Julián woke several hours later. Stone wasn't around but soon the front door of the apartment building slammed and he appeared with some pastries. Pamela was still asleep and they left her there and went into the kitchen.

"How's it going?" Stone asked him.

"Good," Julián said. "Very good."

"It's what you need."

They ate some doughnuts, tearing into them hungrily.

"Why are you looking out for me like this?" Julián asked him. "Why do you care?"

Stone finished his doughnut and wiped his hands, looking at Julián. "You're my friend."

"But why me?"

"I used to listen to you guys talking in the bar. It reminded me of what I was like, when I was your age."

"What were you like?"

"I was like you," Stone said. "Dreaming of escape. I was like Pamela – always thinking that the other side of the world was perfect. Shit, for years I carried on believing that even when I got there and saw what it was like."

Stone turned away then. Julián had the strange feeling that he was trying to cry without being seen. But that was so hard to believe for the Englishman rarely displayed any emotion. Julián knew so little about him and yet he spent more time with him than anyone else. More time even than with Arturo. But he didn't know why he had come to his country or why he cared. About anything.

By and by Julián told him that they were going to climb up the Montegordo this morning and Stone said he'd come: he hadn't been up there since he'd arrived in Santa Fé from Guadalajara. Julián stared at Stone: he hadn't known he'd lived there. It had been a long time ago, Stone told him then, but he'd left after they'd destroyed Comuna 13 and claimed it was to fight terrorism. Julián looked at him blankly: he had no idea what he was talking about, he had never heard of Comuna 13, and Stone told him how he had gone up there afterwards, but no one would talk to him, and it had all been so much silence and loss. Silence and loss. He stopped talking and he walked up to Julián and put his hands on his shoulders to shake them, and he said that no one had wanted to listen, no one: that country that Julián wanted to leave for with Pamela, it was a good country, like this was a good country, full of good people, all the same people. That was what he needed to know.

Julián looked at Stone's eyes. There was too much energy and sadness in this flat, in his friend's slim body and long unshaven face, angled and curved by what it had seen, by what it wished had never existed. There was too much force and too much longing and it touched him. For an instant he had the impulse to kiss Stone, something which he quickly buried, with sadness.

He went into the large studio room where Stone worked and slept and sat on the bed beside Pamela. He had to get out. He had to leave. He touched her gently on the cheek and she stirred, smiling, strands of her hair caught against her face where she had been lying on them.

"What is it?" she said.

"We should go. Up the hill," Julián said. "Come on. Stone is coming too."

Pamela rose and sat up, pulling the poncho around her shoulders to keep warm. "What time is it?" she asked.

"Is nearly ten o' clock," Julián said, nodding at the wall clock beside Stone's map of the world.

"Come on Pamela," Stone said.

He had followed Julián into the room, sensing his longing and self-loathing, as if all this was so obvious and there was no need to talk of it. He gave Pamela one of the pastries and she ate it quickly. Hungry. She washed her face in the bathroom and then they were ready to go. The morning was risen with clouds drooping like cotton tears from Montegordo and behind the clouds stood trees thick and green in rows. The wires of the cable car hung drifting and rattling as the cars came and went and the day broke against them.

They walked past the terminus of the buses and joined the crowds dressed in their smartest clothes, in suits and clean shirts and in ironed blouses. Some had earrings and watches though most people were too cautious for that. They started to climb and the city fell beneath them, some of the pilgrims panting, wheezing, already even in the lower reaches of the hill, and others clambering up the stairs two at a time and other people standing by the side of the steps selling chocolates and drinks and rosaries where prayers could be said for those who would never make it as far as this.

It was soon clear that Stone was much fitter than Julián and Pamela. He bounded on up the steps and then stood waiting for them, encouraging, the glimmer of a smile on his set face. As the steps zipped back and forth across the hill he'd turn the zigzag and wait for them on the next level, telling them that the view was better and better, that you could see for miles. Then one time he stopped still, astonished at the faith and gravity of some of the pilgrims, watching a man in late middle age climbing up with a life-sized cross on his back. No one seemed surprised by depth of what there was to atone for.

"Ah," Julián said, panting as he reached his fellow guitarist, "that's nothing. This one comes every week. He killed his brother. An accident. Ten years ago, and he has not forgotten it."

As they went higher, Pamela struggled. The air was thin and the city stretched out grey and vast in the chasm below them, reprieved from violence because it was the day of rest. Julián gave Pamela his arm and helped her up the steps to the top. There was a large crowd outside the church of the Virgin of Montegordo where a priest was speaking and loudspeakers broadcast his message to those outside. Beyond the crowd there were some white balustrades, and here Stone stood, waiting for them, looking out at the city and the mountains on the far side of the plain that the city had occupied.

"You made it," he said, turning to them.

"At last," Julián said.

"Come on," Stone said, "let's get something to eat. I invite you. Both of you," he said, including Pamela.

It was true: they were famished. They sat at a restaurant playing cumbia to fight off the sermon and ordered the comida from the waiter. While they waited, they each ordered a coffee and talked about the country. Stone held forth: perhaps that was why he had offered to buy them lunch, Julián thought, to buy the right to speak as he wanted. He didn't mind too much: he was too tired to talk much himself. And so Stone expanded: here people were praying, but down in the Plaza San Martín they would be protesting. What were they protesting about? Pamela asked him. Julián laughed, and pushed his dark glasses further up the bridge of his nose. But Stone ignored him because laughter was a coward's response to the anguish of others: it was the indigenous people: they had learnt never to go away, always to remind the country that there were alternatives: they were often protesting because their land was always being stolen and their villages torched by people who the government claimed to be guerrillas. And weren't they? Stone smiled as their coffees arrived: nothing was as it seemed in this country, that was one thing he'd learnt, not the oppressed and not the oppressors and not even the moralizing journalists like him who were too old and too hardened to leave.

"Ignore him," Julián said to Pamela, whispering in her ear and taking the opportunity to put his hand on her leg. "He doesn't mean it."

Pamela moved a little towards him but she did not seem to stop listening to Stone. She stirred her coffee, looking at the journalist. What about him? she asked, was he not what he seemed either? Perhaps he wasn't. She asked him how he had come there: he had come on a commission and fallen in love and stayed even though the affair hadn't lasted long. But had he stayed in love with the country? Stone laughed at that. Countries were like women, he said, winking at Julián. That was his experience. You fell madly in love with them when you first met them and the bliss was an ache and a joy and a replacement for something you hadn't known was lacking. But as time passed you got to know them better and understand them and their negative characteristics. Often you became disenchanted. But if you persevered and accepted those qualities, then you were on the way to a lasting love. And was that what happened with news stories as well, she asked, with stories like Jasmine Purdue's? He didn't answer that.

Julián turned to Pamela. "You're interested in this American. The girl who disappeared."

"Wouldn't you be if you were me? She seems to be following me."

"How?"

"It's not just you, Stone," Pamela said. "Not just because you used to go out with her. But also, you know, she used to live in the flat where I'm staying."

Stone leaned forward then. "You're staying with Leila Halabi?"

"Yes."

He shook his head. "I'm sorry," he said. "I didn't realise."

"I didn't ask you to apologise," Pamela said.

"I'm sorry," he said again.

"Why are you apologizing?"

"Is obvious," Julián interrupted. "Halabi is a nice woman, is not her fault, but this is a coincidence. Here, we might say it is a bad one."

Pamela turned to them both: so, she asked, why did she vanish?

Neither Julián nor Stone spoke for quite a while. They could hear the priest's voice from the loudspeaker. It had become louder. It sounded as if he was coming to the climax of his sermon.

"Don't ask me," Julián said by and by, gesturing at Stone and feeling that one of them had to say something. "If anyone knows, this the man."

And Stone still said nothing, looking into Pamela's eyes. Searching. She needed to start with what she knew, he said eventually, with the company backing Purdue's research about the fibre from the Amazon. Someone was involved. Was it a conspiracy? What about Leila? Didn't she work for them, too?

"But what I don't understand," Pamela said then, "is why you were with her at all."

"Why do you care?" Stone asked her.

"You're an idealist," she said. "But Jasmine worked for a multinational. She never was an idealist in the first place."

Stone pushed his chair back slightly from the table, as if to stand up: "Perhaps I admired her honesty," he said.

At that he looked away and beckoned to the waiter. Soon their lunch arrived and they ate it in silence. After Stone had finished eating he leant forward. He wasn't saying that there hadn't been a conspiracy. He believed in conspiracies as much as the next person. Wasn't there a conspiracy somewhere, in the highest echelons of society, unspoken because there was no need to speak of what was essential, to promote all this violence? She tried to answer but he wouldn't listen: he asked for the bill and then they all left the hill and began to go on down back towards the city.

"This man has been very helpful," Pamela said to Julián as they went. "He has given me some ideas about the American."

Julián laughed. But what was so funny? Pamela seemed upset then, and Julián held her hand, pulling her back from Stone who walked on a little ahead of them. What was it? she asked him. What was the matter? And Julián told her how thrilled he had been the night before, how much he wanted her. But she had to be careful. He didn't know much about Stone. Not really. He didn't even know what he was doing here in the first place. He needn't worry, Pamela told him: she'd find out, he'd see.

Then they sped up until they were running down the steps, until they had caught up with Stone. Pamela asked him straight out, why was he here? Why was he investigating what had happened to Purdue in the first place? Stone didn't look at her. He walked on. He started talking. In spurts. Telling them about his life, which Julián realised was the first he'd ever heard of it. How before he'd come he'd been in Central Africa. He'd gone out to Uganda and heard of the Tutsi bodies floating in Lake Victoria. He'd sniffed an opportunity to make his career out of the violence of others and gone on into Rwanda on the heels of the RPF and started to file stories and then he'd gone on to Goma and the Hutu refugee camps and he'd met the Interahamwe and watched them butchering animals as they'd butchered people and he'd smelt the hunger and the fear and the hatred that seemed to have twisted from out of nowhere and swallowed the world. He'd gone back to Congo as the killings went on. He hadn't meant to stay but he'd filed stories and the first million had died and he'd lived on the coat tails of the UN and witnessed the aftermath of massacres as the coltan mines had opened up and the second million had died. And all of it, all that violence so removed and yet so present had eaten him from the inside and he'd tried to communicate it in his stories and he'd lost all sense of time or humanity and he'd come to think that everyone was a pornographer back home where his dispatches were consumed on computers and cellphones bought and possessed and created with the very coltan whose production fed such terrible violence.

But what did that have to do with Santa Fé? Then he'd got a commission when he had come back to the country. And that was how he had gone to Guadalajara, which was then almost as violent as Central Africa at the end of the 90s. He had met more violence and that was why he had stayed. He looked at Julián, then, smiling. Then he had joined the band and tried to forget about all that. Bury the past. But every now and then a case came up which forced him not to forget. A case like Purdue's.

They had almost reached the bottom of the hill by then. It was the afternoon, and Stone told them that he would leave. He wanted to sleep. He walked along towards his flat, a slight figure, lonely, seeming abandoned and somehow afraid. It was as if in his solitary departure he was trying to remind Julián how important it might be for him to try to stay with Pamela, of how much he had come to care for him and their vampire band: that after everything he had told them about, everything he had seen, it was still possible to love.

# CHAPTER 11

At the rehabilitation centre in the south of the city La Tumbera had become less of a ghost. She didn't look like the dust left behind by some earthquake any more, white and billowing and forgotten by the time the sun has set on it. Apparently, when the Tumbera had arrived in the centre she had sat day by day like some statue on her bed. Pale and silent. Her sole benefit, Ramona had told Pamela, with her habitual smile of disgust, was that unlike most statues she did not commemorate or celebrate murderers or rapists. But she had not been one to enter into the life of the centre. She didn't want to be touched and she didn't want to talk and all she had wanted to do was to eat and to think. When the glass had broken in the window of her dormitory and Ramona had come to patch it with a piece of old cardboard she had said not a word. If she could get her to talk, Ramona had told Pamela shortly after she'd first seen her talking to the Tumbera, that alone would be worth the price of her involvement.

It was foolish to expect them ever to become friends. How could people who were so different have enough trust to become friends? A person who had hurt themselves, almost killed themselves, hostage to some selfish memory of a past that could not return – she didn't seem like anyone that Pamela had ever known. What would it be like to cut into yourself, anyway, to bleed yourself almost to death like a parasite feeding on itself? Would that explain a silence that followed, rich and deep as aeons? There had to be a reason why it was so difficult to talk with her about anything that mattered. That was what Pamela began to think as she got to know the Tumbera, as she showed her the scars on her arms, serried, almost military. Betraying some sort of plan. As if her attack on herself had been part of some wider campaign.

Soon enough the Tumbera liked Pamela above everyone. Ramona said she saw something of herself in the Englishwoman. Pamela did not understand what she meant, forgot it day and night as she went to and from Leila's flat in the Pachinero. What mattered was that the Tumbera liked her. She was starting to talk, making room so that Pamela could sit beside her. She said that she liked to practice her English.

"Why?" Pamela asked her once, as they sat side by side on her bed in the dormitory and listened to the sounds of the patio outside. "What good has it done you?"

"Is true," the Tumbera answered. She gestured at a calendar for an American beer which one of the female inmates had tacked to the wall beside their bed. "Is a language of violence. Colonization. But the best time in my life was with the Northamericans. In San Bonifacio."

"What was so good about it?" Pamela asked.

The Tumbera smiled: she beckoned Pamela to come closer and then said softly: "The sex."

She hadn't opened up to Pamela completely, not at once. Perhaps she felt like an archaeologist herself, excavating her own past. But she liked Pamela, she said, and with that emotion, and the recollection of the person she had been when she had been happy, learning English, she began to recollect more. They sat in the dormitory, talking, surrounded by the empty beds with small piles of belongings stashed beneath them and by the old wardrobes lined up wooden and silent beside trestle tables against the walls. Or they walked slowly around the yard of the centre, the Tumbera linking arms with Pamela, dressed in a shapeless red jumper and baggy jeans that Ramona had rescued from a shop selling dead men's clothes. She liked to drink camomile tea, and shared her mug with Pamela as they walked. Sometimes she chided her that she wasn't dressing up properly, that men wouldn't pay her attention. You had to be like a peacock in this world, not a peahen: to imitate those brash males, even if you never wanted to be one of them.

Pamela tried to laugh these comments off. She never rose to the bait. She listened, eager to learn. And the Tumbera was happy to talk, as most people are when the subject is themselves. She talked of San Bonifacio, almost always of that.

"All those young students from Northamerica," she told Pamela one time, "the professors brought them out as cheap labour on the site. Just like we were. And that was how the professors saw it, as a hierarchy."

"But that's not what they're there for. They're supposed to be uncovering the past of people who had looked at the world very differently."

The Tumbera shrugged. "Well, that was how it was." There they all had been in a valley so beautiful it could only have been made by God, or the gods, where the mountains touched the sky and fell in sweeping layers, like some thick material enveloped in sadness, down to the valley where the farms had spread out and the animals called to one another and shat and the people lived and where the earth steamed cold in the early morning with the dew and the sun making the water rise in twists of mist towards the mountains and the cloud from which it had come in the night. "Yes," the Tumbera said, "there we all were but the professors thought only of power and the rest of us of sex. We were people, after all.

The Northamerican students were desperate for sex, just like we were, but they were discrete. Very discrete. They were not like us, not at all."

"Your people can be discrete," Pamela said.

"Mujer, no sabes lo que digas. Are you crazy? No, these Northamericans were soft. They didn't jump on women like me, but they smiled at us, invited us for beers, made us feel important. It wasn't like it was with the men whenever we went back to Rosario for the weekend, to the salsotecas at Juanchito. It was dangerous there, on the drug route. There was money, and violence, and so we had to be careful."

"I have been to a club here," Pamela said, thinking it important.

The Tumbera ignored her: "There was one man who liked me," she told Pamela. "One night, in Juanchito. He was drunk enough to think that he was funny and big enough that his friends agreed with him. When I told him where to stick his desire he opened his flies in the bar and came towards me. Waving his penis thick and purple in my face. Hard like a plastic gun. I laughed at him. We left soon afterwards. But I didn't forget him. I think I slept with one of the Americans as soon as we got back to San Bonifacio the next day."

Afterwards, after Pamela had begun to sleep regularly with Julián, she wondered if it hadn't been these conversations with the Tumbera that had prompted her. She pretended to herself that it had all been a surprise, that she hadn't had any intentions when she'd arrived in Santa Fé. If men flirted with her in the streets, downtown or in the Pachinero, she felt herself tense, remembering how everything had finished before for her in London. But the time she spent with the Tumbera meant that she had never spoken about sex as much as she did now. The Tumbera seemed to feel free, to want to unburden herself of everything that lay in the past as if this could be the only purgative. The medicine for the heart was its expression, she said to Pamela once. Not to be distracted from itself, as if fleeing from something frightening and obscure. She spoke elliptically as they walked around the yard of the centre as the other inmates played football and shouted at one another, and those who were damaged sat at tables, playing cards, watching the sky grey and lifting the world from its eternal sadness. The Tumbera spoke freely, Pamela realised, because she could speak to her in English: unburden herself in a private tongue which no one else at the centre would share, no one but Ramona.

It must have sounded as if all they had done there at San Bonifacio was screw, La Tumbera told her once. But that wasn't true. Sometimes they walked for hours in the mountains along paths that clung to chasms and passed small farmsteads where mules were tethered to pickets and chickens pecked at corn in a yard layered with sawdust and old women with hair white as snow, tied into a bob at the back of their necks, sat knitting in the front porch and drinking mate de coca, while their sons and grandsons set up the arena for mini-tejo and lobbed weights at the fireworks in the hope of setting off an explosion bigger than any that even they had heard before. These were farms where you could imagine that nothing had ever changed even though they saw day by day as they dug that others had lived there and loved and farmed and disappeared. Even though they knew that the army and the guerrilla were never far away, that probably the year before they had all been there, cleaning. They all knew that, the Tumbera told her, and yet they worked and ate and screwed in that unspoken knowledge, and every day they rose before dawn and had coffee and bread and then they worked and then they breakfasted again at 10 on bread and eggs and potatoes and bacon and drank hot chocolate and then they worked again on the dig until noon. But that didn't distract them from the sex. It could not. Because those old clay pots fired from an ironstone forge that today people could not even begin to make, they often showed how their ancestors loved the pleasures of the body, how they needed that too just like every human being. How they made their own sacrifices and did their own blood-letting along with all the others. How they were people, too, people who had their own view of the world and its time, and their own message to give it. And they couldn't forget that because they worked with it every day. Yes, surely, that was why they had screwed so much.

Perhaps she confided in Pamela because she wanted to shock her. Because she knew she would not interrupt her. "Don't let her talk to you so much," Ramona said to her once. "You English are so polite, you'd listen to anyone, a dictator, Hitler, if you thought you ought to." La Tumbera wanted to talk, and there was a power in talking, in making someone else listen to you. Just because your ideas and your voice sounded important to you. Just because you believed, more than others believe, that what you had to share was important. And once you were used to talking, or listening, it was easy to continue: to lead, and to follow. Why did Pamela think the history of Latin America, was as it was? Was there any deeper inclination towards dictatorship, or political violence than anywhere else? Or was there rather a habit, a cycle extending since the very first rupture of power and ideas on the Bahamas, in 1492?

It was true, Pamela did not want to interrupt. She'd been taught, it was rude to break someone off. She came from a country which had been quite happy to break off other societies, to sever them and their arteries too, but you had to let others talk before you brutalised them, recording their beliefs for posterity. Manners were important. Where would society be without its hypocrisy? That was one of the reasons she'd yearned so much to leave, to come and see what the country she was helping with her work was like. She listened to those she met, to people like the Tumbera, Leila and Julián, because that was how she would learn who and what she really was.

The Monday after she had slept with Julián for the first time Pamela caught an early bus to the south of the city. She walked a couple of blocks from where she was dropped off, past small stores with painted signs on the walls of houses, preaching political slogans in silence where real voices were so hard to get heard. She arrived in time to help serve the breakfast and went to eat her bun and drink her coffee on the same table as the Tumbera, as she always did, and listened to two of the residents arguing over which was the best way to butter bread and eat it, whether butter side-up or butter side-down, and then she repressed a laugh when the Tumbera interrupted, what did it matter?, what really counted was how you held the knife. And then everyone fell silent and Pamela looked at the greying stubble on the faces of the men around the table, the faces drawn and puffy, withdrawn from the world, both men and women, having lived long enough to have made their lives irreversible but not yet long enough to die.

After breakfast Pamela went to sit on the Tumbera's bed and told her what had happened with Julián. She felt herself borrowing from the Tumbera's style, sitting comfortably, talking at length. At the end of the room the trestle tables were piled high with dirty bedclothes which looked over them like soiled chaperones. She described the set of Los Vampiros, how she had gone with Julián to his car in the last of the darkness above the city. There had been the boy, his face clear and fresh and yet also sad so late in the night. Asking for money, and of course Julián had given him something. And she remembered that this had been the act that had really awakened her desire, because she found compassion and generosity the most attractive qualities of all. The night cold: the wind blowing her hair: and with the cold, clutching Julián's arm, wanting his warmth, wanting him more and more. She remembered all the details, as you do when you have an experience or visit a place for the first time.

"And what was the place you visited?" the Tumbera asked her. "Surely you aren't trying to tell me that you were a virgin until last Saturday?"

She burst out laughing. "Ay Dios, tenemos milagros de sobra en este país. No more miracles, please."

"Are you making fun of me?" Pamela asked: asking herself, what had she expected?

"No, of course not."

"Well, perhaps what I'm saying," Pamela said, "was that this was the first time I really identified with your people's cause."

The Tumbera looked at her, then, her eyes red and tired, withdrawing even as she looked at Pamela: "Don't do that," she said. "Many have done that before you, and where did it get them? Usually, the cemetery."

"The cemetery?"

"We are very good at making the cemetery bigger," the Tumbera said. "Look at my name. I should know."

"Well, maybe so, but that doesn't make you better or worse than any other country anywhere in the world. Look at my country. At Britain. Look at all these immoral wars. Fought just for money. To keep us warm. You can't say that my country isn't also an expert in expanding the world's cemeteries."

The Tumbera smiled: "All of those killers, they are just boys. They are no different to people here."

"Maybe so," said Pamela, getting up then: feeling angry: "But it is not funny, none of it is funny."

The Tumbera's approach made her angry because of what was happening at Leila's. Leila never wanted to talk about any of the wars, not the one here, and not the one in Palestine from which her parents had fled. She could not get close to Leila, whatever she did. The day before, when she had returned on the Sunday from the Montegordo, after climbing it with Julián and Stone, she had tried. Arriving with guilt, because she had not called. She had begun at once with her apologies, but Leila had cut her short.

"It's like I told you when you arrived," she had said. "Stop saying sorry. You're not working for me."

"But weren't you worried?"

"Worried?" Leila had looked at her with an amused expression. "Why should I be worried? I'm not your mother."

Pamela hadn't taken it any further, not then. Almost, she'd said what she'd been thinking: that Leila, too, was good at providing work for journalists, as Stone knew, that her previous foreign lodger had disappeared, that she might have worried that there was a pattern here. But she had bitten her tongue and gone to sit in the sofa, sprawled and exhausted in the brown leather cushions.

"You had a good time, didn't you?" Leila had called to her. "I'm pleased. This is a good city for having a good time, provided you've got money and aren't the wrong colour. You should be having a good time." Leila had walked over and sat beside Pamela, putting her hand on her knee: "Just don't tell María about it. Don't let her meet him. I'm going to have enough problems there in a year or two anyway. I don't want it to start now."

That was when Pamela had realised that it was all so obvious. That she was obvious. You could arrive home at two in the afternoon after a night at a club, but whether you were in Santa Fé or in London the chances were that you had taken some drugs or had sex. It was cheapening, as if she was also cheapening the lives of Leila and María. It was like the British in Iraq, in Afghanistan. Everything she touched was contaminated and she could do nothing about it because she was her own virus.

"You look ill," the Tumbera said to her then, as she remembered her shame before Leila. "If I was still a gravedigger, I'd be getting your own one ready."

"I haven't been sleeping enough," Pamela said.

"You should go home," the Tumbera said. "You'll feel better in the morning."

It was true. Pamela left early, telling Ramona she needed some rest. After an hour she was back at the flat in the Pachinero. María was at home, watching television in her bedroom, and Pamela called out a greeting. She went to take a shower and then lay on her bed, with the curtains drawn, trying to sleep, irritated by the lights at the socket which were attached to Leila's computer and showed that it was switched on, that illuminated the bed and the off-white built-in wardrobes that were grey in the half-light. She tried to sleep but she could not. She felt uneasy. She wanted to do something to show Leila that she, too, understood. In spite of all the silences. She wanted to buy the family something, a token of appreciation which was worth more than the commercial exchange which made their relationship what it was.

After a time she drifted off to sleep and when she woke it was almost dark. Cries from the street below echoed in a sort of delayed action, with the growls of the buses accelerating on Caracas. She could hear someone moving in the kitchen. Probably Leila had returned by now. She rose and went to watch. Her host was lifting an armful of washing and slapping it into the sink.

"Puedo ayudar?" Pamela asked her.

"Do you want to do the washing for me?"

Pamela smiled, embarrassed, still standing in the doorway. "I'll go and get a cake from the supermarket for dinner. Something we can all share together." Leila said nothing: she lifted a blouse, dark and heavy with water, and twisted it in her hands. "You look like you've done that too often," Pamela said to her.

"In childhood I did it all the time," Leila said. "Wringing the necks of chickens. Like that" – she twisted her hands suddenly, her mouth following in kind – "until they were dead."

Outside Pamela walked the streets which were so grey and lightless and she felt the eyes of the city on her. Two chancers started trying to talk to her on Caracas, a shapeless and middle-aged couple dressed in ill-fitting clothes. The man was toothless and slightly threatening. Pamela ignored him, smiled at the ground, and she carried on walking and looking at the windows of the clothes shops and boutiques as if she was interested in buying something, at the city as if just by looking at it, just by visiting, she would already understand it. When she reached the supermarket she bought a cake from the bakery counter and paid for it at the checkout and the security guard stamped her receipt and she walked back along Caracas. A man stood on the corner handing out fliers, but Pamela didn't take one. She'd read somewhere that some people laced the fliers with burundanga which drugged a victim so that they became infinitely suggestible. Like a reader of a novel, entering a world which is suggested but which they too have to create. There was something threatening about him, too, pushing the paper at her. She didn't feel paranoid, but she'd realised that you couldn't be too careful in this city. There was a reason why Purdue had disappeared. Probably, she hadn't been careful enough. You had to sympathise with the victim, but in the American's case her misfortune was substantially down to her own actions.

Leila thanked her for the cake when she returned to the flat: "The strawberries look nice," she said. "I've always liked strawberries, ever since I was a girl."

Why was she talking about her childhood so much that evening? Perhaps it was the thought of love, the sense that Pamela might have found love over the weekend – if that was what she had found. Of course she wasn't in love with Julián: not yet. He had texted her that afternoon and she'd sent back a jokey reply. But as yet she had only formed that first stage of attachment when the body asserts itself and guides the blood, pretending that love is nothing but flesh and blood and the imagination all rising together, a vicarious self-possession. But that wasn't to say that she couldn't yet love Julián, where love becomes the yearning for the loved one to be absolutely themselves in a space where you are also absolutely yourself, in a space carved out by desire and built by trust. Leila must have sensed that, and recalled her own childhood: her innocence, such as it had been.

Leila put the cake on a plate and carried it through to the dining room. She asked Pamela to fetch María and when Pamela knocked on the bedroom door she saw that the girl was sitting on her bed, leaning back against the wall. She was staring into space.

"Qué más?" Pamela asked.

"Nada."

Pamela nodded at the kitchen: "Hay torta. With strawberries."

"Voy."

They walked together to the dining table and when they got there Pamela told Leila that her daughter had been dreaming when she had found her: as if she was writing a poem.

"It's because of her name," Leila said.

"Her name?"

"I called her after a famous novel."

"Mami, pare," María said, but her mother went on, about how she had used to love the book as a child, reading it in the south of the country, imagining that condition of violence and beauty that precedes every catastrophe, and seeing herself as the narrator arriving on horseback through the forests with every aspect of the birdsong and the cane fields and the casa colonial, the lives of the African slaves and their masters, all of it so real, depicted with such detail by the author, with the sort of detail with which people used to understand the world when they lived in it instead of reading about it or watching it on TV. But of course, Pamela would understand all that, she must know the book?

But of course Pamela did not: even though she remembered, then, how she had held it in her hands on the night that she had arrived.

"My mother is typical," María said. "She named me after a heroine who was born in Isaacs' novel only to die."

"Like all of us," Leila said.

"Pues."

Leila told Pamela then that María still did not understand. She was too young. But that voyage was not just back into the world that was dead. It was like the voyage her own parents had made, when they had arrived from Palestine in 1948. Into a world that was dying with violence, like their own. Why did they come here? Pamela asked, and

111

Leila said how most of their friends from the homeland who had come to America had gone to Chile, but that a few families had first taken passage to this country, about sixty or seventy people all told, and that when they had arrived, thinking just to stay for a week and then to continue to Valparaíso, a Spanish hotelier had taken pity on some of them and offered them rooms indefinitely until they found somewhere to live, and a group had then found a good price for a clutch of houses in a decent neighbourhood in Rosario. Her grandparents had all died within five years or so of arriving, shattered by their loss and their exile, and she thought that it was this shared experience of injustice and loss that had brought her own parents together, and so they had soon made friends and started a business together, a small shop, and then they had married and had never left. And what did they find? Pamela asked her then, what had the farms been like, when they had gone out into the countryside outside Rosario to visit her parents' friends?

And Leila told her. Her parents' best friends had been the Ramírez family, with a farm not far from the city. A simple farm, not one of the wealthy ones. Apparently, when the violencia had started most families had made for the city but the Ramírez family had stayed there and protected themselves. They had said their lives would be better there than in the city and if they died they died and God would be the judge of them. Old Señor Ramírez had been born in the farm sixty years before and knew little else. At the back of the house there had been a long worn stone where the old man used to butcher chickens and goats if times were good. There were stains which in the city would have been taken as the residue of coffee. But everyone in the farm knew they were from the blood of animals which they had killed and eaten.

Why were they so good to Leila's parents? Her mother and Señora Ramírez had been great friends. They used to sit in the early evenings on two three-legged milking stools near the killing stone, shelling beans or knitting and watching the sun plunge like a red UFO beyond the western hills. The land behind the farm swept down steeply into trees and the red roofs of other farms. Far away emptiness drifted towards the sea. The ladies would talk of the stories of the farm, stories which Leila still remembered fifty years later. Some people said the farm had a bad atmosphere but Señora Ramírez didn't think so. She found it safer and more peaceful to be there than in Rosario. Or, God help her, Santa Fé.

"They were good to your family," Pamela suggested, and Leila agreed.

"I didn't know them at first, of course," she said. "But then, when I was a teenager, when things had become a bit calmer, we used to go out there for a week at a time in the summers," she said. "And when old Señora Ramírez needed to come to Rosario for a night or two she would stay with us. She was sad. Sad because of what had happened to my parents. She'd look at the photos they had brought with them from Palestine. On the dresser in the salon there was a photo of their old houses in Ashkelon. Once I remember my mother sitting down with her and going through the pictures she had, telling her what had happened to them, where they were. Who was alive and who was dead. I remember once, Señora Ramírez was crying, ah, she said, why did you leave one war just to come to another? Couldn't you have found somewhere peaceful, at last? But my mother used to say that we had been very lucky. We arrived as refugees, she used to tell Señora Ramírez. No one had wanted to kill them. They belonged to neither faction. They were just poor and dispossessed and they worked hard as other people killed one another and they managed to build a life for themselves."

When she had finished Pamela asked whether they hadn't hated how their land had been stolen from them, but Leila said that their hatred had gradually faded. Her mother started to say, what was the point of looking backwards, of digging it all up? Didn't everyone live on land that had been stolen from others and whose theft had been legalised by parsers of the law whose authority rose sheer from the shoulders of violence and power? Who was it who used to own this land where our city of Rosario has been built, she used to ask Leila, and lived in it and farmed it and buried themselves in it and found their Gods in the mountains and the trees and the fleet wings of birds flying to a land far beyond? And where did they lie buried if not here? You could dig it up if you liked, but there would be another's memories to strangle you with injustice if hatred was your choice in life. Better not to hate. Better to understand, to live here where you were and think of tomorrow. The hope that came as you crested the pass from the coast and your home valley stretched below you with the plantations green and rippling and horses tethered to pickets on the lanes stretching out into the country, out into the country which they had come to inhabit. From which others had gone.

When Leila had finished speaking it was long since dark but their room also was dark in its biding. Neither of them had switched on the light. "Love is generous," Leila said. "Now you will see. Now you arrive, an exile, like she was."

"I am only staying three months."

"Yes. That is your plan. And my parents' families only came until the war in Palestine had died down. But they learnt to love here. If you can forget hatred, after all of that, you will learn to love." She rose and collected the plates and swept their crumbs into the bin in the kitchen. María went to her room and then Leila returned to the table. She leant forwards, putting her hands on the table in front of Pamela. "That's why I told you the story," she said. "Because it isn't easy to love."

"I've discovered that myself," Pamela said.

"Pues. And like anything, it's something that a person, and a whole society, has to work on. It is beautiful and precious but then – suddenly – it is gone. And then it can disappear and lie buried. For a long time, it can lie buried."

"What's that got to do with me?" Pamela asked.

"It's what you need to remember," Leila said. "Wherever it was that you screwed with your new lover the other night, that's what you need to remember, above everything. Sometimes I wonder if it isn't what Jasmine had forgotten."

"She had a lover, too," Pamela said. "Stone."

At that Leila bristled and rose to go: "Yes," she said. "And he's one person who could easily get you to forget all about that."

"What happened to her?" Pamela asked.

But Leila said nothing. She turned and went and Pamela realised that in all the silence and mystery that surrounded this person she had never met there lay a presence more meaningful and louder than anything that she had yet heard spoken in the city, her new home.

# CHAPTER 12

The comuna was like a being constantly created anew. The sun rising each day upon a changed wasteland where roads had been built and buildings flattened and all of it by night. In a month a new corner of the comuna could have appeared as if by a strange magic. In another month another corner could have disappeared with those who had lived there and no one to say where they had gone or why. In time memories were all that were left.

Three months passed with the Angolan and then another three. Other boys from the barrio came and went but Elvis stayed. The Angolan liked him. He sent him on errands to all the corners of the hill and Elvis came to learn the patterns of the streets and see that they changed week by week, that gradually a new comuna outgrew the old one from within, like a parasite child. He took money where it was owed to the streets farthest from the turning point for the city buses and collected packages and shopped for Rosaura at her favourite corner stores and brought the groceries to her house, opening the padlock on the gate with the key the Angolan had given to him and arriving with a smile and sitting on the hard bench beside the table, looking idly at the roses on the tablecloth as Rosaura brought him a milky coffee or a pastry. Admiring her as she moved in a space which she commanded, where she was at home.

That was the time that Elvis really got to know his world. As an adult. No one had a bad word to say about the Angolan, who always paid what he owed and paid on time. No one wanted to get on the wrong side of a man like that, a man with influence, who never used weapons. Elvis carried a gun on his errands but he never needed it. Not even once. The Angolan's contacts usually welcomed him. Sometimes he was offered beer or cigarettes. He was coming to be thought of as a person worth knowing, a person who would put groceries on his own table as well as on Rosaura's.

In all those months he never spoke once about his father. Not to his mother nor to the Angolan nor even to himself. Of course the Angolan was a readymade substitute, and he sensed that his mentor himself had a need to gather in someone to tend around him. Perhaps taking that chance, recognizing it before others did, was the strategy that all his chess had taught him. He never asked what had happened to the Angolan's children and the Angolan and Rosaura had learned quickly never to ask about his father. One did not ask about that which was present through silence. Others, too, had gone from the barrio like his father and their children, and then others had taken their place until they too might in some future time vanish as if they had never existed and time had covered their tracks and their house and the city entire with the dust of times past. Each generation buried the preceding one and heaped ridicule on them. Pretended that they had never been. The rare thing with Comuna 13 was that this was what had happened to an entire community, the first time that the paramilitaries had come.

It was not just Elvis who did not mention his father. Juaní said nothing about him either. Years of resentment had won out over love. The dependency had been transferred to Elvis, but dependence on a son is always more reliable than dependence on a husband.

There was something light about Juaní in those months. It was almost like she was young again, beyond care. She laughed as Elvira crawled around the house, picking up toys and clutching her food in her hands as she ate. Elvira was so happy. She was not hungry any more. None of them were hungry. The Angolan was paying Elvis and he was paying him well. Juaní said to him once, to make sure that he thanked the Angolan properly, that he made sure that he felt appreciated, for in a very real way he had performed a small miracle.

Elvis wasn't sure, though, that thanks were appropriate. Sometimes you had to express gratitude in different ways. By staying. By listening when others spoke. Not finishing their sentences. The Angolan liked speaking. Often he'd speak all the way from the hill into downtown when they took a bus with a sack of rescued parts for re-sale. And Elvis would agree, and listen, and show through his constant presence that this was respect, and a different form of value. And in the centre sirens screeched and buses revved up and accelerated past others beached by the roadside as arteries of passengers climbed on and off, and the smartly dressed passed in suits, both men and women, talking into their cellphones and window-shopping as they consumed a world which had already devoured itself, and groups of unemployed young men slouched on walls with their faces long and hungry, searching for a chance, anything to make the day better than the one before – young people like him who walked off quickly if they saw the police looking at them – and the air was grey and brown and the dirt from the buses darkened the sunlight, and the green hills ringed the city like a barricade. This was where they came to do business, where their skill in salvaging value from the waste of others was most appreciated. His respect for the Angolan paid well. He got to know the customers, too, the buyers and their manners. This was his future, somehow he was aware of that, the only way that he would ever exile himself successfully from the hill.

And so when Juaní asked him if he had thanked the Angolan yet, Elvis replied that he had his own ways. That being with the Angolan and Rosaura itself was a sort of thanks.

"I've noticed," Juaní said, doing something that she so rarely did: sitting down, on the orange plastic chair by the door, and resting. "You're hardly ever here. But at least you bring the money in. At least you are regular."

"Yes mami. That is what I am."

She loved him, it was clear, but even now her love had its own way of being laced with criticism, with anger at what she could not control: her son and herself, both of them ageing before their time was due.

"But you are losing things," she said.

"What things?" he asked mockingly: he couldn't see it, couldn't really see what he could be missing. Surely she knew that everyone dreamt of leaving. That it was impossible to imagine nostalgia for a place everyone yearned to abandon.

"Elvira doesn't know you like she used to," she said. "You don't hold her, and cradle her like you did when your father went." He shrugged. "What's this? Already, like your father? It's true, then, what my aunt Lucía said when she helped to deliver you: enjoy him while you can, they grow up so fast these days."

He laughed at that, and did not even dignify her with an answer. He got up from the table and went to lie on his bed and looked at the chessboard but then threw it onto the floor. There were other strategies he'd need soon if he was going to escape the clutch of the game. This was why he felt that he was more at home outside the house than inside, why he brought money home but increasingly lived elsewhere.

He usually ate at the Angolan's. He became familiar with the dining room where Rosaura held forth, as if it were his own. On a plywood cabinet beside the dining table – rescued from Julio Campiñas's bar, when the police had closed it down, the Angolan told Elvis – there was a photograph of the Angolan and Rosaura, and another of two boys, an aged photograph now, apparently with none to replace it. There was a vase with plastic flowers on the table, and some orange polyester material sewn into a curtain and drawn across the window. Rosaura always spoke freely, unselfconsciously arguing with her husband about money in front of Elvis. Sending him out into the yard to check for eggs in the hen coop. The smell of the countryside there, of wood smoke and animals, something that he didn't quite understand, that seemed attractive and dangerous at once. The countryside was dangerous, everyone knew that. The city was much safer.

"Do you ever go back to the countryside?" he asked them one evening, eating some spaghetti and sauce. "From the world you came from?"

But they never had: "I prefer my memories," Rosaura said, "of childhood as it was."

Then the Angolan asked him: "Do you ever play football, have you played at all since the match against the barrio of the Cross?" But Elvis had not. He sat silent, his head down. Dogs barked in the darkness beyond them and the Angolan smiled. "Where childhood and the past are concerned," he said, "memories are always better, the best substitute for reality. Look at me," he said to Elvis, "look at my name, the Angolan: itself it's like a memory, it calls up the past, acknowledges it, but doesn't demand any more than that."

Elvis had never thought of it like that before. "It could be dangerous, your name," he said, "if the wrong people came asking. Why bring that all up?"

"It's happened. People have asked about it." The Angolan shrugged. "Because this country still runs as if some people are better than others, as if the race could still be improved if only the others would go away, stop bothering people once and for all."

"What about the paramilitaries," Elvis asked then, "didn't they ever ask?"

The Angolan did not answer. He stood and walked up to the doorway and then looked out at the night. There was a low hum from the alley just beyond the gate. Some people were talking there. Laughing, without fear. It sounded as if they were high. There were dealers everywhere in this part of the hill, though the Angolan had nothing to do with them.

"We've already paid our dues," the Angolan said, turning by and by. "We don't owe them anything."

That could have been one of the reasons that the Angolan cared for him: that he hadn't gone, like so many others, with the paramilitaries.

It was shortly afterwards that the Angolan asked Elvis to go and call in a debt from Bear's sister, Teresa. She worked at the Gloria bakery as her mother had before her when Bear had been an infant, not far from the turning point for the buses down to the city. The bakery was warmer than the other buildings on the hill; the ovens kept it like that. It was one of the busiest places in the comuna, where everyone went to get news with their bread. Even the paramilitaries hadn't raided the building when they'd nosed around; they'd just commandeered a few kilos of bread a day, a contribution for the fight against the terrorists, as they put it.

Teresa worked in the ovens there, sliding trays layered with dough in to be baked and removing others, her hair bunched beneath a plastic hood, her hands sheathed with rubber gloves. Since Bear had gone it was said she'd shrivelled like the plastic in which she kept her hair as she worked, hunched up, ready to jump, like a frog in a TV documentary, something he might have watched at López's store.

Elvis did not wait his turn in the queue as the bread was wrapped in paper bags and customers paid at the till, getting their receipt stamped and taking it back to the counter where the stamped receipts piled up, impaled on a metal spike. He called across the heads of the people in the shop to Juan, the owner's nephew. He needed to speak to Teresa. Of course, he could go on, Juan said: follow the heat, it's rising. And Elvis went into the baking room and saw Bear's sister with her back hunched and her hips shapeless and swollen. Already she had two children. Had it been so long since he had seen her? It had to be months, before the match with the barrio of the Cross, because she had aged. All of them had aged in that time.

Elvis picked up a wooden spatula which lay on a work surface beside the oven and knocked it. Teresa stopped in the act of working and looked at him. She did not smile. He was like the ghost of her brother who did not write and who had vanished like all the days of her life, had become a memory and the sweeter for it. Elvis explained, it was delicate, the advance that Bear had taken: times were getting hard, as she knew: there were shortages: hunger was something most of them knew, who was there who knew what it was like to eat three times a day?

Teresa looked at him: "You do," she said. She leant over and grabbed the flesh of his cheek between her fingers, shaking it. There it was: he was filling out.

"It's true," he said, "life has been kind to me."

"What kindness?" She spat. "You're still here: you haven't had the intelligence to leave. You've never been as brave as my brother."

Elvis did not answer, because there was no need to fight someone who was still living through the triumphs of the past. Now Bear was gone and Elvis was working for the Angolan. He was alive and he was there. He smiled at Teresa. He smiled because that was what life did, changing fortunes. Because you could become absorbed in the triumphs and vendettas of the present and forget the violence from which it had all come, the wellspring of the paramilitaries, and the inequalities of history and property which had been their forge in turn, and the rubbish strewn across the streets and the mansions of Miraflores, the wellspring of ignorance and of the world entire.

"The Angolan needs the money, Teresa," he told her. "That's why he sent me."

Then Elvis left and instead of walking straight back to the Angolan's workshop he climbed up the hill. Past the broken paving slabs. The dust piled up like mountains outside houses of adobe and zinc and corrugated iron. The walls red and blue with graffiti. White, the colour of anger. Past dogs rutting in wastes of houses dismembered and yelping and crying and silent like the world. Signs written on boards outside houses offering cellphone calls, a connection to the outside. And above the sky yawning in blue infinity, like the sea, his imagination of what the sea might be like. His father had seen the sea every month when he had driven to Veracruz but Elvis could only imagine it. His father had gone. He stopped outside where Condor and his family had lived once, remembering. The house had been dismantled and a new family had moved in and built a new one, and the mother was outside sweeping dust away from the entrance. She smiled at Elvis when she saw him and Elvis turned away, part of the waste which she was dispelling. He wondered, would life always be like this?

When he got back to the workshop near the ravine the Angolan smiled when he told him that the message had been delivered. They worked for some time longer and then the Angolan handed him a sandwich and they began to gather the parts together, ready for delivery down to their partners in the city. The Angolan's arms black and glistening in the afternoon sunlight, the scars bulging with the effort of the work. He said that he had not cut himself but how was Elvis really to know what the truth of it was? He trusted him now because he treated him well. Because he was eating. But he knew that people did cut themselves and others disappeared and that it was said they were taken. Taken to some sort of holding centre by people who thought they were helping them, and helping to make the country better with a different sort of disappearance. When the sack was ready the Angolan gave it to him and wished him luck, with his trust and work despatching him down the hill to where the money was.

The Angolan had introduced him to many of his friends downtown and as they had become more familiar he trusted Elvis to take the salvaged parts alone and to strike bargains. This was his training. Most of the mechanics treated him squarely, as a colleague or a collaborator. They didn't offer him bribes but gave him a fair price and treated him to coffee and doughnuts. He usually went towards the end of the day, when things were a little less busy. He had his favourites, of course, places where he'd go to first, where he was usually well received. He was in demand. The Angolan had told him how the mechanics often swapped the older parts they brought for newer versions from the cars they were repairing and made some money on the side. Everyone benefited in the trade, except for the consumer. But they deserved that, didn't they?

Elvis's favourite workshop was owned by Emerson Moralla. Moralla was someone who wasn't afraid to get his hands dirty. He ate well, and he always said that it pained him to see Elvis. He was too thin! He often invited him to go and have a Bandeja, to put some weight on him. That was the only sort of bribery that Elvis was willing to accept, a good meal, something to make him more attractive in the streets of the hill. That was why Teresa had been able to grab the flesh of his face, to point out his good fortune, the way his lot was different to hers. By the time that Moralla had taken him to eat and he had despatched the meat, eggs, beans, rice and plantain he had already expanded. That was better, much better, it was how he would become a man: Moralla always watched him eat approvingly, providing his commentary as they discussed the value of the parts that Elvis had brought. Moralla didn't say much more about his business, not often: only once, pointing at the cars in the workshop, at his cellphone and the computers in his office, at his gut, he had gestured, it was all made of nothing: everything here, he had said, it's all made of nothing, just to keep others happy. He'd never understood it, he told Elvis, and he still didn't. But he was happy, and that was something.

That afternoon when Elvis arrived, Moralla asked Elvis if he could stay late. He wanted to show him what he meant: why the whole world was built on emptiness, and how you could escape it. Elvis was unwilling because he knew that the Angolan would worry but Moralla insisted and Elvis did not want to jeopardise the contact. After six Moralla closed up the workshop and then they drove in his brand new Chevrolet out of the city and climbed the hills in wild switchbacks through the darkening sky. Where were they going? Moralla just laughed. He wound down the window and the night air was cold and made Elvis shiver. They passed a couple of roadblocks and Moralla gave the soldiers some money. The roads gradually emptied of other traffic. Only criminals travelled the countryside at night. They crested the hills and saw isolated lights stricken in the night and then Moralla turned up a track and they drove for some minutes until they reached a single-storey farmhouse whitewashed and shuttered and lost to the world beyond.

"Come on," Moralla said. "You can get out."

Elvis opened the passenger door of the Chevrolet and stepped onto the track. It was so dark and still. Birds called and snakes rustled and shadows flitted past his ears in darts and arrows. Then he thought he saw the shadow of a ghost, a long-vanished ancestor with straggly rushes of hair falling on either side of a face that he could not see: Elvis started. But it was just bats, and Moralla laughed at his fear. He switched on his torch and walked up some stone steps to the old creaking veranda, surveying the silence. So still and quiet was the world beyond the city that Elvis felt himself quivering, in fear and ignorance.

"Who lives here?" he asked Moralla.

"At the moment, no one."

Moralla opened the door to the farmhouse and shone his torch around a square room. In the centre of the room there was an old sofa and two upright wooden chairs. At the back, a long table stood empty except for a candlestick, and to the side there was a hardwood dresser.

Moralla opened one of the drawers of the dresser and pulled out two thick candles; he put them in the candlestick, lit them, and turned off his torch: "There are some beers in the dresser if you want them," he told Elvis. "Help yourself."

Elvis opened a beer.

"How long have you owned the farm?" he asked Moralla.

"Years! It's been a very good investment. I bought it when people were afraid of living in the countryside. Now I've made enough money that they're afraid of me." He smiled, exaggerated in the tenuous candlelight and the flickering shadows on the white plaster walls. "But you don't have to be afraid of me," he said to Elvis. "I want to look after you. Look at this place: you can live in it, for nothing, if you work for me."

"How?"

Moralla burst out laughing and took some time to stop. "By making money," he said.

"Making money?"

"You'll be rich," Moralla said. "Rich. It's like I told you, money is made of nothing, the world is made of nothing."

Moralla rose and beckoned him to follow. They went outside into the yard, Moralla shining the way with his torch. A breeze had sprung up, rustling the branches of the trees and muffling the sounds of the creatures that had come out by night. Elvis shivered again, his body tensing itself and relaxing as it met the cold air. Moralla led them behind the farmhouse to a squat breezeblock building covered with a corrugated iron roof. The door was padlocked; Moralla opened it, and shone the torch around. Elvis saw piles of paper, boxes, machinery piled against the back wall.

"You see," Moralla said, "this is where you can make money. For both of us."

Elvis tried to get used to the light and the works around him. "How?" he asked.

"Because money is made of thin air anyway. Of nothing. The rich know that. That's how they build up their fortunes, by finding ways to get round reality and build something from nothing. Inventing the power they have to consume."

Elvis stepped forward and picked up one of the bundles of paper on the floor. Then he let it go: "But this isn't money," he said.

"No, not yet. But it will be. Why should you and me be closed away from the power to make money? Wealth is just a power of the will." Moralla went up to one of the machines at the back and began turning a handle to the side. "This is the best equipment. I got it from a contact in the police. They know all about it. It couldn't be a safer business."

"How much money do you make?"

"Enough," Moralla said. "Enough to give to the Angolan, to my workers, to the whores. That's how money makes its way into the comunas. Didn't you know that?"

"By fraud," Elvis said.

"Maybe, but that way people aren't as poor as the government wants. Everyone wins."

Moralla's offer was simple. All Elvis had to do was stay in the countryside. Five days on, two days off. Work the machinery and make the money. That was what the National Bank did, anyway. Moralla would give him a nice cut. He'd be able to take it into the city, and spend it every weekend. No one bothered much about where the money came from in those bars, late at night. Not even the police, if they came raiding. They didn't care if the money they were given was fake. It was the parallel economy. It was the real economy, also. It was how nothing became something, and fakery adopted the hallmark of what was authentic.

After he'd finished Moralla shut up the garage and they walked in silence to the Chevrolet with their feet crunching into the earth. There was no moon and the stars were silver strings across the sky. Moralla threw some beers into the car and locked up the farmhouse and then drove them back down the empty road and onto the empty highways of the countryside where few people dared to move. They rode down the switchbacks with the city a neon pulsing monster below them and other monsters stopping them from time to time at the checkpoints, waving them through when Moralla passed on some of his money. They drank beer and threw the cans out of the window and Moralla turned off the highway in downtown and drove up towards the skyline, the rim of the hills, where Elvis lived. The pavements became broken. Men stood on street corners, hunkered down on their haunches, drinking, waiting.

Moralla pulled his car up at the bottom of the last stretch up to Comuna 13: "You can make your own way from here," he said. Elvis nodded, and made to get out, but Moralla put his hand on his knee. "Do we have a deal?" he asked Elvis.

"I don't know."

"What's the problem?"

Elvis wasn't able to say what he really felt: there was this business, deep in the countryside, and yet no one was there to run it: but surely Moralla had had others working for him there too, and what had happened to them? Had they just vanished? And yet all the time the matter and people of the world seemed to be getting bigger.

"I don't know," Elvis said. "I'll have to talk to the Angolan about it."

"Why? What I'm offering you is a way out from here. The Angolan will never give you that." Elvis climbed out of the car. "Think about it," Moralla said. "If you want to work for me, just come down to the mechanic's before the end of the week."

Elvis loped through the streets, sticking to the shadows of the houses. It was so late at night that anything could happen. The streets were empty because even the gangs were scared of them. As he went, he felt released by the events of the day. He didn't have to continue in this place. He didn't ever have to see Bear's family again, to remember that humiliation and the petty feuds that divided his family from theirs, buried somewhere unknown in the past. The Angolan had helped him in his first steps towards adulthood, but he needed more. He couldn't live as a surrogate son for Rosaura and him forever, he was not their son: he was alive. As he neared his house he realised how late it was; even the shutters of López's store were down. This could be his only chance to leave Comuna 13 before it was cleared out again through one of those habits, purgative, that the country seemed unable to dispose of.

Juaní was waiting for him when he came in. She said nothing. Put a plate of rice and sauce in front of him. Moving with the slow, waning grace that sustained her. Coughing and then putting her hand to her mouth so as not to wake Elvira. The child rustled in her bed, groaning quietly. Then she coughed, too, and her blankets twitched as she moved her limbs. He spoke at last, to Juaní, told her that he'd been offered a new job that day, outside the city. Had he told the Angolan? No, the Angolan didn't know. What sort of gratitude was this, his mother asked, to the people who had raised him, who had helped him to come of age? Would he just leave like so many generations of men before him, leave as if marching into nothing, fires of emptiness, rivers of blood, as if that was what they desired? The world was not made of nothing, Juaní told Elvis then, thumping the table: it was made of love. It could be true, he answered at length, but he was not rich enough yet for gratitude.

He went to lie on his bed, beside Elvira. For a moment he dreamed that he was older, that he had managed to make enough money to buy his sister out of the comuna. A contract killer made good: you could do worse in life. He turned onto his side. He could hear his mother cleaning the kitchen. She wouldn't be able to sleep now, and probably neither would he. Yes, she was right, the world was made of love. He still loved his home, and that was why he had to leave it. He couldn't bear to see it disappear when the time came. He knew his country and the world well enough by now, even though this was the first day he had ever left the city where he had been born and had lived every day of his life until then.

# CHAPTER 13

There was somebody Arturo wanted Julián to meet. A friend of his, Vásquez, selling real estate to American investors. "Where are the houses?" "On the coast," Arturo said. "Near the National Park. Those people love it." "But there's nothing there except jungle," Julián pointed out. "And why would anyone want to invest in this country, anyway?" "Who knows? They're American." Julián laughed openly at his father: "Your friend and his Americans must be cleaning up their money." Arturo did not disagree: he finished drinking his coffee and put his cup in the kitchen sink of their apartment. "That makes him no better or worse than anyone else in this country," he said.

It was true. All money was dirty anyway. The Central Bank was complaining about it. The Director had been on the news. People defaced money, he said, they drew beards and spectacles on former presidents and illustrious heroes of the cemetery. Some spidery hands wrote shopping lists there. To-do lists. Names of people for party invitations. There was no respect. No order. But why should people respect money when all of it had been stolen?

The problem was, his father was becoming more serious about his training. He wasn't going to let a good dogsbody go to waste. The plan was simple: Julián could do six months' training with his friend in the real estate business, and then start managing Arturo's books. "You won't steal from me," he told Julián one morning, over breakfast. "I've got several other children I can leave this to if you're a disappointment."

What did Arturo want? It was simple. It had been obvious for almost twenty years, ever since Julián had been able to walk: he wanted his son to be just like him. Like all heartfelt bullies, he couldn't imagine how anyone could resist him. Like all heartfelt bullies, he lacked imagination, which was why he was always angry when the world failed to obey.

Arturo arranged a meeting for Julián at Vásquez's office downtown. It was on 6th Avenue, just opposite a really good lanchonete. You went up some steps beside a secure parking area, and then along a bare corridor with a cheap brown carpet and opaque windows hiding you from the inner patio. The reception area was staffed by a security guard with a face long and drawn and by three secretaries.

One of them led him through to see Director Vásquez, who had a private office overlooking the Avenue: "It's excellent that you can help," he said. "Arturo tells me that you have a real interest in the financial side."

Julián shrugged: "My father tells a good story. He's a García Márquez."

Vásquez laughed: "Your father, a novelist? He's too good at making money."

"That's what he tells me, too," Julián replied. "Like I said, he tells a good story."

Vásquez clearly didn't know what to make of that. Julián knew his type. He was one of those who didn't understand irony, and wasn't used to people making fun of him. There had to be something to it: maybe Arturo was a real fabulist, just like Julián had told him. But Julián could hardly stop himself from laughing.

"Look," Vásquez said, "what I want is someone to help with the financial side. Someone I can trust. There's no benefit in paying taxes to the government which will just be stolen." He rose, beckoning to Julián. They stood beside the open window, looking down onto the Avenue. It was lunchtime, and people were hurrying in and out of restaurants in twos and threes. There was some laughter; a little way down the street, an indigent had let his trousers fall down to his ankles and was heckling passers-by. "You see," he said, "the poor only improve their lot if the rich can spend their money. What I want you to help me with is a public service, if you think about it carefully. In the right way." He patted Julián on the shoulder, like an uncle. They turned from the window and sat again and he offered Julián a whisky. "Nothing cheap," he said. "White Horse." The mark of a failed gangster. Julián laughed again, but Vásquez took it for nervousness. "Your father convinced me. I'm always happy to help old friends when they'll do the same for me down the line." Julián said that he was as well, and drained his whisky.

When they had finished discussing terms Julián agreed to start the following Monday. He'd work there three mornings a week. He'd have to cut down his hours in the taxi, but that was his father's fault. Not that it mattered. Nothing mattered when people like Vásquez were in charge, people who thought that they were doing the world a favour by being rich. They were the real vampires, after all, people whose only logic was to expand or die, like the debt collector he'd watched time and time again in Belo Horizonte on Youtube. People who believed that favours were given out with a view to what would return and not because people could sometimes respond to the angel inside them. Yes, he could do Vásquez's books; he could really screw them up, and leave before Vásquez bothered to find out. *Your son, Arturo, your son is a thief, a scoundrel – where is your son? He's married an English whore: Pamela Oswald...*

After he'd finished at Vásquez's he walked a few blocks up the hill towards the Colonial district. He went in to the grill house run by Cruz's uncle and found his friend and Bontera behind the bar, helping to prepare the drinks.

"What's up?" Bontera asked.

"It's my father. He's making me do the books for his friend."

"Who's that?"

"Some crook selling real estate by the coast to Americans."

Cruz laughed bitterly: "You mean there are still people who think you can put money into this country and take it out when you want to leave?"

"What am I going to do?" Julián asked him.

"You've got to do what the Lizard told you," Bontera said.

"What's that?"

"Write your part of the story. Leave with Pamela and never come back," Bontera said. "You can't live as an accountant. It'll kill you."

He was right. Julián could feel the force leaking out of him just at the thought of what his father wanted. But it was crazy, a crazy scheme. He didn't even know if he liked her. In fact, he suspected that if he spent any length of time with her, he'd find her worse than annoying.

He called in to see Stone after leaving the grill house and they had lunch at a place with pretensions in the Colonial district that served rich students, people like them. They ate soup and chicken with potatoes and Julián drank a coke. He called in to the university to pick up some books and then returned to the apartment to catch some sleep before the night shift. On the way he texted Pamela from the bus and then his father called to ask how the meeting with Vásquez had gone. *It's like I told you already*, Julián shouted into his phone as the bus careered along 11th Avenue, *your friend is a crook*. That was good, he'd offer him good training, his father replied. Perhaps he hadn't heard him; perhaps he had. They were like each other, Julián realised at last, like all rich people. Everyone with money was like Vásquez. They pretended to have no sense of how little or ridiculous all their fantasies were. All he wanted to do was live with something a little like freedom; no wonder his father was afraid of him.

When he arrived at his apartment it was late in the afternoon, and Arturo was lying back on the sofa, his feet resting on a cheap plywood table, watching a football match. He looked up at Julián: "So, it went well." Julián didn't answer; he went through to the kitchen and opened a beer from the fridge, leaning back against the work surface and drinking it in deep gulps. "Vásquez will look after you," his father called through, "he's a man with connections."

Julián made a mental note to ask Stone what he knew about him. Then he walked over to stand in the doorway of the lounge, watching his father and the television with equal dislike. "I don't know if I'm cut out for numbers," he told his father.

"Sometimes it's difficult to accept your vocation. I hated the mechanic's for years, until I got used to it."

"But you left as soon as you won the lottery." Arturo ignored him, watching the match, shouting at the players. "I like driving the taxi and playing my guitar, dad. That's what I like doing."

His father looked up: his eyes were hooded with tiredness and drinking, tired by age, at the realisation that death was nearer to him than birth. "And where has it got you? Where has it got you?"

"I've met someone, now. A girl."

"Is she rich?"

Julián didn't answer. What was the point? He walked past the couch and went into his room and lay squeezed up on the bed and thought about Pamela Oswald, feeling that the computer station was looming over him all the time in the greying light, and then he slept for three hours until it was dark. When he woke he had cool sweat on his forehead, as if he had had a terrifying dream about the onset of malaria: and he was in a farm in the Llanos, a farm run by the paramilitaries or the rebels, he wasn't sure which, somewhere he could only escape from through an act of treachery. He slipped out of his blanket and bent down to put on his slippers and switched on his phone. Pamela had texted him back, suggesting that they meet the following afternoon. Great, he replied: he'd pick her up at the rehabilitation centre and drive her back in the taxi to the Pachinero. Wait for me there, he texted, as if still worried that someone else might come to collect her from the centre and vanish with her into the city, never to return. As if she really was under the same spell as Purdue.

The flat was dark and the sky was moonless and the city lived only with its lights drawing in against the darkness. Offering safety and danger. Like everything in the world, Santa Fé was what people made of it. Often, the city seemed alluring, particularly when he was inside his apartment. But he knew that as soon as he stepped out and collected the taxi from the secure parking lot across the street he'd step inside and switch on the central locking. Because it was impossible not to live in fear, and realise your fears. Because life was becoming increasingly impossible, especially if you were someone like Julián, and tried to hold on to your dreams.

That evening he drove through the city with his eyes wide to the dangers. One time he caught sight of himself in the rearview mirror and was shocked to see how scared he looked. Terrified. His face reminded him of a security guard he'd seen a few weeks before, as he had been waiting in a traffic jam on 7th Avenue, heading north. The guard had been helping to collect money from a bank and had backed into the glass-fronted building, holding so tightly to his machine gun that his finger would probably have frozen if he'd tried to fire, staring with his eyes so wide at the city and the people who might have wanted to kill him as easily as they'd eaten their corncakes for dinner the night before. Without thinking. The violencia had gone on since 1948 and when he'd looked into the eyes of that security guard and seen eyes of such bottomless fear that they could quite easily have caused the guard to fire by accident into the crowd, or kill another who raised his hand in greeting, it had been obvious that it was going to carry on. That was how close money was to violence and fear. That was why people defaced their banknotes, as a small defiance against authorities who killed them with violence, killed them, when all was said and done, because they were worth less than money.

He collected several fares and toured the streets from the Zona Rosa to downtown. Near the Colonial district a young child came and put his face to the window with his eyes so wide with hope and fear that Julián rolled down his window and gave the boy 1000 pesos and the boy said nothing and scurried off like a rat as if afraid that Julián might change his mind and shoot him dead. Yes, things were getting better. There were more generous people around than there had been ten years before and the street children lived longer before they died. Stone had written an article about some of them, he remembered, but the Englishman never gave them money. He thought that sort of generosity was self-indulgent and inhumane. That was the word he used: inhumane.

Shortly after midnight he picked up a middle-aged European from a bar in the Zona Rosa. The man was so thin that at first Julián thought that it must have been from poverty and he almost refused to pick him up. But he'd noticed that some of these foreigners were like that, and hardly ate anything. The man's Spanish was so bad that they had to speak in English. He was from the Netherlands and was an industrial consultant for one of the biggest bakeries in Santa Fé. He serviced ovens which were brought over from Europe. He laughed: sometimes he got on a plane at Schiphol and arrived and his work was done in half an hour. Then he got his local manager to sign him off for a week and went to spend the time with his fiancée. He leant forward, his eyes bloodshot, his voice slurred: his country had very beautiful women, he told Julián, the best in the world. Julián looked back at him, saying nothing: what was there to say? People travelled the world like birds, these days, finding new breeding grounds. This guy had landed here, he could take his place. Julián wanted to leave. No one wanted to stay where their home was, it was too painful. The best girls in the world, the Dutchman repeated. Was that why he came here? Julián asked: surely the work was hard sometimes? Yes, sometimes it was. He'd have to sweat for a day or two and sometimes the oven was beyond economical repair. It was sold off cheap to workshops in the comunas, where people were prepared to work for days at a time for next to nothing. Those were the real masters, the Dutchman said, so much more skilled than he was. They salvaged the ovens and used them in the bakeries of the comunas and that was how the poor ate. The oven was written off on the books and he split the money he got for the oven with the local manager and everyone was happy.

He returned home as usual just before dawn and slept and avoided his father. In the morning he texted Stone and they met in the cultural centre in the Colonial district and Julián told Stone about Vásquez.

"It could be an interesting story for you," he told the Lizard. "What are those Americans doing buying real estate near the National Park anyway? It has to be a front for something."

"Probably," Stone agreed. "Most things are a front for something, especially in this country." He drew on a cigarette and blew the smoke past Julián's ear. "That place offers the new route for cocaine to Europe. It's quite a short route, all in all. You can cut fuel costs for the flight, just as those old slave captains used to cut mortality and wastage by bringing slaves from the nearest part of West Africa." Stone shrugged, stubbing out the cigarette in an ashtray on the table between them. "That's geography, and the romance of history."

"Find out about him for me," Julián said. "I'd like to know whose books I'm going to fuck up."

"Vásquez," Stone muttered. "They're ten a penny here."

"He can't be that important. He's a friend of my father's."

"Oh, he won't be anyone serious. The big shots will have passed on the American buyers to him. He probably doesn't know their real names anyway. But I'll look into it." Stone pushed his chair back, about to get up. "Everything's connected in this country anyway. He may be small beer. A slug in the works. But he may be connected to the people who know where the American is. Purdue."

"You still think about her, Lizard?"

"I forgot for quite a while. But this coincidence about your English girl, Pamela, made me think about her again. Look at a few things." He stood. "Like I said, everything is connected here. That's how this country works. This guy Vásquez could be interesting."

He left, calling goodbye to the staff in the cafe. Julián ordered a coffee and a sandwich and later walked down to 7th Avenue and caught a bus north to his apartment where he slept for a couple of hours before going to collect Pamela.

The Englishwoman had arranged for him to eat with her that evening. There was an old lady who lived in the same block of flats as Leila Halabi, who cooked for her in the evenings. Julián protested that he wasn't hungry when he picked Pamela up from the rehabilitation centre but she insisted that she wanted him to meet the people that she knew, that she wanted him to come to the flat. There wasn't much he could say if he wanted to be pliant, and so he agreed without saying much. What sort of food did she cook? he asked five minutes later, as they passed through the city centre, and Pamela said she was sure he would like it. Julián nodded: it was probably just like what his grandmother used to cook for him.

When they arrived at her street in the Pachinero it was nearly dark. Pamela let them in to the apartment building and she climbed quickly up the stairs. He tried not to look at her buttocks, but it was hard. By not remembering he remembered and that made his groin twitch as he climbed the stairs. But then the thought passed: she was waiting for him at the landing, knocking at the neighbour's door.

Inside, they sat at the old lady's table. He did most of the talking, explaining that Pamela had invited him as a friend. Who was paying? the old lady wanted to know: Pamela paid her 5000 pesos for a meal. Direct, like most women he knew were. She was, Julián said: at least, he assumed she was.

"Sí, pago yo," Pamela interrupted.

"Habla bien, ahora," the old lady said, smoothing her hand through her grey-black curls and across her forehead, still without lines after all these years. "Cuando llegó, no hablaba ni una palabrita, pero ahora sí. Aprendió."

She turned and went back into the kitchen. Julián looked at the bow above her hips where she had tied her apron fast, at the slow caution with which she did everything. These were the people who lived for a hundred years: the people who were so slow and measured in everything they did that they never moved fast enough to get in range of the assassin's bullets.

"It's true," Pamela said. "I've learnt a lot already. A lot of Spanish."

"You understand what I said to her?"

"Most of it."

"But still, you're talking to me in English."

Pamela looked at him, then, her eyes blue and welcoming, with laughter and without fear: "That's because I want you to understand me."

Then they sat in silence until the old lady Fonseca brought them their food. A broth flavoured with lemon and coriander, then some rice and meat. A fruit to finish: fresh mango, the best. It was the sort of food his mother's mother used to make for him when they went to visit her farm near to Rosario, heating the dishes gently on the gas stove, piling their plates high, refusing to take no for an answer. Who was there who was rich enough in money or luck to refuse a meal if it was offered them? Not her grandson, that was for certain. And when Julián remembered his grandmother he remembered in an instant the journey he used to make over the mountain roads with his mother and the time they had been tipped off about bandits on the road ahead and hidden most of their money in the spare tyre and he remembered the view from the farm and the sound of the cockerels in the morning and of bats sweeping past in the gloaming. He thought how strange it was that his world would have been incomprehensible to his grandmother. So full of stress and speed that it might have killed her in a month. If he had been born thirty years earlier he would have lived near her in the countryside and have thought as she did. What had changed his generation so much? Were they so different to those that had gone before that they could not talk? It was so difficult to imagine that world, now, even though he had seen it. He drummed his fingers on the table, tapping the wood, violently.

"What are you thinking about?" Pamela asked him.

"My father," he said. "He wants me to work for his friend."

"What does his friend do?"

"He sells luxury properties by the coast to rich Americans."

"Don't do it," Pamela said to him.

"Why not?"

"Surely, you hate Americans." Julián laughed. He couldn't reply to that, it was impossible. Didn't she realise, that he loved American rock music? They were the first people who had sung of their rage at what the world had done to them – them too. "I hate Americans," Pamela said then. "It's like a religion for me."

The old woman Fonseca came in then to clear their dishes. "Terminaron? Les gustó?"

"Si señora, gracias," Julián said, then, as she cleared the dishes. He broke into a smile. "Me hizó acordar de mi abuela," he said to the old lady then. "Que esté en paz."

"Si Dios quiere, mi niño."

Pamela turned to him then. She said that he should come up to meet Leila and they said goodnight to Señora Fonseca and walked up to the flat but when they entered there was no one there and the lights were off. He waited in the gloom of the salon as she went to knock on one of the doors but then she returned looking puzzled. It was strange, Leila's daughter María wasn't there either. She looked shocked. As if she wasn't used to this silence and emptiness, and felt like a historian or an archaeologist might feel when they opened a tomb and expected to find great treasures of a lost past only to find that everything had vanished and they had only themselves to live with. In the darkness, her eyes seemed fearful. Was she afraid of him? For an instant her fear excited him but then he was disgusted at the wretchedness of his own urges and stepped away from her. He sat down heavily in the sofa and she turned the light on.

"You can't work for the Americans," she said again, as if to pretend that nothing had happened. "Surely you hate the Americans."

"Why do you hate them?"

"All that money and violence. All the power they've shed here. Everywhere. The people they've hurt."

"Yes, yes," Julián said impatiently.

"Like I say, it's a religion for me."

Her constant mantra about her new religion made him feel edgy. It wasn't as if Americans themselves had spurned religion like she had. Stone had told him that the girl Purdue who had disappeared from Leila Halabi's flat, where they were that very moment, had herself been a churchgoer. Who was to say that she hadn't had a truer grasp of her own authenticity than either of them did?

"Their evil turned you religious?" he asked in the end.

"I just can't stand them."

"But there are lots of bastards right here, in my own country. My hatred starts closer to home."

"Look at Leila. You know her parents were from Palestine?"

"What does that mean to you?"

"Look at what's been done to her country."

"Great," Julián said, "and what are you going to do about it?"

She came and sat beside him on the sofa. Leant over and kissed him, her tongue jagging into his teeth, forcing them apart. One fierce emotion became another. She stopped and swept her hair from her eyes and looked at him."I always do the opposite of what society expects," she said. "I never cared what I earned. I just want a real experience."

"What do the Americans have to do with that?" he asked her.

"The girl who disappeared. The one who was staying here. She was American."

"So?"

"Maybe that was why they took her. Maybe that was all it was."

"You think that life is as simple as your hatred," he said, "but it's not."

They looked at each other. At the apartment. Still it was empty and neither Leila nor María had returned. They could have gone together to Pamela's room, and Julián tried to insist. But he could not be too forceful, not if he was to leave with her. So instead they sat quietly, hoping that the owners would return to what was rightfully theirs and put a stop to their intrusion. But they waited until ten at night and still the women did not come and then Julián made his apologies and they kissed and he went down the stairs and out into the street to begin the night shift.

# CHAPTER 14

Leila was always talking of her daughter as an artist. In the salon, or standing in the kitchen, wringing out washing, monitoring the kettle on the hob, her creation was her favourite subject. María was such a skilled guitarist, her natural flowing ringlets made her *look* like an artist. She had a real talent for painting the world, brilliant with colours. She was a spiritualist, too. Sometimes they would be walking along a street, and she'd take Leila's arm and say: Mama, let's not go down this street; Mama, don't trust this or that person, their spirit makes me uncomfortable. She had gifts, Leila would say, gifts that needed to be drawn out. An artistic temperament. And when Pamela asked her one evening in the kitchen what an artistic temperament was, she spread her arms wide, with a narrow smile playing on her lips: it was the ability to create just for the sake of creation, with no other motive in mind, because what was a work of art but something that had no purpose beyond itself? A life could be a work of art. Directed only at itself, if you thought rightly about it.

Pamela didn't understand Leila when she spoke like that. It sounded like she disowned her past – not that Pamela could blame her for that. She embraced art instead, as if that could be a redemption. Leaving activists like Pamela to fight for her cause, while she thought about the cultivation of her own garden. Of María.

María's guitar teacher Carlos came every Sunday, late in the afternoon. By that time María was alert. She played in the salon, sitting on one of the chairs by the dining table, and whenever she played her eyes widened and her upright frame rose, lifted by the music she played. When she was not checking her phone, Pamela stayed to listen, sitting on the sofa and watching the painful honesty and suppleness of María emerge in the music. It reminded her of her own idealism, before she had chosen politics above art. Carlos seemed almost as innocent as she did, listening as if to angels, his jowly face beautiful with its clear dark skin and luminescent brown eyes, the light of which might have been love. He had studied music but was turning to marketing. It was something to keep his soul alive so that he could dream in song, Pamela had heard him tell Leila one week. Maybe the time would come when he'd be able to sell something he loved: something that was art. Leila heard him out, checking through her purse for the money to pay him: and if he ever did that, would it be enough to make him happy?

So did a pattern become set in the city, and Pamela felt at home even though she was not. Perhaps it was because she was connected to the world beyond Santa Fé, because she needed to email her office in London and keep in touch with family and friends there. Because she was never entirely present anywhere any more. With her computer, mimicking the omnipresence of a God that had died long ago. Laughing with María in her room at the Argentinian soap opera that she did not understand, listening as María explained the plot. Something of a shared experience emerging, not because their lives were similar, because they would always be different, but because their experience of a world connected in its living and its dying would unite them even when Pamela had gone. Because of that, Pamela had felt María's absence when she had come to the apartment with Julián and she had not been there. She felt it for days, as María persisted away, until it could not be undone.

The weekend after María vanished Leila was in such a nervous condition that she forgot to ring Carlos and let him know what had happened. He arrived as usual on the Sunday afternoon, and when the buzzer sounded Pamela answered for her landlady. Leila didn't want to talk to anyone, but Pamela didn't have the Spanish to explain what had happened. Once he had arrived, and understood, Carlos set his bag heavy with sheet music on the table and walked quietly to the room where Leila and María had slept these past two months, ever since Pamela had arrived. He opened the door and surveyed the room as if it could have told him something and then after he had looked at the room for a minute at least he turned and walked back into the salon. He asked Leila a question but Leila's face crumpled and her eyes swelled with tears and there was no need for her to answer. She suddenly looked her age, her hair greying fast, the wrinkles set around the edges of her mouth and on her forehead. Had they asked her friends? Ximena? Had they told the police? Then he sighed, his face suddenly taut to snap: but there was no point in that, really, none.

Pamela explained that Leila had not left the flat for three days, apologising for speaking in English. But she knew he spoke the language well, since all the marketing textbooks he had to read were written in it. She hoped he didn't mind, she added, unnecessarily. She had had to ring the rehabilitation centre to explain the situation. She hadn't been able to go to work. She'd cared for her landlady, she'd cooked, shopped and washed, and everything in a void where a life had used to be. "You are caring for her," he said. "What else can you do?"

Carlos moved with the heaviness of a body that can barely support itself. He sat on the sofa and the heavy leather cushions sighed at his weight and his face was downcast. A waning grey light fell on the coffee table before him, where lay the copy of the novel which had inspired Leila to name María. Carlos picked it up as Pamela had done when she had first arrived. He flicked through the pages, and Pamela felt that she was reliving something impossibly distant in herself even though she had only been in the country for a little while. Her arrival felt more remote than many of her feelings and friendships back in England. What was the novel about? She remembered when she had discussed it with Leila and María, and how María had seemed embarrassed at the source of her naming. No one wanted to symbolize a perfect, doomed love, or an idealism born to be destroyed. It was like naming someone after all those old patrician values such as the belief in the soul, everything that the last human century had chased out of life. And when Pamela thought of what Leila had later told her about the book, about the inevitability of María's death, the destiny of an impossible love, she wondered if she had not created for her daughter a tragic path which she could only avoid with great difficulty.

"Voy a salir," Pamela said to them then. "Pueden hablar."

"There's no need for you to go," Leila replied in English. "We can all talk."

"You'll have to stop doing this," Carlos said then.

"Doing what?"

"Having people vanish."

Leila's eyes filled with tears again: "But it's nothing to do with me," she said. "It was María who wanted us to put Pamela up anyway. She was the one who encouraged me that we couldn't have the sadness of Jasmine hanging over us forever. That we had to fill it with another house guest. Yes, it was her idea." Then Carlos asked if they had any idea where she had gone. But how could they know? "When Purdue went, I felt afraid," Leila said. "I stopped eating, and lived off sweet coffee and cigarettes. I assumed it was something to do with work. But María has nothing to do with that. Perhaps it's something else, something completely different."

"What can it be?" Carlos asked.

"Well, the only thing that María and Purdue shared in common is the centre. The centre run by Ramona."

"But who would care about that?" Pamela asked them.

"Oh, that's easy," Carlos said. "Surely people have told you about that?"

But no one had told Pamela anything. She looked at Carlos, at his boyish energy for life when life itself was reluctant to sustain him, and saw then how much of his artistry was a mask. Like all artistry. But everyone knew, he told her, in genuine surprise. Everyone knew that the government mistrusted the NGOs and called them allies of the terrorists. There were fuerzas oscuras in the country. Very dark, he said, all trace of a smile vanished from his face in the gathering twilight. They were the ones who swept through the shanty towns, places like Ciudad Bolívar, places that were much more desperate than anywhere she'd been yet, and just cleaned people up. Cleaned them out. As if they had never existed. Made them disappear. And people who worked for NGOs had a short life expectancy around here. They seemed to have a death wish, he said, holding her gaze with his eyes. Or else they thought that their life was worthless if they forsook morality. Those who survived were usually worthless, Carlos said, still looking steadily at Pamela. So really, it was a compliment to be kidnapped. To disappear. It was traditional.

When he had finished it was almost dark. Pamela rose without a word and went out. There was a cafe twenty yards up the street where she had a drink and sent emails for half an hour, speeding through them as a way of forgetting what had just happened. What was still happening. When she had finished she walked across 11th Avenue and found a bar near one of the private universities where she sat drinking on her own. The students were laughing. She could smell dope in the air. These rich bastards. They could live in impunity not even thinking about what was happening in the same city. She gripped the edge of the table. For a moment she wanted to light a cigarette and burn the edge of their faces. She couldn't bear to see them. She turned the volume up on her i-pod, and the noise helped her to forget them. It was cold. She shivered, and ordered another beer. She'd not understood before why Julián was so desperate to leave this country but now she did.

At eight that evening she called Julián on his cellphone: "We need to meet," she told him.

"What's the matter?" he asked her.

"It's María. She's gone."

"Gone?"

"Yes," she said after a pause. "She hasn't been home for days now."

He said nothing superfluous. Yes, perhaps everything that there had been between them until then had been superfluous. "I'll be there soon," he told her. "Wait for me." And she waited as the night darkened and the streets slowly emptied of light and people. She called Leila but Leila did not answer so she left a message on her answerphone that she should not worry. What was Leila doing? She had to be at home. It could have been the police ringing with information. It could have been María. Probably, she was occupied with Carlos.

When Julián came they had a beer together and then got into his taxi and toured the streets together and talked, more openly and freely than they had ever spoken before. The seriousness of the situation had released them. "If the country was safer, I'd have driven us out into the countryside," Julián told her, "into the mountains." "Let's go there," Pamela said. "Why not?" Julián said nothing and they drove through the rainbow lights with Julián skipping reds, his angular face harsh and unmoved, perhaps afraid of stopping or perhaps just not wanting that moment to be interrupted. By and by he put the central locking on and switched down a side street which was dark and empty and apparently without life. There was no traffic and Julián put his foot on the accelerator and they burst in callous speed through that silence. Her problem, he said as they went, was that she still refused to recognise the seriousness of her situation. But what did this have to do with her? she asked, and Julián screeched the car to a halt and looked at her: what, did she think this was a coincidence, that two people from Leila's flat had gone missing? Pamela felt him moving towards her, and she felt a sense of disgust, at herself and him and at all the emotions that flooded through them: she didn't know if it was a coincidence or not, she told him, but she couldn't believe that Leila had anything to do with it, she was just another victim, like her grandparents before her. So is that what you think? he said, that the world was just of victims and aggressors, just a place for vampires like him?

The car was still shuddering gently from the suddenness with which it had stopped, and she looked at him, overwhelmed by sadness and desire, and that was when she kissed him. Just the need to feel less alone moved her. There was so much solitude in the city, enough to turn you into a cannibal, to consume yourself. Or be consumed. Love as loneliness pierced.

After they had finished they rested together for some minutes. Then she stirred against him. Wasn't it dangerous? she asked him, but he said not. No one dared to walk along these streets at this time of night and only the reckless, lovers, drove by here to stop. It was still before midnight and he said that he'd drive her back to Leila's. Would she go to the rehabilitation centre the next day? Yes, probably, she said. She couldn't bear another day in the apartment. Then they drove back to the Pachinero and she spent some time looking at Julián. She realised that she felt something for him, but she couldn't distinguish yet whether he was the object of her emotion or just a substitute for the country she was coming to love. Or perhaps he was both. She knew that he didn't want to stay, of course, that he hoped that perhaps she might be a route out. But who could blame him?

When she reached the apartment Leila was sitting in the room she had shared with María, watching late night TV. "Permiso," Pamela said, looking in through the door. Leila nodded and Pamela went to sit on the bed with her, as if she had been her daughter. They watched the recording of a concert from Miami, and Leila was scornful. They watched for some time and Pamela felt closer to Leila than she ever had before. She felt as if Leila was talking to her daughter, somehow, through listening to this music that she couldn't stand. Leila began to laugh, by and by:

"She always asks Carlos, can he teach her one of these songs? And he always scolds her. It reminds me that she's still a girl."

Pamela didn't answer for a moment. "Let's hope she's OK," she said then.

"I prayed for her today," Leila told her.

"Why?"

"I know you don't believe in any of that, but I believe that prayer can help."

"Yes I know you do. But I can't understand why."

"One day, you will."

"But your country has been destroyed by religion. By the settlers who have taken it in religion's name."

"This is my country now," Leila told her. "And you forget, I am also a settler in someone else's land. The land of the indigenous people."

And soon enough she said goodnight and left and went to her room where she kicked off her shoes and lay on top of the blankets and wondered why it seemed to be left to her to fight so many of the battles of the world. She fell asleep wondering why she was coming to love this country when it was a place of such casual cruelty, when even decent people like Leila didn't seem to care. Was it something in herself she loved, something she had lost? She dreamt that she was walking in a field of daisies and buttercups, the sort of meadow she had known as a child, and that the field tumbled down towards a broad river beyond which rose mountains serrated and austere, covered with trees, dense, the hillside in darkness and looming. She walked down towards the river and as she did so a band of soldiers poured out of the mountains beyond it in their fatigues, green as the grass, like the trees behind them, born of the world and in the world soon to be interred. And as she watched in horror, impotent, they spread out in a line and pointed their machine guns across the river, at the enemy. She could see their commander giving orders from a promontory to the north. She felt like she was watching a film and that this was her entertainment. They were pointing their guns at her and the commander was pointing at her, as if she was the enemy, but she knew that they could not see her, that to them she was invisible and that they were hunting her precisely because they could not see her and desired to confront her all the more because of that. She watched as the commander gave the order to fire and she saw the guns twitch, like men's penises, full with desire, the desire for death, which after all was only a step away from lust. But she heard nothing and that was when she woke and listened carefully to the city and the fridge in the kitchen, humming, and her heart beating hard inside, and the sense that she could hear sniffs, that in her room Leila was crying for her daughter who was gone and whose return could not even bring back the childhood and innocence that was gone with her.

Pamela could not get back to sleep after that. Early in the morning she rang Ramona. Things were bad, she told her, very bad. She had wanted to come in to help today but she just couldn't, and please, could Ramona apologise for her to the others, to the Tumbera. Ramona laughed then, hard, brittle: was she scared? Pamela could not bring herself to answer. Perhaps they hadn't told her, Ramona said then, and perhaps they should have done. But it was always hard to talk about the things that were most important.

When Pamela had finished the call she went out to buy some bread. Next to the bakery was a cheap café where she ordered a coffee and a pastry. She sat by the window and watched the owners of the shops selling rosaries and holy books roll up the metal shutters and open for the day. A cripple with deformed legs sat outside one of the shops, holding out a plastic cup. Schoolchildren were walking slowly past, bags pouched on their hips. At the table next to her, a group of women sat wearing the uniform of a chain pharmacy which had a branch further up 11th Avenue. Three of them were talking to their friend, trying to persuade her of something, Pamela heard the woman answer them, quite clearly, que el problema era que su novio tenía una manera de hacer el amor que a ella no le gustaba. Then the others laughed. There was more banter about her sex life and they got up to leave. After they had gone, Pamela felt terribly alone. Who was there here who would really look after her? There was only Julián, and even he was not disinterested. Perhaps she really was in danger. She had never even thought of it before. She had thought that all that talk was exaggerated. She had even been irritated when Julián had implied that the dangers were more than she realised.

She had thought he was trying to ingratiate himself. But now, things were different. Perhaps the only way she could protect herself was to find out what had happened to Purdue and María. To make sure that the same thing did not happen to her.

She ordered another coffee and texted Julián: she needed to meet him downtown that morning. After he'd replied she gathered up the bread she had bought and took it back to the apartment and laid it out carefully on a plate which she put beside the green-and-white vase on the dining table in the salon. Still Leila had not woken. Probably she hadn't fallen sleep until almost dawn and now the day was running by her. Pamela wrote a note which she put next to the bread, urging her to rest. She'd be back in the evening. There was nothing to worry about. Then she left and caught a bus south along 11th Avenue and looked out at the city without thinking. There were boutiques and restaurants and kiosks just like in any other city. There were traffic jams and security guards. She put on her i-pod and tried to block it out, and that was when the bus driver allowed a barefoot child wearing what looked like a sack to board the bus and pass down, placing photographs of himself and his younger sister on the seats beside all the passengers, both of the same colour, a colour that did not allow of forgetting. The motor of the bus growled, guttural, a smoker's voice. But above it the boy sung with his voice still high, somehow peaceful. Pamela switched off her music and listened, and gave him 1000 pesos when he passed nearby. Still, she couldn't quite imagine his world, even after everything that she'd seen. What was his world like, the shantytown? Probably he was one of those who had been cleaned out by the paramilitaries. One who had escaped. His world was so close and yet it was impossible that she would ever see it. As far as she was concerned, it might as well not have existed. It could be erased without trace. If you made something invisible, intangible, unmentionable, soon enough everyone could pretend that it had disappeared, that it had never even been.

When she reached the Colonial district she went to the cultural centre. Julián was waiting for her there, with Stone.

"This is getting serious," she said as she sat down. "Very serious."

Stone laughed: "Violence only becomes serious when you think it might affect you," he said.

"Do you know anything about it?" she asked him.

Stone shook his head. "But it must be connected," he said.

"He thinks it's the rehabilitation centre," Julián said to her then. "That's what he's told me."

"It could be," Stone said. "Or it could be something else again. Even that friend of your father's, Vásquez, and his connection to the money launderers."

"Bontera said it wasn't that."

"What does he know?" Stone challenged Julián.

"He thought it sounded like a bad story. One of the ones he discards because it comes to him late at night, after too many drinks, trying to take over from all the many voices singing in his head."

"The guy thinks he's a poet but he can't even have an idea without being an asshole," Stone said.

Julián laughed at that, and brought them back to Vásquez. He'd found out a bit more about it, he said. He didn't think it was money laundering, but fake notes being cleaned up. Vásquez had said something about business interests in Guadalajara, and there were rumours about one of his associates there. Stone chuckled: there were rumours about lots of people in Guadalajara. Plenty of people had disappeared there. Whole neighbourhoods, as Julián knew. There were plenty of rackets there too. Enough to produce the country's first tennis champion before long.

"But what does that have to do with the centre?" Pamela asked.

"Who knows?" said Stone. "But if you follow one problem to its source you may clear up the other one, too. Everything is connected in this country. The good, and the bad."

"Especially the bad," Julián said.

"What I hate is that no one cares," Pamela said.

"Who can blame them? Life's a comedy."

"To you, maybe, Stone."

"Why do you care then?" Stone persisted. "Because at the end of the day, it's not your problem. You can leave, and it'll just become your job back in London. That's why these days right-thinking political concern is just a luxury for the liberal elite." Pamela hated him just then: he must have seen it on her face, because he tried to joke: "That's why I say, there's no need to worry about it. Life's a comedy. But if you want to get to the bottom of the disappearances to make sure it doesn't happen to you – that's sensible."

Pamela looked at him then. He was so thin and nervous, eaten up by what he had learnt of the world. He said life was a comedy but he didn't look as if he meant it. He lived on fear. And yet she needed him, because he understood the country. He understood it better even than Julián. If he could help her to escape whatever danger she might face, maybe she would leave with his friend for Britain as a sort of thank you. Probably, he'd be the one who stayed here, living on in his fantasy of violence and beauty, subsisting by preying on the stories and fears of others.

Could he help her? she asked him by and by. Yes, he could. The key was money: who was making it and how much they hoped to make in the future. People in this country made all sorts of noble comments about ideals, and progress, and the future, but each of them had a bottom line and it was getting lower and lower, as low as hell. All they cared about was money, and getting the rest of the world to help them consume the country and its products. All the disappearances, and kidnappings, and cleansing, every piece of scarlet violence, came from that, he said, lighting a cigarette, and blowing the smoke into Pamela's face, came from the act of buying a piece of the country, emeralds or oil, whatever it was. But provided they had no illusions, they might have a chance of saving María, and of making sure that the same thing didn't happen to her. Because they ought to be honest, he said then, as he stood up to leave, that's all she cared about. She didn't deny it. He'd call, he said, some time in the next week or two, when he had some information. In the meantime, she needed to watch her back. He gestured behind her and then walked out into the street and strolled across to buy some cigarettes from Don Octavio's kiosk outside his flat. Pamela realised that she had been left alone with Julián, which was what she had wanted all along: but they had nothing left to say to each other and soon agreed tacitly to leave, to meet again in a day or two, when the silence and loneliness had again become too much for them to bear.

# CHAPTER 15

He didn't say anything to the Angolan and Rosaura until the night before he was leaving when he went to eat with them as always and knocked twice on the front door and stamped his shoes on the old wooden crate by the door and greeted them and sat on his usual chair and put the key to the padlock for their gate on the table before him. "I didn't want you to think I was ungrateful when I never came back," he said. He wasn't sure what he'd been expecting, anger perhaps, or tears. Like all teenagers he overestimated his own importance. And when he saw that they weren't crying, that Rosaura just picked up the key and tucked it into her bra and served out the stew as always, that the Angolan bowed his head down as he served himself with his spoon, hunched as if in prayer, the reality of the new phase of his life, the one he was about to enter, assaulted Elvis for the first time and he sat still with his head down as though copying the Angolan for he knew that if he looked up he would cry.

Rosaura served him liberally. "Eat," she said, "you'll need lots of food where you're going."

And he started. "What do you know?"

"Don't worry," she assured him. "Don't feel guilty. Humberto and I are not surprised. No one stays in the end, and who can blame them?"

He began to eat and as he did so Rosaura settled herself on the bench across the table from him, toying with one of the roses inlaid on the plastic tablecloth. It was true, she went on, the money they were able to give to people like Elvis was good when you were young, and it gave you a sense of independence, but it wasn't enough. How could you feed a family on 150,000 pesos a week? It wasn't possible, you'd end up dead from hunger or murdered because of your debts. People who had ambitions moved on and she couldn't blame them but she also knew that people who had ambitions in this country had to pass through dangerous territory, territory that she'd been lucky enough never to have to enter.

He ate and when he left he tried to look the Angolan and Rosaura in the eye but he wasn't quite able to and he walked out of the house and along the alley and heard the door shut behind him. It was still early, then. The street near to the Angolan's house smelt acrid and sweet, like marijuana. He walked past friends and greeted them and then crossed over the football pitch where he used to practice with Bear and Condor who already had gone where he was going. He said good evening to Juanchito López who was leaning against the doorway of his mother's store, smoking a cigarette, and when he returned home he went straight to bed. He kissed Elvira when he woke in the morning and boiled the kettle on the stove and took his mother a cup of hot water for her morning herbs and that was when he kissed her and she embraced him before in a few moments he was gone, walking down to the turning area for buses which went downtown and rattling down the hill and towards the workshop of Emerson Moralla.

Moralla was in a hurry. He had to get back to Guadalajara for an important meeting with the police. They ate corncakes and eggs which he'd cooked in his office and then they got into his Chevrolet and drove out to the farm. As they went Moralla talked non-stop about the country, politics, change and the future. The future was going to be good, he said: it couldn't be worse than the past. When they came near police checkpoints he slowed to clip in his seatbelt but as soon as they had passed he unclipped himself. With his stomach, he said, they didn't suit him and though people chided him for taking risks he didn't agree: he knew someone not even as fat as he was whose gut had served them in a crash, wedging them fast against the steering wheel so that all they suffered was some inner bruising. Moralla laughed loudly then. Had it been a joke? Elvis couldn't really tell. But soon Moralla was off again on another tangent and as he spoke he looked at Elvis almost as often as he looked at the road, one arm lightly holding the wheel and the other free.

Elvis couldn't understand why he was talking so much. He should have wanted to make a connection with him, the person he was trusting his money-making business to, but the connection was in his mind only. Or he should have been interested in making sure they got there safely, when so much money was at stake. But he seemed only to want to impose his personality, to make Elvis afraid. Elvis was not yet old and he knew there was much yet for him to learn but he understood that. He was used to being afraid.

Actually, though, Emerson Moralla did not frighten him. He knew how to deal with bullies. It was the countryside outside Guadalajara that was frightening because he had never seen it before. When they had driven out before it had been dark and the headlights of the Chevrolet had only picked out trees and the road before them. And then when the car had stopped by the farmhouse and the lights had gone off he had only just made out the shadow of the mountains rising dark and jagged against the night sky. But now he could see the verdant fields and the variety of the trees and the languorous plumes of grass and these scenes so bucolic that they did not seem real. All this life. It was not normal. Things he had never seen before, although he had heard of them. Campesinos guiding donkeys up sand roads and pressing them on with their switches and the donkeys swishing their tails against the flies and trotting and passing others on horses, and fields with horses and cows grazing, and clean white cruisers growling past them in puffed-up clouds of dust.

As they neared the farm, Moralla looked at him. "You've never seen the country before, have you?" Elvis shook his head, and Moralla laughed. "There's a first time for everything," he said. "There's nothing to be frightened of." They pulled up outside the farmhouse and Moralla got out of the driver's seat. "Sit here," he said. "I'm going to clear up a few things inside." He unloaded a box of provisions and went inside and came out soon afterwards with a beer. "In a minute, I'll show you how the printing machine works," he said. "But first, we need to agree the rules."

"The rules?"

"Yes, the rules about you're being here."

"What are the rules?" Elvis asked.

Moralla leaned his arms over the door of the passenger seat and looked down at Elvis as he sat in the car. "You need to make up two blocks of notes per week, and you need to make sure that the farm is safe."

"That's it?"

"Wait, wait. What does keeping the farm safe mean? That means that you don't wander very far and you don't invite friends that I don't know and you say nothing to anyone about the work. In return, you'll get the weekend free and 500,000 pesos to take home for your mother and to spend yourself."

Elvis rubbed his eyes, still tired with the early start and the newness in everything. "But who will look after the farm at the weekend?"

"Don't worry about that," Moralla said, "that's not your concern. Your concern is to make the money and to make sure no one finds out about it. I've brought enough food to last the week. If you want to, you can walk across to old Señora Frankl's farm for some company. It's a kilometre away, towards the mountains. She'll give you some fresh eggs and butter if you need them. But you can't leave." Moralla looked at him with what seemed to be an attempt at kindness. "It wouldn't be safe for you."

Of course, Elvis agreed. He told Moralla that he had nothing to worry about but he did not look at him as he spoke and instead looked out from the veranda at the dirt road which led away from the farm and the thickets on either side. A goat was tearing at the thorns on one of the bushes just beyond the fence by the roadside, shaking the whole bush with its determination. A bird with blue-and-red wings darted away from the bush in a spray of colour and the noise and the colour startled Elvis and he realised that the land around the farmland was laden with birds whose calls echoed, like the voices he used to hear calling across the comuna, that there were so many of them calling that it was like music and he had never heard this music before. "That's great," Moralla said, interrupting his thoughts. "I knew I'd be able to count on you."

Elvis got out of the car and stretched and Moralla took him to the sheds where the presses were and gave him a half-hour lesson in operating them and then they walked back again to the farmhouse and Elvis sat on the steps as Moralla went inside with the box of food he had brought over from Guadalajara, and all the while Elvis looked at the small and delicate flowers that lay open yellow and red in the bushes, as if waiting for someone to pick them, and he heard the birds call and dogs barking in the distance and he realised that half of what he could see was so foreign to him that he could not even name it.

He heard Moralla come out of the farmhouse behind him and felt his hand on his shoulder. He'd see him on Friday evening with 500,000 pesos, Moralla told him and Elvis nodded agreement and asked him to say hello to the Angolan for him. Moralla said that he would and climbed into the Chevrolet and drove off in a spray of dust, hooting his horn. And after the sound of the engine had gone Elvis sat for some time on the veranda listening again to the birdsong and the distant calls he could hear people making to one another. He looked out beyond the thicket of bushes and saw how the land curled up in tongues and bunched into hills where the trees thinned and how beyond the hills was a mountain range that shone grey and gold as the sunlight hit the rocks high above. He watched it all in silence for half an hour and then realised that never before in his life had he been so alone in the world.

That was when he felt afraid. He stood up and walked around the farm, as if just to check that no one was spying on him, and then sat again and tried to accustom himself to the solitude but he could not. Who was there here who could protect him? He tried to banish the thought and remember that the comuna was dangerous and that it was dangerous because people lived there, but he could not. He thought then of how angry he was if Elvira woke him at night and how often he had longed for more space as his father had made Juaní creak and moan on his returns from his journeys to Veracruz. What seemed narrow and confined seemed beautiful to him then. There was so much space here, but no one to share it with and a pervasive fear that someone might attack and try to take it from him. Perhaps that was what it was like to be rich.

By and by he cooked himself some spaghetti and tuna fish and in the afternoon began the process of printing the first batch of notes by cutting the paper and loading the ink and when he had finished for the day he drank some beer and continued drinking until it was dark. Then he sat watching the stars pulsing as if like the blood inside his head, an energy to keep him breathing when it would have been so easy to have just given up. Perhaps this was how Bear and Condor had felt when they had escaped from the comuna, the freedom and the fear eating them up in equal measure, their emotions cannibalising themselves before they could even speak. Who knew where they were, anyway? Probably somewhere like this, if they were still alive. And as he thought of those friends of his who had disappeared he realised that right then there were people in the comuna who were thinking of him as he had once thought of Bear and Condor, that for them he was the one who had disappeared.

In the morning he woke and decided to go to Frankl's farm as Moralla had suggested. He needed to talk to someone. There was an old mule trail that led from the back of the house towards a valley and Elvis followed it until after a few minutes he felt that someone was looking at him. He turned and saw a blonde, middle-aged woman standing beside a stunted tree. She was staring at him with her eyes deep and hollow. He moved back towards her and then she vanished and he realised that he had been dreaming. But he had never dreamt like that, of someone who had never been there. Of someone who had not even disappeared.

He turned and continued towards the neighbour's farm. There was some fresh horse dung on the path and flies had congregated. He waved his hand around his head to disperse them and the flies skittered across the sharp morning light and then flew back to the dung. The path passed some rocks and then went down a steep hill into the valley where the old lady's farm stood beside two stone-walled corrals in which some horses and sheep were penned. He passed the corrals and knocked on the old wooden front door and Frankl came and answered and invited him in without a word and poured him some hot milk and gave him some warm bread and told him to feel at home. Her white hair was tied up behind her neck and she wore a floral apron above a grey blouse that was heavily stained and her hands were brown with ingrained dirt and she smelt of animals.

Elvis sat on a long wooden bench beside the kitchen table and looked at her. "How did you know I was coming?" he asked her. "The milk's still warm."

"It was about time. Moralla hasn't had anyone to guard the farm for a couple of weeks now."

Elvis drank his milk, thinking about what she had said. "Who usually guards it?"

"Oh, he always has somebody. He doesn't bother me. I suppose he thinks I'm harmless."

"And are you?"

She laughed; there was a gleam in her eyes, of knowledge and also of the wisdom not to share it. "You don't need to worry about me," she said then. "I know what your job is, and I know what goes on up there, but I can tell you that my neighbour could be a lot worse than Moralla. Much worse. He keeps the place tidy and he looks after the land and that's enough for me."

After he'd finished eating she took him to the hen run and found four eggs laid in the straw and gave them to him in a paper bag. He asked her what he could do in return and she laughed and said that he needn't worry. Moralla helped her with practical things around the farm, things that needed doing, and she returned the favour. Elvis couldn't help wondering whether he didn't pay her something just to keep an eye on the place. But he thanked her for her hospitality all the same and walked back up the track. He moved slower this time, because the heat had risen, and he looked at the rocks beside the path and saw that some of them had been etched with representations of animals he did not recognise, deities perhaps, creatures to respect and to hold and to fear: yes the rocks were as roadsigns laid down millennia before by people who had known that others would come, and others would see. Those people were as seers who had their own view of time, in which it did not move in one direction only.

By and by the gradient levelled out, and he came with a feeling of heat and mystery and the heaviness of his body that would not let him rest, that told him it was far too early for that in his case. And thus he came towards the farmhouse and as he neared it he remembered that strange mirage of the blonde woman standing beside the tree which stood stunted with its roots twisted up out of sandy and rocky soil, clawing onto the earth as if worried that it was about to let go, but then he banished the thought and made his way to the house and went inside and fried himself some eggs which he ate with bread and sweet coffee, sitting on a stool in the kitchen with his legs raised onto the table, before replete he started on the day's work.

Elvis had been anxious about how he would find the work but in fact it didn't take him long to get used to it. There was a satisfaction that came with making money. Contributing to the economy, that was how Moralla had put it. And the money would find its way back to the comuna through Moralla and through him. He spent his days working and eating and then slept when it was already dark and the stars were like frozen ice from the mountains and once he dreamed that they were tiny droplets of moisture from the breaths of the Native American peoples who had breathed and then died and left the stars as their memorial. Winking quietly in the darkness when most were sleeping. In the mornings he visited Frankl and sat watching the steam rise from the stove and helping the old lady to feed the fire with logs from the carefully woven basket which lay on the floor nearby. She fed him warm bread and quince jelly and he left with fresh eggs after they had talked about her life and his. Once she talked sadly about some people who had owned Moralla's farm many years before, about how the owners had had trouble, and the woman had died suddenly, or no one had seen her again, and some people said that her husband had killed her and others that she had left and returned to Holland, which was where she had been born, probably near the start of the 20th century, so long ago that it seemed in almost a different dimension of time. Frankl did not know what had happened to her. But soon he had gone too and the farm had been abandoned and no one had wanted to occupy it in those violent years and empty it had remained until Moralla had bought it.

Moralla arrived on the Friday at lunchtime. He inspected Elvis's work and ceremoniously counted out 500,000 pesos in 10,000-peso notes and gave them to him. Then they drove back to the city and when Elvis reached the comuna and walked into his home Juaní looked at him as though he were some sort of ghost. "I didn't quite believe that you'd be back so soon," she told him. "Your father never was." "I'll keep my word to you," he answered. He looked in his pocket and gave her half of what he had earned and they both eyed the money, which sat in a small pile on the table, untouched and somehow unloved. "You've been working hard," she said. "I told you, mamí. I had to leave the Angolan." Juaní did not answer him but she rose and put the kettle on the stove, They were almost out of gas, she told him: later on he'd be able to go to López's store for a new canister.

The kettle took a long time to boil but eventually she brought him a cup of coffee and he spooned in three sugars and then as he started to drink it Elvira woke from her afternoon sleep and started to cry. Her noise stifled his thoughts. He rose and picked his sister out of her bed and handed her to his mother and told her he'd be back soon. He'd go down to get the gas from the store.

By then it was nearly dark. The comuna looked grey and sad in the waning light as the light closed over it and the city and its noises ground on in the gathering darkness, the sounds of families preparing to eat what they could and dogs seeking out their infinitesimal pleasures and the cable car wires sparking overhead. He had never seen it like that before. It had just been life. He walked down the hill and called out greetings to the neighbours, but he noticed that not everyone replied and that those who did spoke with a respect which he had never experienced before. When he reached the store, López greeted him with a shout:

"We weren't expecting you," she said. "We were told you were working away."

"I am," he said. "But I have the weekends free."

"Still, we didn't expect you again." She looked him up and down, measuring the person he was becoming. "You're getting bigger," she commented. "They feeding you well?"

"OK." Elvis shrugged; he couldn't admit that he was cooking for himself.

"You're no longer the little boy Elvis. So slight you could make him disappear with one punch."

"No," he said. "That was long ago."

Elvis pulled up a stool beside the counter and ordered a beer. He was in no hurry just then. All that was so long ago and now things were different. He could feel his arms getting broader, his body fuller. He was becoming like the Angolan, someone the Angolan would have been proud of, someone to respect. He still had over 200,000 pesos in his pocket. Almost 100 beers! That was what Moralla had meant by contributing to the economy. He'd buy things, and that would help. It would help López. He ordered a second beer. He felt happy.

"Do you have any gas?" he asked her.

"None in," said López.

"Where else can I try?"

López sighed: "It will have to be the store run by Bear's mother."

"Bear's mother." Elvis splayed out his lips, sighing. "Has Bear been back?"

"No. He's left like the others: that was why I didn't expect you back."

Elvis sipped his beer. An argument started outside, loud and bitter. López walked over and shut the door. "Excuse me," she said to him, "but I have to protect this" – she gestured around her – "as you know, it's all I have."

"I can't go and buy gas from that place," Elvis said to her then. "As you know, my family and Bear's don't get on."

"Of course."

"I've never understood why. My father hated them. Really hated them."

"Ah," she said, "it goes back to when you were little."

"Was it sex?"

"No, not that," she said. The argument had abated outside and she opened the door and brushed aside the beads which hung in the doorway and stood inspecting the silence for a moment, as if to see how silent it really was. "It was really an extreme time," she said then. "People did things they shouldn't have done. Everyone did."

"The paramilitaries?"

"Let's just call it what it was, a war. People came into the comuna and whole streets vanished overnight. As if they had never existed. We all lost people. And some people can never forgive that."

"My parents?"

But López did not answer. "There'll be some more gas in by the middle of next week," she said then. "Tell Juaní I'll keep a bottle for her."

"What did my parents do?"

López turned to look at him: "Afterwards, they did a lot."

"Afterwards?"

"Your mother. She helped the foreign journalist when he came to look into it. When your father wasn't here." Elvis felt his eyes turn to a different intensity as she spoke. "And I'm sure the journalist was well-intentioned. He got a lot of information from your mother. But it was as he told her: no one would really care."

Elvis drained his beer and stood, ready to go: "That was the usual condition of my childhood," he told her.

Every experience was intense for Elvis that weekend. The streets toured by packs of rangy dogs and young men, hungry both. Young women waiting on corners and in doorways. Watching. He could have bought one with the money in his pocket. Soon enough he did. But that first weekend he called in on old friends and bided his time with Elvira and Juaní. He felt as if he was taking his leave from his childhood. And on the Sunday he went downtown to buy his Bandeja and bought some new clothes and met Moralla as they had arranged and Moralla drove him back out to the farmhouse through the winding coils of the city's lights. And as it had been once so it was soon again the following week and again soon after and within a month Elvis was used to the life and to the money it brought him and he became used to being able to buy things, whatever he wanted, and he lost his virginity and bought clothes for his family and drank beer, all the time with money he had made, with a purchasing power that came from nothing.

One weekend he decided to buy Frankl a present. She was so kind to him, cooking him food, treating him like a grandson. She never asked for anything although he cut logs and milked her goats without being asked, sometimes spending half the day with her. She always said that there was nothing she needed, but he doubted this. He knew she would like a radio and so bought her one and put it in his rucksack. He did not say anything to Moralla about it. He sensed that Moralla might not have liked him getting too close to the neighbour. That perhaps he would worry in case Elvis found something out.

On the Monday morning he took the present down to her farm. As he descended the valley he saw Frankl in the yard in front of her house, throwing grain to the chickens. She seemed very happy but he realised just then that he knew nothing about her life. Whether she had been married or had children. How she had come to the farm in the first place. There were many mysteries and his life was increasingly a mystery, used as he now was to this double existence between the farm and the city where a month before he had never even left Guadalajara.

"I've bought a present for you," he told her when he reached the yard. She smoothed her hands on her apron and smiled.

"We'd better go inside," she said. When they went into the kitchen he sat on the bench and gave her the radio. "Has it got batteries?" she asked, after she had thanked him, and he told her yes, he had thought of that. "We'd better put it on." She turned on the radio and they listened to a local channel, high-pitched and hectoring, and for once they did not talk to each other as she boiled his milk and served him food, all as if nothing had changed and as if nothing ever would. Finally, she turned it off. "I haven't listened to the radio for years," she said. "Not since I was a child."

"Why not?"

"Pah," she said angrily, "who can bear all these lies they tell us?"

They said nothing and then Elvis asked if she had been a child on the farm. Oh no! She laughed at the thought, she'd been born in Austria and her parents had escaped in the 1930s. They had told her something of this past when she had been a young girl, in the late 40s, and ever since then she'd felt alone, even when she'd married her husband and they'd come out to live on the farm. He'd died young. There had been the Dutch neighbour but then she had gone too. All that was left now in her mind were memories of a past which seemed increasingly unreal. Peopled with ghosts who could come up to you if you weren't careful, to remind you of what the world had once been. But these days, even the ghosts came less and less often.

By and by he left. He walked up the path, past the gnarled old tree. There was an instant when he thought the blonde woman might have been behind him, but he turned and she was not there. And then he stood for some time, looking at the sky gold with the morning sun and white with clouds, flooding the valley with light.

# CHAPTER 16

Starting something new was a way of making time disappear. An hour could last for a month and a day for a year. But if experiences were all the same, if all you did was to stare at a screen, then it was impossible to tell when the days had changed into months and when the months had become years. It was impossible to tell if anything had happened at all.

That was how it had been with Los Vampiros. The first two months leading up to their debut gig had been the best time of Julián's life. New friends changed your perspective on life, or at least allowed you to discover something in yourself that you had not known was there. At length they had played at a restaurant in the north of Santa Fé where the owner knew Cruz's parents. It was the sort of place where you could see more make-up than flesh, where nothing was real, not even the money they received at the end of the night. But who cared? They'd each left with 100,000 pesos, and Julián had taken the cellphone number of a girl called Carlotta.

After the gig they had spent time trying to record their first CD, and that too had been new. Even Stone hadn't been able to kill that with his cynicism, though he had tried hard enough whenever they had met to work through the lyrics at the cultural centre.

"What's the point?" he'd asked, more than once, "there's no point in anything except playing."

"It's our mission," Bontera had replied once, when they were sitting at their favourite café in the Colonial quarter, "you know we've got a message that needs to be heard. That we've got our voice now, one that's in the story and can't be made to vanish."

"Hah!" That was when Stone had choked on his coffee: Julián could remember the disgust crunching his face. "For decades people have had messages that need to be heard, voices that they thought wouldn't be crushed, and what difference has it made? More and more books. More and more CDs. Everyone consuming them. And more and more violence, more and more inequality."

"So what, that's our fault?" Bontera had asked him.

"I'm not saying that."

"Is it even connected?"

"Like I've told you," said Stone, "it's all connected."

"No," said Bontera. "You want to mess us up with your anger, but you can't. So you want to lead us to it instead, like you're some Pied Piper, just a leader actually."

"So what? So you believe the message we all hear, that material contentment leads to inner peace? That's bullshit." Stone spat onto the cobbles beside their table. "Anyone who believes that, they should come to meet all of us."

By and by their sparky anger dissipated, though, and they got on with the business of playing. As the weeks had gone by a slow ennui had settled over them. Nothing new lasts forever. There was only so much that they had to say, to the world and to each other. Once people reached their third or fourth book or CD, it was all downhill. Time started to drag. Counting the weeks as if he was learning slowly the numbers, still in school. Perhaps Arturo had sensed it, and that was why he had sent him to Vásquez's office.

Even that had been a novelty. The first week there had settled slowly for Julián. There were always points of interest in a new routine. The revolting cheap aftershave that Vásquez used, and the fact that none of the secretaries seemed to mind. For a moment he'd wondered how anyone would be able to have sex with that sphere of lard smelling of rancid strawberries. But of course they did. Julián could tell that Vásquez was highly sexed. Prostitutes did have a useful social function, after all.

One of the secretaries there attracted him more than the others. She was tall and slender, like he was, and had dark wavy hair which fell on either side of her temples and sometimes hid her eyes if she moved her face suddenly. Her name was Roberta, and she came from the flatlands beyond the mountains. She was very composed, the sort of person who feels that the world will ask nothing impossible of them. Her breasts rose round and firm under her blouse and Julián found it hard not to look at them as he talked. He wanted a visa for Britain, that was true, but he wasn't going to stop looking at women just because of Pamela Oswald.

Roberta had been working for Vásquez for over a year. After a couple of weeks Julián suggested they had lunch together and they crossed the road to a lanchonete just across from the office where the tables were pressed together and waiters dressed in white shirts brought bowls of stew and plates of chicken and rice from the serving hatch and people ate, greedy and noisy, rejoicing that they were not hungry. Julián asked her what she knew about his business, and she told him about the apartments for North American investors. "It's like all the best and most beautiful things in this country," he said, holding her gaze, "we can't stop selling them to foreigners. We're like an old whore who can't refuse herself even though we're near death and there's nothing left of us to take." She simpered, and that was when Julián saw that she was not at all an innocent. He could have had her if he'd wanted to but he didn't care. He just wanted to find out about Vásquez. "Have you met any of the Yanquis?" he asked her then, but she shook her head: she hadn't. "How do you know they exist then?" "I've seen the books," she said. "The money doesn't come from nowhere, it isn't a conjuring trick out of thin air. Of course, the Americans are there. And then, there's the cash that comes in from the girls' school."

Julián had just been letting Roberta talk. That was how people told you about things that they were meant to keep hidden, Stone had taught him that. He asked her about the school but she did not say much and began to eat more swiftly and it was not long before she looked ostentatiously at her watch and told him that she needed to get back to the office, there was an email she had to send to a client in Guadalajara. Julián was all smiles. He didn't let on that he was aware of what she'd said but stood up and helped her into her jacket with fake courtesy, the sort that a dumb manipulator like her appreciated. She asked him if he was coming back with her but he declined: he didn't work in the afternoons, they could do it another time.

After she'd gone he tried to call Stone but he had no credit left. He walked up 12th Street until he found a call centre but Stone was engaged. A girls' school couldn't bring in that much cash, could it? Education was an expensive habit and the wealthy despised it because it taught you to distrust wealth, and to hate them. You couldn't afford to educate people well if you wanted to be rich. You'd have too many people competing for your money. No, it was impossible that Vásquez would have bothered investing in a girls' school that was just a girls' school.

He saw Stone early the next morning. He drank two tintos straight and told him what had happened.

"The school could be a lead," Stone said. "Who knows what goes on there?"

"Almost certainly, Roberta doesn't," Julián said.

Stone shrugged, drawing hard on his cigarette: "If it's a boarding school, it's the sort of place that you could take people to disappear. People like María and Purdue. Although that probably isn't it."

"It could be."

"No." Stone shook his head decisively. "Probably, that isn't it at all. But the connection could be there, and if you want to impress Pamela Oswald and show her how to stop anything bad from happening to her, this could be the right way." Stone looked at him, then. "If that's what you want," he added. Julián looked away: the truth was that he didn't know what he wanted, and it seemed to him that this made him just like everyone else in the world, that these days no one knew what they wanted because what they wanted was too much. "Just find out what you can," Stone told him, interrupting his distraction, "but look after yourself."

Over the next two weeks, Julián looked meticulously through Vásquez's accounts to build up a picture of the school. It was the one time in his life that he had been pleased to have his training. The school was easy to identify, named after St Teresa of Ávila. In fact there were two branches, one in Guadalajara and one in Rosario. It was the only branch of Vásquez's business that had nothing to do with the real estate, but when he asked his boss about it he was so forthcoming that Julián knew he was lying. The school was the charitable arm of his enterprise, he told Julián, the part that made him proudest of all. It was set up by the Americans for poor girls of Rosario and Guadalajara to give them an education, something that would be useful to them in later life. But the schools turned a profit, Julián pointed out. Vásquez ignored him: that was right, a real charitable foundation, the sort of thing that was best about the country. When he told Stone about it later Stone told him that he needed to watch out. Vásquez might be rich, but he probably wasn't completely stupid.

Julián didn't care. Vásquez was a friend of his dad's, so the worst that would happen was that he'd be taken off the job. But there was no sign of that. Vásquez became more friendly. Two days after he'd mentioned the schools, he asked him to come into his office so that he could make him an offer. He took him into his confidence, showing him plans for the future of the condominium developments, the encroachment on the virgin forest, development of high-speed boat links for clients so that they could easily visit nearby islands, spending projections, growth forecasts. "In ten years' time," Vásquez said, "the development by the coast will be a real goldmine." He laughed. "So how do you mine a goldmine, Julián? How? You open a new seam." A new seam? Vásquez clearly had fantasies of owning emerald mines in the mountains. "Yes," he went on. "We'll start a tour company to offer bespoke services to the Americans in the apartments, taking advantage of the boat links we've set up. You can come in on it too, if you want to. Your English would be a huge advantage."

Vásquez was grinning, and Julián felt himself responding. "It sounds interesting," he said.

"It will be the making of you."

"But will those foreigners really want to tour around a country as dangerous as this?"

Vásquez smiled at that question, sitting back in his office chair and resting his hands on the back of his head. He expanded, slowly, confidently: with the air of someone who is used to being listened to. In these tours, there'd be no danger, he said: no danger at all. Julián would clean up, and then he'd have enough money to launch the music career he was always dreaming about. How did he know about that? Oh Arturo had told him plenty: plenty! But that was the problem with artists like him, Vásquez said then, leaning forward and suddenly looking with extreme intent into Julián's eyes so that he felt himself edge back into his seat as if somehow in an interrogation in which no questions may be asked and no answers may be given and safety is assured by the most profound of silences. The problem with artists like him was that they were bankrupt, they had no vision. No money. They dreamt of becoming famous through their art, they dreamt of earning fortunes through their art, but very few had the talent to realise that the only true artists are ones that have already sold out. Sold out. Vásquez emphasised the phrase, drumming his hands on the table with suppressed hatred. They couldn't see, he said with the blunt disgust of someone who has always hated art and artists, who has never been able to understand it, that in order to make true art an artist had to be free of the need to earn a living and that in order to be free they needed already to be rich, already have sold out, or belong to a family that had.

Julián heard him out and said he'd consider it, though he was not really sure what he was supposed to be considering. "You can be a partner," Vásquez said. "Think about it. Next week, I'm going to Guadalajara to inspect the girls' school there and you can come with me if you want to."

Julián thanked him and went back to his desk and when he left for the university he felt so tired that he stopped to buy a fruit juice and fell asleep for a few minutes as he waited for his drink to come, slumped in his chair as if he had been shot. He collected his marks and prepared for the night shift and drove his car in anger, burning petrol pointlessly by revving the engine at traffic lights, offering nothing to his passengers but a hollow face and the dark silence of a city filled by dark silences, threatened by death. He felt like falling asleep at two o'clock but he took some heavily cut cocaine and drove on and the city pulsed like his heart and there was so little life left, just the throttled fury of his engine and Pancho directing him from his sad solitary room in the basement which he occupied on 25th Avenue, directing him to collect other solitaries like they both were, people who might have borne witness to the ugliness and injustice of a city shorn of light and built on bones and trampling on streams and meadows where flowers once had grown and other peoples long since dead had dreamt like people have always dreamt and died like people have always died with the soft promise that their dreams might still come true, if only their death would come. If only the death wish could be realised. If only so that another society could be born from one that has nothing more to give to the world from which it has only taken.

When he told Stone about it the next day, Stone just laughed. "It's obvious," he said. "How do you buy off someone on your case? Someone you can't get rid of? You bring them on board." He leant forward; his limpid blue eyes still held a glow of mirth. "Are you going to sail with that ship?"

"You bastard, Lizard." Julián was angry, really angry: he almost got up to leave.

"But seriously, why not? Is there a choice?"

"There's always a choice."

Stone shrugged: "Not really," he said, "and not always. If you believe that, you've never been in a really impossible situation." Of course, Stone had. Julián remembered, then, that time they'd come down from the Montegordo and he'd told them about his life in Africa. How did you survive in a time like that? You had to choose your friends, and there were no perfect choices because no one was perfect. "Look," Stone said, "don't get angry. You're angry because you're worried that I'm right. But hell, I may be wrong."

"So you think I should go with him to Guadalajara next week?"

"It depends why you're going there."

"He wants me to join the team, to make money."

Stone laughed derisively. "It's always possible to make money if you have to. Don't go for that reason. No, you go because you have your own ambitions, not because you want to do his bidding."

"But I don't want to go."

"No," Stone said, "but you do want to impress Pamela. There are two missing people in her life, María and Purdue. You go, telling her that you think you're on the case. You impress Vásquez. And maybe, just maybe, you'll find something out."

Julián sat back in his chair, looking at the Lizard. He was even thinner than usual, and his cheeks were pale and a little sunken. There was a matting of stubble curving either side of his chin like a saucer. His eye sockets seemed to have become deeper over the past few months, as if life was really beginning to sadden him. "Why do you think they've disappeared?" he asked Stone.

"I don't know," Stone said. "Every time I realise that someone has gone, that they're not there any more and that no one can say how or why they've gone or if they'll ever come back, it reminds me of all the parts of myself that have died off these past ten, fifteen years."

"Which parts?"

"Only the parts that matter." Stone was smiling as he spoke, as if it were all a great joke. "Hope, love, authenticity. Or the ability to write something that isn't full of clichés, or catchphrases masquerading as thought. The ability to think. Things that just sometimes you can still glimpse, if you try to learn something new, perhaps, or play a game of chess for the first time in years. Nothing that makes me different to anyone else." He stood up. "But mostly," the lizard told Julián, "these are things that have just gone and will never come back."

"And does that happen often?"

"That people go?"

"Yes, how often can it be?"

They were leaving the cultural centre, and Stone nodded across the street: "Don Octavio's kiosk: have you seen it this week?" Julián noticed now that it was gone. "I suddenly realised yesterday," Stone said. "Realised when I saw his face slapped up on the lamp-posts around here as a missing person. I realised that he hadn't been there for ten days." They strolled down the hill towards the city. The sky was light and the streets flickered with people and the colours of passing buses and taxis. "That was when I realised how angry I was," Stone said. "When I knew that I really had to get to the bottom of all these disappearances."

"That's what Pamela's been saying to me," Julián said.

"Of course. She's worried. She didn't have that in mind when she decided to come here, to help out as she saw it."

They parted and Julián walked slowly down towards the Plaza Bolívar. An elderly couple were walking with great effort up the hill towards him. The man was dressed in a synthetic brown overcoat that was several sizes too big for him, and his wife held onto his arm tightly. They looked as if they didn't quite know where they were going. The man looked up with hunted eyes into Julián's own gaze and asked him the time, with his eyes shifting evasively away and looking into the distance as if this was not really what he had meant to ask him at all. Julián checked his cellphone: it was a quarter to twelve, but when he looked up to answer he saw that already the couple had pushed past him. Only madmen behaved like that, or comics trying to substitute bewilderment for meaning. Or people who were afraid.

That was what reminded him of Pamela. Stone was right. Over the past few weeks she had lost her enthusiasm. You wouldn't have known this to speak to her, for she would still tell you how much she believed in the work of the centre, how much she loved Ramona and Leila, and enjoyed her meals with Señora Fonseca. She still sounded out the same trite platitudes. Some switch had probably flipped in her brain and could only send her thoughts in the same endless circles. But her skin did not look as shiny or as fresh as it had when they'd first met. The lines which lay latent on her forehead, as they did of everyone aged thirty and above, had become more prominent. Sometimes when they slept together in a hotel he'd booked for them in the Centro Internacional or the Pachinero he'd hear her teeth grinding in the night, anxious, like the city. María had not reappeared and no doubt the atmosphere in Leila's apartment had darkened and Pamela had understood the true gravity of what had happened and of what she had come to do. She was learning so quickly. One night she cried out in her sleep, in Spanish: no quiero ir, no voy a ir con ustedes, déjeme aqui donde la gente me pueden ver, donde aún puedo ser.

When they went out for dinner later that week at a vegetarian restaurant downtown, Julián told her about Vásquez's plan.

"Don't do it," Pamela told him.

"Why not?"

"It could be dangerous. Surely you won't go to Guadalajara with someone who's just cleaning up money?" He looked at her, eating, saying nothing. "We need to make the most out of the time we have together, Julián," she said. "My time in the country is almost through. In three weeks I have to leave for London."

She was already getting ready to go, already thinking about the report that she had to write: the "objective account", as Bontera mocked it behind her back, sniggering, this was what objectivity was, an excuse for truth. Julián looked at her. He suddenly felt flat and heavy. What sort of fantasy had this been that the lizard had helped him to cook up, that somehow they would fall in love and that he would be able to leave with her, leave the country behind him and disappear through his own volition? What sort of fantasy was that? Manifold were the ways of refusing to confront reality, of refusing to conceive of one's dismal fate as it was. That was when it hit him that in thirty years' time he would be just like his father, if he was lucky. Large and tired, proximate to death without daring yet to taste it, unloved and unloveable and disappeared from the memories of all good people, for when all was said and done what was there to love or admire in someone who had wasted their youth in pointless schemes, schemes which lacked all larger ambition? Perhaps Stone was right: Vásquez's offer could really be his last chance.

"You're not going to go?" Pamela asked him.

"Why not? It may give us a lead on María and Purdue."

Pamela looked unhappy: "It's a bad idea," she said.

"But you could come too. Have you been out of Santa Fé yet?"

She shook her head: "No."

"Why not?"

"It all seemed too risky," she said. "I found life interesting enough in the city."

He sighed, finishing his food. He could feel anger and disappointment swelling inside him, like cancers. He thought she had wanted to understand the country, really understand it. People like him, the urbanites she hung out with, they were like washing hung out to dry in the rain. They weren't really supposed to be there. Their parents had flocked in from the countryside and swarmed like flies around the dungheap where the plutocrats had shat long ago and left their stools to fester. They loved the city, or pretended they did, but even they didn't feel at home in it. That was why it didn't work properly.

Pamela looked as though she were crying. She wiped something from her cheek and put her fork down.

"What is it?" he asked.

"It's just María. That's all." They were silent for a moment, and then she carried on. "Sometimes I'm worried that I might forget all this."

"What?"

"You. The city. María. It can all seem unreal, so suddenly. As if the only person really making any of it true is the person remembering."

"But this is real, Pamela," Julián said; he leant forward and took her hand.

"But soon I will be gone."

"I can come and visit you." She laughed. "My father has money, you know."

"But he won't let you spend it on that."

They looked at each other across the table and the candle hissed and wax spat into the holder and they listened to the chatter of other couples, nice people like them and on dates like them and able just for that evening to forget everything that made such evenings possible, even though what made it possible was so terrifying.

"This has all just been a statement for you," Julián said then.

"A statement?"

"Sex with me. Just to show that you came here, you fucked a local. You can tell everyone about it later, share your memories. Make yourself authentic."

"You're being silly."

"You believe in your ideals so much that you'd do anything for them."

He got up. He wasn't even sure why he was so angry. He walked out of the restaurant into the cold night with the air so thin and cutting like little knives sharpened by time, by hate. It wasn't true, she said, she had always been interested by him. He turned: so it wasn't just a pretence, like her fascination for this country, another man, another place that she'd known? Of course not: she was fascinated. She stood before him, moving nearer, trying to make him kiss her. But he stood back: all she cared about, though, was herself and the life she had made for herself in Santa Fé. She hadn't even dared to see what the lives of others were like elsewhere. She stepped before him and agreed: he was right, OK, he was right, she'd come with him to Guadalajara. She waited there longing for his kiss and when he bent forwards he felt her mouth, ardent and supple, her lips parted, desiring him for some reason neither of them could understand.

# CHAPTER 17

At the rehabilitation centre, Ramona was always busy. She wore blouses of which she'd roll up the sleeves, untidily, so that the cuffs were splayed out at funny angles on her short, hirsute forearms. The cuffs jerked with her arms as she moved around the centre, giving orders. The new dormitory block was almost complete, but you had to keep an eye on the workmen or else there would be delays. There were always bargains that had to be struck with the local stores so that the food could be bought as cheaply as possible. Sometimes her voice rang out from her office as she berated the supplier. Someone would come and ring the entrance bell an hour or two later. Usually it was Pedro, the simple man that one of the local stores used for deliveries: smiling apologetically, unshaven, his frame a little stooped, Pedro would wheel the trolley of groceries into the centre and unload the boxes as Ramona looked on, showing them all that this was her demonstration of love, that this was how she cared for them all.

Pedro had a wide, gentle face. His eye twitched at times with nerves and he only spoke when he was spoken to. He reminded Pamela of a boy who used to get bullied by his peers at her school. He had been dyspraxic, and found it hard to keep his life ordered. She had tried to be kind to him sometimes, or as kind as the bullies would permit without turning on her. She tried, too, to show her kindness to Pedro. She always smiled at him, but at that he often as not turned away. Probably, he never understood her Spanish anyway, no matter how hard she tried. One time, after she had unloaded the groceries in the refectory's kitchen, she walked into Ramona's office and stood across from the desk while Ramona thumbed through a sheaf of papers, and asked her, "Can't I do something for him?" But Ramona was brutally dismissive: "He lives with his mother. The brute controls him like an animal, but that's what he wants." "What he wants?" Ramona rolled her eyes; it always seemed to Pamela that she was trying to withhold something, something unpleasant: disdain, if not outright disgust at the world. "She feeds him," Ramona said slowly, tapping the pen she was holding onto the desk in time with the words, "she tends to his needs. Like the baby she never wanted to relinquish. And if he's too much of a coward to stand up to her then he's been born in the wrong country."

There was something admirable enough about this straightforwardness, and Pamela had recognised this when she had arrived. It was the sort of commitment to a cause that she longed for herself, an energy for life which flew from her short frame with a power that was surprising. Ramona wasn't one for graces, that was well-known. She chain-smoked, and the sandy yard of the centre was filled with her cigarette butts. She never treated Pamela as if she was important. But Pamela quickly shrugged off any annoyance, for how could you keep a place like the centre going, how could you do any good in the world at all, if you weren't completely single-minded? Ramona demanded a similar commitment, and perhaps this was why Pamela hadn't minded coming on her weekends, staying late, showing that for as long as she was in Santa Fé the centre was her life. Hadn't she said that she was there to help? The only way of showing that it was true was through action.

As the time neared when Pamela was due to return to London, though, she noticed that Ramona became more and more slighting. She didn't do pretence well at the best of times, and it seemed as if the moment had passed when she cared to pretend with her at all. She'd stand talking to residents, a yard or two from Pamela, and completely ignore her. She didn't share the latest news or the circumstances surrounding the latest person to be admitted. It was as if she didn't want to talk any more about the pain that went with all these mutilations that people had done to themselves. As if Pamela had already left.

Pamela felt betrayed, but she tried her best not to show it. Why should her organization try to help these people if they didn't care anyway? It was hard to feign indifference. When she told the Tumbera about it, she listened with a soft smile on her face. With sympathy. Yes, she had come to help, she was helping, and yet did nobody realise it? "Perhaps they don't," the Tumbera said. "Why not?" And then the Tumbera explained, that it was easy enough to be suspicious of the motivations of others, God knew that. All those genteel North American archaeologists had arrived in her country in their elegant clothing, with the latest electronic apparatus, saying that they wanted to uncover a forgotten past and restore a voice to the voiceless. But many of their in-country helpers hadn't been able to help wondering whether their concern was not really their own status and authority. And then the past had intruded, and one of them had been taken. Just as if they were a local! And then they had all disappeared, never come back.

That was the problem with the Tumbera: you asked her about one thing, and almost invariably she told you about something else. There were less than three weeks before she was due to go back to England and still Pamela hadn't told Ramona that she planned to go to Guadalajara with her boyfriend at the weekend. She hadn't even told the Tumbera about it. She sat on her bed, not even attempting to fill the silence which the Tumbera's little speech had left. Outside, some of the men were playing football. Birds were hopping over the dust, calling to each other. The workmen were painting the roof of the new dormitory block and the corrugated iron clanged as they moved across it.

"Why do you let people call you the Tumbera?" Pamela asked her then. "You didn't choose the name."

"I like it."

"Why?"

"It sums up part of my past. When I helped to sift through the tombs. When I pieced together bits of a past that was dead. Dead."

"Why does it matter to you, though? It's all gone. Finished."

"We've talked about this already, Pamela," she said, crossing her legs as she lay back on the bed. "You already know that we don't agree about it."

"Still, the name...the Tumbera. It's so ghostly."

That was when the Tumbera leant forward. She grabbed Pamela's hand and dug her nails into it. Pamela cried and tried to pull her hand away but she couldn't. The Tumbera's eyes were hollow and pale: they looked through her as if she wasn't there. Again, Pamela tried to pull herself away but this time the Tumbera leant forward and pinned her to the chair, digging her nails in further. She brought her head up to Pamela's ear. She was panting, heavily, like a dog in the heat. "That hurts," she whispered, "but it's only a thousandth of the pain that I did to myself just to get here." She let go then, slowly putting her hands on her lap and sitting back. "When you realise," the Tumbera said then, "when you realise that my choice was between that pain or not being there at all, being as thin as air, then you might understand why I don't mind my name." She waved her hand at the dormitory, at the blankets piled up on the other beds and the grimy sheets which there wasn't the money or personnel to wash regularly, at the trestle tables lined at either end of the room, where the residents kept their wash bags and at the heavy old wardrobes where all their clothes were kept. This, she waved her hand, this was already a sort of a grave: for the past was always with us, whether we liked it or not, and people tried to violate it by developing their own objective narratives. And it was our duty to deny that: to make the story of the past disrupted, as complex and intrusive as possible, so that the voiceless could speak.

There was a cry outside, and the Tumbera rose to see what had happened. An aeroplane climbed over them, heading towards the

Montegordo hill and clear away from the city. The noise rattled the building gently, like a minor earthquake. It reminded Pamela of the pain and fear of all arrivals and departures. "Ha," the Tumbera laughed, "that idiot Ramírez has spilt his paint all down the side of the new building."

Pamela didn't say anything. She did not acknowledge her and she did not reply. Her hand still hurt, and she could see the imprints of the Tumbera's nails deep in the flesh of her hands, standing out red on either side of her veins. She got up to go, and the Tumbera called out: that was what this place was like, it was the land of the unexpected. Then something burnt inside Pamela and she turned, angry: Someone I know calls it Colombian Roulette, she said, because you can always run into danger: and perhaps that was true. Perhaps it was, the Tumbera said, perhaps it was, but was it in the end any concern of someone who would leave?

To that Pamela said nothing, and she was still rubbing her hand as she got on the bus north towards the city centre and as a little boy climbed on and set out tiny calendar cards on their laps and then sang with surprising beauty about the Virgin Mary. Here the city was big with devastated buildings and the pavements were disintegrating and rubble mixed with rags and the bus bumped over the potholes. Some of the passengers gave the boy a few pesos and he got off just south of the centre, calling out thank you to the driver. Soon after he got off another boy climbed on and sang as the bus hummed like a hornet in the traffic, shaking with the effort just of keeping on. The traffic was so bad that a few blocks south of Tucapel Pamela climbed off and decided to walk home instead. She texted Julián, how would they get to Guadalajara anyway? He replied brutally, just the two words: By Plane. Just as she had arrived. Just as they had met. She walked along the streets long and grey and reflecting the clouds which hung overhead. Usually Julián was freer with his texts, he liked to make jokes. But of course, she remembered, he had been hoping to leave by plane with her to somewhere more distant than Guadalajara.

She walked past the Museum of Gold. An ugly building which seemed to be turning slowly brown, with age. Just opposite the side of the museum there was a small square where some acrobats were performing. A couple of middle-aged men were sitting on a stone bench. One of them was strumming a guitar and the other was clapping his hands in time. They were both stooped a little forward, as if drunk, but no one seemed to care. Julián, Leila, Ramona, they all told her how awful the situation was in the country, but life went on. One of the most insufferable things about life, Pamela had realised, was that terrible things happened all the time and yet life went on. Some people could even be happy when the world was like that, but she was not one of them. Perhaps Ramona had really been talking about her when she had mocked Pedro for being weak at heart.

Just past the little plaza was a craft market housed in a converted old colonial building. Pamela had been meaning to buy some souvenirs for weeks. There were some remarkable crafts produced here, it was something she admired the country for. People were not deskilled, as they were in Britain. They used their hands. There were the beautiful little cars made of clay and painted bright colours and decorated with baskets of fruit and people hanging out of the doors, such as you might have seen in the countryside still, where the traditions had not been destroyed, where the city had not encroached and you could still hear birdsong at the end of the day. There were dolls designed with long, spindly legs and decorated with outrageous jesters' outfits, dressed in red or white, with long hats in a style long past. The jewels of the country, the emeralds and rubies, had been set in rings and on bracelets and necklaces and lay like beautiful garlands protected by locks and alarms. Some of the stalls had been set up by artists who had appropriated something of the cubist style and fused it with brilliant colours and mystical beasts of another world and another time. The beasts that still rode furious in her mind when she was asleep and which she loved and hated and pretended were long dead, but which lived on and reared their heads when you were not looking. Wasn't that what the art critics meant by primitive art?

She bought some dolls for her nephews and a necklace and a handwoven jumper made of llama wool for herself and put them in a thin white plastic bag and caught a bus back to the Pachinero. It was almost dark in the city and the lights of the cars switched like sunbeams across the streets. There was still plenty of life when she got off and walked down from 11th Avenue. The students were drinking beer and people were shouting into the phone booths at the call centres or into cellphones attached to a padlock on the kiosks which had set up as if spontaneously on side streets. Salsa blared out from the music shops and the streets were thick with the music and with people and forgetting and just for an instant Pamela felt sad that she would be leaving before too long.

When she reached the apartment it was dark. She turned on the lights in the salon and saw that Leila was sitting there immobile on the brown leather settee. She was looking ahead as if there was nothing there to see and nowhere to go. She did not acknowledge Pamela and so Pamela went to her room and put her new things carefully in the suitcase which she kept at the bottom of the built-in wardrobe. When she went back out to the salon Leila was still there. "Quieres un té?" Pamela asked her, but Leila did not reply. Pamela went into the kitchen and boiled the kettle. The water rattled, and Pamela realised that all this sadness and all this silence, the fearful sense of a death approaching or already past, a death which nothing could be done about, was another reason why she would be glad to leave. She had needed to come, to see what the life was like which she was trying to make better. But now she needed to go back to London, so that she could help.

She went back out with her tea and sat at the table in the dining area.

"I bought some presents to take home with me," she said. This seemed to rouse Leila. She sat up, and looked at Pamela, as if realising for the first time that she had come in.

"Ah," she said, "qué compraste?"

"Good things. Toys for my nephews and something for me to wear."

"Yes," Leila said. "You feel better now."

She often said this to her, Pamela had noticed. It was annoying. "Did you go to church?"

"Of course. On my way to the office."

"So, now you feel better."

"Yes," Leila said. "I do."

"I never see you in the mornings any more."

"No. I leave early. I have to go to church."

"Were your parents Christian?"

"Christian?"

"In Palestine."

"They were not."

Pamela didn't say anything more, then. One of the things she felt most uncomfortable about in Leila's apartment was Palestine. When she had found out about Leila's origins she had felt pleased, or rather pleased and angry. But Leila hadn't offered her what she'd expected.

"The priest told me today that we would find María," Leila told her then.

"Did he say when?"

Leila's face tightened. She stood up and came to sit at the table next to Pamela. "He doesn't have a direct line to miracles," she said. "He is just a man of faith."

All this crap about faith. Pamela felt the blood rushing to her head. Hadn't Leila learnt anything? María had been a kind young woman, someone helping out the mutilated in her free time: it hadn't stopped her from vanishing. There was no personal God who could stop any of it. There was just society, there was selfishness and there was violence.

She felt the anger rise in her, looking at Leila. Accepting her fate. The strands of her long dark hair curled around two of her fingers as she fidgeted as some substitute for action.

"You can pray as much as you want," Pamela said then, "but it won't do you any good."

"Thank you," Leila said.

"You don't need religion," Pamela said, putting her mug on the table with a little anger. "You need action. Religion stops action. It stops people finding María."

"Do you think so?" Leila asked.

"I just can't understand..."

"No. You can't understand."

Leila rose and went to the room which she had used to share with María and Pamela heard her turn on the television. She sat in the living room but the light seemed too harsh now that Leila had gone and she turned it off and saw there in the darkness as Leila had done and tried to experience what Leila might have experienced, all that sadness and all that loss and the world darkening by the moment, so intense, but she could not. So she rose and went to her room and called good night to Leila as she went. The woman was to be pitied, really. She couldn't live here much longer, though. It would be heaven to get out of the place, to leave it all behind. She was glad, too, that she was going to Guadalajara. She needed to leave, if any of it was going to have any meaning for her.

The next day she rose early to catch her bus to the rehabilitation centre. The light was only just rising over the mountains to the east and the trees up above seemed full of shadows. She stopped by a news stand as she waited for her bus and bought the International Herald Tribune. She boarded her bus and went towards the back and sat down to read. After five minutes, a businessman came to sit next to her and put his briefcase on his lap. Smartly dressed, a little oily. So many successful people here looked like that to her, she couldn't see what the country's women saw in them. It wasn't what she was looking for at all. She felt a hand on her leg and so moved herself to the side, but it followed her. Probing. Moving upwards. What could you do to these predators if you didn't want to scream and make a scene, if you wanted to retain your dignity? You couldn't retain your dignity. You had to scream. You had to scream if there were abuses, you had to get angry.

Pamela remembered the Tumbera. She put her hand on the hand and stroked it. It was a hairy hand, smooth and hairy. Like an ape's. She stretched her fingers out and then dug her hails as hard as she could into the man's hand so that he yelped in startled pain, yelped like a dog, and she dug her nails in again and he yelped again and Pamela felt a warm glow in her thighs and a sense of triumph, of pleasure even. The man pulled his hand away and smoothed his hair, as if this were what he had been wanting to do all along. He looked at her, his brown eyes livid with his emotion, angered and disappointed. Soon he got off the bus and she rattled on southwards through the city centre and the bus slowly emptied and filled like an artery of its blood, and the suits and blouses were replaced by jeans brown with grime and patched and threadbare jackets, but it made no difference to the bus. It carried on, on the same journey it made every day.

When she got off she rang the bell at the centre. Ramona answered, which was something she hardly ever did. "Oh," she said when she saw Pamela there, "are you still here?" Clearly she was expecting someone else. Probably it was Pedro, bringing things for lunch. After a moment she stood aside to let Pamela in. Some of the residents were sitting on stools beside the courtyard playing cards. They called out to her when they saw her and she smiled. She went through the double doors into the old dormitory block and was about to go through to the kitchen when the Tumbera called out to her.

Pamela turned: "I brought you a paper," she said, "something to help you practice your English" – it was true, this had crossed her mind when she had picked up the Tribune.

"What use is that going to be to me?" the Tumbera demanded. "I'm never going to need English again in this life, and once you've gone I might well never speak it again. And besides," she said, more slowly, sitting down on the bed again, "whenever I speak it or read it I feel sad."

"Even with me?"

"Yes, even with you," the Tumbera said. "Because English is a language which reminds me of death."

Pamela walked into the dormitory then and stood at the end of the Tumbera's bed: "I don't think much about death," she said.

"No," the Tumbera said: "but I think about it all the time."

It had begun in those mountain graves where they'd dug with spades and disinterred people who deserved their rest more than most. Once, she'd heard one of the archaeologists say that they shouldn't feel only sadness when they picked out the bones and found hands still with rings on them. He'd read that the African slaves of the French colony of St. Domingue in the 18th century had found the same, bones and hardened skulls of the Arawak peoples who had long since died, sometimes horribly mutilated by the Spanish. They had found these remains as they'd dug the holes in the moist earth for the sugar canes and they had never forgotten them and so the world had never quite forgotten the people who had disappeared so utterly from the earth, for when the armies of former slaves had defeated Napoleon's troops on the island, who were molten with fever and running sweat like creatures of the deep, Jean-Jacques Dessalines and the other generals of the victorious army had chosen to call the new independent republic of freed slaves Haiti, which was the name that the Taíno had known the island by, those Taíno whose bones they had moved aside as they had planted the sugarcane and sown the seeds of the revolutions of the future. So the bones too could be some sort of testament, a memorial to people otherwise forgotten, otherwise lost, disappeared all these centuries and yet never quite absorbed by the mulch of the earth's oblivion. That was what he said, the Tumbera laughed, but of course he too wanted the selfishness of his own version of events: a sanitized history, so as finally to get rid of it, to make the past and its lessons disappear once and for all.

When the Tumbera had finished speaking Pamela found that she was still standing, holding out the copy of the Tribune. She withdrew it, and the Tumbera laughed.

"Was that your last gift for me?" she asked.

"No," Pamela shook her head. "There are still two weeks before I leave."

"Perhaps," the Tumbera said.

"Do you think I'm leaving now?" The Tumbera said nothing. "What has Ramona said? What does she know?"

"She hasn't said anything. I just had a sense, that's all. Sometimes, when you live like this, that happens. The future swaps places with the past, in some unaccountable way."

"What sense do you have?"

The Tumbera shrugged. "I understand you. You're not sure what you desire but one of the things you desire is what I desired when I came here myself. But you can't bring yourself to cut into yourself. You want others to do it for you. If you are going to make a sacrifice, rediscover the meaning of religion and do something to recover the sanctity of the world, you need someone else to make the first cut."

Pamela felt herself flush, and she rose to go. Again, her generosity thrown back in her face! Was that her lot in this country? "I don't think you understand me at all," she told the Tumbera. She turned, about to go through to the kitchen, but the Tumbera would not let her go.

"But I do."

"And everything that you've done," Pamela said, "has that somehow been wiser? Do you really think that all that work you did with the American archaeologists in San Bonifacio could really act as some sort of atonement for all those people who died so long ago, like you said to me when we first met?"

"It might have done," the Tumbera said. "But who is going to do the memorial for us?"

Pamela had no answer for that and she said nothing, making a sad gesture with her hand. She went into the kitchens and greeted the cooks as always. She could hear her voice: it sounded heavy and sad. The cooks were peeling potatoes and Pamela joined them, gouging out the eyes with quick, brutal thrusts. They talked desultorily and their voices echoed gently around the room, bouncing off the aluminium saucepans and the gas stove. But they only made the room sound hollow. There was only so much sadness, so much reality, that it was possible to live with. That was why she would be getting on the plane with Julián on Friday, heading for Guadalajara and dreaming of the world she had first imagined when she had arrived and Julián had met her at the airport.

# CHAPTER 18

One week he arrived as always in Moralla's Chevrolet and spent the day at work and ate spaghetti and sausage for dinner sitting on the veranda and looking at the grass cropped by animals and at the bushes and trees drifting up to the mountains where the sky was already pale with fleeting light. Voices carried across the plain from the village of Santa Clara and there was the roar of a motorbike's thrust churning up dust and something opaque hung over the evening as it darkened. He drained two bottles of beer and then went back inside the kitchen to put the empty bottles in the bin but there was no bag there so he walked down the steps at the front to the barn where the trash bags were kept before Moralla drove them off to the municipal tip at the weekend. One of the bags wasn't properly tied up and as he stopped to tie it his elbow knocked into the side of the wall and he spilt some of the rubbish over the floor and saw piles of used condoms still sticky and deformed clinging to the concrete like ticks. The rancid smell stored up in the bag and spilt like wasted seed across the barn floor made him gag and he ran out of the barn breathing hard.

The sky's blue had turned purple with the darkness and he looked at it with a stiff neck and that smell still fresh, thinking of his house in the comuna in the days when his father had come back to spend some time and of the filthy mattress in the concrete room down in the rubble where he had gone the last few weekends with some of the girls of the hill, girls who admired him now that he was a person with connections and with money, now that he was becoming bigger, and they were willing to spend time with him and teach him how he could become a man physically, now that he was ready to pay his way. Luisa Fernanda with her wide eyes and young, hard breasts, her slow rolling gait that excited him whenever he saw it, and Pati with her shy evasive gaze who found it hard to turn away from him now that he was becoming what he was becoming, and Amalia with her enormous breasts large enough to suffocate a man who had just come for some protection, and there were some who said that some men liked that and paid her good money to eat chocolates and sit all day on the wall outside her parent's shack, waiting. He knew that smell and it was the smell of love and it wasn't even a surprise that Moralla came here to have sex at weekends, but who would have thought that he had so much life in him? There had been at least twenty condoms spewed out onto the floor and Elvis almost retched again at the thought that he would have to clear it up and pretend that he had seen nothing. That was what making money really entailed, pretending that you knew nothing about where it came from and spending it to forget your pretence, and others pretending that they also knew nothing as they accepted the force that came with the money that you had.

Elvis went back to sit on the veranda and watched the gloaming glitter with fireflies and he listened to the crickets and frogs singing from the marshes beyond and he thought of all that life reproducing itself in the darkness and Moralla, coming here weekend after weekend and leaving the farm with that sad and urgent atmosphere which he'd noticed, the atmosphere of a place that had seen too much and yet which often hardly saw anything at all, and he lit a cigarette and saw the red glow of the tip as he inhaled and listened in the silence and his loneliness. He couldn't bear that loneliness, not tonight. Not after seeing how Moralla used the place, that glimpse of the life that was here whenever he was not.

Perhaps he could go down to Santa Clara and find a girl to bring back there. Something to ward off that loneliness. But Moralla would know, of course, he would surely have friends in Santa Clara, people who kept watch. Maybe that was what had happened to the people who had worked at the farm before him and Elvis could understand that because he'd never been as lonely as he was here, not when he'd been in the comuna with its vendettas and its fears and the sense that always people were alive, and always they were dying, and scheming or drinking or shooting up or thieving something which was barely worth anything but which made their lives a little more bearable. In the comuna people were working or they were watching, on the streets, or they had gone and their house had been dismantled and another had risen in its stead like a seedling, and no one knew where they had gone or who the new arrivals were, or where they had come from, and what appalling crimes had forced them to leave there, either that they had committed or that had been committed against them, but soon enough they were a part of the comuna just like everyone else. Soon enough they were just like everyone else, even these people who had appeared instead of disappearing. You longed for peace when people were all around you, dying, fucking, vanishing, appearing, but actually peace was silence and the silence was quite terrifying. That was when you might turn to violence, as a defence against all that loneliness and fear, the sense that your neighbour might now be coming themselves and you could not see them, you could not hear them, they would creep soundlessly through the plain, behind trees, and murder you in your sleep if you did not strike first to protect what you had and had taken from others. And so that was when you might kill your neighbour.

He chain smoked for two hours as the stars deepened their light until his head spun like the world around them. Then he was able to sleep and he dreamt that he was back in the comuna, sleeping with Bear's sister, when her mother came in and started beating him with her shoe, screaming that he was ungrateful, from an ungrateful family, collaborators, a family who tried to take everything. But what had they taken? Elvis asked. Only the bread that they ate. People fight just as desperately for nothing at all as when fortunes are at stake: the key thing is fighting.

He woke hot and with sweat gathering in his chest in a film that grew and grew, as if he was slowly condensing. When it was light he walked back down the path towards Frankl's farm. There were fresh hoof prints in the earth and the triangular mark of a nocturnal wanderer already back sleeping in its hole. The sun was low above the mountains and the shadows were long on the petroglyphs and the light was brilliant and fine. Hummingbirds were already at work hovering around the flowers that hung still in the breathless morning. There was a string of smoke rising from the buildings in the valley. Frankl always rose early, before dawn, and had changed the horses' hay and cleaned out their shoes before it was light. That was when it was time to rest for a moment, to enjoy the fire in the kitchen and to break the fast.

When Elvis arrived she greeted him fondly, and he sat on the bench in her kitchen with his knees squeezed under the table, waiting as she heated the milk. Had it been noisy at the farm over the weekend? No more than usual. Had she ever been there? She didn't go somewhere if she wasn't invited, and she hadn't yet been invited there at the weekends. She didn't want to go where she wasn't welcome. Her entire life was a welcome, a blessing, ever since one official in an overheated office in Berlin made a decision to help her parents, a decision that on a different day or even later in the morning, or if that official's bread had been a little stale at breakfast or his coffee a little tepid, he might not have made. And ever since she had heard that story as a child she had known never to press her luck, that life itself was luck.

Elvis listened in the rising heat, drinking his milk. Already it was hot enough in the farmhouse that the flies were bothering, circling randomly in the kitchen with their fizzing drone. After the old lady had finished talking the flies provided the only noise for some minutes. In the distance, then, they heard the accelerating roar of a chainsaw breaking trees into logs. It was the neighbour on the other side, Paulo Millar. Probably the son of a Scotsman, Frankl told him. It reminded her of the man who had owned Moralla's farm and whose Dutch wife had vanished. He had always been outside the farm in the evening, splitting logs with maximum efficiency. And now when she sat alone in the evenings she wondered sometimes if this wasn't the same skill he had used when dismembering his wife and burying her under some tree in the wasteland around the farm. Perhaps that was why he had never come back. Why the farm had something of it that was evil, at least that was how it seemed to her.

One of the horses whinnied outside and Frankl clicked her tongue like one of her chickens and looked at Elvis with the fond and disinterested gaze of someone who wanted to help. It reminded him of why he liked talking to her, because often she would do what she had just done, talk of places and times which he had never heard of and which should have meant nothing to him and which yet somehow brought the vastness of the world to him and helped him to realise how strange and mysterious its distances of time and space really were.

After some time he rose, making as if to go back up the hill to Moralla's farm. But she stilled him with a gesture of her hand, a gesture of age and authority.

"Wait," she said. "There's the whole day yet to work." He lingered by the table, waiting for her to speak. "What disturbed you about the farm?" she asked. "What did you see?" Elvis didn't know how to answer and then the old lady laughed with joy and amusement: "I haven't always been this old! You'd be surprised. I know a lot more about life than you do, young man."

Elvis realised that probably she did, and it made him soften. Perhaps she was trying to be kind. "Do you know what happens at the farm at weekends?"

"Not exactly. But I have heard the cars arriving loudly, late at night, and the laughter of young women. Many of them."

"Where do they come from?"

"Moralla once told me that there's a school he's involved in that uses the place for away days."

"Away days?"

Frankl shrugged; she gestured to him to sit down again, and he sat on the bench across from her and looking into her eyes and wondering what she really knew about the farm, and the world. "He said that I didn't need to know any more."

"Was he threatening you?"

"He was preparing some firewood then. For me. With an axe. He'd offered to, then."

"Is he good with an axe?"

"Not bad. He knows how to use one. But I've lived long enough not to worry about threats any more. People say that the countryside is threatening but to me it has always been welcoming. Dangers only appear if you start to fear them. If you laugh at them they soon go away. And that's my advice to you."

"What advice?" Elvis asked her.

"Don't believe that Moralla is capable of what he pretends." She rose and went over to a store cupboard where she rummaged about and emerged with a glossy brochure. He looked at it and then looked back at her. "I did some research," she told him. "One day I went to Guadalajara and went to the public notary's office and asked to see their files for private schools. I searched through the registration documents, looking for Moralla's name, and found it associated with the private girls' school of St Teresa of Ávila. Moralla's on the board of directors."

"What school is it?"

"A smart school for children of the executive classes. The people who administer the money of the people who are seriously rich in this country. The blind bureaucrats who find that the best sort of reality is in the numbers that they tot up. Wealth creators. Wealth protectors."

"I've never met them."

She smiled sadly. "Well, young man," she told him, "they pay a small fortune to send their daughters to the school of St Teresa of Ávila and Moralla and his co-directors bring them here and fuck them into the bargain. That's what this country is like. The rich despise everyone who hasn't stolen enough to build a condominium in Miami."

Elvis sat by the table and brooded, and Frankl continued. She wanted to tell him about how this corner of the earth where he had ended up really functioned. These conversations opened his mind to a different world and the old lady, who was as lonely as he was, knew it and took advantage. She had not told him what Moralla was like, not straightaway. She had let him move a little closer to the truth weekly, until she felt he was ready. And that was what life was like, he realised, no one really wanted to tell young people, people like Elvis, what it was really like and why there were vendettas and people hated each other, so that when you were a child there were just these curious bursts of anger and fury which seemed like ghosts, rattling about the home and attached to nothing and yet able suddenly to appear as if at will, at any time, to destroy any peace that there might have been. No one could bear to tell children the truth until it was too late for the innocent at heart to remain so. Ah, Frankl said then, rising by pulling herself up on the kitchen table, but it was a good world that the Lord had made and for that she thanked God. Didn't she live in a beautiful place?

At that they went outside and leant against the dry wood of the picket fence and watched the chickens pecking at corn in the dust and the flies buzzing around their necks and around their droppings that lay on the yard and the sunlight brilliant and silver reflecting off the tiles on the roof of her house which rattled in a gentle breeze and they listened to that noise and the birds calling in the trees like children swinging rattles with joy and they heard a woodpecker in the distance and the sound of an engine fading and they both looked up the hill towards Moralla's farm and saw that the path was empty and that the flowers on either side of it chequered the long grass of the meadow with the colours of the rainbow, giving them a quiet joy as they watched them in the morning. Some people said, Frankl observed as he made to go, that the ghost of the old Dutch woman who used to live on Moralla's farm was still there, and appeared to some who lived there. Others too had gone there to work and had disappeared as the Dutch woman had done and it was possible that there was great psychic harm abiding in that place. But had he ever seen that ghost? Elvis looked at her and then looked away, bowing his head. If that was what he had seen he should observe everything carefully for just as the silent were not always as silent as they seemed, the generous were not always as generous.

Elvis took his leave from her and walked alone up the path and when he had reached the farm house he started working and cut the first batch of paper and prepared the inks and then left them to soak into the printing press and stacked the paper correctly and then rested on the veranda and smoked his first cigarette of the day and saw the heat rising. He could hear his heart loud between his ribs, loud with anxiety. When he'd finished the cigarette he lit another and then he felt his head buzz and went to lie down in the cool of the farm house. He wanted to sleep but this was no time for sleep. How could he rest when the old lady had gently laid his future before him, showing him the only thing he could become? The best that someone from the comuna could hope for was what he had. And what he had was so lonely and so terrifying that the only way to make it bearable was somehow to make it his. Still his heart slammed like a drum and the blood raced inside him. He felt himself grow hard and thrust into the mattress to displace that force if he could. His pulse subsided, then. He listened to the flies again. Somehow he'd make this world his.

Elvis worked remorselessly all week, harder than ever before. By Friday lunchtime he had produced three batches of notes and stacked them neatly in packing cases as Moralla instructed. That afternoon he sat on the porch, drinking. Usually Moralla came in the mid-afternoon so that they were back in Guadalajara before dark, but this week he was later and Elvis was quite drunk by the time he arrived. Moralla didn't care, though. When he saw the bundles of notes and realised how hard Elvis had worked that week he gave him a smile, complicit, and said that he deserved an extra cut. Something special, he said. He'd give him an extra 100,000 pesos that week so that he could have a really good time back in the comuna.

"I don't want to go back to the comuna this weekend," Elvis told him.

"Ah, you don't want to?" Moralla came and sat beside Elvis on the veranda. He stared hard into his eyes, trying to divine how much he really knew. "There are good girls in the comuna," he said. "Look at you. You're filling out. You're becoming a man." He grabbed Elvis's forearm and gave it a shake, moving it back and forward. But Elvis pulled his arm away. "You see," Moralla said, "you're getting strong. You're the sort of young man our army needs."

"Still," Elvis said, "I don't want to go back."

"You want to stay?"

"I want to stay."

Moralla sighed and stood up and went inside the farm and came back out with two bottles of beer which he opened with a sharp flick of the bottle opener. The bottle tops fell onto the wooden floor and they drank in silence. The beers frothed over the tops of the bottles in foamy waves. After a time, Moralla turned: "You've been talking with Frankl, haven't you?" Elvis said nothing. "Pah! The old hag is harmless enough. I've never done anything to hurt her, but she has a mouth the size of Guadalajara."

"She has been good to me," Elvis said. "She gives me milk and eggs."

"She's lonely," Moralla said. "She likes talking. I don't mind if the people I have working for me here go and talk to her, humour her. But I wouldn't believe much that she tells you."

Elvis looked down as Moralla spoke. The important thing was not to challenge him. It was how power games had always worked in the comuna and he recognised it again now. The people in authority had to convince you of their lies. They had to believe in the importance of their lies themselves, that they were for a greater good. That was when they were most effective, in fact. So they spoke you into submission and you accepted what they said even though it was obvious from Moralla's irritation with Frankl that what she had told him was true, that somehow, by wanting to stay over the weekend, Elvis was challenging Moralla's authority but also offering to become more dependent on it. Moralla was talking more widely now, about business, and foreign investors, and the crooked path taken by money, any money, whether it was printed here or anywhere else. People thought he was a crook, granted, but money was just abstract these days anyway. Ever since they got rid of the gold standard. If you made money here or in the National Bank it was all the same. It just depended on who had the power to print money and the power to get others to accept it.

As he talked it got late and the light faded behind the mountains. In spite of all the beer he'd drunk, Elvis's head was clear. He walked over to take a pee by the bushes next to the drive and Moralla joined him. Two hares sprang away from them and Moralla laughed: "We frightened them," he told Elvis, "we certainly frightened them." Elvis said nothing. "So you're staying, are you?"

"If you'll let me."

"Of course," Moralla said, as if suddenly resolved. "It would be good to have you here. I've got some friends coming over from Santa Fé. Some foreign investors in a school for the poor that I help out with. That one is the twin of an executive school, St Teresa of Ávila. They are bothgirls' schools." He shook his penis out and then zipped himself up. "You can have a good time here too," he said, looking at Elvis, "that's for sure. Now that you're with us."

They walked back to the farmhouse together and drank another beer as the night darkened and then Moralla drove off to the city saying he'd be back with his visitors in the morning and Elvis listened to the night animals calling and watched the lights of the stars sharpen and thought of his life in the comuna which now seemed as distant even as those stars, and as inaccessible. So, he was one of them. And this was how so many others before him had gone from the comuna without a word and why people had wondered what had become of them, what wars they were fighting in and on whose side, whether they were alive or dead, whether they had been buried or left to rot, whether they still had their dignity and if so for how long they could keep it. That was what had passed through his mind when he had heard that someone had gone from the comuna, even when Bear had gone, and that was what right now people were saying about him. That was when he realised that for him the comuna was already long in the past and that this was all he had. He drank until he passed out on the veranda steps and when he woke in the morning the flies were buzzing about his head as if he had been a dead animal.

# CHAPTER 19

The night before they were due to go to Guadalajara Julián dreamt of a desert of lava red and jagged where only a few stumps of trees remained and he walked alone and picked his way over the rocks with care and even so his feet were jabbed by the edges hard as diamonds and if he called out it was only the wind that heard him. He dreamt that he slept in the desert curled beneath a promontory of lava on pumice stone that was grey and wrinkled by time like the face of the dead and that when he woke it was not yet light and the sky was fading from black into purple and there were few stars left. He set off while it was still dark and banged his feet into lava so that they were bleeding red as he crested a rise and discovered a city silver with light below him, a city that he had never suspected was there. The lava was transformed into concrete and he ran towards the eddies of light but when he got there the city was empty and everyone had vanished and it was impossible to imagine who had built this damaged city of light and why it had been made and what had happened to the souls that once had inhabited it.

When he woke from his dream it was already light and Arturo was making breakfast. For the first time in many years his father smiled at him when he saw him come in to the kitchen.

"What is it? What have I done?" Julián asked.

"Vásquez told me," Arturo said, pouring him some coffee. "That you're going with him on a business trip."

"That's right."

Arturo patted him on the shoulder

"That's good," he said. "So things are going well." Julián shrugged. "That was always the right way for you."

"The right way? You sound like one of my clients in the taxi."

"But still," Arturo persisted, "all that music is not a real job. It's not a future for you. Not in this country."

Julián looked at his father, looked at him carefully for the first time in a long time. He was tired and he never bothered to shave properly any more. He didn't have to impress anyone, he was the one with the money. But he looked sad and shrunken. He was getting old, Julián realised, and for all his bluster Julián was his last hope. Perhaps he really did want the best for him and thought that the best he could hope for was a deal with Vásquez: that was the ceiling of his expectations in life.

"This country," Julián said, "you're right, it's not a place with a future for music." He smiled back at his father. "But it's excellent for many other things."

Yes, for him it had been a place of luck, where his father had won something on the lottery and made his life easier. It was like any place in the world, it had war, misery, joy, happiness and the tedium of every day. It was whatever people chose to make of it for that was how people were different to other animals, they were creatures who always transformed their environments.

After breakfast he prepared his bag in his room, made sure that the computer terminal was switched off at the mains, and then walked out into the salon and closed the door of his room behind him. "Goodbye," he said to his father, who was sitting on the settee and watching highlights of baseball from North America.

"Enjoy your weekend," Arturo said. "I'll see you at the end of next week."

"Where are you going?"

"The coast. On business." A leer cast his father's face in ugliness.

Julián looked at him, expressing nothing and yet worlds with that silence, and then he turned and left. At once he felt released. He caught a bus downtown and felt as if he was starting out on a new chapter of his life. He had not texted Stone. He hadn't even told Jhonny Cruz and Bontera that he was going. That morning he would meet Pamela and leave with her and Vásquez and drive out of the city and the traffic would subside and be replaced by the roadside restaurants and stalls strung out along the highway and it would all feel like a new beginning. It was supposed to be serious, of course, he realised that. There was this strange idea that maybe this could all be connected, that they might find clues to what had happened to María and Purdue. But Julián didn't believe that, not really. It was just a story that he had invented together with Stone, a story to make their lives more interesting and perhaps also to make Pamela come along too. But the objective reality was that María and Purdue had vanished and they were not going to find them in Guadalajara: that was the fact of the matter, whatever other voices tried to intrude on it with a different version of events.

He got off his bus in the Colonial district and walked towards Vásquez's office. The sky was light and grey and people were wearing coats. Some labourers were working on a building site, shouting to one another. A businessman stood by a roadside stall, drinking tinto fresh from a thermos and looking with disdain as a dog slunk across the rubble of the building site looking fearfully over its shoulder, its eyes dark and sad. Julián looked at the dog too for a moment and there was something in its gaze that touched him and made him start humming a few bars. It was a nice tune, a tune that expressed something of that moment: with lyrics that could tell a story, one that would make sense for him, for their band at least. He'd work on it when he had time, when he wasn't still dreaming of what he knew was impossible, thinking of Pamela when he wasn't wondering what would happen to them in Guadalajara.

When he reached Vásquez's office he went into a little side room off the corridor and put down his bag. Roberta came to see him and asked if he wanted coffee. When she brought it she lingered and her body seemed languorous and light as she stood before him and invited him to ask her something, to make a proposition. Julián made a show of looking through his papers, and sipped from his coffee as Roberta waited. When he looked up, she was still there.

"You've probably heard," he said, "I'm going with Vásquez to Guadalajara this weekend. We're going to show some clients around the girls' school there."

"Yes," she said, "but who are you going to spend the weekend with?"

Julián looked back at his papers. "Not with you," he said, "not with you."

Roberta did not seem at all flustered. "Why not?" she asked. Julián put his folder down on the table next to his coffee and looked at her. She was very beautiful, her face angled and her cheekbones high and pronounced, offsetting her sharp profile. She would go a long way because she was desperate to go a long way. Her heart would not rest until she was dead and secretly she longed for that oblivion and used others ruthlessly to advance her cause towards it. Her ambition was the death wish transformed. "Why not?" she asked again.

"Look," he said, "you've come to the wrong person. You don't need me. You need Vásquez."

She looked at Julián with complete disdain. "I've had him already," she said.

When Vásquez arrived it was still early. He was in a hurry, chivvying Julián out of the office. There was no need to say goodbye, he told Julián, laughing, they'd be back soon enough. His jowls expanded and shrank like a concertina as he gave orders. He didn't want any phone calls forwarded, he told his secretary, if anyone was going to call and leave messages it was going to be him. It was obvious to him, he told Julián, as they made their way to the car park, all this new technology was just an excuse to create a new form of torture, a new type of control. It was certainly very useful to co-ordinate torture, so he'd heard. Who'd told him that? Oh it was well known: everyone knew it.

They walked down to the car in silence after that and Julián found the bars he'd composed that morning returning to his head and sticking there like a glyph of beauty that had already vanished. The vanishing and the potential for vanishing were qualities of beauty, of course. Nothing permanent was beautiful. Was God beautiful? Vásquez was the type who went to church, and Julián didn't think that he was capable of believing in anything beautiful. Rape on Saturday, church on Sunday.

They'd arranged to collect Pamela from her flat in the Pachinero. He knew that she had been impressed by the aeroplane, so he had only told her about the change of plan at the last minute, that they would be going by car instead: he suggested that it would be more dramatic a journey, that she'd really see something of the country, and the ranges of mountains that separated Santa Fé from Guadalajara. Vásquez had been enthusiastic. Yes of course they should bring her, she must come. He'd heard all about this English girl from Arturo. He knew everything about her! Had she been out of the city? he asked, as they climbed into his car. She was worried about the security aspect. Oh, there was no need to worry about that.

They drove through the city and Vásquez sped in the outside lane and showed little regard for speed limits. Once he crashed through just after a light had gone red and Julián felt himself grab onto the passenger door for protection. Vásquez drove like a lunatic and talked freely, hardly seeming to look at the road. When they got to the Pachinero, Julián began to give him directions but Vásquez wouldn't let him: he knew where she lived. He pulled up outside Leila's apartment and Julián went to get Pamela and they got back into the car together and left with Vásquez and as they drove through the city and the city fell away behind them Julián wondered if this wasn't what his dream the night before had all been about, that somehow he had meticulously been preparing himself to vanish from the city and to lose something of his soul as he did so.

Shortly after they'd left Santa Fé behind them Vásquez put on a CD of Cumbia and they drove with the syncopated beats and trumpet flourishes in their ears past melancholy strings of roadside farms with dogs chained up outside them and chalkboards offering meals and fresh fruit and past green signboards for towns that straggled away into hills and the sky. The music meant that they did not have to talk to each other. Pamela held Julián's hand and after a time she rested her head on him and they watched the land together which was green and broken with mountains and forests and beautiful. After five hours they stopped for lunch at a restaurant called La Fonda Siqueña set fifty yards back from the highway. Several buses had stopped outside and the restaurant was dusty and busy. An awning had been set up over a terrace at the back where they ate and looked at fields where fat horses grazed and the sky rose big and empty behind them.

"Who are we going to meet in Guadalajara?" she asked by and by.

"Yes, of course, you'll want to know that," Vásquez said to her, wiping his lips with a red serviette. "We'll start with my colleague Emerson Moralla, one of the co-directors of the girls' school. He's arranged everything. He has a farm in the countryside just outside the city. We'll go there on the Saturday for a barbecue."

"That sounds great," Pamela said, imagining the glimpse into the countryside which she had anticipated that first night in Santa Fé, alone in Leila's flat, alone without her luggage. But Julián did not seem so impressed.

"Why do we need to do that?" he asked.

Vásquez laughed. "It's a great place. Moralla has told me about it often." He leant forward looking at them both with a shadow of cruelty. "He's a good man, you see, a charitable man. He hires kids from the shantytowns to look after the place for him, kids who had no futures. And sometimes they let him down, too. He has a good kid, now, but the kid who was there before was some kind of thief. He got into trouble with the men of the nearby village, a place called Santa Clara. Moralla didn't want to talk about it, but one weekend he'd arrived as usual on a Friday afternoon and found the kid hanging from a tree behind the house, blue and bloated and his body already picked at by vultures. Who could say why he'd done it or indeed whether he'd done it at all?" Vásquez laughed. "But you don't need to worry about that, anyway, the new kid is a good soul, Moralla has assured me. We'll all have a nice barbecue when we get there."

As he was finishing, Julián excused himself. Pamela watched as he went to the bar and ordered a shot of rum which he drained at once. There was something agitated about him, hyped up. He had wanted her to come, but now he was distant, as if he felt she shouldn't be there at all. She didn't understand him anymore. She just wanted to enjoy these last experiences, and then to be free of them.

Julián left the bar and went to the toilet which smelt of stale shit and buzzed with flies. Vásquez was a hopeless bully. His threats were so obvious that they weren't enough to make you afraid. What made people afraid were things that they didn't understand, but Vásquez was easy to understand. He resolved to turn on his MP3 player when they got back into the car to continue their journey and share his music with Pamela so that they didn't have to listen. When he got back to the table Vásquez was still talking and Pamela was nodding as if she understood more than she did. Vásquez paid the bill and they continued and Julián and Pamela listened to the music which bound them together and brought their own views of the world together, spliced their stories of the world and so repeated their histories of constant splicing, as they shared in the music and the country slipped by them and the road crept by precipices and over high passes where the world for a moment seemed light and all its problems easy to forget, as long as they listened to their own music and did not have to listen to Vásquez, as long as they had their technology and were prepared to submit to its control. When finally they descended towards Guadalajara it was late in the afternoon and the city glittered before them and Julián remembered his dream from the morning and wondered for a moment if they would find anyone there.

Vásquez drove them downtown in tails of cars lit up red and orange by their own lights and the flaring sunset beyond the hills that circled the city like crenellations of a primeval world. They drove forwards with a momentum that seemed to be gathered from the cars all around them and downtown all was glass and waning light and shouts as people climbed onto buses and waited at metro stations reading the city's press. The cheap eateries gave way to banks and supermarkets and then after a time Vásquez turned off one of the main avenues and they drove past a string of mechanics' workshops fronted by thick tyres and groups of men dressed in blue overalls sitting on small metal chairs, their forearms black with grease, watching as the city lights came on and the frenzy of the workshop behind them subsided and they gathered their energies to finish the day.

Vásquez pulled up outside one of the workshops.

"This is the one Moralla owns," he said. "Wait here a moment. He's co-ordinating the visit."

Once he had gone Julián switched off the MP3 and turned to Pamela: "Thank you," he said. "Thank you for coming."

"It was a beautiful trip."

"I did not think it would be as bad as that. Sorry."

"It's OK, Julián," she said. "It was beautiful." She meant it. There was no need to say anything about how ghastly Vásquez was or his blundering threats. Perhaps she had not even taken them in, he thought. Although she was always telling Julián how quickly her Spanish was improving, he hadn't seen much evidence of it. To him her grasp of the language was of a piece with her grasp of the country: she understood what she wanted to understand, whatever suited the ideas she'd arrived with in the first place. "Even if we don't find out anything about María and Purdue, the trip was worth it," she said then.

Yes, after all, what did it matter to her? She'd be leaving in a couple of weeks anyway, when the whole experience and its human meanings would fade quickly. Consumers were all the same in the end: they devoured whatever it was, food, a product, an experience, and shat it out soon enough behind them before moving on to the next one. And who was there who remembered what any particular shit looked like? They were parasites feeding off the inherent expanding violence of the system in which they lived. They wanted to create a universal narrative that excused their parasitism, that was their deepest ideological aim in life. That was why terrorism was so appalling to them, it challenged the veracity of the story they told themselves day after day.

Julián remembered then the lean, sardonic frame of Bontera and how he'd first met him, ranting about this very sort of thing. He'd just come fresh from some poetry workshop or tertulia in Buenos Aires where he'd got into trouble, and was in deep need to start again: we tried in that workshop, Bontera told him, we really tried, but no one wanted to hear our message because it was so fragmented.

Vásquez came back then with a large man who he introduced as Moralla.

"Great to meet you," Moralla said, gripping Julián's hand and smiling across at Pamela. "The foreign investors are arriving later on this evening. You're all going to stay in a house belonging to the school in a nice neighbourhood, Miraflores." He stopped, and the sense of welcome evaporated as he talked to Vásquez. He seemed a little edgy about something. He rubbed his paunch as he talked and his face quivered slightly with something that seemed like anger or excitement. "I'll see you tomorrow, then," he said, turning to them both, "at the barbecue."

They drove through the streets and Vásquez dropped them at the large condominium in Miraflores and called them a taxi to take them out to a restaurant. He said that he was too busy to go with them, but they should enjoy themselves that night. They put their things in one of the rooms set around a pool in the grounds of the house and then went to a pizzeria where everything was catered for. Julián asked Pamela, she hadn't seen much of this side of the country, had she? No, but you had to see as much as you could of a place to understand it, rich and poor. As she spoke she threw him a sharp, flirtatious look. She was excited by the money and power she had glimpsed, even though she couldn't admit it to herself. She wanted him that night, and in spite of the disdain he was beginning to feel for her he felt aroused.

As they ate they talked about the band and the rehabilitation centre and then he asked her if he would ever see her again after she had gone back to London. Of course he would: she wasn't just going to disappear, like Purdue. She laughed and there was something ugly there and Julián wondered why he had ever imagined that he might want to escape with her. A life as Vásquez's sidekick was probably the best option: his father was right. Was she going to miss all this? He gestured around him, and she said she would, of course, and whenever she read one of Stone's despatches she would think of them all and feel sad. Ah, Stone: Julián smiled when she mentioned him, nodding, and his respect for Stone increased when he realised that all along Stone had been teasing him, testing him, was he really prepared to go off with someone like Pamela or was he able to see through her? Perhaps that was what Stone had been asking him. If he recoiled now, they might really become friends. He sensed then what Stone had been through, everything, and he remembered how Stone had told him that he had lived in Guadalajara when he had first come to the country and had been in comunas where half the population had disappeared and the other half could not talk about it for fear that they might vanish too, how that silence ate a whole neighbourhood up, like all silences, and cities and whole countries were poisoned by it and fell into cycles of war which sustained parasites like him. Of course he was a parasite, Stone had once said to him, but at least he made no pretence about it. Julián thought of all that and of the things he had seen in Rwanda and Congo, all the expanding violence of the world which no one seemed able to restrain, like the urge for sex, or death, something that could be transformed into art when the power and will of artists were there but otherwise sat so desolate and destructive upon the world that as Julián thought of all that experience he almost cried as he looked at Pamela before him, still talking, her eyes lambent with desire.

When they had finished their meal and were about to leave, Pamela noticed that there was one other customer left in the pizzeria, a foreigner like her. He looked up then, and their eyes met. He nodded, and came over to their table.

"I heard you speaking English," he said.

They both looked at him. Pamela gestured for him to pull up a chair.

"That's right," she replied. "Where are you from?"

"I'm Dutch. From Rotterdam."

"How long have you been here?"

"Five years," he said.

"Welcome," Julián said and they both looked at him as if he were the one who was out of place in his own country. "Let's get some beers," Julián said. He clapped his hands and as the waiter brought the beer over he looked at the Dutchman's face, bloated and its veins cracked like an autumn leaf's, distorted by drink. He had sandy hair and ate too much and breathed heavily and greedily, wheezing like a hog.

The Dutchman seemed to have little interest in Julián. He asked Pamela why she was there and she laughed, and said something about her NGO and about the work she was doing in Santa Fé. Why was he there? she returned.

"I've been here five years," he repeated. "I got into business with somebody from this country back home, whose cousin ran a shop in Rotterdam. He got me interested in the country, and all the opportunities there were here. I've been here ever since."

"In Guadalajara?"

"No, down on the coast. On a boat."

Julián interrupted: "You been living on a boat five years?"

"I came from Peru," he said. "Importing fish meal to Veracruz. Port captain and my crew turned on me. Said the boat was stolen and demanded a bribe to let me leave. Armed militia tried to storm the boat three times when I refused. My lawyer and the trial judge were assassinated. Now the government may pay compensation."

They put their drinks down and looked steadily at him. His eyes were blue and limpid and there was a sadness that had settled over him like a nightfall that would not lift. Julián felt that there was something eerily familiar about him, about his whole story, his countryman in Rotterdam, the sense of something withheld: hadn't he always been taking people like that to the airport in Santa Fé?

"A lot of fuss about a fishmeal deal," he remarked then, thinking of his dad in Veracruz: perhaps they knew each other, perhaps even his dad was mixed up in this fishmeal trade: it would make sense of how he was connected to Vásquez and Moralla, that was certainly the sort of business they'd like.

The Dutchman almost smiled. He tapped the table with a thick finger. "After two years I rang my wife in Peru. I used to live in Tumbes. She told me she had bribed a lawyer to transfer the deeds of my house into her name. She was divorcing me. 'I didn't marry you to be poor,' she said."

Then Pamela asked him why he was telling her all this and he said that he had to tell someone. He'd seen her sitting there and had been able to tell straight off that she'd only just arrived. He looked pointedly at Julián and then said that people often came to this country looking for beauty or to make money or sometimes aware that they'd lost something inside themselves and hoping to find it. But when something was lost it very rarely returned and often enough didn't even want to be found. There was no point in wasting life on a meaningless project and everything that had made his life solid had vanished as if it had never existed and he didn't want the same thing to happen to her.

Julián interrupted. He asked the Dutchman what it was that used to make his life solid? He was in import-export, right? Probably he used to wait months to make each trip, to get his cargo together. That time couldn't have been solid. The Dutchman asked if Julián was doubting him? He'd been married, he'd told them that. He'd had dreams that he'd make a pile of money plying the Pacific coast and then buy a hacienda in Mexico. He'd believed in providence even though it was obviously irrational and he couldn't believe in a personal God. He'd felt as if something had been looking after him from the numinous ether but then he'd spent five years on the boat and he'd seen innocent people die and drugged-up militias waving machine guns on the quay with their eyes smeared red like a bullethole. Now he just felt empty. He wanted the government to pay him his money and to leave this country and to spend it on trash.

They sat in silence for some time. It was late and the pizzeria was empty but for the waiters and the security staff. The street stalls had closed and the world was turning in on itself, silent and afraid.

"Where are you living now?" Pamela asked him in the end.

"The Dutch consulate has lent me some money," he said, "because I've got nothing at the moment. I've found a cheap hotel."

"Whereabouts?"

"Downtown."

"What's that like?

He grinned. "It's interesting. You can get anything here, from a liver to a transsexual. Downtown, the transsexuals are everywhere. Near the Cathedral. The best place for them."

That was when Julián snapped. He ordered a taxi and it came within a few minutes. It just gave him time to turn to the Dutchman and ask him if he had been to church since he got off the boat. He laughed at that and they bade him farewell and when Pamela asked him in the taxi, why the religious turn?, he said that she ought to understand that, living with Leila, that there were things that people needed and that if they did not meet their needs they would come out in violence and blame. The Church offered the cosy mirage of a universal story, and humanity needed that more than anything now, when life had become so fragmentary and voided of meaning, overturned by a narrative not of its keening.

It was late. They were let into their condominium by the caretaker and after they had gone to their room Julián went to ask her about the arrangements for breakfast. The lady who ran the establishment had her hair tied up in multi-coloured curlers, as if she was always about to retire to bed or had only just woken. She was kind and her smile made her face shine and she laughed and said that she expected they'd be hungry. They had travelled far, and it was late, so late. All the people who stayed at the house seemed to be hungry, ravenous, and she always made sure to get a good spread for them, ham and eggs and cheese and jam and fresh bread and coffee, he needn't worry. He hadn't been worried, he told her. But she answered that people said they weren't worried but in her experience they were, even though life was so beautiful, and that was the thing that made her saddest of all in the world. There were many sad things in the world, though, Julián said, thanking her, and he went back to the room and closed the door behind him and saw that Pamela had already taken off her clothes and lit just a dim bedside lamp and was waiting for him there with her body so soft, inviting him, and although he cared so little for her any more he could not resist her desire or his own desire, he could not resist her, and he came over to her and what had to happen happened as it had ever since humans had first trodden the earth in countries the world over, countries just like this one.

# CHAPTER 20

Miraflores was a district which like most of its kind was the cleanest in the city. Of course Guadalajara bubbled with a suppressed roar here just as it did downtown and up in the comunas which circled like a sore of conscience or memory but there were also quieter streets where the houses sat squat and inert like statues of a culture already vanished in a museum for the victors behind high walls topped with broken glass and automated metal gates guarded by watchtowers, where there were side gates through which the serving staff could pass early and late to and from their homes high in the comunas and memories of a childhood in the hills beyond from which they had been taken by some ineluctable force or consuming power to their current place of abiding.

Pamela had heard so much about Guadalajara. She remembered when she had first begun to read Stone's articles in the British press, when she had first really taken notice of the country. She couldn't place exactly how long ago that had been: six years ago, perhaps eight. It was before she had got her first proper job, when she had been doing work experience at an NGO in East London and still living at her parents' house. And in that tall and elegant house – Edwardian, or late Victorian, her parents could never agree on which – she had spent whole mornings each weekend consuming the press and those stories of Stone's which seemed ripped from another world like an unborn foetus striped with blood and hatreds so long and deeply meshed with the fabric of a country of which she knew nothing, but which seemed nothing to do with her. Stories which seemed just that, of story, fantastical in their violence, their gleeful detail, as if designed to insult the person reading them simultaneously with their lack of concern and their pornographic interest.

Gradually, her interest waned. New wars of empires superseded old ones and old ways of thinking, the media expanded into those pathways of thought to replace them with arguments that sprouted bitterness and the very old ways of hatred, always in the guise of something new. The new situation offered certainty, right or wrong, something that everyone could agree on. And only occasionally, she remembered, at the same time trying to suppress the memory, had she thought again of this country and of those articles by Stone when she or some friends of hers leant forwards with their bearing one of prayer in some elegant flat in East or South London, where the cocaine had been divided equally into lines which lay like thin white troughs upon the table.

Guadalajara wasn't, finally, as she had imagined it. That night at the house of the school of St Teresa of Ávila she woke just before dawn and was surprised at the silence. That was what people paid for here, she imagined, the security of silence. That nobody would shout or shoot or think unless it was them. There were sounds in the complex, though. She could hear someone shuffling about, setting out plates with a gentle clatter. It must be the caretaker. She nudged Julián with her elbow: perhaps it was time to get up, but he did not respond and just stretched out his arm around her and murmured something in his sleep and continued to breathe heavily and in regular sighs as the light crept across the night and under the door of the room where they had slept together. When it was clearly day she rose and drew back the curtains of the window which looked out onto the courtyard. Some birds were hopping near the swimming pool, looking for worms, and the sky was clear and none of the other guests seemed to have risen.

Julián woke eventually and they breakfasted. He went to speak with the caretaker for some minutes, and he asked her about her family. They weren't here with her any more, she said, they had gone some years ago, though she still saw one of her daughters now and again. They had all moved to Santa Fé and vanished. Yes, Julián responded, that was often what happened when people moved to Santa Fé, and it often happened to those who were living there as well.

When he came back to the table, Pamela was checking her phone. "Qué más?", he asked, and she showed him a circular text message that she had opened from a peace-building organization. "Qué atroz," she said, and her face was heavy with anger and impotence at the iniquities being carried out by mining companies and oil exploration multinationals. His finger suddenly moved across the phone and touched the screen as if to delete the whole thing, but she grabbed his hand and stilled it: that would have been moral cowardice.

Moralla arrived at about nine o'clock. There had been a problem with the Americans' flight, he told them, and they had had to stay overnight in Santa Fé. But it was no problem. They'd head straight out to the farm and the Americans would join them later with Vásquez. He helped them to load their bags into the car and then they reversed out of the gates and drove through the city and as they went Moralla talked to Julián about the school and the business arrangements. This was what a business trip was, after all, the chance to make a deeper connection, a shared bond that would be harder for greed to break. It was how all groups functioned. Pamela switched off and looked out of the window as they climbed out of the city and Guadalajara fell away into a grey shining ball below them. Mountains hung from the sky like drapes of green curtains flowing with rock and the red tiles of farms and small villages of a uniform height except for the white churches which thrust up from them. As the road climbed they passed villages straggling along the highway and military posts where they were waved through even as the same soldiers stood alongside a bus whose passengers stood with their hands against the bus as they were frisked. Perhaps it was true, it was a country at war.

By and by Julián and Moralla fell into silence and they drove along roads with potholes in the tarmac past small roadside stalls sheltering beneath awnings of thatch where piles of fruit were on sale. Moralla seemed unhappy about something. Pamela asked him some halting questions in her Spanish about how long he had owned the farm, what he used it for, but Moralla did not answer. As they turned off the main road onto a sandy track he called over his shoulder: "And how is Mr Stone?" "Mr Stone? Do you know him?" "Of course," Moralla told her, "and I haven't forgotten that Stone lived here some years ago. I got to know him then. I've always taken an interest in his work." The car carried on, bouncing on the track and sending up dust as if it had been filled with explosives, dust that flooded the car through invisible cracks and stuck to their clothes and to their hair and in their nostrils, which lay on the tongue, coarse and fine, and crunched if you moved your teeth. "Stone's fine," Pamela said in the end, "but I haven't seen him for a few weeks." Then Moralla lapsed into a final silence and they drove along the track until it gave out by a low whitewashed building with some barns attached to it. Moralla slowed down and as he did so Julián turned from the front seat, he felt white with fear, and he looked at her with a foreboding which she had never seen before, a fear she had always read about but never known. It was too late. The car had stopped and a teenage boy was walking towards them from the barns with a face thin and hungry, the face of someone who looked like he might want something from them before long.

They climbed out of the car and Moralla introduced them to the boy, Elvis Jaramillo. She remembered what Vásquez had said on the drive from Santa Fé, that this was a boy who had been stripped by birth of every privilege and raised up by a charitable hand. It was the sort of moral that she could understand. She smiled at Elvis, rich and welcoming in intent, but he turned away from her and spoke very fast to Moralla and went behind the back of the farm from where a plume of smoke was rising into the sky. It reminded her of a funeral pyre, something she had seen on the Internet when looking at a documentary about funeral customs in the East. Moralla and Julián began to talk and she walked around to the back of the house and saw Elvis standing with his back to her and a long fork turning red bricks of meat over an open fire and rubbing his eyes; he sensed her of course, but he would not turn because he was dedicated to the task that he had been given, pliant and unwelcoming in his desire to follow orders, to become one with his superiors. It was why he and his family were as they were, Pamela thought. Perhaps it was why the work of the rehabilitation centre had to go on. People harmed themselves above all by not challenging those who were above them. She was about to move forward and challenge him herself when she saw a figure about a hundred yards beyond him standing beside a young tree, a blonde lady with her hair tied up in a bun and the skin around her eyes stretched into worn circles which made it look as though years had passed since she last had slept. Pamela was so surprised that she walked towards her but then the figure vanished and Elvis turned and looked at her, and she felt the empty hatred of unrequitable violence, his gaze forming a question, and she asked him if he needed her help but he just laughed and his laughter was his answer to the place he had found in the world or that which had been allotted to him.

She turned, then. Julián was walking towards the barbecue place. He looked like she felt. "This is bad," he said to her in English.

"Bad? It's so beautiful here."

"Fuck that. There's something bad here. Rotten. It feels like ghosts."

"Don't be silly, Julián."

"I'm afraid. Why's he asking about Stone?"

"Stone is famous."

"No," Julián said, "here in Guadalajara, for people like Moralla, Stone is infamous."

Julián went to sit on a wall and looked out at the bushes and pasture, leaning forward and with his hands clasped together as if for prayer. Pamela came to sit beside him but he shrugged her off and told her that she still hadn't realised how bad this situation was and that he'd come with her to protect her and also because she had been worried, worried because of the disappearances, because all that abstract concern formed by memberships and letters of protest and campaigns had become for her something tangible and, who knew, had perhaps knotted her insides together like the ropes on the old sailing ships from which her ancestors had once controlled the seas, and he had thought that his connection to Vásquez through his father would be enough protection. All the threats and formless posturing hadn't put them off, and he didn't think that she hadn't sensed them, but the fact was that they were trapped here on a remote farm without their friend, Vásquez, and that this was how some disappearances began. And the worst thing of all, Julián told her, was that he felt now as if he had been preparing for this all along and in some way had even longed for it, like she had, a death wish, perhaps, or a keening to belong with all the sadness and violent force where so many had vanished nameless before them into the black hole of destruction which was yet the vortex into which the world also would spiral when its time had come and all the pain had become numb like a limb so dead from a ceaseless pressure that it is ready for amputation, that you might as well sever it yourself.

"What are you doing?" she asked him. "Are you inviting me to do that?"

"Do what?"

"Harm myself. It sounds like an invitation."

"No, no," he said, angry, "people who want to mutilate themselves, who are preparing themselves to be mutilated by others, they don't wait for invitations, they just invite themselves. It's like the history of this continent these past five centuries. You should know that. It is like everything in this country, people who want to sell it off to the Americans, hectare by hectare, don't wait to be asked. They create the demand. They're quite happy to sell off everything that's beautiful, a few young women from an elite school to go along too. Why not? All-in. What a deal."

As they were talking, Elvis called over to them. "Veanse," he said, "está casi listo."

"Está bien muchacho." Julián stood up. "It's ready. I'll get Moralla," he told Pamela. "We have to pretend that everything is normal."

"You're being silly," Pamela said. "It is normal."

But he walked quickly away. She watched, passive, as Elvis pierced the steaks with his fork and moved them expertly onto plastic plates that sat beside the barbecue pit on a clean stone: "Estas experto," she said. He shrugged. "Hace cuando que eres aqui?"

"Acá?" He looked at her: this figure almost a fantasy, like the ghost he had come across between the farm and Frankl's, perhaps her rebirth: what did she care how long he had been here, why did she even pretend? Still, he considered her question, counting on his fingers to signal the months that had passed. "Tres meses ya."

"Te gusta?"

"Es muy solitario." But then he smiled, because he did like it after all, in spite of the solitude. "Pero el jefe me paga bien y ahorrita eso sí me gusta."

He leered at her then, and she felt herself stiffening. "No soy en venta," she told him.

"Por ahora, no. Por ahora no estas en venta."

That was when Pamela saw that Julián had spoken to her in all seriousness. Had they been somewhere safe, at the rehabilitation centre, for instance, this was the sort of boy she might have been trying to help. That was her job. But he hated her, and hatred would never give way. He had said as much: he thought she was for sale. She wondered if all that loneliness of working out here on the farm hadn't hardened him and made him more likely to accept a warped view of her, idle talk that she was dangerous, perhaps, that she couldn't be allowed to escape. It was easy to create an army, and after isolation and indoctrination everything fell into place. What a strange schooling place the world was for soldiers fighting in struggles which sought only to make their lot worse. She felt like crying, then, and pretended to Elvis that it was the smoke from the barbecue and turned away from him with the plate in her hand and began to eat with her right hand shaking as it tried to grip the meat.

By and by Moralla came to sit with them and she looked more closely at his face and saw that across his cheeks it was pitted by the scars of a childhood pox whose marks had never left him and that his dark hair was streaked with grey, which might have lent his face distinction but really only made him look old. They sat on a stone bench set into the wall which lay opposite the house and ate the meat with some bread and a salsa laced with tomatoes and chillies. Elvis had turned the radio on to a local music station which played ranchero music from Mexico and as they listened to the music it suddenly seemed to Pamela that they had been excised from the world like an unnecessary growth and removed to somewhere far from everything where it was quite possible to be forgotten. And this thought which should have terrified her in fact made her feel quite peaceful. Perhaps that was what María had felt when she had been taken from Santa Fé, perhaps she had not minded becoming lost for becoming lost to the consciousness of the world was the one fate which all human beings shared and in that oneness there was a sense that the prefiguring of that experience was actually quite beautiful.

"Así es la cosa," Moralla said then, putting his plate to one side.

"Y Vásquez?" Pamela asked him.

Vásquez? Vásquez wasn't coming. Moralla had just had a text from a friend in Guadalajara who'd told him that the security situation on the road to the farm had deteriorated that morning and there had been two attacks on civilian cars and so it was far too dangerous to travel. Vásquez would have to show the Americans around the city instead, and they could enjoy the farm. A holiday, he said, with a quick look of amusement. But wasn't it dangerous here, too? Pamela asked and she saw Julián throw her a glance close to disgust and Moralla laughed: "Quién te va a maltratar acá?" he asked: no one was going to touch them here.

At that his eyes became more distant and he added that speaking of ill treatment made him think of Stone, of the lies that he had written about his city, something which made him quite angry, because they were not written by someone who had the best interests of the city and even the country at heart. All that violence, he had made it seem as if they had wanted it. And hadn't they? Julián interrupted then, and Moralla replied quickly and brutally that he should not criticise either, not if he knew what was good for him, that something had needed to be done with all those young men and after they had gone there had been peace, so sometimes you had to be murderous if what you really wanted was peace. And anyway that was all so long ago now, and no one remembered those young men who were picked off in Comuna 13 by the helicopters and the crack troops, and since then it had been peace, and so who was to say that it was not them all along who represented the forces of good and not evil? And as he spoke Elvis rose as if there were something that made him angry and he did not even excuse himself but left the barbecue area and Moralla said that this young man represented the new problem, that people like him had been infants when Stone had been writing those stupid articles but now they had grown and they had their own urges and their own needs and responsibilities creeping up on them like age, and they would exact their own demands for violence and a new war would need to be found for them if society was to continue. And what war did they suggest: should they be at war against themselves then? Who else could be attacked? Was anyone willing to sacrifice themselves? Moralla laughed. They were not ancient Americans here who had Gods who could readily be appeased with the hearts and entrails of friends and enemies: the Ancient Americans had gone and left only their inscriptions in the earth and mausolea for their cultures. They were not ready to sacrifice themselves because who was there today who really believed in a higher purpose beyond themselves? Who was there who had enough faith to make a sacrifice of themselves, requiring others to do it for them? So someone else had to be found. Someone else like Elvis, Pamela said. Like Elvis, or like you, Moralla said, like you. Though Elvis was also a good possibility. The right age. No prospects. He didn't know it, but his family had a long history of collaboration, they had moved into their stinking hovel on the hill after the last cleansing operation when the family that lived there had been butchered, they had moved in without worrying about it and there were many on the hill who had never forgiven them.

Moralla stood and stroked his belly, looking at his empty plate with regretful pleasure: "Eso sí que fue un buen asado," he said. That was the thing about violence, once it had started, ever since 1948, or 1492, if you preferred, it sowed hatreds like a farmer his crops, year by year, spring by spring, they came growing without even needing water or tending, they grew of their own will, so it was never hard to give the war a new direction when it was needed, that was its nature, and it always would be.

He left, then, saying he needed to see what had happened to Elvis. Pamela turned to Julián: "Well," she said, "perhaps the situation will be calmer tomorrow and we'll be able to go." Julián laughed: "You really are stupid, aren't you?" he said, and he felt total disdain when he looked at her, she was someone who in the war of disappearance was at the top of the list of those to be sacrificed, someone who almost deserved it, if anyone did. "Don't you get it? That game Bontera talked about, Colombian Roulette: we're playing it now." And when she saw the revivified hatred within him, she felt her loneliness reborn, with the sun falling close to the distant mountains and so few sounds and lost on a farm so far from anywhere or anything that cared, and that was when she did cry for the first time since she had arrived in the country, cried for herself and for everything that like her had vanished from the world.

# CHAPTER 21

High up on a string in the kitchen of Moralla's farmhouse lay a plait of onions whose stalks dried and curled as desert grass reminded Elvis of the messy paths intertwined on the hill, running through people's yards where the women were cooking and the smoke curled up and through it they watched their sons kicking a ball around the yard and sometimes against the house of one of them. Whereupon they joked: in ten years' time, he'll be kicking your door down. It was always the boys who left in the end, always the women who stayed and bore their posterity and tended it and then had to watch it leave as he Elvis had left. Something that plait of onions reminded him of, that his mother had said: that all paths met up in the end, that no memory was ever completely forgotten.

He'd gone to the kitchen when Moralla had mentioned the comuna and he hadn't listened any more because people talked of things that they knew nothing about. And that was why they chose them to talk about, it was less likely to hurt them. What did he know about cooking? Moralla had forced him to learn to cook the basics, as if he was training him up for something. Training him up to be a woman, to tend someone else's hapless posterity. A woman, or a politician. Talkers, promisers, shit-sayers. Like Moralla.

Here he came now, big and full of meat, like a giant burger swallowed up by a flabby bun of flesh. "Don't leave for the moment," he said, "it's all under control, they're going to sleep here like lost children gently in the forest."

"What about the girls?" he asked Moralla.

"Ah yes, I promised you girls, and I gave you foreign clients. And are you excited?"

"Not excited, no," Elvis said, "but I'm wondering why I bothered to stay."

"Because you wanted to be one of us," Moralla said, moving towards him, "and you still can be, for what you're thinking of is only one sort of rite of passage. Things haven't turned out as we imagined, you see, Elvis, things rarely turn out as we imagine. And now that you're one of us, you understand that accidents can easily happen."

Moralla stood, leaning back against the doorframe with his arms clenched across his chest, defensive, or barring an exit. Elvis could see his stomach expanding, with desire and the will to crush him. He looked like Bear might be, if he lived long enough. A vandal in a world where vandalism was the correct ticket. And Elvis lost his mind to thoughts of Bear and others he had known in the comuna, to the whole body of the disappeared, which itself could have been an army, the sort of army that Moralla was trying to forge if only he hadn't colluded in disposing of them, and that puffball of pride was saying to Elvis, just think, the boy I had here before you, he did not do what he was supposed to do, he did not stay quietly here but went down to Santa Clara on some donkey with rags cinched up for a saddle and drank himself to a standstill on aguardiente and slept in the stable like Jesus himself, next to his donkey, using those rags for a pillow and stinking of that donkey's piss to heaven itself, and, Moralla said, he was so drunk that he couldn't remember anything of the previous evening when he woke. But he'd spoken as volubly as if it were his last testament before God. He'd said everything there was to say about this place in the bar which was the meeting place for all the village wastrels who watched television as if it were God because they hadn't the brains left to speak, or think, there was Tiger and Puma and Cat, they all called themselves after animals, and drank like animals and couldn't keep a secret even if they were so drunk when they were told it that they couldn't remember it either, yes, his predecessor had told them all about this place and what it was used for although of course he had denied it on the life of his mother. And soon enough he had his own accident and was strung up outside this place like one of those plaits of onions, twisting round in the sun and dried out and crumbling, gone.

With that Moralla seemed to relax, he unclenched his arms at least, cast his eyes towards Elvis as if he might have listened, if he had had something to say. So, Moralla said, he could see, accidents happened easily, especially when people did not take precautions. That was what happened to boys like Elvis, people who didn't know their place in the world: they found out that the world wasn't the place for them and they disappeared from it. And it was better. Moralla moved towards Elvis then, and put his hand gently on his shoulder. "You see," he said, "it's better to know your place."

"Tell me what I have to do to find it," Elvis said, moving back, and Moralla came towards him again, and Elvis could see a light of excitement in his eyes and it sickened him and he shoved his boss in the chest then, as if pushing away an image of something he could never forgive: "Tell me what I have to do," he said.

Moralla stepped back, his smile gone. "You're such a delicate boy," he said then, "I never thought you could be so angry. It was your weakness that made me notice you in the first place."

"But you don't really want me to be weak," Elvis said, "you need me in the army. You want me in the war."

"War?" Moralla said.

"The war," Elvis said. "The war we're always fighting in the comuna. The war on disappearance."

Moralla laughed: "It's true," he said. "There is no war without peace, and no peace without war."

Elvis could not wait there any longer listening to his lies when he thought of all the grief his mother had endured and of Elvira who was getting stronger and never cried at night and slept with her arms stretched out behind her head in complete trust of the world and when he thought that the money which bought all of that was all fake and bought by Moralla's lies, that it was money that didn't really exist when you thought rightly about it and was just the product of a fantasy and a game, that didn't exist just as they didn't exist, on paper, he spat instinctively onto the floor of the kitchen and pushed past Moralla and walked beyond the barns to a little knoll where he could watch the sun as it fell like a golden coin that some deity far wiser and more noble than any human artisan of money paper or metal had created. It was a quiet time of late afternoon when there was no breeze and the flowers hung still as paintings in their rectitude before the bushes and the grazing cattle and horses that cropped them without mercy, without caring less how upright they were. It was such a beautiful moment and that was when he realised that Moralla was right and that this beauty could not have existed without the war and that he too would have to commit to the war if he was to know his place and preserve himself and what was yet left of beauty, for without commitment there was nothing and life voided itself in laxative distress and the soul was lost and disappeared and everything became nothing as if inverting the gift of creation which was all that there was to the world.

Moralla had not given up on him. He came then and put his arm on his shoulder and they both sat quietly in the gloaming and then Moralla asked if it was true, and he wanted to be in the war himself, and Elvis said that he did.

"That's good news for your family," Moralla answered, "because I'll be able to increase your wages once you're in the army and you won't spend anything, it'll all be provided."

"But who will we be fighting?" Elvis asked him.

"Haven't you realised who the enemy is?" Moralla laughed and his laughter pierced the stillness and Elvis saw a flash of blue, white and purple as two birds flew past the knoll and away from the noise as if in fear.

"What's so funny?" Elvis asked him.

"It's them," Moralla said, pointing down at the farmhouse, "it's those two."

"But who are they?"

Moralla spat with the sort of savage disgust that Elvis had only ever seen directed with hatred in the past. Rivers of hatred which flowed in the comuna without ever being dammed, even though there was love. At times even his mother had seemed to hate him, hate his pretensions when he was pretending to learn chess and her dependence on him when all those lessons had borne fruit. Who were those people? Moralla spat again. They were the sort of people who spread lies about the country. They made people afraid, they put off investors. And how were people going to be fed in the comunas if foreigners didn't bring their money? They threw up their arms in horror, they criticised honest citizens like him, Moralla, as murderers, but they had enough money themselves to buy a thousand hit-men, and they just spent it, more and more, they wanted more and more things, and whoever wanted more things had to be a conservative to have enough money to buy them with, whatever they might pretend, and they could only have them with violence, theirs or someone else's, because a human being hadn't yet been created who'd work for next to nothing to make things for others unless they were forced to by circumstances, and all circumstances were conditioned in the end by violence and the will of God, violence, theirs, Moralla said, or ours. And so they come here wanting to create their own objective history, to bring together all the fragments which their own violence has created. But they can't do it: the silent truth of each voice always overcomes them in the end.

Moralla looked out then at the farmhouse and at the smoke which rose from it and at all the strings of smoke hanging between the clouds and the countryside like plumes of a heavenly peace about to be burnt into a terrible fire. "I'll tell you who this war's against," Moralla said, then, "it's a war against hypocrites and homosexuals, for all hypocrites are homosexuals. There, and homosexuals are condemned by Jesus Christ. It's the same old war, a war that has always been so difficult to win."

"But I'm scared," Elvis said. "I'm scared of fighting."

"That's natural," Moralla said, standing up. "But you have to learn how to be hard and to resist your feelings: that's what being a man is all about."

When it was dark they returned to the farmhouse and Moralla laughed and joked with the prisoners. He kept on telling them not to worry. There was plenty of food, plenty of drink, and they would wait for the situation to improve. If things weren't better in a couple of days, he'd text his friend and see if they could get a helicopter in. Then they ate cold meat from the barbecue and just before they went to sleep Moralla took Elvis aside and told him to leave at dawn for Frankl's farm, because that was where his real training would begin.

"What does she know about it?" Elvis asked him.

Moralla laughed: "I don't know what she's told you," he said, "but she certainly knows everything."

That night he dreamt the strangest dream he had ever dreamt and first he saw his mother standing quite clearly in the yard outside their house on the hill with Chico at her side and Elvira in her arms and she asked him if he would ever be coming back and he told her that he would not, that the world was vaster than a person could compass in their lifetime and there was not enough of it in the comuna where everything was hard and the houses were strewn with rubble and the streets with rubbish and the doorways with threat and fear and you never knew how far you would be able to trust a friend if you had some piece of fortune in which they wanted to share, and as he spoke he saw rivers of gold flowing down the hills of the comuna and he picked up a sheet of corrugated iron from outside López's store and waved at Juanchito and floated gently over the golden stream of light until he was outside Moralla's workshop and Moralla was standing there with a gun, pointing it at his chest, telling him to get off the river and to give him the gold, to do it now, before it was too late, and then as he did as he was told he saw that his life had gone before him like water down a drain into the fetid sewer of the past from which it could never return.

When he woke it was not yet light and there was a fetid smell in his nostrils. Outside the window of the room where he slept, he could smell someone's urine. It had probably been Moralla. He rose and went to the bathroom and threw some water on his face but when he went outside there was no one there and so he sat alone on the veranda until the first grey streaks of light crept across the mountains. It was time to go. Moralla was still sleeping, he could hear him snoring. He was amazed that the prisoners had not tried to escape, but then where was there for them to go to? Elvis sat there for some time yet, thinking as the day lightened and the others still slept.

By and by he left and walked down the path towards Frankl's farm and passed the spot where the ghost lay and the petroglyphs which glinted in the rising light and spoke of the breathlessness of time and the speed with which it seemed to pass. He saw that Frankl was already awake and that the smoke was rising from her chimney as it always did and that she was waiting there for him as if she had always known that he would come that morning. She looked tired and drawn, as if she had not slept, and gestured wordlessly towards the kitchen where some warm milk was waiting.

"Moralla told me to come," he said.

"Of course," Frankl said, "and the others will arrive not long after dawn."

"Others?"

"Every month or couple of months they come," she told him. "They remind me of photographs I've seen of starving children. Their cheeks are hollow. Ah, their clothes look like burial shrouds, they're so big."

"Where do they come from?"

Frankl shrugged. "Who knows?" she said, pushing his milk towards him and bidding him drink. "Maybe Moralla picks them up by night on the roadside or sleeping in mud and filth in farms where the world smells of shit."

"Maybe," Elvis said, slurping the milk; it was warm, and cheered him, although the world seemed so desolate just then.

"Or else he picks from comunas like yours," she said. "From families like yours."

"Like me," Elvis said.

But Frankl would not be silenced. She warmed to her theme, trying to educate him, perhaps, or make him feel less solitary in the world: people criticised the atrocities of this person or that person, of this nation or that one, but weren't all peoples the same, by God, beneath the light of the world that had been created? "Or they're dragged in helicopters from the swamps near the coast to these high plains," she said to him. "I've seen those ones. They shiver by night. You can hear their teeth chattering if you listen carefully."

"What do they come here to do?"

"The same as you," she said. "They want to join up, to find a purpose in life. Because a purpose is better than any alternative they have, better than a life in poverty."

"And what happens to them?"

"Oh, they're sent off. That's the fate of young men." She looked sad then: he realised it was the first time he had seen her like this, with her face drooping and withholding its light. "They go off. Their officers send them away with no provisions into the high plains and I never see them again and doubtless some die and others survive."

He finished his milk and laid the mug on the table with a gentle thud. "You think about them, don't you?" he asked.

"I don't mind them," she said. "They keep me safe from the war and allow me to live out my years here in peace where by God you don't see the face of the Devil and his violence. All that can happen elsewhere. Yes, by God, as far as I'm concerned all that can happen somewhere I don't have to be. My parents saw enough of that violence and so by God now it's someone else's turn."

"My turn," he said.

"Your turn," she said.

As they were talking a whine grew from the sky. Frankl leant across and grabbed his arm: this was it, here they came. They went outside and Elvis saw two light planes coming in to land in the rough field behind the farm. Twenty young men climbed out with a man who seemed to be their officer. He ordered them into rows and walked up to Frankl and asked if this was Moralla's recruit and she said that he was. He smiled. There were chickens in the yard feeding on corn, their beaks deep in the mud. There was a mottled pig in a sty behind the adobe house and beyond the sty was a picket fence and then the land rose steeply into the sierra. The officer, whose name was Bonifacio, called the young men all together and told them that this was the last part of their training. They were given two sausages and a bottle of water and they had to climb the sierra alone and cross it and on the far side was another farm where he would wait with the Cessnas.

They set out beyond the picket fence and then the trees thinned out and there was a high cold plateau above them thick with bogs and moss. There were some wild horses who fled from them and condors circled. They tried to keep together but some of the men were not so fit and suffered at the cold. They fell back and vanished into the mist. Elvis never saw them again. Some of them did not make it down.

They kept the high mountains to their left as Bonifacio had told them. The plateau was long and dreary. There were clear pools of water in the moss where they drank but there was nowhere good to sleep and Elvis spent the first night curled up in the shelter of some rocks. In the morning he saw some deer and tried to shoot one but missed and the laughter of the crows who started from his gunshot echoed from the mountainsides like spirits of people long dead.

The day was dank as they set out. Some of the men had blisters and shivered and wanted to turn back. But if they tried to turn back they would be shot. They carried on but their feet were heavy and the pinnacles above them were oppressive. Their muscles ached. Those who were still together by the end of the second day slept huddled up for warmth in a low cave where water dripped and the floor was green with moss.

They woke early and after two hours reached the far edge of the plateau as Bonifacio had instructed them. Here there were cliffs where rocks skittered down a chasm and goats clung to ledges chewing thorns. There was no path. Some men tried one way, others another. They did not keep together. Elvis followed some animal tracks over a ledge and edged down and when the clouds broke a plain appeared so distant beneath him that he felt that he was flying. He could see the farm on the plain with corrals nearby built of dry stone from the mountains and the Cessnas parked on a field. He followed a narrow gully down to a sandy path where it was still cold and when he reached the farm he was the first one there.

Bonifacio greeted him as an initiate with aguardiente. The owner of the farm was a criollo with a huge belly. His peón had killed a sheep and it was roasting on a spit over a fire. As the others arrived they celebrated and drank toasts and ate meat. Now they were ready to fight the enemy, Bonifacio told them. Elvis asked who the enemy was and Bonifacio laughed. They were fighting the enemy of the people, he told them, and their enemy was violent and cruel and wicked and had to be pursued without mercy. Someone else asked if their enemies were in the country or somewhere else. They were everywhere, Bonifacio said, they'd soon find that out. Their enemies were those who wanted to destroy society: they were anarchists, communists, drug dealers, terrorists: they'd soon learn to recognise them.

After they'd eaten they climbed into the Cessnas and flew close to the clouds as birds and then gradually came nearer to the land and Elvis recognised the folds and forests that he had seen from Moralla's farm and he saw the whitewashed buildings where already he had spent much of his life and he felt afraid. He did not want to go back there, in his mind he had already bidden farewell to that part of his life and moved a step closer to death, which is the way of all changes.

When the plane had landed he climbed out with the others and could smell the meat on the barbecue and Moralla was there with a grin on his burger face. He came out, pumping his hand hard but there was a coldness in his eyes, a sense of distance that can come with renewed power. He'd made it, they'd all made it, or most of them had, and they were all going to help in the struggle. They sat around the walls where Elvis had spent so long alone and looked out at the land and joked with each other in a new-found companionship which made everything they had been through seem bearable. It was good to eat, to have your stomach filled without worry or fear. All of them knew what it was like when there was no food, when there was that fear and you could not sleep for it or for hunger and the insistent pain of the stomach which had its own demands, when all the senses were heightened and the slightest sound knotted your insides together.

By and by Moralla came to sit beside him.

"What happened to the prisoners?" Elvis asked him.

"They were taken away and they won't come back here." Moralla looked at Elvis with something like avuncular concern. "Like you, they won't come back."

"Where are we going?"

"It depends. On where the war moves. Where the enemy is. Bonifacio will tell you about that."

"He knows a lot," Elvis said.

"Of course, he's a man of experience. But the main thing is that now you're one of us. We'll send the money back to your family, to the collaborators in the comuna." He called over to Bonifacio: "This is the kid I told you about," he said. "My new recruit. Already he wants to find out about the military situation."

Bonifacio eyed him carefully, he'd better come inside, he said. They walked into the farmhouse and sat at a table in the dining room. Bonifacio asked him to sit down and offered him some aguardiente. Moralla had told him all about him, Bonifacio said, and they were both impressed. He smoothed his hand over his tight dark stubble and opened his mouth. He laughed. There were some things that were not told to all the recruits. Only those who had distinguished themselves in service were instructed about the non-governmental actors. These organizations and human rights lawyers and international academic consultants were a dangerous wing of the enemy. They could not so easily be bought off, unlike governments. They had to be dealt with differently. Bonifacio raised his glass and they toasted one another.

As they went outside after their meeting was over the sky was darkening and Moralla had switched on the radio. They listened to the news. The guerrilla were under attack.

"They're terrorists," Bonifacio told them all, drinking rum from an old coca-cola bottle. "Like fleas on a dog. They need to be wiped out before they spread."

The radio announcer said that dozens of terrorists had died. "Who dug the graves?" Elvis asked.

"Those animals dug them themselves," Bonifacio replied. "Pah! They were going to be at rest soon enough. That was the best use of energy. Why should the rest of us care?"

By and by they all settled down and the radio was switched off and Elvis sat on the veranda next to a recruit from the coast, a tall man with a long nose and several teeth missing. Elvis didn't feel as dwarfed as he might have done six months before. He looked at the man's ebony skin and compared it to his own café con leche and wondered at everything that had made them different and the same to each other. Then Elvis asked him why he had volunteered and the man said that he hadn't volunteered and that he didn't hate this enemy and that any enemy of Bonifacio's was his friend. He started to sob and his body quaked even though it was tall and strong and he and Elvis had never shared friendship before then. Elvis was sad. The man from the coast asked him if he would kill the enemy and Elvis replied that he had been surrounded by death ever since he had been born and that he was used to it and that he would play his part as he had learnt no other.

# CHAPTER 22

When the land surrounding the farm had at last become too silent for those still living there to bear, it had been obvious that it was too late. The planes had swooped low over the farm and landed down in the valley in a churn of dust whose plumes had risen into the morning and then they had departed over the rim of the mountains that severed the world between here and the beyond. The young boy, Elvis, had been gone in the morning, and the farm eerily quiet. And then it was too late to leave and too late to be rescued and too late to regret the anger that a country like this could produce in you, the anger that made you dangerous, a cancer to be eliminated, and it was too late to turn back because if you turned back another would take your place, since that was the umbilical violence of a country that expanded into the lands of others and could only expand by creating enemies.

Yes, it was too late. They waited with Moralla on the stone wall and felt the sun warming on their skins and the sweat hanging there waiting to fall. Moralla talked jovially, threatening them and consoling them as he spoke. Those planes had come to airlift old Señora Frankl to safety because the threat was closing in all around them. But they had no need to worry, he'd get them out. They ate stale bread and fried eggs which Moralla cooked himself and when Pamela finally rose Julián turned away from her. There was nothing she could say which could interest him and the more he looked at her the more he realised that he could only survive through betraying her.

"What is it?" she asked. "Didn't you sleep well?"

He smiled at her, and that gave Pamela something like hope. She was still trying to pretend to herself that everything was normal, that they could carry on with their ordinary lives as if nothing was happening. "I slept very well," he told her.

She went over to the wall where Moralla had left the frying pan and served herself some cold eggs. "Perhaps they'll come to get us this morning," she said. "All we need to do is get to the airport and we can be back in Santa Fé tomorrow. By Monday morning at the latest. Then there'll be no need to let head office know all about this."

He had not realised how blind she really was: still she was not concerned about her situation, but only about how people thousands of miles away might think about her if they thought she had been unwise. He drank the last of a cup of cold milky coffee and threw the dregs in the direction of three rangy cross-bred cats  lurking in the hope of scraps. "You haven't got a message to them about this?" he asked.

She shook her head: "There's been no chance yet."

"So if we don't get back, as far as they're concerned, you'll just have disappeared. Like the American before you, Purdue."

"That isn't going to happen," she told him.

He rose and gathered the dirty plates and dishes and took them into the kitchen. Just to get away from her. It reminded him of living with his father. Already they were like an embittered married couple. Thank God, he was never going to leave this country. He had been born to die here, that was his fate, and sometimes you had to accept your fate for otherwise you tried to take fate into your own hands and died anyway, with the fist of fear in your heart, without ever being able to forgive the world for what it was.

Moralla was in the kitchen and as soon as Julián looked into his eyes there he knew that the old murderer wanted to save him if he could, that his friendship with Vásquez counted for something. That perhaps even his father, the lottery layabout, counted for something.

"Put those down in the sink," Moralla said. "The plane will be coming soon."

"Where are we going?" Julián asked him.

Moralla laughed: "I thought you knew about that," he said, "that Stone had told you."

Julián looked him hard in the eyes since there was nothing to be gained by avoiding them: "This is all about Stone, isn't it?"

Moralla shrugged: "It's all about protecting the country from people who want to lie about it."

"And friends of Stone – me, Pamela Oswald, Jasmine Purdue, María Halabi – they're all dangerous."

"I've not decided about you," Moralla said. "Vásquez says your father is a good person. But we don't know about you." He walked past Julián, then, and filled the sink with water. "We have recordings you know, recordings of you and your girlfriend talking about things. And talking with others. Even with Stone. Recordings which sound disembodied. Tortured even." He turned to face Julián. "Really, it's very unpleasant, Scary, even."

"This country gives fear to everyone," Julian answered.

"So really," Moralla said, "everything is up to you."

"Yes," Julián said, "I've known that for some time. But why didn't you just take Stone out years ago? Why bother the rest of us?"

Moralla laughed. "But of course, Stone has been very useful, as well as dangerous. He has taken us to people like you."

It was too late not to choose. What did he owe her, finally, when she had planned just to leave and never see him again, when her betrayal added to all those which had torched his country for centuries? She thought she had come to help, and that was the worst betrayal of all. He tidied the kitchen methodically, remembering in passing his attempts to tidy up after Stone in his flat in the Colonial district. Here, it was even worse. It was filthy. The boy, Elvis, who'd been living here before: obviously he hadn't known how to look after himself. The sink was caked with grime and the cups and plates were black with rings of dirt. The windowsill was grey with a finger of dust that made the kitchen suddenly feel frozen in time and as if all the terrible sadnesses which had destroyed so many lives in the decades just past had afflicted a different world entirely. If only he could have stayed there, a part of him felt, never leave. But surely the sadnesses outside that dust and the window lined with years of dust, cracked, would make even the kitchen unbearable and he'd never be able to cope with the solitude. Probably he'd have ended up eaten by mastiffs or swinging from a tree and buried with no ceremony beneath the bushes or one of the trees in the pastures beyond the dry stone wall and to stalk the land as a ghost and frighten those who came after him with thoughts of everything that they had lost in all the years since the violence had begun.

As he tidied up he became so distracted that he cut his hand on the jagged edge of a tin that had been opened savagely with a knife. He walked out holding his hand out at a distance, red and throbbing. When she saw him coming like that, like a demon from a late night horror movie she might have watched in south London, Pamela started back. "What happened?" she asked him. "What did you do to yourself?"

"It's nothing serious," he said.

"It looks terrible."

"It's the least of our problems, frankly," Julián replied. "You don't seem to care about disappearing, so why bother about my hand?"

This was typical of him, typical of the man he was becoming. And what was all this talk about disappearance? Pamela couldn't bear it, she couldn't bear this sense that there was a narrative in this journey which she had not grasped, which was not her own objective creation, nor of her own making. The story she had imagined telling to her friends would never be told. It was not hers to tell any more. It would not be the one that came bidden from her own fantasies, but instead one that came from somewhere else entirely, from a different voice. A cluster of voices were coming together, breaking down her force of purpose. She looked at him, shaking, bitter, defeated. "Is that it?" she said. "Is that all you can say?"

"Don't worry about it," Julián answered. "It's nothing serious. I'm making an application to join the rehabilitation centre."

She looked at him as cold as stone: that was the problem with these worthy do-gooders, they had the sense of humour of the condemned, and they were useless when it came actually to helping. For it was Moralla who found a bandage and some disinfectant and cleaned the cut, just in time, for as they sat there they heard the noise of metal violence in the air and saw a Cessna launching itself towards them and then preparing to land, the dust and the bushes scattering as it came down. They ducked behind the door of the house until the dust had passed, and then Moralla turned to them and told them that this was it, this was their way out of here.

"Come on," Moralla said, and he shepherded them up to the Cessna where the propellers were still whirring their swivel blades through the air and blasting it with dynamite force, blasting the sky as it prepared to rejoin it. They climbed into a cabin with men younger than they whose faces were copper and cocoa, smoothed and hard. They were barely any older than the boy Elvis had been and Elvis was destined to be one of them, Julián realised with a sudden gulp of sadness, and that had been his destiny ever since he had been born. He smiled at them and they did not return his friendship and their eyes seemed empty as they looked at him, at his jeans, his long hair. Julián was not in fatigues like them and he had a European grandparent unlike them. He was not like them and they knew it. They must have hated him, as he had been born to hate them.

When they were all in Moralla tried to find them seats and he gestured for Pamela to squeeze next to one of the soldiers and when she looked at him uncertainly, as if in reply, Julián heard him shouting that she should not worry, these were the people who the government had sent to protect her. Yes: it all depended on how reassuring you found the presence of the army and their fighters. Julián smiled to himself and Moralla came up to him and said that there was nowhere else, he'd have to go and sit beside the pilot. Julián walked forward and buckled himself in and the Cessna flew low over the farmland and over the mountains and then the land fell away as if they might never see it again, and it seemed broken, broken by rivers, broken by feuds between villages clinging like leeches on either side of mountains which separated them like some final barrier between the living and the dead.

It was loud in the Cessna but it was bearable and after a time he shouted to the pilot and asked where they were going and the pilot looked at him with cold blue eyes and said nothing, eyes which were sad and beautiful, eyes which had forgotten how to love, which perhaps had never known how. They reminded him of someone but he couldn't remember who and suddenly, from nowhere, the pilot said to him that the land serrated and bare and dangerous reminded him of Mozambique. Mozambique? When did he go there? A while ago, after the end of the civil war there, he'd had a contact in the army who'd swung him a UN posting and they'd been paid a fortune and a three thousand dollar-a-month food allowance as well and he'd lived in a small concrete house in a town called Cuamba and flown out to villages in the bush and dropped food from his plane often without landing, as if what he'd really been delivering had been a bomb. He'd spent six months there and he'd seen men without arms and women without legs and children bloated with malnutrition and their eyes swollen and pussy and he'd seen towns shot away by disease and death and an empty land of sand and bushes and sierra high and bare like this one, where no one dared go for fear of the lions, and from high up in the aeroplane it had seemed beautiful, so beautiful. Yes, Mozambique had been great: he'd made a fortune, enough money to start a haulage firm when he'd come back here, and that had been some years ago, and now he owned a Cessna.

He looked at Julián again and that was when Julián realised that the pilot reminded him of Stone. Stone who had also been in Africa back then, another leech making money off the tragedies of others. Stone with his coldness and Stone with the impenetrability of his experiences, the reality of what it was like to be so fascinated by the suffering of others, to be drawn in by their story and to want to tell it and so to come to depend upon and need that suffering with a yearning and a sadness that cut very deep, that sang something of the song of how and why the world was. Stone with his silences and Stone with his longings and Stone who might very well disappear one day and not regret it, never to be seen again, when he was at peace with all that tragedy and no longer needed to speak of it. Stone with his longing and fascination for death and the dying and the dead, who wanted to preserve them embalmed for the future. Stone who was crazy.

So, Julián asked the pilot, didn't he want to go back to Africa and do the same again? No not any more, the pilot said. He'd seen enough. But his business partner, he was different. He was an investor, someone who was also buying up real estate near the National Park. He was still saving: he had dreams, the pilot said, dreams of buying an island, something that might come cheap in some parts of Africa, of going somewhere where he could be in complete control, and live without depending on anyone. If he ever does it, he laughed, looking at Julián for a moment, maybe I'll go there too: but that was in the future.

The plane banked east towards the high mountains then. They flew low over the tops of the hills and forests and huge scars where the mines were with their trails of dust and effluent and across small towns pierced by church towers and across land empty and silent where not even lone fires broke the sense that nothing and nobody lived there. They flew for half an hour, an hour. The pilot did not speak to Julián after his memories of Mozambique and Julián watched his country pass beneath him with the sense that when they came in to land it would have changed forever. Or that he would have done. The thing was, he was aging. He saw it in himself, and he did not resist. He was thinking like his father. He owed Pamela nothing, and the main thing when he got to their destination would be to survive. Without survival, there was nothing. He looked over his shoulder to see how Pamela was and was astonished to see that she was sleeping as peacefully as if she had been a bird. Surely, she knew that they were not going to Guadalajara airport, that this was their disappearance. But maybe this was what she had wanted all along.

By and by they banked again and they had crossed the mountains and were into the Llanos. The land became heavy with thick forest and the extravagance of banana trees and palms and of forest throbbing with the absence of people. They came in to land at a small airstrip where there was just one small concrete building standing empty and forlorn in a thick heat. Three pick-up trucks were waiting as they climbed off the plane. The recruits followed Moralla's orders and climbed into two of the cars and sat in rows on the trucks and put their bags under their feet and their machine guns between their legs. Moralla reminded them to put the safety catch on their guns, and then he beckoned to Julián and Pamela and wordlessly they followed him to the third pick-up. Then they drove for over an hour on bad dirt roads between thick stands of trees and clearings of savannah where cattle grazed and drank brackish water and banana trees grew in clumps and parrots wheeled and screeched in the sky. There were some small farmsteads and Moralla blared his horn as they approached and then waved at the children and old men and women who watched them pass.

After half an hour, Pamela turned to Moralla and asked him where they were. It was a safe place, he said, a place where they would not be troubled.

"Have you kidnapped us?" she asked.

"You are safe with us here," he said, "safer than in many other places in this country."

"But we can't get any word out," she said, with the irritating whine Julián had become used to. "Who can we speak to? who will listen? who will know even that we have gone?"

Moralla laughed. "You have nothing to worry about," he said. "You won't be forgotten. The embassies will make sure of that, and so will your friend, Stone. He's an expert in making sure that nobody forgets."

Pamela sat in brooding silence and looked at the world beyond: "Still, I don't understand why we had to be taken."

"Of course you don't."

"Why did we?"

"Don't you see?" Julián interrupted, shouting. "Just shut up."

"Why?"

"You're so stupid. Just shut up." She said nothing and he saw a veil passing over her eyes as if already she was becoming someone else. "Can't you see?" he said, more gently then. "Perhaps there is no reason, no really good reason. Perhaps it's revenge and perhaps mistrust of people like you who come to help and go back. Perhaps it's hatred of journalism and perhaps it's because Stone slept with the American, Purdue."

Moralla laughed at him then. "It could be," he said. "Or perhaps it's because Purdue is lonely, so lonely, and needs company." He looked at Pamela: "She can't survive as she is," he told them, "she needs more than the cocks of the bored recruits that she meets here to deal with her loneliness."

Eventually they pulled into one of the farms and climbed out. There was a collection of single-storey adobe buildings each with its own veranda sheltered by a sloping roof, and a clutch of animal pens deep in mud and excrement. The owner of the farm was a harsh, lean man, but his peóns were softer. They looked at Julián and Pamela with kindness, pity even, and offered them some meat from the barbecue they had made. The meat was cold, but they both were hungry and ate it with gratitude. There was a long, low barn where the recruits slept, painted green and white, and behind the barn was a path between animal pens and a row of chicken coops which curled behind a stand of banana trees. There was a bridge over a sluggish stream and on the far side of the stream was a long low building. This was where the hostages lived, Moralla told them: this was their home.

Then Julián asked him who was there and he shrugged and said that the American Purdue was there, sleeping interminably in these afternoons and probably if they went there now they'd find her curled up with sweat forming on her brow and their sheets damp and soiled. That was the life of the people who'd disappeared, unless they died whereupon they were wrapped in those sheets and carried beyond the fences around the farm buildings and buried in the earth where it was heavy work enough to dig the grave. Julián looked at Moralla and he asked, was that a threat? Pamela looked at them both and Moralla did not answer but he was smiling and he beckoned to Julián and told him to come with him.

Moralla told some of the recruits to guard Pamela, to wait with her, and then Julián went with him and they walked into a small building beside the barn where there was an office with a plain desk and three straight-backed chairs, one of them peppered with holes from woodworm as if once it had been used for target practice.

"Sit down," Moralla said, and Julián sat. "You can make your decision now. You can join the war against the guerrilla, against the communists, and anti-capitalists, if you want."

"If I want..."

"We're waiting for you to decide. If you agree, you'll be trained for work in the city and we can get you a job. You'll join the network and your life will be good, as your father's has been."

"And otherwise?"

"Otherwise..." Moralla waved his hand in the air. "You can join the hostages in their prison."

"How long do I have to decide?" Julián asked.

Moralla looked at his watch: "About ten seconds."

After they'd finished Julián went outside. Pamela was still there and she looked at him but he looked away. Three of the peóns were smoking and he asked one of them for a cigarette and they smoked outside and then ground their filters into the earth. Julián asked the peón nearest to him, a wiry man with bloodshot eyes that spoke of the aguardiente which allowed him to live and hastened his death, asked him if he had been born in the lowlands and he said that he had, and this was where he had learnt to tame horses and kill snakes, it was where he had married his wife and he had never gone any further since the day he had been born. Julián told him that the world was great beyond these confines, that there was so much to see, wasn't he greedy for it?, didn't he yearn to have it?, to know what it was like?, wasn't that something that everyone wanted in these days when no one could trust anything or anyone except what they had seen? But the peóns just laughed then, all together, like a clutch of chickens clucking in a yard, and his neighbour said that all that was worth nothing, not even the smoke of the cigarette they had just blown into the plenitude of the clouds thick with impending rain of a heavy afternoon in the Llanos, all that would pass and be as nothing and then what would remain, the peón asked, what would remain except for the people that they themselves had been?

All that would pass, the peón said again: everything passed, even hatred. He looked then at Pamela, whose head was set down now, low and lost, and who had nothing to say. She could not raise her eyes to meet Julián's and he could not stay: he excused himself from the others and turned and walked towards the barn where Moralla had told him to sleep beside the others. Soon it would be dark. Soon he would be beginning his life again, and everything that had marked him out and defined him until then would be less than a memory. And that, he realised, was how the past could disappear, how stories could be constructed that occluded it. That was when he thought of Bontera, that he might never see him again even though this was what he had always said to him; and his face crumpled in sadness at the loss.

# CHAPTER 23

When Julián Restrepo left she realised that there would be no way out of her disappearance any time soon. He'd hardly spoken to her for days, hanging out with the farm workers and the paramilitaries in fatigues. He wasn't even sleeping with her in the prison block. Not that she wanted that. All her desire had gone. Something in her life had been cut off and she could feel it and knew that it had been there. But she didn't know how it could be restored and it was as if all her memories of what her soul once had been had been mutilated.

She was a prisoner in the farm but they did not keep her in shackles. Where could she go to? Beyond the farm was the road which the paramilitaries used as a freeway and beyond the road was an emptiness where she would die. So she conspired with her own disappearance.

Sometimes she could not bear it any longer and she felt like dying or burning the farm down, trying to raze it all from the earth so that no being present or future would ever sense the directionless suffering and games of power which had taken place there. She screamed, insisted. She asked again and again, why had they taken her? On those days she was given an audience with the commander who told her that they were fighting people just like her, they were the enemy. Was that so? she asked him once, and his sad dark eyes widened a little, and she could see that he believed in her evil. Then she felt sad. That afternoon she went back to the long, low building which was her prison and tried to sketch him: a successful shadow of a man, the sort who believes that the ideologies of the past will again serve the future.

The worst thing was the boredom. Time became telescoped into the present which passed thickly, slowly, without love. And that scared her. Things died if they were not loved, and sometimes she feared that that would happen to the world, too. At first there would be the warning signs, the loveless announcing their sadness, trying to consume themselves into oblivion or mutilating themselves in surprising, grotesque ways. Then they would flaunt their dismembered souls before society and if society ignored them they died and with them the world that disdained them. She thought about this in the farm because she was asking herself, every day, how much longer she'd be able to love this world. If she stopped, she realised, she might die. Was it really the paramilitaries who might kill her? Perhaps they wouldn't be the guilty ones at all, and were just symptoms of a struggle that was going on day by day inside her.

Thinking about the mutilations made her think of the rehabilitation centre and of the Tumbera. The holding block was not unlike the dormitory she had sat in so often these past months. The same lack of possessions, bare mattresses and sheets, the sense of people having arrived there under duress but finding it difficult to leave. Was that one of the things that the Tumbera had been trying to communicate to her, how similar the rehabilitation centre was to a prison? Pamela had come there to help, but perhaps she had just been like a prison orderly, assisting offenders, the violent, those who mutilated themselves as a philosophical statement, before their own country had the chance to. The violence of the state and its actors was always imprinted like tattoos on the skin of those it marked. Like the slave brands of centuries past. Perhaps the Tumbera had been right: perhaps you could not exorcise the violence of the present without digging up the violence of the past, exhuming it, interring it, laying it to rest by restituting its voices. Why was this such a violent country, after all? People talked of the violencia as beginning in 1948, but the Tumbera was right: the country had been at war for over 500 years, that was how old its mutilations were.

Instead of the Tumbera as her roommate, though, she had Jasmine Purdue. Purdue slept on a mattress beside her. When Purdue first introduced herself, on the evening of Pamela's arrival, Pamela cut her short:

"I know who you are," she said. "I know all about you."

"Do you?" Purdue asked.

"I know what you were doing here! I even know Leila Halabi and her daughter María. And your boyfriend, Stone."

Pamela thought that perhaps this sharing might create a sort of intimacy between them but she had not yet realised that there was already too much intimacy in the camp. Purdue did not thank her. She withdrew that night to her bed in silence, and later Pamela saw her crying.

A couple of days later, Pamela tried again.

"Have you seen María?" she asked Jasmine.

"María?" Jasmine replied: "Is María missing?"

"Yes. We thought she had been taken. Like you were," Pamela answered.

But Jasmine just shook her head sadly: "I haven't heard anything about her," she said. She stood on the veranda of the holding block looking at the rising heat. "María is missing?" She spat onto the dried grass beyond the boards. "That's the saddest thing I've heard for a long time. I feel worse about María's disappearance than I do about my own."

"That's funny," Pamela answered. "You sound as if you've disappeared from yourself."

"Yes," Jasmine said. "That's possible in the world that you're about to enter."

"What's possible?"

"To vanish to a point where the person who has once been can never come back." Pamela was silent then, touching the sadness of Jasmine's confinement. "María," Jasmine said again. "That girl was so elegant, so beautiful, and she had all of life before her. But she was like a heroine in a novel, she was too sensitive to the world. Perhaps that's the trouble with people here, they're too sensitive."

"It's terrible," Pamela agreed. "And especially after everything that family has been through in the past sixty years."

"That's war for you," Purdue said

"And then what?" Pamela asked.

"Then?" Jamine laughed. "You can't reconstitute the voices of the war-dead once they're gone."

"So we just accept that?"

Jasmine shrugged "Mostly. Or then it's up to others to give all the energy they have to replenish the voices. The voices like María's. Did you ever hear her sing?"

"No," Pamela said slowly, "I never did."

After that sad exchange they had slowly settled into a routine where they tolerated each other, but rarely spoke. Pamela alternated between an immense lassitude where she could spend several days and even a week without leaving her holding building, and a desire for action. When she could bear her prison room no longer she snapped. The first time she blew everything away, decided she would die in the wilderness beyond the farm. She left in the thickest afternoon heat when everyone was asleep, crept behind the banana trees and was gone into the forest. She walked for twenty minutes with the pain in her heart and chest building until she was constricted and could not breathe. That was when she screamed and shouted, collapsed, and sobbed into the mulch of the forest floor; that was where she was found, half an hour later, after her screams had brought people to her.

After that, she no longer tried to break free. She recognised that freedom as just an idea whose time was done, that she could never have such a thing here. By and by, she asked to be taken on walks instead.

They passed groves of guava trees and pineapples half-submerged in the red earth with their spikes protruding like green porcupine quills. Sometimes her guards would point at holes in the ground where snakes lived. They followed the tracks of spiders and sat on gnarled boles of the lowland trees and smoked cheap tobacco which made her lungs rasp. Always the air pressed down heavy as a lid always in the process of being closed. Sometimes she talked with the guards, and it was almost possible for a moment to forget the differences in their condition, the captured and the capturers, those who in theory could still do things with their lives and those who were officially nothing.

After a few weeks, she recognized one of them. It was Elvis, the boy she'd met at the farm near Guadalajara in that twilight zone between being captured and being free. He looked at her with a little sympathy now, something he'd never shown her before. She wanted to hate him, to hate everything he stood for, but she could not. He was still delicate and slight in body but there was already a hardness and a repressed lust in his expression that made her very sad. How was it possible for the world to fail a boy like Elvis so badly? How was it possible for human beings to be so inept at running their affairs? Really, if they had been halfway competent, there would have been no need for people in her line of work at all.

By and by, she got to know Elvis. He persuaded her to play chess with him, and slowly she remembered the moves of a game she had not played since childhood. She started to joke with him as the Tumbera had with her. Perhaps this was the natural response to their guards of someone who has been institutionalized in captivity. So was he from Memphis? she joked one day, asking him about his name. No señora, he was from one of the slums of Guadalajara, she knew that. But he had Native American ancestry like the King, didn't he? Yes he did, and African too: it burst up in him sometimes, would not be ignored. And didn't he miss his family? His father had vanished some time before, he told her, and he doubted whether he'd ever see his mother or sister again. Sometimes you just had to get used to life.

Slowly, she got to know Elvis better. He was a gentle man in conversation. He never tried to make advances, even though her body must have had its own animal scent, and at times what she longed for above all else was contact. Yet he never tried to touch her, he never threatened her at all. He was like a captive audience. He was solitary like she was and like his colleagues, all of them alone with their emotions and their histories, and that was what made them human. Elvis was alone and so were his comrades and what had brought them together and given them some sort of direction was a community of violence. She remembered over the weeks that this community was what she had wanted to flee from when she arrived, that was why she had burst out into the forest that day. But now it was what gave her a sense of security: the community of violence was what gave her peace.

Other than Elvis, her only outlet in the whole farm was Jasmine. They had been thrown together by a shared experience but really they had nothing in common. Pamela worked for an NGO, and was caught in the wrong place at the wrong time. Jasmine was a research scientist at a big American university, doing the bidding of business. She had deserved what had happened to her whereas Pamela had not: the fact that they were both together just went to show that there was no God. They had nothing in common other than the fact that they had disappeared.

One response was denial.

"Isn't the freest thing of all being able to think without being able to answer to anyone?" Jasmine said to her once.

"You could be right," she said.

"Who do we answer to here, then, Pamela?"

It was true: they could think what they liked, write what they liked, and no one looked over them or corrected them. No one even read their notes. But you could prove anything by sophistry, and it didn't make you happy.

"What are you saying to me?" Pamela said angrily, after some moments, "that we're freest once we're forced out of the life that we've shaped ourselves, once we know no one, when we're entirely alone?"

Jasmine said nothing to that and instead returned to reading the Bible, which the Commander had given her in order to help maintain order. Jasmine infuriated Pamela at times, and they baulked at discussing religion just as they baulked at politics. Jasmine thought she was naive and selfish.

"If only everyone could see things as you do," she mocked her once, "you really believe there'd be no more violence."

"Maybe there wouldn't," Pamela said.

"And is that what you really want?" Pamela swore that it was and Jasmine laughed at her, her contempt big in her voice: "But what would idealistic people like you do for a job if there was no more violence or suffering? What would you do with your desire to help others? You'd be able to consume nothing and instead you'd consume yourself."

So Pamela rowed with Jasmine all the time and yet she was the only person there who could sense what she was going through. She was the only one sharing the most immense experience of her life. No one else cared.

After the rows she tried to forget Jasmine. That was when her lassitude came on strongest, when her acceptance of the impotence of her situation overpowered her the most. She would sit for one day, and then another, and then another, and not leave the holding block. She had an old iron bed, and on it a lumpy soft mattress covered just with a couple of sheets and a pillow. It was so hot in the evenings that there was no need for anything more. The bedclothes were changed every three weeks, which was not often enough. Spiders crafted their webs in the corners of the room and there was an elongated rectangular window which gave out onto the worn grass between the buildings and the thicket of bushes and low trees which bordered the farm. Her world was still, so still, for hours at a time until it seemed that nothing would ever move any more and that nothing ever had, as if there were no inner urges driving people to commit loathsome and pointless acts of violence, as if there had never been any sadness or atrocity and the whole history of the world was a myth invented by a long-lost people to answer the terrible quandaries which were prompted by the mysteriousness of being alive.

But after all that stillness the change came. A flock of brilliant green parrots swept across the horizon. One of the guards of the holding block switched on their radio and they listened to the world, so far away, where a teenager in Santa Fé had called in to an agony aunt on the radio because her boyfriend wanted too much sex. Then a caravan of pick-ups swept into the farm and young men in fatigues jumped out with their machine-guns to stand in serried lines for inspection. Those in authority assigned them to different blocks and they accepted the assignations with good grace and shouldered their kit-bags and moved off with their companions into long shapeless buildings topped with corrugated iron beneath which bats hung and chattered late into the night. The recruits accepted everything. That was how they had been conditioned. For the prospect of freedom and violence and perhaps some money to take into the future they had relinquished the capacity to question. It was a bad deal, but it was the only one they had been offered.

The soldiers seemed to arrive in gangs, every week or two. Usually most of them moved on to some unspecified new front in the war, and Pamela rarely got the chance to get to know any of them well. But one of the exceptions was Elvis. He stayed where the others left. Like Julián, he seemed to have been selected for special training. He had regular shifts on guard. Perhaps he'd been instructed to get to know her although she couldn't think why. They thought that she embodied the enemy, she understood that, but still she thought it was laughable.

By and by Elvis asked her if she'd like to help with a constructive project. They were going to dig a new plot for growing vegetables behind the holding block, and she could help if she wanted. Why not? she said. It might be better than sitting in the holding block most of the day long, watching Jasmine read the Bible. The plot at the back of the holding block was extensive. The cadets were charged with breaking the earth and turning it over. Pamela was given a rake by Elvis and asked to smooth it all over once the earth had been turned to prepare it for sowing. It was hot work, the air close and thick, the rake heavy. Pamela was not used to physical work and her hands blistered during the first couple of days but she persevered. It was good to be outside. It was good to be doing something. There was a sense of togetherness and friendship that came with collective work and every hour or so a canteen of water was passed around and they drank together, the prisoner and her guards, and they felt that they were not at war with each other.

After a week the plot was prepared and Pamela was given the seeds along with the cadets and they moved slowly over the soil burying them in tiny holes and moving on to bury some more as if in remembrance of the interment which was the end of all humanity. With each miniature burial you touched your mortality and might have been terrified by it had you not been planting something which would grow and give life, something which would not disappear. As she helped to sow the seeds, Pamela felt for the first time an answer to the question that had been haunting her ever since she had been brought to the lowlands: yes, she would be able to love the world, even after all this was done: perhaps she would love it even more than when she had been living and working successfully in London, and Santa Fé, thinking without thought.

When the seeds were sown the work gang had a celebratory meal. One of the peóns lassoed a steer out in the enormous paddock which stretched through savannah and thickets down to the watering hole. It was a long-horned steer with a rangy neck and a fleshy belly that bucked and quivered in the golden afternoon light as other peóns grabbed its legs and hobbled them, as the soldiers helped to truss him tightly and move him to the pick-up which had come to transfer him to the killing place. Such grace and expertise in the arts of butchery! In the appointed corral the steer was carried to a worn board and laid there and two of the peóns held his head, gently and almost as if in a caress, and the animal had ceased its struggle and was quite still with its eyes open and watering and watching with curious resignation by the time the peón who would kill him unsheathed his machete and sharpened it on a whetstone and then passed it into the beast's neck. A soldier was waiting with a bucket for the steer's fresh blood which was passed around the cadets and the peóns and then, vampires all, they began to butcher the carcass and light the coals in readiness for the barbecue. For so many decades and centuries these men and their ancestors had developed these arts and yet fewer and fewer of them lived in the countryside and could practise them. And so piled up in the cities like armies of soldier ants, they turned to butchering people, and they turned to butchering themselves.

Pamela ate the meat with them when it was ready, lacing it with a spicy pickle. Elvis walked her back to the holding block when they were done. It was another clear, loud night, furious with the calls of crickets and the hunters of the plain. They did not speak much. Elvis said goodnight to her and then she went into the block and lay on her bed, a prisoner again. At least she was alive; the steer was not. The moonlight that night was so pellucid and the air was so still that her mind quietened and with it all the dilemmas that were racing in it and all the thoughts that once had fascinated her. She felt that she was losing her expertise, and that worried her. If she had been transported back to her office in London she would not have known what to do next. What was she a specialist in any more, except living and dying? Who was she really equipped to help?

Jasmine stirred on her bed. She was awake. She called out:

"So, you've been eating with the enemy, then?"

Pamela laughed. "I'd rather do that than read what you're reading," she said, nodding at Jasmine's Bible.

"Why do you hate religion so much?" Jasmine asked Pamela.

"I just don't understand how people can believe this stuff any more."

"Why not? People have always believed strange things."

"It makes no sense. It's like saying, human beings have always been ostriches. We'll stick our heads in the sand and ignore the real world."

"So what's the real world?" Jasmine asked her. "Does it happen to be the same thing that you believe in?"

They lay there for some time in silence. It was late. There was no sound from the farm although the duty guards would be awake, watching for enemies who were never there. They never slept on duty. That was an offence which led to execution. Pamela forgot Jasmine as she drifted towards sleep, turning over memories. She thought of Leila and she hoped that in her sadness and loneliness she still thought sometimes of the beauty of life, of why it was such a joy to be whole even as a prisoner. She thought of Stone and his bitterness, the misanthropy of someone who has seen too much ugliness and has made a profession of casting it out, and judges everyone as himself. She wondered where Julián was, stuck in an office in Santa Fé, his guitar in a cupboard, consigned to a life he had always wanted to reject. Now that he was gone from her and she would never see him again, there was a strange way in which she was more attached to him that she ever had been before. Before, he had just been an attachment of the moment, a keepsake for her future to prove that she had been to a country such a long way away, that she knew what it was like.

Then she thought of the meal with the cadets that she had just shared. Several of them had been missing fingers, she'd noticed, although not Elvis: she wondered if this was a mutilation that they had inflicted on themselves or rather a punishment that had been part of their training, an unseen act of violence which no one discussed and yet which bound them all together as they travelled into the future.

# CHAPTER 24

The blisters came from training. Loading and holding and aiming the machine gun and grabbing it close by to squat in the thicket and observe the enemy imaginary as in all war games. The work of holding the shovel low and digging the earth out, preparing for planting. "Keep it close by, lean hard," Commander Bonifacio said: "if you need to dig a grave quickly, before sunset comes and the body scavengers with it, you need to know how to dig hard, otherwise the bodies might have gone by morning and with them the chance of burial. And let me remind you, burial is a sacred act."

In the comuna, burial was a quick affair. At times the priests were busy for so many were the dead. At others they lapsed into a torpor from which it was difficult to raise them as if they felt a secret resentment that they were not needed. Sadness was the province of the living, it was said, the distress of grief with it, but who was sad at leaving? That was why people talked of the disappeared and the dead in the same breath, because both had gone to a better place. Father Milton - the Brazilian who had lived in the comuna for nearly 15 years, longer than half of the comuneros – usually gave the sermon for the dead. There by the broken land near the ravine which separated Comuna 13 from the barrio of the Cross. He insisted on a corpse before he would perform the ritual of burial and if someone had just disappeared he would say that the history of this continent this past fifty and five hundred years, was a history of disappearance, that he could not expiate all those souls daily in individual ceremonies of despair, that the very rituals which were performed daily were a sort of requiem for all those who had gone. Without a corpse there was no sanctity in death. God help him, he had buried so many in 2001 when the military moved in to liquidate the neighbours, people they called terrorists or collaborators with the urban guerrilla, because such a thing had been easy enough in those days, and there had been so many bodies then and he had helped to dig the graves and his hands had blistered into swollen puffballs of skin that left their scars for years after. That was when he had learnt that the soul was immortal but could not be immortal without its body, that without the body also there was nothing.

Eventually Commander Bonifacio moved on and with him went some of the cadets who were needed elsewhere to fight. But Elvis stayed. His new commander was Franco, a veteran of the war with the guerrilla who had tired bloodshot eyes and a jowly face bristled with stubble. He was constantly talking on his cellphone and listening to the radio. On his third day as Elvis's commanding officer he summoned him and told him that Bonifacio had singled him out for training. He needed to get to know the enemy to know how to defeat them. He was going to stay on the farm and guard the hostages on a duty roster. As he knew they were two, an American and a Briton called Jasmine Purdue and Pamela Oswald. It was known that he had worked with the English woman, Oswald, and so he was marked out to get to know her and the danger she might represent. That was his task.

When Elvis took his first shift as guard he sat on a wooden chair next to the other soldier on the veranda and looked out across the yard with his back to the prisoners. He didn't want to reveal an intimacy that was not there, or pretend that the shared time on the farm near Guadalajara and here digging the vegetable garden made them anything more than what they were, guard and captive. Franco had told him already that Purdue spent most of her days reading the Bible, so he ignored her also. He spent most of the time talking to the other guard, Dionysio, a talkative man from the south. On their first shift together Elvis asked him how he had come to this farm in the Llanos, and Dionysio explained, he had been picked up from his barrio on the outskirts of Rosario and flown by helicopter to a nearby camp where along with others he had been fed meat and given weapons and instructed that the land needed to be cleared, that the communists did not produce properly on it, they didn't care, that there were huge international markets for the nation's coffee and flowers and textiles but the communists weren't interested. The land needed proper stewardship from people who understood how to build a future. It needed to be protected. They spent three weeks at the camps, Dionysio told Elvis, where they were told about the international dimension of the communist terrorists and that there were people all around the world who sympathised with their aims and wanted to destroy the country, to keep it poor and mired in peasant agriculture so that they would stay rich. Then by and by they were singled out and sent on secret missions said to be related to the international terrorists, on 3-week assignments to various districts. They had never seen the enemy, Dionysio admitted, who always fled from them before they arrived, and so they torched their villages and their vegetable patches and grilled their pigs and their chickens in the ashes of the fires that were left with their eyes smarting from the smoke and the acrid smell of their work fresh in their noses as the cold grey dawn beyond a mountainside broke over the smouldering destruction. That was life, Dionysio told Elvis, they cleared the land and made it useful and then they moved on, and after six months they flew him here and this is where he had been ever since, like Elvis, waiting for the next move.

Had he been back to see his family in Rosario? Elvis asked him, but Dionysio said that he had not. Neither had he seen his, Elvis said. They sat in silence then, that first shift together, in the heat thick and close that made their fatigues cling to their bodies, clammy and warm. Elvis then felt very sad for he realised that ever since he had agreed to Moralla's suggestion and gone to the farmhouse with him he had agreed to the desolate logic of his life where every emotional connection was severed so that he could prepare for death, his death and the deaths of others. Elvira probably remembered him still but soon she would grow and forget, and gradually like his father he would come less and less to Juani's mind and she too would forget, and then he would be forgotten unless the world itself possessed some latent facility for memory.

Without adaptability, his life would have been impossible. He had got used quickly enough to making the money for Moralla, money that made this war possible. In the end it was money that had driven his disappearance and those of all others like him, always money. And now, even though the prospect of money had receded, and he hadn't seen any for weeks, Elvis got used to being a guard. Every couple of days the officers would instruct them about various aspects of the enemy's ideology. He learnt that they were against freedom and the nation. They were communists and funded the insurgents and their supporters through the NGOs. Elvis learnt all about this and then he would return to guarding Purdue and Oswald and accompany them on their exercise sessions and to the toilet and occasionally on walks into the forest where they went in silence and the only sounds were animal both their footfalls and birdcalls and the humming of insects chattering like thoughts in their brains. She was an easy mark, after all: she had tried to escape at first, like all the others, but then she had seen how hopeless it was and she was quiescent, passive, like a sheep taken to the killing stone.

On one of these walks Oswald asked them to wait while she went to relieve herself in the bush. Elvis waited five minutes with Purdue and Dionysio. Then he became worried that Oswald might again have tried to escape, though he knew that if she had finally managed it this time it would only have been to her death, and for that he pitied her. Where could she have escaped to in the lowlands and what could she have eaten and how would she have died? He couldn't believe that she had run off and when he went to find her he saw her at once, bent over and sobbing, again, in the shade of a low tree.

"Why are you crying?" he asked.

"Don't you ever feel like crying?" Pamela answered. She felt desperate, so desperate, and yet her voice was thin and weak and she did not know how best to ask for help. She asked with her eyes, devouring him in the wish for some humanity, a gesture, anything, but he didn't answer her and instead looked at her thin face and greasy blonde hair which she had tied in a ponytail behind her neck and at her vivid blue eyes. She could see that he thought she was quite pretty. In another world, one in which they had not been born and would never live, he might have made a proposition to her. "Don't you ever feel like crying?"

"You're not crying because you're unhappy," he said.

"Why am I crying, then?"

"In grief," he said. "Grief for the person you were before you came here."

Pamela sobbed again, more loudly, uncontrolled: she sobbed because she knew he was right. "What do you know?" she said.

"It's change," Elvis said, "and every change is a form of death. It's hard to accept that."

"Just shut up!" she screamed. "What do you know about any of that, to start lecturing me? What do you know about what it's like to disappear?"

Elvis told Dionysio about the exchange that night, their cigarettes flaring like machine-gun fire. But she was right, Elvis said, for him, she was right. He hadn't killed an enemy in battle yet: what did he know about what it was like to make someone disappear? He could hear Pamela and Jasmine stirring on their mattresses. Probably, they were listening. Anything to torture their captors who would not let them go because they could not. He hadn't killed anyone? Dionysio drew hard on his cigarette and then sighed and blew the smoke into the darkness. They must have been saving him for a special mission, he suggested, something of a secret importance.

Elvis wasn't sure about that. The war mattered, he believed that. How could he not? Moralla had told him that he was on the right side, and he even believed that. It was easy to believe people when they fed you and gave you money so that you could have things you had never had before. Conviction through bribery: he could almost hear Moralla's voice in his ears then, that's a language that everyone understands. Opinions are convenient: he could hear his mother, too, shouting at his father on one of his occasional visits: "Your opinions are just a convenience, Federico, you think that they protect us, protect me, but haven't you seen how many of the neighbours hate us for being newcomers? You said that this was our chance to find a place to live, that we should just come, but what chance will your son have when he wants to work? Who will help him out? Not you, husband: not you. Haven't you seen how that family look at us, the parents of his friend, Bear? It is as if they want to eat us alive."

There were too many voices in his head. His past was so vague that those voices meant little to him. He could not separate them. That past was a meaningless babble which seemed increasingly just like a story of no consequence. His mother had told him that they had moved into the comuna with him still young, that his grandparents had been farmers who had been forced out of the countryside after the violencia had begun in 1948. But what did any of that matter? That past had vanished and it was not coming back. It had been amputated from the world, like a rotting leg. It meant nothing to him now. He had to live with what he had, in the present, a permanent war and a latent threat of violence which meant that he could never live without fear.

The only release he had from that fear was when he and Dionysio escorted the prisoners for their exercise walks in the forest surrounding the farm. The plants stuck to their fatigues like animal claws, savage and hungry, and birds chattered like pneumatic drills and the choir of the priest Milton's church in the high branches. Commander Franco had drummed it into him that the enemy might still be out there, that they had to be careful for there had been cases where prisoners had been abducted. If that was possible, he had added, laughing. But neither Elvis nor Dionysio really took that threat seriously, they knew it was just made to keep them alert. The guards liked the damp, rotting smell of the lowlands full in their nostrils and watching swarms of ants sharp-toothed on the dried-out stumps of trees and listening to the birdsong and watching the prisoners walk. The more time they spent with them the more beautiful they found them, and Elvis sensed that the attraction was mutual. One time he rested his hand gently on Pamela's shoulder as they sat on a tree stump, smoking, and she did not move away but allowed his hand to rest there. Elvis felt a surge of desire, and for a moment it seemed the same as his lust for the girls on the hill, and the same surge of energy and feeling came to his cock. But then that sense passed and he looked at Pamela again and thought how strange it was to desire someone you did not have to buy.

Elvis did not act on his desire, not then, but he did not forget it either. The world was forged by pulses of desire that could not be undone even when they had gone. He knew, too, that Pamela had not forgotten. She looked at him with a distant, wistful gaze. But if he tried to look back at her, she turned away, fighting her memories. Franco had told him, he had to get closer to her, closer to her memories. For months she had been working in Santa Fé for a subversive organization which looked after people who had no right to be looked after. People who had cut off their fingers and people who had cut off their hands and savaged their legs. People who gave the country a bad name, and yet they were gathered in and tended there. That was the way the world was going! So you could see how dangerous these people really were. Franco had told him, they had to find out as much about the centre as possible, to get as close to her as possible. Elvis obeyed, and remembered the rumours he had first heard in the comuna when he had been a child, rumours that there was a centre that helped in gathering in all the people who had disappeared from the hill. They had always thought of it as a mysterious and dangerous place, collaborating in their tragedy.

Was Pamela really as sinister as that? An enemy. She was not as Elvis had imagined the enemy. Still he felt the pulse of desire when they walked in the bush. She had been unable to rid herself of her yearning for him either, and sometimes wanted just to take his hand and pull him with her off the path: if she could not escape her captors she wanted to possess them, to be possessed by them. She was so close and yet seemed so distant, impossible to be with. One time when she looked away from him he had a fleeting sense of how sad her confinement made her, how it was eating up the old person that she had been, how if she stayed any longer that person might be completely exterminated. It was only then that he realised how hard it was for her to come to terms with the fact that the only objective story of her time in the country was not one that she had made, but was that of her disappearance: this is what had been produced by all the voices in her head, the voices she had pretended to listen to but had tried to crush.

One time she had had enough, she could not bear the prison of nature where she found herself, this place which she had thought would be so beautiful, she felt convulsed as she walked, and ran off the path saying that she had to shit, and when she did not return he went to find her and again she was sobbing, she felt her chest heaving like a sea with her sighs, and the sounds she made came in gulps, muffled by the arm she held across her mouth to hide her suffering. He held her then, and she told him that she was frightened, that she felt like nothing, that she could talk to no one since Jasmine and she had no belief to share, that she felt that she herself was vanishing before her own eyes. That was how he felt, Elvis told her. They looked at each other and kissed, and tore at each other's clothes until they were bare and still like all the other animals of the bush beneath the sun, and then they kissed again and his lips and teeth were on hers and in hers so that they were together, and it felt as if they were that moment the same.

When they had finished they dressed and he kissed her eyelids and the bridge of her nose and then they rejoined the others. Dionysio and Jasmine were sitting on the log with their backs to each other, not talking. What had taken him so long? Dionysio asked with a smile. They walked back to the farm and stopped by the vegetable plot where they picked some beans and then they carried them in bags made of twine and took them over to the communal kitchen which stood beside the dormitory where Elvis and Dionysio slept. Then they went back to the prison cell and Elvis took Pamela's hand just as she was about to go back inside and he kissed her. She kissed him softly, and she thought how strange it was that she could find this emotion with her captor, with someone who really was her enemy. This was not the moral that she had imagined, not at all; and still the violence continued.

That night Dionysio teased him, jealous and happy at once for his friend.

"I'm worried, though," Elvis told him. "Franco will punish me."

"Punish you?"

"For breach of discipline."

Dionysio laughed at that. "He'll be happy," he told Elvis. "Unless he's jealous he'll be happy. Didn't he ask you to get closer to her, to find out what you can about the centre?"

And of course Dionysio was right, for he was older and stronger than Elvis. Franco called him in a few days later and Elvis told him how the centre was funded from international donors, that they worked with local stores in the south of Santa Fé, that Pamela did not seem to have any knowledge of the wider conspiracy which it was a part of. "But she does," Franco told him, "she does: you just have to cut deeper into her. Find out more."

So Elvis asked her on those walks why she had started to work there and what made her sympathetic to that cause, and Pamela felt liberated by everything that had taken her to this point, and she talked to him about injustice, and history, and solidarity. And what did she know about that? he asked her. He hadn't understood her answer, he told Franco later, it confused him. It didn't matter, Franco said. He leant forward and offered Elvis a cup of aguardiente. They were finding out from other sources. New volunteers had gone to the centre, people that they had planted. The seeds of the future. The young man that he had met on Moralla's farm outside Guadalajara was working for them now, he had gone to volunteer there himself, and they were getting closer to the answer all the time. Was there an answer, mí comandante? Franco looked at Elvis with tired and empty eyes, eyes that had seen too much and longed for rest, and drained his glass and still turned those sad and hollow eyes which had been stripped of something which they had already forgotten, turned them to Elvis, and he said to him that there always was an answer, that the one thing that the world needed at a time like this was certainty.

But there was no certainty in being two people, lover and guard. This was something Franco did not understand, for he had only ever wanted to be in command and this made it hard for him to consider the subtleties of those who were commanded. Subtlety was the tactic of the weak, he told Elvis at one of his debriefs: you could learn a lot from language, a lot. He had studied history, he had learnt how language was the biggest traitor of all. The Brazilians used to call their slave ships that came from Angola "*tumbeiros*", floating tombs. He wished that more of them had died, Franco told Elvis, for he was the poor fool who had to deal with the consequences of that evil today, with people like him, Elvis. Evil is a rapist, it is someone like you are, he said again to Elvis, begetting more and more evil. That was certainty, Franco told Elvis: good and evil, as their grandparents had been taught before the violencia began.

Sometimes after those meetings Elvis could not help tears rising into his throat and to his eyes. He did not know why. It made him think of the times he had found Pamela crying in the woods and always, on those days after he had met with Franco, she found that he was very tender towards her, that he did not pressure her for sex and instead sat on the veranda of the holding block playing chess with her, that if they did make love he was always so gentle, going into her welcome little by little, closer and closer until she wanted only to be tight around him with her love.

"Franco believes in right and wrong," he told Pamela, on one of those evenings, after he had been called in and after they had made love, as they sat on the veranda of the prison block and looked at the stars thick with brilliance above them.

"Yes," she answered. "And so does Jasmine."

"Jasmine?"

"Yes. She reads the bible because she can't deal with reality, can't understand that the only truth is a violent, disappearing one."

Jasmine: he had barely thought about her, leaving her to Dionysio to take care of. "Does she know about the centre too?" he asked.

"Of course. She volunteered there, like me. She even slept with Robert Stone."

"Who is he?"

"Ah, you don't know." She sighed. "Your commanders don't like him."

"No. Probably they don't."

"He's not unusual. He's a journalist. There are thousands like him."

"Like him?"

"People who neither of us have heard of. People who shaped our lives although like us they've gone already and can't come back."

Elvis rose. "I've never thought of that." he said.

"No," she said. "But it's up to us to remember them all if we can."

Elvis stood leaning against the wall of the prison block. There was a part of him that wanted to go to the centre, too, he told Pamela then, he had this strange feeling that he might meet many people there that he had known long ago on the hill and who had since vanished from his life. People who had been beautiful and who made him feel sad when he thought of them. Condor and Bear who used to play in the same football team in the comuna. His father and the families who had vanished when the paramilitaries had come, people that he had not known well but whose loss had marked him when their faces had gone from his life. And then the children of the Angolan and Rosaura, even his mother Juaní and his sister Elvira, small people like him, people who counted for nothing: people whose stories rang in his head and helped him to construct his own song of the world, one in which they both were now, both of them disappeared. Would they be there? he asked Pamela. She could only tell him that she did not know, did not know if their voices were heard, interrupting the sort of stories that were usually told. What she had found when she had worked there, what she knew was that there was only one way you could go to the centre and that was to mutilate yourself. Elvis laughed: yes, he said, and Franco would love them for that, he was longing for more and more spies there, he might even let Pamela go if she agreed to that. That might be her route of escape. Yes, but she did not know if either of them were desperate or strong enough for that, strong enough to cut into themselves. But he knew, Elvis told her, and he reached into the belt of his fatigues and pulled out a sharp knife with a blade that was dark in the night light and he held it out between them like an offering before a shrine, a prayer for the future. He knew that they could be strong, he said, and make this sacrifice as a kind of rebirth of belief, and he knelt down on the veranda and put the knife on the wooden boards and they both looked at it and felt that it offered at once a memory and a cure for the memory of everything that afflicted them, that it was a fetish for all that had been so terrible about the world and for all that was beautiful. "Your ancestors knew that there was reality in fetishes," Pamela said to him then, and Elvis picked up the knife and sat beside her on the veranda and rested it in her palm so that they could hold it together, so that they could cut into themselves and so be granted their freedom, before the opportunity had gone.

END

Printed in the United States
By Bookmasters